MY OWN

Personal

SOAP OPERA

Looking for reality in all the wrong places...

Libby Malin

sourcebooks
landmark

Published by Sourcebooks Landmark, an imprint of Sourcebooks, Inc.
P.O. Box 4410, Naperville, Illinois 60567-4410
(630) 961-3900
FAX: (630) 961-2168
www.sourcebooks.com

Library of Congress Cataloging-in-Publication Data

Malin, Libby.
  My own personal soap opera : looking for reality in all the wrong places-- / Libby Malin.
       p. cm.
  Summary: Frankie McNally doesn't just write for a soap opera, her life resembles one. Head writer for the soap opera, Lust for Life, Frankie is being courted by both Victor Pendergrast, a dashing older man sent in to save the show's sagging ratings, and Luke Blades, the soap's totally hot leading man. Just when she thinks life can't get more complicated, a jewel thief starts copying the show's storyline—a development that could send the show's ratings soaring if it doesn't get Frankie and Victor arrested first. Can Frankie write her way out of this one? And can she put make-believe aside long enough to discover the truth of her own heart?
  1. Television soap operas—Fiction. I. Title.
 PS3613.A4358M9 2010
 813'.6—dc22
                                    2009051112

Printed and bound in the United States of America
VP 10 9 8 7 6 5 4 3 2 1

*In loving memory of my grandmother, Nanny,
who was an avid soap opera fan*

Beyond the veranda and swaying palms, moonlight shimmered on hypnotic waves. Nearby, the soft, insistent thrum of a guitar beat to the rhythm of the longing in Terri's heart. She sat on the bed, arms locked around her knees, waiting.

Her dark hair cascaded down her back. Her bright eyes shone with anticipation. Her fingers slid over the satin sheets, twisting the corner into a knot she rubbed slowly, ever so slowly, along the length of her long, tan shin.

A breeze caught the plantation shutters, bursting them fully open. She rose from the bed and glided to the window in her diaphanous white negligee, the wind dancing around her tigerlike body, blowing the chiffon taut against her shapely breasts and sweetly curved hips, and arching up into angels' wings beyond.

Through her mind, images of their tumultuous courtship played: the night she slapped and cursed Donovan, not knowing he was only pretending to love Alicia while on an undercover assignment; the morning Donovan scolded her for being too prissy and she'd longed to prove him wrong; the summer afternoon she'd found him near death at the bottom of the ravine; the midnight they'd shared their first kiss and he couldn't leave her until they'd both satisfied their desires…

She trembled at the memory, looking out over the rustling palms and white sands.

"Donovan," she called over her shoulder in her velvety alto. "Your princess awaits!" When he didn't answer, she walked to the door of the adjoining sitting room and opened it. "Donovan?"

Chapter 1

"JUST KILL HIM OFF!"

"Are you crazy?" Frankie shifted her cell phone as she strode along Manhattan streets, heading for her favorite coffee spot. "Criminey, Ma, I'm powerful, but even I can't just snap my fingers and have him go dead."

She rushed by a man in a leather jacket and sunglasses, who did a double take as she made this pronouncement.

Arriving at the double doors of a trendy coffee bar, she stopped and turned when she saw the long line. Okay, second-favorite coffee spot this morning. She kept walking.

"Just get rid of him," her mother said. "Have the count pop him."

"Wow, that's brutal." She laughed. "What would that bring his body count up to? He's already responsible for half a dozen deaths in Crestview. He does have that arsenal in his basement, though."

She thought she saw a policeman look her way at this last statement. She hurried around a corner and saw her coffee mecca. Good, no long lines. Hoisting her heavy laptop-laden attaché case onto her shoulder, she marched on.

"Besides, the count never gets his own hands dirty," she said into the phone.

"Then have that half-wit of his do it. What's his name?"

"Mittbul." Frankie spit it out like it was a bad olive.

"What kind of name is that?"

"I don't know—something foreign."

"Ohh, you mean Swedish, like meatball?"

"No, Ma, *Mittbul* like... like... well, Mittbul," she said. "He nearly did himself in with that arson attempt on the Reilly Tavern. Maybe I'll have the count get rid of him, too." A woman wearing earphones and a trench coat glanced at her as she heaved open the door to a coffee bar.

"Have him taken off somewhere and tortured," her mother said. "You know, by some group of half-naked women."

Frankie laughed, finding her place in the queue. "A sex ring, huh? Yeah, I think a lot of folks would like that."

The man in front of her stared over his shoulder at her. She looked down. "I mean a lot of people would like to see Donovan half naked."

"Just have him snatched, and sit him in a room with a dozen slave masters."

"Whoa—since when were you into the bondage thing?"

The man in front looked around again, this time with a disquieting gleam in his eye. Frankie glowered at him.

She lowered her voice. "We could do a hostage situation, I guess." She slid her heavy case to the floor beside her, rolling the ache from her shoulder.

Her mother snorted. "Like that's not been done before. I thought you were more original than that!"

Frankie bristled. "Hey, nothing's new under the sun, okay? Hostage, kidnapping, sex ring, arson, hit job..." Without realizing it, her voice was rising. More people stared. The man in front of her left the line and was talking to the trench-coated woman who had followed her in.

Red-faced, she moved up in line. "I have to go," she mumbled into the phone. "Love ya." She forgot about her bag as the line pushed forward. By the time she ordered her double cappuccino and turned to leave, the woman in the trench coat had called in a dog to sniff the abandoned tote and was motioning for Frankie to come her way.

"Ma'am, would you please step over here and answer some questions?" Trench-coat lady flashed a badge, and Frankie heaved a sigh.

It took Frankie nearly a half hour to explain she was a head writer for the daytime serial *Lust for Life* and to demonstrate that her bag contained nothing but her laptop, a half dozen one-hundred-calorie snack packs, tissues, perfume, and the latest issues of *Soap Opera Digest, Daytime Serial, Soap Opera Today,* and *Soaps 'n' Suds*. The delay didn't bother Frankie so much as the last question trench-coat lady put to her before letting her go.

"You say this show's been on how long? I've never heard of it."

You and half the soap-watching universe, groused Frankie to herself as she was finally released.

———

"Kayla!" Frankie called to her secretary from her office as she let her bag slide into her chair. No answer. The woman must have left her post. *But she was just there a moment ago when I came in!* Frankie swore under her breath. When she'd taken over as head writer a scant six months ago, Frankie had rejoiced at the thought of having her own administrative assistant. Joy quickly had turned to confusion when she'd discovered Kayla's mysterious talent for disappearing whenever Frankie wanted to use her services. The gal must have had some sort of cloaking device.

One of these days, Frankie was going to have a talk with Kayla. But not today. Not until she read up more on how to manage the problem employee. She had put several books on the topic in her online shopping cart and had a list in her purse for others she'd noticed at the bookstore, but she hadn't yet decided which ones to order.

Grumbling, Frankie sank into her chair, bumping against the bag she'd just put there and spilling coffee onto her blouse. "Damn!" She moved the bag to her feet while looking over a just-released ratings report placed on her blotter, presumably by Kayla. No, more likely by executive producer Brady Stephens's efficient staff. They were always at the ready with bad news.

No wonder *Lust for Life* wasn't on anyone's radar screen. They were barely a blip, coming in a distant last behind the *General Hospital, Young and Restless, Days of our Lives* crowd. She sipped at her coffee, the magnitude of the challenge looming before her: bring *Lust* back from the grave, back to its heyday position, the one it had occupied years ago when Peggy McNally, Frankie's mom, had started watching the show.

Frankie McNally's mother had been a fan of *Lust* even before Frankie was born, and now that her daughter worked for the daytime serial, she talked with her regularly to get the inside scoop. Already this week, mother and daughter had spoken several times about breaking news concerning Luke Blades, the dashing heartthrob who played Donovan Reilly on the show.

"Breaking news" was a spot-on description for what had happened to Luke. He had decided to boost his career that winter by appearing on *Dancing with the Stars*, doing extremely well, too, by making it to the final four couples. That's when victory was snatched away in a snap. Literally. He had jived his way into a broken fibula just three nights ago, when he'd jumped off the platform and landed, not gracefully in a grand flourish of kneeling slide, but awkwardly on the edge of the bottom step, his shin cracking so loudly there was a unanimous gasp from the live audience.

But Luke—always aware of his assets—had managed to turn his best side toward the camera as he worked his jaw muscles furiously, telegraphing strength and vulnerability at the same time. Luke had told Frankie in a phone call from the hospital that he'd hardly felt anything. He was too much in shock, and, besides, he'd taken a few "supplements" before the show to calm his nerves.

Gone in a bone-breaking snap. The lovely plot she had concocted for Donovan and his lady love, Terri (known secretly to Donovan as Princess Terese du Valmont-Scaiyovnova)—who had been kept apart and thrown together in a succession of wild and exciting stories designed to raise viewers' libidos to a fever pitch as they cheered Donovan on to the bedposts of sexual victory—was now shattered, like Luke's leg. And it had all been scheduled to air during sweeps week, a mere month away. They had just taped the initial scene with Terri waiting lustfully on the bed, the "breakdown" for which Frankie had written herself. She alone among the writers infused her story descriptions—the breakdowns, or outlines, of stories she passed along to scriptwriters—with a novel-like sense of narrative and description, as well as… something more.

Her cell buzzed. Her mother again.

"Yeah?"

"I thought of something. Why not just use old footage of him and the princess rolling around? Why do you have to shoot new stuff?"

Frankie smiled. Her mom was always trying to be helpful. "The fans will know." Yeah, all five of them.

"How fast do you need to come up with something?"

"By today. We'll redo the scripts and shooting schedule immediately." She finished her coffee and tossed the cup into the wastebasket beneath her desk. "Hey, you don't need to worry. I'll think of something."

"I know you will, sweetie."

Frankie sighed and looked at her watch. "But I've got to get going. A meeting—where we discuss the jitterbugging Donovan's fate."

"Yeah, I gotta vamoose, too. Scheduled a hair appointment for my day off."

They finished the conversation like lovers parting by train, with quick bursts of promises about visits and calls and notes they'd forgotten to send via email, ending with "love ya's" as they leaned into the phone chugging along toward its cradle.

Even though their talk was brief, it buoyed Frankie for the meeting ahead, and she now scooped up pen and pad and walked to the conference room with cheer rather than the gloom that had afflicted her when she'd called the meeting. At that time she was facing tough choices—abduction, coma, amnesia, runaway, false death— all stinking of a manipulation that curdled her true-blue character-drives-the-plot principles. But her mother's cavalier attitude toward Luke gave her a sense of perspective. It wasn't the end of the world if she had to reconfigure Donovan and Terri's story. She'd make it work, whatever "it" ended up being.

"Give me what you've got," she barked as she entered the room, looking to Hank, a lean, ghost-faced newbie who'd interned with them the summer before. With his big eyes and dark hair curling around his forehead, Hank always reminded Frankie of Jethro from *The Beverly Hillbillies*, good-hearted and eager. His white shirt bore the wrinkles of a week in the laundry basket, his blue tie didn't match the blue in his pants—*yuck, why is he wearing blue pants anyway*—and his fingernails looked like he worked a garden with his bare hands in his spare time. She glanced away.

"Uh…"

Frankie sat at the head of the table, already moving on.

"How 'bout you, Nory?" Frankie turned toward gothlike Lenore, slunk in the corner away from the light as if it would melt her skin. She wore a tight black sheath the same color as her ragged black-marker hair, Cleopatra eye makeup, and ankle boots. At least the multiple piercings had disappeared. The one in Nory's tongue had always freaked Frankie out. Frankie would be happy when Nory got entirely past this stage. She liked her new country music phase a lot better—well, at least the parts when Nory wasn't quoting song lyrics all the time.

"Just shoot him from the waist up."

"He can't move around much," Hank chimed in. "I checked with a friend of mine studying to be a doctor. He says these kinds of breaks are very painful and Mr. Blades will likely be incapacitated for six weeks or longer."

"Great," Frankie said.

As if that were the green light for more, Hank continued, "This friend of mine, by the way, would make a terrific consultant when we need help with medical stories, Ms. McNally. He'd be very reasonable, too. I know I could work something up that wouldn't bust the budget. I could give you his name."

"Uh-huh. Sure thing. Leave it with Kayla." Frankie couldn't keep track of all the people Hank knew who could be of use to the show. Lately he seemed to focus more on pushing people into the biz than on actually doing the work in front of him. She figured he must be so proud of his job he told everyone about it, and they in turn tried to use him to get gigs. She didn't hold it against him.

"I hear he's practically paralyzed," Raeanne drawled in her Mississippi twang. Sitting alone at the opposite end of the conference room, she leaned into the table, revealing even more than usual of her Marilyn Monroe figure squeezed into a thin spandex-like wrap top of sea-foam green. She bit her lip. Frankie could swear she saw a tear bead up in the woman's baby blues. *Well, that's why she's good at this. The woman knows sentiment.* With a shag of blonde hair framing her face, porcelain skin, Kewpie-doll mouth, and a bod that every straight man in the office lusted after, Raeanne merely had to breathe to get attention. "The poor soul must be just devastated, in pain and unable to work. He's devoted to *Lust.* Absolutely devoted to *Lust. Lust* is the most important thing in his life."

The same could have been said of Raeanne. She was always willing to work late and go the extra mile. Well, as long as she knew she was getting credit for it. If Brady Stephens wouldn't know of her efforts, she remained still and mute.

The three of them—Raeanne, Nory, and Hank—were *Lust for Life's* breakdown writers, the people who put together the story arcs for the shows before they went out to the half dozen scriptwriters who worked from their homes on contract, penning the actual dialog. *Lust for Life* was a lean operation. Only three breakdown writers, with the head writer—that would be Frankie McNally herself—doubling as story editor. She suspected they'd have a bigger team if they had higher ratings. Until then, she had to make do.

Right now, she didn't mind. Frankie often liked to map out stories on her own, throwing them to the team for fleshing out and brainstorming details. She liked being in control. But desperate times called for fresh strategies. She needed every brain cell in the story department working this problem fast. Executive producer Brady Stephens had already called her a number of times with his own ideas, which, unfortunately, were limp retreads of things they'd done with other characters in the recent past. Brady, like Frankie, was a recent promotion. *Lust for Life* was a cocktail shaker for careers.

Frankie shook her head. "I've talked directly to his doctor. He can move, but it would be awkward. He was supposed to be really heating up the sheets with Terri this week. Lots of rolling and writhing and…"

She drifted off as she described the now-useless scenes, thinking of Luke, the man-candy actor who played Donovan Reilly on *Lust for Life*, rolling around in *her* sheets.

She blushed. It had been after the office Christmas party two years ago, and she had just signed the divorce papers ending her three-year marriage to Brian Aigland. She'd had too much to drink, and Luke had shared a taxi home with her. She had been relatively new on the job, still the assistant head writer, and he was so sweet and attentive, and one thing had led to another and another, and, oh baby, those fingers of his, those rock-hard pecs, chiseled chin, and that wicked, sweet tongue. Surely, she was allowed that one mistake, after the much larger mistake of marrying Brian.

"Frankie? You were sayin', honey?" Raeanne interrupted like an evangelical clairvoyant reading her dirty thoughts.

"It was only one night!" Frankie blurted. They all stared at her. She cleared her throat and rustled papers in her notebook. "I mean, it's one night, but it was going to stretch over a week or more. We had some good stuff here, guys. Great stuff! And now it's all wasted."

"Look, seriously, we can shoot him under the sheets," Nory repeated. "You know, moving around with his shoulders or something." She demonstrated, doing some weird elevator movements with each shoulder and twisting her neck back and forth, making her look like a bobblehead in a tornado. Awkward silence followed. No one knew whether she was joking. "No one will see his leg," Nory continued.

"Oh, gosh, Nory, they'll see it perfectly well." Raeanne clucked her tongue. "It'll look like some big, throbbin', pulsatin', hard, rigid mass of, of…"

All eyes turned to Raeanne, waiting for the punch line. "What?" she asked, wide-eyed.

Frankie resisted the urge to point out that many fans might enjoy seeing Luke's hard, rigid mass of something under the sheets. And not all of them women, either.

A soft knock at the door shifted her attention. The mysterious Kayla poked her head in.

"You're wanted in Mr. Stephens's office," the secretary said in an odd conspiratorial voice.

"Right now?" Frankie asked.

"He said he wanted McNally up there pronto." Kayla gestured to the hall with dramatic flair. She was a tall woman, a blonde like

Raeanne. Or at least today she was. In the past couple of years Frankie had also seen her as a brunette and as a redhead.

"I'll be right there." Frankie sighed. As Kayla left, Frankie turned her attention back to the group. "Give me a dozen different ideas—each of you—by the close of business today. Write up some treatments, too." She flipped her leather portfolio closed and rushed from the room.

———

Before heading to Brady's suite, Frankie first made a quick stop in her own office. Closing the door, she slid into her black leather chair, pulling a cosmetic bag from the bottom drawer. Whenever Frankie was around Raeanne, she felt the need to recheck her own appearance.

She stared at the fold-out mirror. Yup, the same Frankie. No transformation into sex goddess in the past half hour. Frankie looked at a long, slim face; thin mouth; narrow green eyes; freckled cheeks that only industrial-strength makeup could hide; and long, reddish hair on the fulsome side of curly. It now frizzed around her face like an electric shock aftereffect. Damn, it was damp out today. She scrabbled through various pieces of head hardware and chose a tortoise-shell clip to secure the frizzy mess at the nape of her neck, hoping it didn't make her look like she needed a prairie bonnet to complete the ensemble. She applied a little powder to her nose and some too-pink gloss to her lips, kicking herself for not remembering to change shades. This would have to do. At least it was something.

After scraping everything back into the bag, she stood, dusted the shoulders of her charcoal silk pant suit, pulling the jacket over the coffee stain on her umber shirt, and strode with all the confidence she could muster past Kayla's empty desk. While she walked, she thought of the story ideas they'd just discussed and how she'd present them and more to Brady, steering him away from his own ideas for Donovan Reilly—fall down the stairs (done that with Donovan's brother Kyle just last year), satanic possession (Donovan's half-sister Belle had suffered through that seven months ago), and coma (even though this had been on Frankie's original list as well, she'd quickly nixed it when she'd tallied up the recent coma victims in *Lust for Life*'s town of Crestview, a number that probably made it the coma capital of the world).

As she waited at the elevator, Hank approached her.

"Ms. McNally," he began in a soft voice indicating a request was coming.

She smiled at his boyish deference. "Hank, how many times do I have to tell you, you can call me Frankie?"

He blushed and looked down. "Ms. McNally—Frankie—I hate to be a pest, but I sent you an email about my cousin, and I was wondering if you had a chance to consider it yet. He's called me several times asking."

Hank's cousin? Was this the medical student he'd just mentioned? No, no, somebody else. Frankie did a quick flip through her mental files. She had a vague memory—a cousin who wanted to audition for a part. A big fan of the show. She couldn't remember anything else.

"Nothing's open right now," she said. "But as soon as we have a casting call, I'll let you know, and he can be included in the bunch." She gave him a quick reassuring grin, which he answered with his own beaming smile.

"Thank you so much. He's a real actor, you know. Not just some wannabe. He's studied and all. Been in some plays."

The elevator arrived, and she stepped in. No harm in letting Hank's cousin in on a casting call when it happened—it was the least she could do to keep the staff happy. There were so few occasions to dole out favors.

One flight up, the elevator whooshed open onto a plush executive suite as silent as a sanctuary. Two reverent secretaries—Bob and

Serena—typed at computers, their backs to each other, separated by an exquisite Persian rug of rusty hues. Bob finished a line and turned to Frankie, saying in hushed tones, "Mr. Stephens is in with someone right now," but Frankie wasn't sure if he was talking to her, because he had a Bluetooth on his ear. Whoever he was talking to, Bob gestured for Frankie to take a seat on the long low 1950s-style leather couch just beyond his and Serena's desks.

This was typical of Brady—making it seem like her job was on the line if she didn't arrive in a flash, and then keeping her waiting. Nonetheless, a knot curled tight in her stomach, and she picked lint from her knee in nervous anticipation.

No daytime serial was lighting the ratings world on fire these days. They'd all been losing market share over the years. But *Lust for Life* was losing it at a prodigious rate.

Yet once, years ago, the show had shone like a beacon at the top of the mountain. It was the network's longest-running daytime drama and had been through every transformation the genre had experienced, often leading the way. Starting out as a quarter-hour radio serial, it had jumped to television with a half-hour black-and-white offering in the late 1950s. From there it splashed to color, doing the first location work in the mid '60s, including one fabulous shoot in Hawaii in the late '80s when then-heartthrob Keir Michelson lost and then recaptured his beloved Amelia, only to see her whisked away by a tidal wave (reappearing years later after he'd remarried).

That was the story that had first captivated Frankie, addicting her to it years ago when summer vacation meant sitting in the club basement drinking cola and eating chips and watching television while Peggy McNally worked as a nurse at a downtown Baltimore hospital. *Tell me what happened*, Peggy would say to Frankie when she got home each evening, and Frankie would spill out the latest, as if reporting on the inhabitants of Crestview were her summer employment. In fact, it became that. As long as Frankie could keep her mother entertained with *Lust for Life*'s stories of love, death, and near-incest, Peggy didn't bug her daughter to get a regular summer job. She let her mow neighbors' lawns instead. Frankie became Scheherazade during those lazy summers, entertaining her mother with daily recaps that often enhanced the lamer stories playing out on the screen.

Lust for Life was her baby-sitter, counselor, friend, teacher, fantasy builder, dream starter—it was a place where women were beautiful and sophisticated, where true love always won (eventually), where lost love could come back from the grave, where loneliness and trouble were banished.

It was a world where people got to say what they really thought— hurling accusations, unleashing resentments, sharing secrets, and blurting out confessions with a liberation that Frankie's long-gone hippie father would have cheered. Frankie often used the treatments she now prepared for the show to work out her own innermost frustrations, having characters on *Lust* give voice to her deepest feelings, saying all the things that civilized people in polite society withheld from each other.

In fact, she had often wished she could live in *Lust for Life*'s fictional town of Crestview, where everyone knew one another, where you could walk into the Reilly Tavern and run into family and friends any day of the week and know that people loved (or hated) you. Frankie was first inspired to write, filling marble-covered notebooks with melodramatic stories, after becoming entranced by *Lust for Life*.

Over the years, *Lust for Life* had pioneered shows that included abortion, rape, UFOs, out-of-body experiences, and even the first openly gay character on a daytime drama. They'd been the first to introduce the "super couple"—a pair destined to be together yet pulled apart for years until the final consummation (and even then smooth sailing was never guaranteed). They'd gone to an hour and a half in the late '70s, only to pull back to an hour five years later.

Despite her great affection for the show, Frankie had never set her sights on working for it. She'd stumbled into this career after first marching down the path toward a career in *Lit-rah-chure*. Academic skill rewarded by scholarships had lifted her out of suburban America into the heady halls of upper-class academe (Wellesley, then Columbia for her MFA) and then into editing jobs at a prestigious publishing house. Frankie had even thought of penning her own Great American Novel one day... if she could just make the time and figure out what story she wanted to tell. But editing other people's novels was good enough while she waited for inspiration. Reality had interfered, though, when her brief marriage to a similar dreamer and aspiring novelist had jeopardized her credit rating with debts she didn't even know she had accrued.

She could have forgiven Brian the money problems, though. It was the knocked-up graduate student Brian "tutored" in the afternoons that had finally sent Frankie to the lawyer. She was glad for *Lust for Life*'s steady money then.

Steady at least for the short term, that is. Frankie had been hired just two years ago as an assistant to the head writer and was quickly promoted when he had a nervous breakdown. She was the fifth head writer in six years.

And every time Brady Stephens called her into his office, she expected to hear him say, "The network's pulling the plug. Tell the staff." And every time, she sat here berating herself for not putting more in savings, for not getting her resume out there, for not finishing that Great American Novel that would surely sell for millions when it went to film.

Good lord, in the time Frankie had been playing in the daytime TV sandbox, even her ex had finished and sold a novel that was coming out this month. Then again, Brian's father being a golfing buddy of the publisher probably helped get that new author moved to the front of the line.

A door opened. A gregarious voice boomed. "Frankie, come in, come in. You weren't waiting long, were you?" Brady was always obsequiously polite in front of others, so it didn't surprise her to find someone else in the executive's office when she entered. Standing by one of the butter-yellow designer armchairs was a tall, dark-haired man in a black pinstripe suit, white shirt, and coal black tie. It was hard to guess his age, but Frankie pegged him on the sad side of fifty. His craggy face gave him the air of an old gunslinger, and she half expected him to greet her with a rich, baritone "howdy, ma'am" when he held out his hand.

She had the vocal tone right but the words wrong. In a deep but cultivated voice, he said, "Hello, Ms. McNally, I'm Victor Pendergrast."

As if propelled by an unseen magnet, she crossed the three miles of plush carpeting in Brady's office and shook Mr. Pendergrast's hand.

"I bet you get kidded a lot," Frankie said by way of suave intro- duction. At his curious look, she explained, "Pendergrast Soaps. The sponsor of *Lust.*" When he didn't respond to that, she offered up one of Pendergrast's best known slogans: *"When you're feeling dirty, you'll want Pendergrast in your hands."*

It was a bane of her existence that her blush was as uncontrol- lable as it was intense. Now, as she looked over broad-shouldered, masculine Victor Pendergrast, she imagined he had been kidded quite a lot with that slogan and hadn't minded it one effing bit. She was sure the color of her face was matching the color of her hair about now.

"I'm sorry," she murmured when Victor cut her off with a smile and a wave of his hand. "The soap is the sponsor of *Lust for Life*," she explained. "Not lust itself. And I didn't mean—"

"I did hear my fair share of that," he said, his eyes twinkling. (Wow, Frankie would exchange wild blushes for eye twinkling in a New York minute. Maybe there was a self-help book on that.)

Brady walked over and finished the introductions. "Vic is here to help us out," he said, gesturing for Frankie and Victor to sit while he leaned against his parking-lot-size desk. "So I thought you could take him around, introduce him to the team." For Brady, "team" was a euphemism for "peasants."

Help us out? She looked Victor up and down. Maybe he'd been a head writer for one of the competition and was now retired? No, more likely he'd been involved with *Lust for Life* during its heyday, which meant she'd have to find diplomatic ways to steer him away from stories featuring big hair and kids who said "groovy."

Brady was going on to extol Frankie's background to Victor, surprising her with the accuracy of his memory. Her degrees, her literary fiction mentors, her stint as an assistant editor at an artsy independent press editing fiction and a few play anthologies, which led her to a playwright who wrote for *General Hospital* under a pseudonym, which landed her some script writing for *Lust for Life*, which got her on board as a full-timer as assistant to the head writer, and the prompt promotion when that fellow left for "personal reasons." Sometimes it was hard even for her to believe that she'd evolved so far, from working-class product of a single-mom household to network television. Or perhaps this was really devolution?

While Brady prattled she stole glances at Victor. He listened with a benign, friendly smile, nodding at Brady's occasional jokes. Whatever his real background, he clearly didn't need the dough. His suit was no off-the-rack polyester blend. It had the suppleness and gleam of silk, and you don't buy off-the-rack for a physique like that anyway. *He must work out. Or he has big bones. No wedding band, but a big school-type ring with a few diamonds glistening on his right hand.*

"I'd be happy to take Victor around," Frankie said at the end of Brady's dissertation. She looked at Victor. "Do you want to schedule something? I can ask my secretary to call you." After a call to the Missing Persons Bureau located her, of course.

"No time like the present." He smiled back, already standing.

"I—" She wanted to get back to work. She didn't trust the peasants to come up with anything for Donovan that was quite right, and if she could just have one uninterrupted hour, she knew she could work something out.

In fact, if she could get the Donovan stuff out of the way, she could get started on a new idea she'd been itching to write—a provocative story line for the show's latest ingénue, Faye Reilly. The character of Faye had been introduced on the show only in the past year. Oh, she'd been around as Donovan's little sister for years before that, but they'd decided to give her the soap-opera "rapid aging pill" and turn her into a hormone-beaming college freshman in order to create some love triangles and angst-ridden tales sure to appeal to the younger crowd. But Faye's summer sizzler story concocted by Frankie's predecessor had fizzled. He'd paired her with a geeky type whose bad acting and skeletal frame made him the gossip of the fan blogs. Now Frankie had plans, though, big plans.

Brady stood as well, signifying the meeting was over.

"Good, good… you two get going." Brady walked them to the door. "I'll have Serena set you up with an office by tomorrow, Vic. Great to see you, great to see you. Say hello to your aunt for me."

In the hushed hallway Frankie walked at a good clip in front of Victor. Okay, she'd do a rapid-fire tour and shake him free. And Serena could stick him in some cubicle tomorrow, and she'd hand him busywork—continuity checking, condensing Raeanne's summaries, and editing out Nory's tendency to throw in a country music line or two as she powered through her breakdowns. That would be enough to keep him out of her hair and contributing.

"So," she said to make small talk as they waited for the elevator, "how long have you been a writer?"

Victor stood with his hands clasped in front of him as if he was a soldier at ease. "Actually, I've never written teleplays."

The elevator arrived and they stepped on. *Oh, good.* She smashed the button for her floor. *This is far worse than I could have imagined.* "So you're a soap Pendergrast?"

"As a matter of fact, I am." He flashed a smile, then stared straight ahead, adopting his military at-ease stance once again.

An explosive-detecting ping went off in Frankie's brain. Brady had told Victor to "say hi" to his aunt. With wide eyes, she looked at Victor anew.

"You're Augustinia Pendergrast's nephew?" she asked in a reverent tone.

"The one and only."

The elevator whooshed open and they stepped out while Frankie absorbed this new reality. There were two Pendergrasts on the board of the soap company, and Augustinia was one. Victor must be the other.

He was no flunky slumming it while he figured out what to do with retirement. He was a Pendergrast agent come to monitor their moves. She'd shake him as soon as she could and get back to work.

––––✶––––

It took her exactly twenty minutes to "shake" Victor Pendergrast. That's the moment she stood outside Raeanne's cubicle, introducing the two. She'd already taken him on the nickel tour of the writers' suite, including a stop by Kayla's empty desk and her own cluttered office. She'd caught Nory and Hank in the coffee room and blitzkrieged from there to Raeanne's "palace of pleasure." At least it seemed that way to Frankie. New Age music drifting from the woman's hard drive, a lavender-scented room diffuser in the corner of her desk, a poster poem on the cubicle wall. And Raeanne herself, all soft and curvy, sticking out her bust, er, hand, for Victor to shake.

"Why, how nice to meet you! I've been a Pendergrast products woman for forever," she gushed, hand fluttering to her chest. "When I was in college, I couldn't wait to get home on weekends to soak in Pendergrast Milk Bath. My goodness, my skin would be so soft after that you could have used me as a pillow!"

Pillow. Raeanne. Pillows. Raeanne's…

How did she do it?

"Well," Frankie interrupted, "that's nice. But I have some work to do so…"

But Raeanne didn't budge. "You go right on, Frankie, darlin'. I can take Mr. Pendergrast around and show him the set and all. You haven't seen that, have you? And I can tell you all about our audience share and how we're plannin' on expandin' it."

"Victor. Please call me Victor."

Raeanne was already brushing past Frankie, linking her arm through Victor's as she went.

"I'm sure you'll be as starstruck as I was the first time I set eyes on the set." She looked back over her shoulder at Frankie. "Don't you worry yourself. I'll take care of him." And then to Victor, "Frankie is such a workhorse. Dedicated to her job as the day is long."

Workhorse? Why did that sound so unexceptional and ugly?

Faye grabbed Carla by the arm and pulled her away from the party, but especially away from Gabe. Fury rose in her eyes.

"What did I do?" Carla sputtered as they stepped outside the Reilly Tavern. She put her hands on her well-rounded hips and thrust out her ample bosom, accentuated by a skin-tight leopard-print dress. Carla always wore slutty clothes designed to draw attention to the part of her anatomy a man's eyes lingered on.

"You know exactly what you did, you brazen hussy!" Faye slapped her.

Carla rubbed her cheek. "Why, you…" She lunged at Faye, but Faye stepped back, causing Carla to fall into a trash can. When Carla stood, wet noodles and orange rinds hung from her arms, and an onion peel decorated her nose.

"You're just jealous, you little twit," Carla raged. "You'll never be able to keep him."

Faye laughed. "Oh, I know how to keep them, Carla. You might know how to get them. But I know how to keep them."

She stormed off.

Frankie flicked off the television late that afternoon, trying to remember when she'd plotted that scene. Oh yes, now it came back to her—it was right after the last *Lust* anniversary shindig. That was the one where Raeanne had been flirting with the fellow from network, the new guy everybody thought was such a hottie.

Watching the scene ignited a twinge of discomfort. She had to stop using the show and her breakdowns for it—even if a lot of them eventually ended up in the recycle bin and not on air—as a sort of therapy for her wounded heart and bruised ego. Surely there was something wrong with that. And surely someone would notice at some point.

Doesn't matter, she said to comfort herself. That hottie from network didn't last long enough to figure it out. Nobody associated with *Lust* lasted long.

And that, m'dear, is why you shouldn't worry about Victor Pendergrast breathing down your neck. He'll probably stick around for a week, get bored, and go back to his hedge funds and polo meets.

She really couldn't spend time worrying about him. She had too much other work to do, most notably the whole Luke Blades fiasco. None of her writers were beating down her door with ideas. In her short tenure as boss, she'd noticed already they weren't quick to respond to ASAP requests, and she needed to fix that, to learn better managerial and leadership skills. They had to understand that when she said "jump," the correct response was "how high," not "ho hum."

More books, that was the trick. She was clicking her way to a business management site when Kayla buzzed her.

"Mr. Pendergrast was wondering if there's an office space he can occupy," she said, her tone a whispery hush, quite different from the dramatic tones she'd used to fetch Frankie to Brady's office.

Office space? What was she—building management?

"Um, tell him to check with Brady's people on that one, okay? They're supposed to set him up, not me. I'm a little busy here." As soon as she flicked off the phone, she regretted abdicating power. *That's not the way to be a leader*, she thought, *by palming off a problem*. She hit the button for her secretary. Voice mail. Kayla must have already been making the call to Victor.

Frankie stood, looking at the piles of papers, books, scripts, and more that were littering her office. All right. She might not be able to give Mr. Pendergrast an office, but she would be able to keep him busy. She gathered an armful of materials about the show and dumped them on Kayla's desk, penning a quick note she affixed to the top of the bunch: "Background info and some work for Victor. Please deliver." Kayla looked at it and nodded, finishing her call.

Frankie brushed her hands together. There, that was managerial. Right?

She threw herself back into her work, pushing aside thoughts of Raeanne, Victor, Kayla, and the thousand petty difficulties that beset her. For the rest of the day, she was lost in *Lust*'s stories, moving the characters around in her head and on the computer screen like chess pieces, consulting story bibles about past relationships, looking up notes on actor contracts to see where renewal negotiations would fall within a story arc, even plotting out ratings upticks against a rough outline of past story climaxes. By the time she realized she was the last person in the office, dark had descended.

Chapter 2

"You are coming for the weekend, aren't you? I told Dane to make up your room."

Victor stared out at the gray early morning light beyond his new office, smiling sadly at the sound of his aunt's frail voice on his cell phone. He'd come in early to get a fresh start on organizing his notes, his desk, and his thoughts in general before the secretary Brady promised him arrived, but his aunt had interrupted him twice already with calls.

"Yes, I'll be there. Friday evening if I can get away."

They made quick small talk and then he hung up, getting back to the task at hand, which was a cram course on the workings and stories of *Lust for Life*.

Victor Pendergrast was not only related to the Pendergrast family whose soap products underwrote *Lust for Life*. His aunt Augustinia Pendergrast was the slender thread by which the drama's survival hung. If it had been up to the board of the once privately held soap and household products behemoth, Pendergrast sponsorship of *Lust for Life* would have been dropped five years ago when the ratings hit an all-time low. But Augustinia—Gussie to her nearest friends and relatives—used her considerable clout to manipulate any marketing guru who dared suggest there were better ways to spend the company's massive advertising budget. And "manipulate" really meant "fire" to Gussie Pendergrast.

A procession of marketing experts, who made compelling

PowerPoint presentations on why the show should be dumped, crumpled under Augustinia's withering scorn. She had enjoyed her fellow board members' grudging support as long as she'd served. But each year it was tougher to corral new directors to the cause. And this past year, her vigor and influence had waned considerably. She might be forced to give up her seat before long.

Victor wouldn't let this last joy burn out in her life. She'd done too much for him over the years, acting as the one steady influence in his life when his own parents decided that saving the world was more important than saving him, both before and after their eventual split. The Pendergrasts had money, all right. But that didn't buy wisdom or the normal bonds of familial affection.

Damn, he needed coffee. But no one else was about to either get him a cup or tell him where to get one himself. He'd have to remember to stop on his way in tomorrow.

Before him were the head writer's breakdowns for possible shows. She'd given him a cursory tour the day before and then had her secretary load him up with show bibles and breakdowns and scripts. He suspected she just wanted him out of her hair. He couldn't blame her. It was always tough when a new person came on board.

He had a lot of catching up to do, but he was capable of it. He'd faced worse. Rebellion in his youth had sent him enlisting in the Marines after college—to the horror of his friends, the dismay of his aunt Gussie, and the disgust of his parents—and once he'd mustered out he'd decided to tackle a business career, becoming a first-class marketing consultant. And, oh, yes, somewhere in the middle of all those projects tackled and goals achieved, he'd married, had a beautiful daughter, and divorced.

He stared at the pages before him and exhaled. On the far corner of his desk were the morning newspapers, which he'd rather be perusing instead of the tortured tales of Crestview's inhabitants.

"It's all for you, Aunt Gussie," he whispered under his breath as he began to read, pen and notebook at the ready.

He'd already taken a cram course on the show, watching old episodes online in preparation for this gig. His sweet aunt Gussie had been a fan of the soap opera since girlhood, first hearing it on radio and following it through each of its transformations. He knew she was sometimes vocal about her story ideas and had even saved an actor or two from being cut when she developed a fondness for their characters.

In reviewing old episodes, he also smiled at how writers worked around her passions.

When Victor saw characters speaking disparagingly of golden retrievers, he knew that even if the characters were among his aunt's favorites, they were destined to leave. Besides *Lust for Life*, his aunt's other great love was dogs, that breed in particular. If his aunt wanted to keep that character and the writers did not, they threw in some dialogue bad-mouthing puppies, a surefire way to land them on Aunt Gussie's expendable list.

His cell rang, and he quickly answered when he saw it was her.

"You are coming for the weekend, aren't you?" she asked as she'd just done twice before that morning. "I told… oh… what is his name…?"

"Dane."

"Yes, Dane. I told him to make up your room."

Victor didn't smile this time but merely clenched his jaw. "Yes, Auntie, I'll be there. I'm working on *Lust for Life* right now and might not be able to get away until late Friday."

Her voice strengthened, gaining in focus as she talked. "I'm so glad Donovan and Terri are together again. But what about that Faye? She's not going to get involved with that gadabout Gabe, is she?"

He let her chatter on about the soap opera she loved, the one light that continued to flicker brightly in her increasingly cloudy world.

———

Gabe or his father—which one should Faye go for?

This was the story Frankie had wrestled with the afternoon before, the one that had kept pulling her away from the crisis of Luke Blades, that she just couldn't ignore. She thought that in the seeds of the Faye/Gabe/whomever story, *Lust*'s ratings would bloom.

Gabe was a rebel-without-a-cause type, and they had landed the perfect actor for the job—slender but not emaciated, odd angular face, muscular shoulders, and a hushed rough voice. He was so good, in fact, that Frankie worried they'd lose him to the big screen before long—yet another, very practical reason to create an attraction between Faye and the father. If the actor who played Gabe left the show for greener pastures, Faye could fall into the father's arms.

Not even cast yet, the father was just a stranger in a fedora and raincoat for now. Frankie wanted to cast him very carefully, looking for just the right combination of sexy and sage. She'd have to lean on Casting to keep her in the loop. One of *Lust for Life*'s problems was its lack of communication. If she didn't keep on top of those things, she'd write a blue-eyed blonde character and get a brown-eyed brunette in the part.

Right now she was envisioning Gabe's father as tall and muscular, with dark hair and twinkling eyes—no, wait, that was Victor! Okay, so he could look like Victor. Frankie often drew the essence of characters from real people, just changing and molding and sculpting until she had what she wanted.

Frankie sipped her coffee, staring out over the Manhattan skyline. A dreary mist had turned the whole city steel gray, the river a flat, cold band in the distance. Unlike many of her colleagues, Frankie wasn't really in love with the city. Sure, she enjoyed the restaurants, the hustle and bustle, the sense that everything one could want was at one's fingertips. But it also overwhelmed her. All that availability only seemed to make her more aware of her lacks. Not material things—she could pretty much acquire what she wanted. No, a sense of belonging, of being an organic part of a whole, the way Donovan, Terri, Faye, Gabe, and the others were all as much a part of Crestview as the fake earth upon which they trod. New York wasn't home. And at this stage of her life, home wasn't even home.

Starting with her final year of grad school, she'd been vaguely discontent. At Wellesley, surrounded by highbrows, she'd begun to think she should aspire to be one, too. Always a good study, she'd put mind and soul into absorbing all she could about the greats of literature and style, making up for her lack of exposure to such luminaries during summers past when her high school reading list sat untouched by the TV remote.

But when she'd met Brian and they'd married, well, someone had to pay the bills. He was so absorbed in his writing he could hardly remember to eat, let alone go to a job. Besides, she'd had a good one, and in the literary world to boot. So she had achieved her dream after all, right? For a while, besotted with love for him, she'd thought her destiny was to be his muse. Muse and breadwinner rolled into one. As their debts mounted, she began the freelance scriptwriting.

She remembered the day she packed up her office at the publishing house to move to full-time work at *Lust for Life*. She'd had the beginnings of a stress headache, brought on by worry about whether she was doing the right thing. Part of her was thrilled to go to bigger money, to a new challenge, to… home. But that was the very thing that sparked worry. Was she retreating to the comforts of childhood by taking the *Lust for Life* job? Or had she given up too easily on bettering herself? Why couldn't she think of a Great American Novel to write?

She still felt between worlds. Her best friend, Gail, despite her own humble background, was a literary lawyer working with tweed-jacketed prizewinners. The college chums she kept in touch with had similarly moved on to prestigious jobs, working for magazines like the

New Yorker or the *Atlantic*, or they'd earned spanking new PhDs and were starting their climb up the tenure ladder at small colleges hither and yon. When Frankie read of their accomplishments in alumni magazines, it made her hesitate to submit her own job news. It was crazy, she knew, but when you've moved from one social stratum to another, you always felt you had something to hide.

"Ya busy?" A familiar male voice mumbled into the room.

She twirled her chair to face the door, where Luke Blades stood on crutches, his left leg in a cast up to his knee. Despite his injury, his rugged face didn't look the worse for wear. If anything, his five o'clock shadow and slightly pained expression made him look well-worn and heroic, as if he'd been involved in an important struggle. His hair was spiky and tousled, and his eyes—usually a blazing blue—telegraphed his discomfort. They were red and puffy, and every so often his brows twinged. He'd rarely looked so strong or so needy.

"My god, Luke! I thought you were still in the hospital." Frankie leapt up, pointing to a couch against the wall. "Come in and sit down. Get off your feet. I mean, foot. When did you fly in?" He must've taken a red-eye home.

He hobbled to the sofa and plopped down, rubbing his face with his hand after stowing his crutches against the armrest.

"Couldn't stay there. Couldn't get any rest. And I've got lots of dialogue to learn." His voice sounded ragged.

Dialogue? What is he talking about—Luke has no dialogue to learn. Not now, at least. Not until we figure out what to do with him and his rigid, hard mass of... plaster cast. Frankie was still mulling options for him from the paltry list Raeanne and Hank left on Kayla's desk for her late yesterday. Nory hadn't submitted anything.

"Are you okay?" She peered at him. His red eyes were blurry and unfocused. "You taking any more of those supplements?"

"Yeah, yeah." He waved the air in front of him as if flies were buzzing round his head.

"And meds from the hospital?"

"Huh?"

Good grief. The guy is stoned on prescription drugs.

"Luke, honey, I think you should head home and get your roomie to make you a nice cup of tea." Last Frankie had heard, Luke had a live-in girlfriend, an actress doing a nonrecurring part on another soap.

"No can do," he said in his Donovan Reilly voice, all clipped and manly. "Walk-up."

"What do you mean 'walk-up?' There is no such thing as a walk-up these days!" But of course there were. She'd been to them.

"No roomie. Flew the coop."

Or had Luke's roaming eye chased her away? Frankie stared at him, her own eyes narrowing. He was just like Brian, except he made good money. Before she could ask him what he wanted, he grunted out his request.

"Need place to stay." He sounded like a patient who'd just had dental surgery. His eyes flickered. He was falling asleep!

"You're asking me if you can—"

"Elevator. Two rooms."

Yes, her building had an elevator. And yes, she had two rooms—her bedroom and the living room. But Luke living with her?

"Only for a few weeks," he babbled, his eyes shuttering as drowsiness overwhelmed him. "Desperate here, Frank."

And he did look desperate. He looked homeless. And she had to admit to being a teensy bit flattered that heartthrob Luke had chosen her for this request. *Only a few weeks.* She could keep an eye on him, make sure he didn't bang up his other leg, or do something stupid to jeopardize the show.

As she crept up to the possibility of Luke Blades as a roommate, a large dark shadow passed her door. Victor. She grabbed her phone and hit Kayla's number to ask her to grab Victor and send him in.

But as usual, Kayla didn't answer, so she stepped out and called Victor in herself. She noticed Kayla was at her desk after all.

"Victor!" Frankie called. He stopped and came back.

Frankie looked at Kayla. "You didn't answer," Frankie accused. "I just buzzed you."

Red-faced, Kayla closed a binder with a quick slap. "Sorry. I was, er, studying."

Studying the show? The binder was the kind they used for show bibles. Okay, so maybe Kayla was trying to be a well-informed assistant. Props for that.

Frankie nodded to Victor. He wore a pleasant smile on his face and a slightly lighter version of the suit he'd had on yesterday on his bod. She'd have to tell him the dress code was casual.

"You have a car?" she threw at him. Before he could answer, she shook her head. "Doesn't matter. Take a cab and get a receipt—or get petty cash from Kayla. I need you to take Mr. Blades here to this address." She quickly jotted down her Chelsea apartment info, grabbed her key, and held it out to Victor. He looked bemused, his smile now lopsided and his eyes doing that twinkly thing again. He held a cup of coffee in one hand and a newspaper in the other. Recreational reading on the job? Oh brother. Maybe that would keep her from having to baby-sit him, though.

"Could you stop in my office first?" he asked. "I have something to show you."

A few minutes later she was sitting in Victor's spacious corner office, sipping a cup of coffee that his secretary—Bob, from Brady Stephens's office—had fetched for her.

That's right. Victor had an office three times as big as her own and a well-trained, obedient administrative assistant to boot. She kicked herself for delegating the office hunt to Brady via Kayla.

What had she been thinking? She should have relegated him to a tiny cubicle herself, showing him who was boss. Darn it, but she had a hard time showing herself who was boss, let alone anyone else!

And what had Brady been thinking giving him this office anyway? It had previously belonged to the assistant producer, who, like the former head writer, left at an alarming rate. She should have moved in here as soon as she was promoted, but, no, she'd focused on the job, not the digs. The digs were important. They communicated power and leadership and "ASAP means ASAP"—all that good stuff she needed to sell to her staff. Why was she always seeing these lessons in the rearview mirror?

It grated that already-wealthy Victor Pendergrast was ensconced in the high-rent equivalent of the soap's office space. She had come from a small tract house in the unfashionable suburbs of Baltimore (as if any of its suburbs were fashionable), with a single mother supporting her through twelve years of parochial school and helping her out beyond that. It had been a cruel blow to learn, during her first year of college, that people got places on the strength of their names alone.

Victor handed Frankie a copy of the *New York Post*, opened to a page where a story about a burglary was circled. She read it, sipped her coffee again, and set the paper aside.

"We don't have current events time here, Vic. We have work to do. I have to get the breakdowns to Brady and the network for approval so I can send them out to scriptwriters."

Victor just raised his eyebrows and steepled his hands together in front of his face.

"You didn't notice anything familiar in that article?"

She picked it up again and scanned it. "I don't have time for tests. Just tell me what it is."

He leaned forward. "A thief breaks into an apartment in Central Park West, robs an absent woman of her expensive jewelry, and leaves a single rose."

So what, she thought. *A thief with sentiment. A jewel thief, no less.* And then it hit her.

A jewel thief with heart, mysteriously leaving roses on his victims' beds as the camera closed in on his gloved hand...

Oh, no! It was one of their stories!

"It wasn't my idea," she found herself murmuring, as if she needed to apologize. The previous head writer had concocted the story, and now it was still dangling out there, unresolved. They hadn't even decided who the thief was going to be, or why he was robbing people. Frankie had even considered letting the story peter out to nothing and moving on.

"This is—" she began, but he cut her off.

"An opportunity. I know. I've had someone leak it to the press—the association with the show. And I've been looking over past episodes, reviewing the story. I thought maybe you could tell me where it's ultimately going, and then we can decide—"

"*We* can decide?"

What was going on here? He was taking it upon himself to chart out plot direction, to direct marketing efforts, to imperil public safety with a lame story whose arc hadn't even been adequately mapped? And since when had this operation become a democracy? Sure, she asked for input from the other writers, but for crying out loud, he'd just landed on the team, and *she* was the boss. This office had gone to his head. She squared her shoulders and put her coffee on his desk. Time to show him who was boss.

"I never liked this story, Victor, and had been planning on letting it fade away, or wrapping it up quickly. Now we have even more reason to do so. It's a public safety issue." She tapped her fingers on the arms of the chair. She stopped tapping when she realized how weak it sounded. So she stood instead.

"And you shouldn't have done anything with Publicity without checking with me first, dammit," she said. Yes, cursing. That was the answer. That showed who was in charge. "I know you're new, but the way it works is anything that has to do with stories, plots, or character development goes through the head writer. That's me. Especially publicity. That should go through me, too. The head writer."

He stood as well, but she got the sense he was doing it not as a power play but as a courtesy. Woman stands, man must stand. "I'm notifying you now," he said, his voice not sounding at all remorseful or uneasy. It was confident. "That's what I wanted to talk to you about. I was in early, so I got started on a few things."

"Yes, but…" She cursed again but regretted it immediately. It made her sound like a teen, not a team leader. She shook her head, as if that would erase the image. "This is my job, to vet stuff like that. It should go through me first, before action is taken. Me. The boss. The leader. The head writer." Was she saying that too much?

At last—a reaction. He opened his mouth to speak, then closed it again, clearly at a loss for words. Good. She was establishing her authority over him. It was hard, but she could do it. She was learning. She'd never managed an older employee. This would be an important experience. She congratulated herself on getting past the first hurdle. Her point made, she was about to leave when he held up his hand. With the other, he punched a button on his phone.

"Bob, make sure I'm not disturbed, will you?"

What the…?

He gestured to the chair she'd just vacated and came around to occupy the one opposite it. The classic "bad news" setup. Uh-oh.

"I'm really sorry, Frankie, for any confusion," he said after she was settled. "Our meeting with Brady Stephens was so brief, I just assumed he'd filled you in before we got together."

"Filled me in on what?" Her hands prickled, and she breathed fast. *Who was she kidding? She knew where this was going. She was getting fired.* Brady must have been firing her the other day but had bungled it. Victor was taking her job. She probably shouldn't have even come in today. Oh jeez. She'd really made a fool of herself.

How to reclaim her dignity. Deep breath. Get up slowly, thank him for his time, let him know her beef wasn't with him, it was with Brady; tell him where she kept everything; offer to write up notes.

How much did she have in savings? Would she have to move home? Would her mother even have room for her anymore—she'd converted her bedroom into a sewing room—would one of her friends take her in? Aw, jeez, she'd just offered Luke her apartment to crash in. Maybe she could sell Avon or Mary Kay or… mow lawns. Her mother's neighborhood was good for that sort of thing. Yeah, she'd be all right, land on her feet. Just take some adjusting. She could do it. *Oh, god, help me, please.*

"*Lust for Life* has been struggling—" he began.

"I know," she said, blinking fast. "I don't take it personally. Don't worry. None of the head writers do."

He looked confused but kept going. "And the Pendergrast board believes there are far better ways to spend their advertising dollars, more effective ways."

"I know, I know." *Why didn't he just get it over with? Poor guy. He shouldn't have been put in this position. It was Brady's fault. The coward.*

"I'm on the board. And I think there might be enough votes to finally override my aunt Gussie. For her sake, I want to find a way to keep the show going as long as she is going."

"But you're not a writer, not this kind of writer. You said so," she said, touched by his devotion to his aunt.

"But I am an expert in marketing."

Aha, so that was it. They brought in some big so-called marketing guru to take over. Well, poor guy, let him have the job and see how long he lasted. He would never be able to get through a writers' meeting, let alone a month's scripts. Yes, in a short time he would be running for the exits while she would be settled into a new career, a successful, top-selling Avon agent, perhaps even pulling market share away from Pendergrast's Milk Bath line. She made a mental note to put Raeanne on her pitch list.

"Well," she said, standing. She might as well get this over with. He stood, too. "Thanks for explaining it to me. I'll have my office packed by the end of the day."

"You're quitting?" He sounded not only surprised, but a bit panicked.

"I thought—" She stopped. He *wasn't* firing her. She was just supposed to work with him, this big-shot marketing guru. *With* being the key word in that sentence. He wasn't reporting to her, as she'd assumed in Brady's office. They were equals.

Thank god, thank god! Glory Hallelujah! No living in her mother's basement! No business start-up for her. She'd been reprieved, her execution stayed!

She let out a little giggle, then cleared her throat.

Okay, rewind. How to recover…

"No, no. Misunderstanding. I meant I'd have my office cleaned up. So we can meet there. To go over procedures. It's a mess. Been meaning to clean it for a long time. In fact, I won't be the actual one cleaning it. I'll have Kayla clean it. My secretary. I have one, too, being head writer and all. A secretary, that is." She swallowed. "But back to this thief problem, Victor. If we're to work together, then we should have hashed out strategy together before you ran off to the folks in Publicity." There, that was better. She'd reclaimed her position, hadn't she? Sometimes she wished she could watch reruns of herself, taking notes to avoid future mistakes.

"I apologize. I'm used to working alone," he said.

Relief warmed her. He wasn't a jerk. That was a good first step, at least. "Go over with me again what you've already done and what you know."

He began to summarize the problem and his actions again when Bob knocked at the door, letting him know Dwayne was here.

After telling Bob he'd be a few minutes, Victor turned to Frankie and apologized again. "I set up a meeting with the website manager."

Frankie hadn't even known they had a website manager, let alone his name.

"Ah, yes, Dwayne," she said with a knowing wink.

"I was going to tell you about it," Victor continued. "But you were busy, and I decided to be proactive." He held out his hand to shake on this new arrangement. "Let's talk about the thief later today."

"Yes, absolutely," she said, shaking his hand with vigor. She moved toward the door. "Today. No delay. Have your Bob give my Kayla a buzz, okay?" Why was she rhyming?

"Sure thing."

Frankie wasn't quite sure, but the twinkle in his eye might have entered his voice.

She left, marching past Bob and the waiting Dwayne as if she were commander of the regiment, a posture unfortunately ruined when she nearly tripped on a carpet snag.

"Bob, call Maintenance about that," she barked over her shoulder.

She was both relieved and unsettled as she made her way back to her office. The good news—she wouldn't have to look into that other career thing. The bad news—she'd have to put up with his marketing stuff, with being a co-leader instead of a leader. And she'd not even mastered the leader skill set, let alone how to share it!

It wasn't until she was back at her desk that she realized the other bad news—he was operating on the premise that this thief story should proceed. She had been so distracted by her fear of unemployment that she'd let that completely fly by.

A thief imitating their silly story on *Lust*? It hardly seemed possible. And she really wasn't comfortable with Victor's approach at all. Maybe the thing to do was to rally the troops and beat his idea down before it had a chance to take hold. None of the writers had been happy with that thief plot. They'd talked of jettisoning it in the past, even spending some writer meetings mocking it. Raeanne had said it was from the "Dark Ages of Daytime," Nory had snarked that it was so boring they should caution viewers not to operate heavy equipment while watching it, and even Hank had joined in the fun, saying they'd run out of old ladies for the thief to rob unless they merged the show with *Golden Girls* repeats. Come to think of it, his comment had stopped the laughter. At least she knew she had backup on this one.

She hit a button on her phone to reach Kayla. Voice mail. A new message, too, something in what sounded like a British accent. "Leave your name and number, luv." Frankie really had to talk to Kayla.

"When you get back, Kayla, call all the writers for a meeting in a half hour. Oh, and tell Victor to be there, too." If he wasn't finished with his web meeting by then, too bad. She would show him she was still the captain of this writing ship.

As if to emphasize that point, a foghornlike blast came from the sofa in the corner. Luke! He was still there, snoring loudly.

She ignored him, clicking her way into the *Harvard Business Journal* page to see if they had any online articles about managing problem employees. Nope, but another article caught her eye: "Savvy Meets Sage: Young Leadership/Older Team."

Chapter 3

WHEN SHE WALKED INTO the conference room nearly an hour later—she knew everyone would be late—in her hand she had the previous day's pages, which Victor had delivered with his comments twenty minutes ago. His markups were light, but he'd caught some inconsistencies in voice and continuity as well as a big fumble on a family relationship (they were all so tangled on soaps that it was hard not to have some male character lusting after his own half-sister). Victor had obviously studied.

Nory, Hank, and Raeanne waited in the room in their usual places, Nory sipping on a coffee, Raeanne with a bottled water, Hank munching on peanut M&Ms. Nory looked different. Frankie stared for a few seconds.

"Washed out my hair dye," Nory volunteered.

"Nice," Frankie said, still trying to process the new look. The hair was no longer jet black, just dark charcoal. And Nory had on a gray tee instead of her usual black. She was edging her way out of the shadows, Frankie guessed. Good for her.

Raeanne looked up. "Victor was here earlier. He said to buzz him when you came in." Raeanne, alone among the crew, had a stack of papers in front of her along with some file folders and a ratings report from a year ago. What was she up to?

Frankie stepped out to tell Kayla, who, miraculously, was at her desk, to fetch Mr. Pendergrast. "Remind me to talk to you about your voice mail," she added, before rejoining her team.

While she waited for Victor, she chided the writers for not providing more ideas for the Donovan story line.

"Nory, you didn't even give me one," Frankie said.

"I still think we should just shoot him from the waist up," Nory said. She started humming some unrecognizable tune.

"Did you like my abduction idea?" Hank asked, eager to be rewarded. "I thought we could integrate it with the new Faye story, making that shadowy figure the kidnapper."

Raeanne clucked her tongue. "No good, Hank. That shadowy figure is Gabe's long-lost father. Gabe's got enough yin-yang goin' on. He doesn't need more to complicate his tortured soul." When Raeanne drawled "yin-yang," it sounded like "yan-yan." She continued, "And we have a great triangle potential there—does Faye go for Gabe or for his father, the sexy, experienced, cultivated yet hunky sophisticate?"

At that moment Victor walked into the room. He nodded his greetings and took a chair next to Frankie, who sat at the head of the table.

His entrance threw Frankie off her stride. She was supposed to be the one to enter last. Or maybe it was Nory's humming. *Would she please stop humming?* Or maybe it had been Raeanne's comment about the potential for a love triangle with Gabe's father. Frankie had thought of that but not yet voiced it to the team. She was very proprietary about her ideas. Now a jealous fear curled up her spine— that Raeanne might be able to execute the idea better.

Raeanne continued to prattle in her hypnotic drawl, smiling at Victor as she spoke in a conspiratorial way. It was as if she were saying, *I have to explain this to Frankie, the dear, feeble-minded, plodding, ugly old workhorse.*

"To make Gabe's father Donovan's kidnapper intersects the stories in a purely manipulative and imposed fashion. What on earth is Graystone's motivation for having Donovan kidnapped? (Because

I surely don't imagine the man dirtyin' his hands to do the deed himself. He'd hire someone, for heaven's sake, with his trunks full of treasure.)"

Raeanne was the only woman Frankie knew who could successfully talk in parentheses.

"Graystone?" Nory asked.

Thank god, she's stopped hummin' at least.

"Oh, that's the name I keep imaginin' him havin'," Raeanne said, again nodding toward Victor, proud of herself. "It's very Gothic. Should appeal to our demographic." She tapped the ratings report in front of her.

At the word "demographic," Victor focused on Raeanne. "Great point," he said. "But we need to stretch the edges of that demographic. Younger would be better."

Raeanne sucked in her lip as if Victor had murmured something dirty in her ear. "That's why Graystone and Faye will be involved." She patted him on the arm. "Faye's the ingénue. What young woman doesn't fantasize about gettin' it on with an older, more experienced man who can open up the world for her? Faye would be a willin' student to his expert tutelage, eager to lap up whatever Graystone shoots her way." She batted her eyelashes and straightened, accentuating her cleavage, which today was encased in soft white cashmere.

Frankie blushed. "We're not here to discuss Faye," she interjected.

"Oh," Nory said, disappointed. "I was wondering how you liked what I wrote about Gabe and her."

"Were those your pages?" Victor asked her, genuinely interested. "Where you had Gabe tell Faye that 'at seventeen, it's hard to see past Friday night'? I wish I'd had that line when my daughter was that age." He smiled. Nory glowed.

Ping, ping! Two alarms went off in Frankie's head. One shouted, *Victor has a daughter—so what, so what?* The other zeroed in on Nory's line he'd just quoted.

She scrunched up her eyes, thinking, and then it came to her: *"You got so much going for you, going right / but I know at seventeen it's hard to see past Friday night."* She looked at Nory and said, "Brad Paisley. *Letter to Me."*

Nory sank in her chair. "I didn't realize…"

Victor looked at Frankie, clearly confused.

"It's a country song. Nory's become a fan."

"I only listen in the mornings," Nory murmured.

"I thought we'd gotten past this, Nory," Frankie scolded. "I can't be scouring everything you write for remnants of Rascal Flatts, Toby Keith, Kenny Chesney, or Brad Paisley."

Nory continued to keep her head down, as if waiting for the executioner's axe.

"Or LeAnn Rimes," Victor said, looking at Nory. "I like her."

Nory looked up and did something with her mouth that resembled a smile. Victor had managed to be Mister Congeniality while Frankie was feeling like the Wicked Witch of the West.

"We can go over all that later," she said, consciously lightening her tone. "Right now we need to discuss an important event that has far-reaching implications for *Lust for Life*." She passed out photocopies of the *New York Post* article and spoke as they each read silently. "As you can see, we have a problem. Someone is imitating one of our stories, and it could have serious consequences. I know we've talked about this story line in the past, and you've been less than enthusiastic, so I thought we should continue that discussion now that we have a very serious concern associated with it."

Silence hung over the room as they finished reading the article. Frankie suppressed a smile, waiting for the deluge of thief story criticism surely to follow. She couldn't look at Victor. She was afraid she'd start giggling. Who needed management articles? She knew her staff, knew their likes and dislikes, and now she'd let them plow under this despicable story, leaving her looking like the serene and wise moderator of the whole process. She imagined herself raising her eyebrows and saying to Victor, "Well, I certainly didn't expect *that* strong a response," when they started the kvetching. She could hardly contain herself.

"Wow," Hank murmured at last. "Someone's paying attention to us!"

"What a great opportunity," Raeanne said.

"Cool," Nory chimed in.

What was going on here? Had they forgotten so quickly how they despised this thief? How they'd made fun of Jack, the last head writer, for coming up with it? Maybe that was it—they didn't want to say anything negative for fear Victor would think she was the originator of this story. Aww, that was sweet.

"This was Jack's idea," she reminded them. "He hadn't even mapped out where it was going, remember? It was a sweeps grabber. No one would get killed, but there'd be a suspense element. He hadn't even decided who the thief was. And—don't forget—none of you liked it. Dark Ages of Daytime. So boring we should warn viewers about using heavy machinery."

They stared at her blankly.

"None of you liked this story," she said. "None. Of. You." She waited for them to affirm this statement.

Silence.

Raeanne sighed, eventually speaking in a dreamy voice while twisting the corner of a paper in front of her. "Jack was a seat-of-the-pants kind of guy. Very intuitive. Very of-the-moment. He had some real talent, of course, But he never liked plannin' or plottin'. It was his downfall."

Frankie wondered what Raeanne thought her downfall would be.

"Whatever the backstory, we have to figure out fast how to end this thing. We've got to wrap it up so that this guy"—Frankie jabbed at the article—"stops doing what he's doing. Just like we want to stop the thief doing his thing on the show. Like you all have said. A thousand times. A million times. We don't have enough old ladies on the show for him to rob, remember, Hank?"

Again she waited for them to chime in with their agreement. Again, nothing.

She tried repetition. Parenting experts said it worked on kids, right? "Stopping our thief will stop the real thief. And you all hated our thief. You mocked him. Oh, I vividly recall how you mocked him."

"How will ending the story stop the real thief?" Hank asked. Not sarcastically. As if he really wanted to know.

Nory turned to him. "If the thief is inspired by the show, we remove the inspiration and he—"

"Goes berserk," Raeanne said. "Oh, lordy. He could just snap. It could be dreadful. A nightmare. And all our fault. It could be that this story is the man's lifeline."

"Or woman's," Victor said. "The thief could be a woman."

Raeanne smiled. "True, Mr. Pendergrast, but—"

"Call me Victor."

"All right, Victor. But I just keep thinkin' of that Pendergrast Milk Bath whenever I see you," she cooed. "Victor, while the thief could very well be a woman, he is more likely than not a man. It is clear on the show that the thief is a man, after all."

"Who says?" Frankie asked. "The thief was never seen. Just his hands. Or her hands. Arms. Sometimes a leg." Why was she suddenly arguing for the distaff version of the thief? She wanted *no* version of the thief. "But no arms and legs is better. I mean, no thief."

"A woman—like Grace Kelly in *To Catch a Thief*," Nory said, enthused.

Oh no. Frankie had wanted to dampen any enthusiasm for this story, not feed it.

"Maybe the thing to do is to find ourselves a nice, strong policeman to talk to," Raeanne suggested. "See if they think the fellow would do somethin' really harmful if we pulled the plug on his favorite story. That seems to me to be the most careful and professional thing to do. I'd be happy to handle it."

"Funny how the police didn't notice it themselves," Hank said, eyes shining with innocence.

"I doubt they're soap watchers," Nory said, slumped in her chair.

"But, yeah, well, I mean funny how no one pointed it out to them, called it in, you know," Hank huffed. "You'd think that one of our fans would have seen it and let them know. Or let this newspaper know."

"For that to happen, it would have to have been a fan who also saw the news article. Statistically unlikely," Victor said with grim finality while Raeanne trembled at his use of the word "statistically."

"Police or not, we can't keep this story going," Frankie said, her voice rising in frustration. What was the matter with them—had they forgotten how stupid they thought this story was? "Come on, people! You hated this story. Hank, you told me you thought it was duller than reruns of *Teletubbies.*" Well, maybe she'd said that. No matter. She was desperate.

"Did I?" Hank pulled out a tiny notebook, searching handwritten notes.

"And Nory," Frankie continued, "you said, 'What was he thinking?'—when Jack came up with this story."

"Knew what he was feeling, but what was he thinking," Nory said, bobbing her head to an unheard song before shifting focus to Frankie. "Huh?"

"And Raeanne," Frankie said, staring at the blonde bombshell, "you thought the thief should be pulled faster than a heretic at a preachers convention."

Raeanne smiled and blushed. "Why yes, I did think that at the time. But things change. Even heretics can be saved."

Ready to growl, Frankie leaned on the table. "Look, we can't keep this story. None of you liked it then, and I know you don't like it now. We can't keep it. If we do, we're aiding and abetting criminal activity!" Frankie stared at Victor now. "It's unconscionable."

"It's unconscionable to help a criminal, yes," Victor said, his voice calm. "But I think it's quite a leap to say that a story on *Lust* is doing that. As Hank pointed out, even the police didn't make the connection."

"So you think it's just coincidence?" Frankie asked.

"I have no idea. All I know is that the parallel exists," Victor replied. "We can point it out and possibly bring more viewers to our show, and it might have absolutely no impact on the real thief. Or we can say nothing, and it will have absolutely no impact on the real thief."

"Well put," Raeanne said.

"Let's start brainstorming," Nory said. Nory loved brainstorming. Brainstorming for Nory meant she could digress into talking about her live-in boyfriend, Tom, and his latest film project.

But Frankie had no intention of brainstorming about the thief. She'd come into this meeting intending to use her team's previous objections to the story to make the case to Victor for pulling it, now that a real thief was imitating theirs. But she was surrounded by traitors, who were all just as giddy about the publicity possibilities as he was. Had they no conscience? Apparently not. She'd been blindsided. And to make matters worse, it was all her fault. She should have thought this through, talked to them privately before the meeting to reaffirm their opinions and make sure they jibed with her own. Another leadership lesson learned.

She looked at each one of them in turn, eager Hank, seductive Raeanne, geeky Nory—she'd get no support from them now on jettisoning the thief. Oh hell. She'd deal with the thief later, one-on-one with Co-Captain Victor, away from all these quislings. Now she'd reclaim this meeting, fixing another unresolved problem.

Frankie held up her hand. "If we're going to do any brainstorming, it should first be about what to do about Donovan. We'll tackle the thief later. On to agenda item two: Luke's broken leg."

Victor, who, to his credit, showed no signs of gloating about his temporary victory, chimed in first. "The choices are simple. We either go with the abduction plan—which I think is quite good, even if Grayson isn't the kidnapper—or you hire another actor to play Donovan while Luke is on medical leave."

"Graystone," Raeanne simpered. "That's the name I liked for Gabe's father."

"I like Grayson more," Frankie said. "Grayson it is."

"Abduction or new actor?" Victor asked.

"I don't want to deal with Luke's agent right now. Abduction," Frankie said, feeling a weight lift off her. Okay, that decision was made, for good or ill. Surely that proved her leadership bona fides. She looked at Hank. "Start sketching out the story. I'm open to who the abductor is. There's plenty in Donovan's past to work with there. You can talk to me about it in the morning." She felt herself hitting a stride, now that one big decision was out of the way, a decision that she had made… decisively.

She looked at Raeanne. "I've got the Faye/Gabe/Grayson story," she said. "You can do up a treatment for… for Terri's mother." Terri's mother's story was a slow-moving filler plot involving a beloved older actress who worked only one day a week.

Raeanne's mouth dropped open at this boring story thrown her way. Before she could protest, Frankie turned to Nory. "Get together with Hank to plot out the Donovan abduction."

Nory looked at Hank and visibly cringed. Hank didn't see.

Victor. Now Frankie turned to him.

"The thief story involves more than just plotting out characters and a story," she told him. "It involves policy. You and I will handle it first. We should meet with Brady."

Victor smiled. "I have a call into him."

Of course he would, good ol' *proactive* Victor.

She stood. "Meeting's over. I'll check with the police about the thief and we'll talk again."

As she moved out of the room, Victor caught up with her and lightly tapped her on the elbow.

"A word," he whispered and followed her to her office without waiting for her response.

Once at her office, he started talking before they were over the threshold.

"I would like to handle the contact with the police, if that's all right with you." Although he was giving her the chance to object, his tone indicated he'd rather not have a protest.

"It's not all right—"

A loud grunt and snore alerted them to the fact that Luke was still in the room dozing.

"My office," Victor said, leading the way down the hall.

Damn. His office shouts power. No snoring actor in it. No matter. I'm the boss. I'm doing okay. And I haven't even ordered one of those books yet.

She squared her shoulders and quickened her pace so that she was walking right next to him rather than behind him. In a few seconds they were in his spacious and neat office, and he was telling Bob to get him some coffee. He looked at Frankie, raising his eyebrows as if to say, "Want anything?" but she shook her head no and sat down in front of his desk.

"Look, I don't want to tell you how to do your job," he began.

"But you're going to anyway."

He gave her a half smile and sat in his own chair.

Bob tapped on the door and entered with Victor's coffee, placing it in front of him in silence. *How'd he do that so fast?* Victor thanked him, sipped, and waited until he left before continuing.

"Let me try that again," he said. "Look, I have no intention of subverting you with your team. You'll be working with them long after I'm out of here."

"I would hope so," she said defensively.

"What I mean to say is, you can relax." His tone softened to that of doctor-talking-with-deranged-patient. "You don't need to demonstrate to me that you're the boss *with them.* I know that."

A warm glow flooded Frankie's face. He thought she had been unnecessarily harsh for *his* benefit. What an ego! She tried to recover by laughing, but it sounded like a pitiful phony cackle, so she ended it by clearing her throat. And then coughing.

"Thanks, Vic, but you really haven't been here long enough to catch the vibe," she managed to sputter at last. "If I don't stay on top of their mistakes, they'll keep making them. Like Nory and the country music. Did you catch that?" She smiled.

"Obviously, I didn't." His smile and air of superiority were gone.

"No, I don't mean the Brad Paisley reference you skipped in her notes. I mean when she was talking about Jack, the previous head writer, and the thief."

At Victor's bewildered look, Frankie went on. "Nory had wondered what Jack was thinking. She knew what he was feeling, but what was he thinking? It's a Dierks Bentley song."

"Oh, I see." His facial expression relaxed. "You're good at that."

"I'm just in tune with popular culture. Lots of it. You really have to be, you know, in this job."

"Point taken."

Once again, she was impressed by his willingness to back down when she pointed out he was wrong. Maybe she didn't need to have her dukes up so much around him.

"Look," she said, "I'm not trying to throw my weight around, but I really would like to be the one who controls this thief thing. That's why I'd like to talk to the police."

"Perfectly understandable," he said, now smiling. "I just have some contacts, people I trust. That's why I wanted to do it. But if there's someone you know…"

He had contacts. People he trusted. Of course he would.

All right, she would let him do it. She'd *delegate* it. She was the boss.

"Okay, okay," she said. "Go ahead and use your contacts. And tell Publicity we're cooperating. I think it's safe to say that about this story, since you've already gone and gotten the publicity ball rolling. I'll insist to Brady we cooperate with the police!"

"Brady's office is supposed to call me with a time for our meeting," Victor said. "It'll probably be late this afternoon."

She nodded while rising. "Okay. Let me know what you find out from the police first, if you can."

"Will do." He stood as well.

Did he sound deferential, or was he mocking her?

"It still could turn out that this has nothing to do with the show, like you said," she told him.

"Possible."

"And we have bigger fish to fry right now, with Luke's leg."

"Then the thief will be my assignment," he said. "Don't worry about it."

———

"You might be rich. You might have gone to Harvard or Yale or Princeton… or the Avon School of Business for all I know. But here in Crestview, you're no better than anybody else." Faye wiped off the Reilly Tavern counter, staring at the handsome stranger.

"I didn't mean to offend," he said, his face hidden under a fedora. "I just wanted to know how much you'd take for this handsome establishment."

"You think you can buy anything you want just because you have the money?" She stepped back, putting away the washrag and fetching

the coffee carafe. She poured him a cup of coffee. "You can't buy respect. And you can't buy the Reilly Tavern. It's not for sale."

The stranger sipped at his coffee, eyeing her over the rim of the mug. "Point taken, Ms.—"

"Faye." She turned toward the back, drying mugs and putting them away "The Reilly Tavern has been in our family for generations. We know how to run it. We don't need to take any management courses or read special books to do it, either. It just comes naturally to us Reillys." She paused, before turning. "Say, what's your name anyway, mister?"

He was gone. A twenty-dollar bill lay on the counter—and a card.

"Grayson," she murmured, reading it out loud.

Frankie's finger hovered over the "delete" button on the Faye/ Grayson breakdown she'd been staring at on her computer screen as a series of crises washed over her that afternoon: the loss of their best scriptwriter (the woman was moving to California and taking a full-time job on staff for a prestigious cable drama series), a major rewrite of dialogue from a new writer who'd completely misinterpreted a breakdown written up by Hank, and an actual call from the set to straighten out some scenes with Faye.

"That's not quite right," she said to herself, finally saving the document to a "maybe" file under Faye stories. "It'll come to you later."

Before she headed to the set, Frankie picked up Luke's sweater from the couch and stowed it in her attaché bag. Kayla, of all people, came through on the Luke problem, offering to take him to Frankie's Chelsea place and get him settled. Frankie didn't care if Kayla was just looking for yet another excuse to be away from her desk. She had happily handed over her apartment keys and corralled Hank into helping get the drowsy actor into a taxi.

Now it was off to the set, a few floors below the offices. The head writer didn't often visit the soundstage. In theory, Brady Stephens should be more of a presence there than Frankie. But Brady wasn't a hands-on type. Brady was more of a "passing through" kind of guy, with one eye on his career horizon and the other on his date-book. He'd probably jumped at the chance to let Victor be his eyes and ears. A win-win for Brady—please the sponsor, which, in turn, would please the network.

Frankie, on the other hand, enjoyed visits to the set. In spite of her best efforts to become jaded, the bright lights, the cameras, the reality of the walls and tables and chairs that had previously existed only in her mind's eye as she'd envisioned stories always sent a quiver of excitement through her as she stepped into the vast room, dark except for the splash of light by the stage. That quick thrill sparked a few minutes later as she pushed through the double doors with the "Do Not Enter When Flashing" sign above a now-dark red light.

"Jason, you called?" she asked as she walked toward a tall, burly man wearing a headset and holding a clipboard in his hands. Jason was the *Lust for Life* stage manager. With a tenure of eight years, he was probably the most senior employee around, save for Dame Roberts, Crestview's matriarch. Speaking of Dame, she sat in a brocade wing chair by a phony fireplace in the Kendall living room with young Sassy Maslin standing in front of her, hands on her hips.

Dame—which was her name, not a title—frowned while admiring her fingernails. Sassy—which was her name, not a descriptive adjective—tapped her sneaker-clad foot. Sassy played Faye Reilly, and Frankie knew this was the scene where Faye begs Anne Kendall not to press charges against Gabe, who'd gone through Anne Kendall's things looking for the secret to the identity of his real father.

"Thank god you're here," Dame said, seeing Frankie approach. "But where's Jack?"

"I'm the head writer now, Dame," Frankie said, approaching the set. "Jack left, remember?"

A better question would be, where was Maurice, the director? Frankie asked Jason, who shrugged and said "coffee break," meaning the director didn't want to deal with this annoyance, the last camera blocking before cameras started actually rolling for the afternoon's taping. The mornings were reserved for dry blocking, with Maurice taking the actors through their scenes and marks; then there was the camera blocking, which included directions for the cameramen; and then the taping began, with little chance for do-overs. Most scenes were taped in one take, which wasn't as difficult as it seemed. Scenes were roughly two to three pages these days, a far cry from earlier soaps, when actors might have scenes as long as seventeen pages to memorize.

Sassy heaved a sigh, shifting her weight. "Can we get on with it? I've been standing for an hour." She flicked her short reddish hair out of her eyes and tugged at her denim jacket. She was picture-perfect pretty, a natural beauty with no need of enhancement by plastic surgery or makeup. But *with* makeup, she was the type of woman you couldn't look away from. Pixielike face that could be innocent or seductive. Shapely body. Creamy complexion and bright green eyes.

Jason handed the day's pages to Frankie, pointing to the offending lines. "Sassy is convinced that no teen would utter these words. She wants a change."

Unspoken was the real source of the conflict: Dame. Coming from the "grand tradition of the *theater*," she refused to move forward with a scene if an actor didn't scrupulously stick to the words written on the page. "The words are sacred," she'd admonish young actors, as if issuing a proclamation from the Mount. Thank goodness she wasn't in many scenes these days, or taping would take forever.

Frankie read. Faye/Sassy was supposed to say: "Give Gabe a second chance, ma'am. I know he scared the living daylights out of you. But he's good at heart."

As soon as Frankie started to read, Sassy grabbed her chance. "No way would Faye say 'scared the living daylights.' She wouldn't say 'ma'am,' either. What kid uses the word 'ma'am' nowadays?"

"Well, they *should* use it, and often," Dame interjected in her play-to-the-back-of-the-house voice colored by a slight British accent, even though she was originally from New Jersey. "And we can set an example here."

Sassy ignored the older woman and looked right at Frankie. "I'm telling you, a teen would say—"

"Scared the shit out of you," Frankie finished. She quickly glanced at Dame, "Sorry, but that's probably what a kid would say." Back to Sassy, she continued, "But we can't say that on network daytime, now, can we?"

Sassy scrunched up her mouth. "She wouldn't say 'living daylights.' She'd say something like 'scared the crap out of you' or even 'scared witless' or 'scared silly.' And she wouldn't say 'ma'am.'"

"All right," Frankie agreed. Who'd written this dialogue anyway? She'd have to check the books and make sure the writer had a better read on Faye. Oversensitive to snobbish views of the lower classes, Frankie suspected the scriptwriter had too much Courvoisier and not enough Rolling Rock in her background.

"Use 'scared you silly' and say 'Mrs. Kendall' instead of 'ma'am.'" Frankie was about to step away, but stopped. "Or better yet—use 'Miss Anne.' That's how we talked to mothers in my neighborhood. Didn't matter if they were married." She smiled at the memory.

Sassy smiled, too. Dame looked straight ahead.

"Anything else while I'm here?"

Jason shook his head. "This is Dame's only scene today." Meaning any more delays due to minuscule word changes were unlikely.

Problem solved, Frankie headed toward the doors again, but before she reached them, she passed the prop mistress coming into the room, her arms full of odds and ends. One in particular caught Frankie's gaze—a dark red rose, just the kind that the thief used.

Frankie pointed to it. "When's the next scene taping using that rose?"

Meredith, the property mistress, shrugged. "Dunno. Wasn't on my list this morning, but then I got a call."

"A call from who? And about what?" If it had been Victor, she'd have his head. He couldn't just insert thief scenes willy-nilly. She thought she'd made it clear they were teaming on this one. Then she remembered him saying he'd handle things. *Well, Frankie, if you create a leadership vacuum, looks like you know who will fill it.* Frankie turned on her heels and stormed back to Jason, who was shepherding the actors through their last dry block of the day before shooting began.

"Jason, where's Maurice exactly?" she asked. "And let me see your sked."

Jason slipped one earpiece off his right ear, holding out his clipboard to her. "Okay, okay. Maurice has another migraine." He rolled his eyes. Maurice was probably hungover. "He's napping till taping." So the truth came out.

Frankie skimmed the day's schedule. Handwritten at the end of the day were directions for silent shoots of the thief leaving a rose on Anne Kendall's bed. The shoot was marked as a teaser for the weeks ahead. Every Friday *Lust for Life* did a longer preview section at the end of the show, with teasers for episodes a week or more away.

"Who authorized this?" she asked, pointing to the thief scenes. "And who's playing the thief?"

"Brady okayed it," Jason said, rubbing his forehead. He probably had a real headache. "He stopped by about a half hour before you did."

Brady on the set? Was Victor a Svengali? He'd gotten their absentee executive producer to actually visit the soundstage. She couldn't override Brady. She'd have to talk to him first. And Victor had told her he was setting up a meeting for the both of them—had he gone without her? What a traitor! For someone who'd assured her that morning that he wasn't out for her job, he was sure acting as if he wanted to step into her shoes.

Fuming, she turned on her heel and rushed out of the room, pushing through the double doors with such force that she thought she might have bruised her palms.

Chapter 4

VICTOR, IT TURNED OUT, hadn't had a meeting with Brady. When Frankie returned to her office, a voice mail from Victor informed her that Brady had canceled but was "okay with setting up the possibility of more thief stories." So that's what had prompted Brady's visit to the set. Frankie was amazed the man even remembered how to get there.

She tapped her fingers on her desk, again berating herself for not taking charge. A canceled meeting meant Victor had had the opportunity to speak with Brady alone, on the phone. He'd probably made the case to the executive producer to keep the story moving, wringing every publicity possibility from it.

She stood, crossing her arms as she stared outside. It wasn't that she was against trying to get publicity for the show. She wanted it as much as the next person. Maybe more. She knew *Lust*'s potential and she wanted others to see it, too. It just made her skin crawl to think they'd be luring in viewers with such a cheap trick. A trick, by the way, which carried with it some very real potential public safety issues.

She couldn't stand still. She rushed out of her office in search of Victor, surprised to see Kayla once again at her desk studying notes in a binder.

"Hey, about your voice-mail message," she began, remembering the weird British accent.

"I changed it," Kayla said in a hurry, covering the binder pages with her hands.

Frankie wanted to ask her what the big secret was, but Kayla's phone rang, and it was immediately clear it was a call for her, not Frankie. Frankie moved on, looking for Victor.

But Victor was not around, she discovered. Bob told Frankie he'd left early to meet his daughter for cocktails, but he was going to "call you later about a press conference that Publicity wants to set up."

A press conference? Oh, c'mon, they'd talked, they'd sorted things out, they'd determined who was in charge and how the thief thing was somewhat on hold. Right?

She sighed. Not really. She replayed as best she could their brief conversation. Had she once said, *The thief story will stop*? No, she'd argued. She'd expressed an opinion, but not issued a fiat. *It's no wonder Victor is acting as if he owns the effing show*, she thought as she made her way back to her office at the end of the day. She had to read those leadership books! Oh hell, she had to buy those books!

Leadership skills or not, Pendergrast Soap Products does own the show in a way, after all. There might not be a book about how to deal with that.

In a glum mood when she returned to her office, she shut the door, flipped on her TV, and brought up the recording of the day's episode. While she watched Terri and Donovan preparing for their vows, Anne Kendall telling off Gabe, and Carla trying to double-cross Faye, she sighed. Yes, she was capable of being a good leader. She had just hoped to inch up to it while she was dealing with all the other *Lust for Life* problems. With Victor on board, she was having to go through a crash course on management skills. She really didn't need this extra burden. And here he'd been brought in to help. All he'd done so far was contribute to her workload.

She noticed her message light blinking and pressed through the code, letting the call play on speakerphone. It was her friend Gail. "Hey, chica, I had to call your mom to get your personal number—I lost my cell, and it had all my numbers in it! Tried leaving a couple messages but guess you didn't get them."

Thank you, Kayla.

"Call me and let's get together for drinks or lunch or whatever. I'm sure you saw the news about Brian's book."

No, she hadn't seen the news. So while silence curled through the office as cubicles emptied and everyone went home, Frankie Googled her ex's name and saw he'd received a good review from the *Times*. "A sweet and sorrowful story," the critic called her ex's debut novel, *To Love Faithfully and Well*, while another author hailed it as "a great book that works on two levels—as a fantastic yarn and a thought-provoking examination of the meaning of forgiveness."

At this, Frankie snorted. *Forgiveness?* During the divorce proceedings, Brian had somehow gotten it in his head that he was the one who had to forgive Frankie—for her anger at his adultery. She placed a quick call to Gail. When voice mail clicked on, Frankie left a perky message.

"Saw the news about Brian. And being the generous soul that I am, I couldn't be happier. Really. Lunch would be good. Or breakfast. Name the time and place tomorrow."

Off the phone, she went back to Googling, looking up Victor Pendergrast as well. Article after article about his marketing prowess, his ability to do wonders with small companies, nonprofits, theater groups. *My, my, quite a reputation.* Turning *Lust for Life* around would be another trophy for his wall.

She wondered if she'd been a trophy for Brian. Oh, not in the conventional sense. Brian's blood ran blue enough that he didn't aspire to better things—he thought he *was* the better thing. No, if she had been a trophy for him, it was more a "shabby chic" one, a Pygmalion he felt he had lifted to his level. The last few months they were married, she'd begun to suspect he might have thought like that.

Her cheeks burned at the egotism of it all. She'd become used to little "corrections" he'd make of her pronunciation, or explanations he'd dole out about cultural events they attended. She'd found these habits charming when they'd first wed, and had often let them pass even when she was fully versed in the subject he was attempting to "school" her in. But in those last days she'd begun to realize he truly did believe he was a superior person—or artist, at least. It had burned her to the core.

Don't think about it, Frankie.

"You know what I love about you most, Terri?" Donovan's voice came from the screen.

"What, darling?"

"You treat me like an equal."

"You are an equal, Donovan."

"You're royalty," Donovan continued. *"Not some pretend highbrow who thinks she's better than the rest because her family made some money back in the day. You're real royalty. But you treat me… like a prince."*

"Oh, Donovan, anyone who would treat you as less than equal is nothing more than a small-minded drone who obviously has to make up for their own inferiority by casting you below them. People like that are empty no-talents. They don't realize it, but they are the inferiors, not the people they seek to raise up to their level. They are feeding their insecure egos by trying to help people like you be like them. Don't think about those people, darling. They are nothing but pond scum."

The sounds of their slurping kisses smacked the scene to a close.

Frankie clicked off the show before the teasers and credits rolled. She'd written that breakdown herself. Now it sounded a tad awkward.

Well, Terri is kind of wordy, she consoled herself. *It's how we built her character.* Surely, it sounded natural for Terri to say those things.

And Frankie just couldn't seem to stop herself from using the show to say all the things she wished she could say in real life, to make all the injustices and slights she suffered right.

She grabbed her case, turned out her lights, and left, splurging on a taxi because she was too damned tired to ride the subway. She sank into the backseat after giving the driver her address, angry and sad.

Brian had come from an old blueblood family whose sense of entitlement had grown as their financial picture had faded. The Aigland family house in Connecticut might have been furnished with threadbare furniture and rugs, but priceless paintings hung on the walls and books with dedications from presidents sat on the shelves. What they lacked in money they made up for in attitude. Mother Aigland, as Brian's mom liked Frankie to call her, had barely accepted Frankie and had insisted on calling her "Frances" throughout the brief marriage.

Frankie wondered how Brian's mother would look upon his literary success. Would she be happy for him, or recoil that so many people would now know who he was and buy his book? The Aiglands eschewed publicity or anything that appealed to "the masses." Brian never did tell his mother when Frankie went to work for *Lust for Life* full-time. She was probably still under the impression that Frankie worked for a publishing house. *Yes, Mrs. Aigland might celebrate Brian's literary reviews, but not the commercial appeal of his book*, Frankie thought glumly. Hell, she'd have enjoyed both if it had been her. And her mother would have practically taken ads out in the local paper to trumpet her success.

Maybe she should write a book, like Brian. She wrote a lot as it was, why not something more serious? She still had that feeling, buried deep inside with girlish fantasies, that she was a slacker for not penning her own "brilliant novel of insights on the plight of humanity." After all, of the two of them, she had more "plight" in her background. Reviewers should be celebrating her "sweet and sorrowful story." Yet here she was, overseeing tales of raging passion and far-fetched dramatic conventions. Brian wrote literature. She wrote cartoons. *Dammit.*

By the time she put her key in the lock, she could think of little else but her own squandered talents and the unfairness of life. So when she opened the door and smelled something cooking, her first thought was that she'd finally left the toaster, coffeemaker, or stove on and was about to burn the building down. She rushed around the corner, ready to stop an inferno by beating it back with her small designer handbag.

There, Luke stood at the stove, his crutch leaning against the counter while he balanced himself with a free hand, the other tasting something that smelled heavenly.

"You're up!" Frankie said, going back to the hallway to loop her trench coat on a hook. She'd forgotten he was even going to be there. "And you're cooking!" She walked the few steps back into the tiny kitchen, sniffed dramatically, and offered, "Mmmm, that smells good."

"I worked in a restaurant before I got steady acting gigs," Luke said, his voice a bit gravelly.

"You feeling okay?"

"Just a headache. And I'm hungry." He stirred the sauce and flipped something in a frying pan. "You didn't have much."

"I order out a lot." Frankie peered past him into the pan, trying to remember what she had in her refrigerator. Oh yes, chicken. And it had only been there a day or two. No salmonella tonight, thank you very much.

He looked at her. "You look beat."

"Just stressed. Lots going on." She poured herself a glass of red wine. Luke sipped at bottled water, she noted, and didn't ask for any vino. He was far more disciplined than many people gave him credit for. He was downright ruthless when it came to his career, in fact. "It's awfully nice of you to do this." She nodded her wine glass toward the food and managed to slosh some on her and the floor.

"Dammit," she cried, placing her glass on the counter and reaching for a wet cloth. "Wine stains are a bitch to get out."

"Take it off," Luke said.

"What?"

"Take off the blouse. You need to soak it right away." He put down the spoon and turned to her, unbuttoning the blouse.

"Luke, really," she joked, "this is so sudden." But she let him finish the undressing, and she slipped out of the garment. He hopped a step to the sink with it and ran water into a bowl where he left the blouse to soak. When he turned back to her, it was as if he were seeing for the first time her figure sweetly caressed in its pink lace push-up bra. She might not have an actress' body, but she did okay.

"You might wanna dress," he said, swallowing hard. "Dinner's almost ready."

—⁓—

It would have been a romantic dinner, too, just the sort of thing her bruised ego needed, if she hadn't spent it complaining. Luke made some sort of chicken piccata thing he served with rice and peas. He even whipped up a cookie and ice cream thing for dessert. It felt good to be taken care of, and she thanked him more than once—in between her complaints.

"I mean, here I am head writer, and he's telling Brady what he thinks we should be doing."

"He works under you?"

"No, no. I told you—we're equals."

And after a few more bites: "He is undercutting my authority with the team, too. He made Nory feel all gooey and gushy when she'd made a mistake, and Raeanne is ready to have his children."

And after another bite: "Brady thinks we need to keep the story going. Even though someone could get hurt! And that means on top of getting this new Faye/Gabe/Grayson thing launched and redoing your pages, I have to—"

"What's happening with Donovan?" Luke perked up.

"Abduction. You'll do most of your scenes tied to a chair, blindfolded."

"Shirt off?"

"Sure."

"Sweet." He went back to eating.

By the time the meal was finished, she'd talked way too much about things Luke shouldn't have been privy to. She told him to stay put while she cleaned up and made fast—and shoddy—work of washing the dishes and pans, continuing occasional commentary on what was wrong with Victor Pendergrast.

"I mean, he acts as if he owns the place," she said, back to the living room. "Okay, so he kind of does, since we're practically a Pendergrast Soap Products subsidiary. But still, you'd think he'd be a little more deferential. After all, he might have the name, but I'm the one with the experience. He should be respectful of that at least."

She rinsed the last pot lid and wiped her hands. "Oh, be a pal and forget everything I just told you. It's inside baseball. Doesn't affect you and probably won't mean anything in the long run." She turned to look at Luke.

He was prone on the sofa, eyes closed. "Well, no need to worry about you hearing too much, I guess," she murmured to herself.

She walked over and placed an afghan over his body. His eyes flashed open, and he reached up, grabbing her arm, pulling her toward him into a hot, wet kiss. He smelled earthy, like a man, and she was hungry now in an entirely different way. He was the perfect consolation prize for such a crappy day. That thought overrode the blaring alarm bell clanging in her brain warning her of bad judgment calls ahead. She fell on top of him, feeling underneath her the "hard, rigid mass of something" that Raeanne had talked about in their story meeting. And it wasn't the cast on his leg.

It felt awfully good to be wanted.

—⁓—

Victor Pendergrast sipped at his Glenlivet, watching his daughter, Courtney, leave the restaurant. The more he saw her, the more he missed her. He'd shared custody of Courtney with his wife when they split, and it had occurred to him early that the price for his divorce was the open wound of not having Courtney under his roof, protecting her, guiding her. He'd done the best he could during their shared custody visits, and she'd turned out all right—cheerful, self-confident, intelligent. Now she was going to get married. That was why she'd asked to meet him, to tell him in person that she and her steady boyfriend, Roman, were officially engaged. She was off to meet Roman for dinner, where they were going to discuss wedding plans.

Roman—what kind of name is that for a guy? Victor tossed back another sip and stared at the menu without reading it. Sounded like something out of a story book. He thought back to his days in the Marines. Somebody with a name like Roman would have had a lot of defending to do.

Whenever Victor was feeling wounded or alone, he often retreated to the persona he'd adopted in the military—tough, no-nonsense, uncompromising. He'd loved those years, loved the sense of brotherhood, of shared purpose, of hard work—harder than he'd ever done in his life. He missed that, just as he missed his daughter even when she was in front of him.

He had put on a good front when she'd shared the news, congratulating her, telling her she'd found a good fellow, and that he'd beat him senseless if he dared hurt his little girl. She'd smiled, teared up, patted his hand, and said, "Oh, Daddy."

Roman was a good guy, as far as he could tell, but Victor had met him only twice. The young man would provide well—he worked in medical engineering, while Courtney herself didn't do too shabbily in an advertising firm.

The waiter came by as his phone buzzed in his pocket. "The prime rib," he said to the waiter, pulling out the phone. "No potatoes."

"Salad, sir?"

"Oh, sure." He looked at the number. Aunt Gussie again.

"Dressing?"

"Whatever the house dressing is." He hit "reply" but heard only silence. He'd missed the call. Oh well. He was headed out there tomorrow night. She would have forgotten by then that she'd even called him.

While he had the phone out, he looked at the voice mail record. One. He punched into the message and listened while *Lust for Life*'s Publicity head told him she'd set up a press conference for ten the next morning. "I know this is short notice, but it's the best possible time and you said you wanted something quick. I'm emailing you drafts of statements. Call me when you review them. We can pull this off, Victor." And she'd left a number.

Had Frankie gotten his message about the press conference? He'd told Bob to pass that along. Even if he had, Victor still needed to talk with her about it, especially if it was going to be so early in the day. He punched in the number of her cell, which he'd had Bob retrieve for him earlier.

———

Frankie was moaning with delight as Luke stroked her arms and nuzzled her breasts. He had already removed, with her help, the denim shirt she had donned after the wine spill on her other blouse and had his right hand firmly planted on her ass, kneading it slowly as he moved his other hand around to undo the clasp of her pants. She started to wriggle out of them, remembering with a jolt just how exciting their previous coupling had been after that holiday party. She managed to nudge her trousers to her feet and discard them like a snake's skin, grateful she'd actually matched her underwear that day, the pink lace bra complemented by pink lace bikini panties. Luke glanced at them appreciatively, slipping his finger around the delicate waistband, pulling them down the side of her leg.

"You'll have to help me here, babe," he whispered, nibbling at her ear in the process.

"Mmmm," she answered, moving to the side to finish the job. Before she could complete the undressing, the jingle, bangle, bangle of her cell phone cut into the room.

"Don't answer it," Luke murmured, his hand cradling the back of her head, pulling her face to his for another deep kiss.

"Oooh, yes, hmmm, yeah, aah." She couldn't *not* answer it. Frankie McNally had what she liked to think of as "phone genes." She was genetically wired to reach out for a ringing phone—or, rather, for communication of any kind. "No, have to," she mumbled, falling off Luke onto the floor. She rummaged through her pants until she found the pocket where her phone was stashed. She didn't even look at the number before hitting "answer."

Victor Pendergrast's voice came over the line. "Frankie, I'm just calling to make sure you got my message about the press conference. Mary in Publicity wants to do it at ten and is going to coordinate statements with us. Can we meet in about an hour? I could come to your place."

Frankie looked at the clothes strewn around the floor, at Luke's waiting body. No, they couldn't meet at her place. And what was this about the press conference anyway? This last thought she voiced to Victor.

"You said to keep you in the loop," Victor said, not hiding his exasperation.

"No, you said you'd keep *me* in the loop. That didn't mean you have control over the damned loop. I'm the boss. I control the loop. The loop is mine to do with what I wish. I'm the—"

"The loop executive."

Was he laughing at her? His voice did not have a twinkle in it, though. His voice sounded impatient.

"The head writer. I'm the head writer!"

"Yes, I know. I get it." His voice was hushed as if he was in a public place. She heard voices in the background, the tinkling of glasses. "We don't have time to argue over this, Frankie. The press had the story. It's better if we get in front of it."

"The press had the story because you leaked it to them!" She stood, pacing the small living room in her underwear, now tugging her panties back into place with her free hand.

"They would have figured it out eventually," he seethed.

"Maybe not!" Way to go, Frankie. Acknowledge the ratings were so low that no one would have caught the parallels between the real thief and the *Lust for Life* thief. "Besides, this is totally irresponsible, Victor. I can't disagree more with this strategy. We should be announcing that we're cutting off this story. I don't think I've been quite forceful about that. You have obviously misunderstood my desire to discuss this with a willingness to compromise."

Victor sighed. "Whatever we announce, we can't go in without any preparation. Look, can you meet in an hour? If you can't, I'll handle the call with Mary on my own and report in to you. Since you are the boss, the loop leader, the head writer."

Red hot with rage, Frankie grabbed her slacks from the floor. "Where do you want to meet? I'll be there."

Luke called after her. "Frankie, can't that wait?"

—⁓—

"Drink?" Victor asked her a half hour later in his Central Park West condo. He held up a glass of amber Scotch in one hand while he loosened his collar with the other.

"Water's fine," Frankie said. She sat on his leather sofa in jeans and sweater, her hair tousled and damp.

He could have met her at the office, or even at the restaurant—he wouldn't have had to rush through his meal then. But after Courtney's wedding news, he'd been in an ungenerous mood. Playing on his turf would give him the advantage. It would get them to the goal faster.

"Thanks for coming to my place," he said as he poured her a spring water over ice. He walked over and handed her the glass, towering over her, another power play. "Hope I didn't interrupt anything." He knew damn well he had. He'd heard Luke Blades's voice in the background when he'd called, and from the tone he guessed what had been going on. That was unprofessional of her—a relationship with the show's star. It disappointed him. He'd wanted to be impressed with Frankie. Something about her had charmed him during their first meeting. And even her insecurities seemed sweetly self-effacing.

"Well, I didn't have much choice," she said, not hiding her irritation. She looked up at him and stared him in the eyes. "A press conference, Victor? That's way beyond where I thought we were going with this. You've overstepped."

She was meeting him toe to toe. Victor always admired a fighter. That's what had impressed him at first—her feistiness.

He looked at his watch. "Mary said she'd be sending us statements in a couple minutes. I'll check my machine." He walked out of the living room down a corridor to his small home office, sliding into his desk chair and waking up his laptop. Nothing from Mary. When he turned, he was surprised to see Frankie right behind him. She leaned in the doorway, arms crossed over her chest.

"Did Brady give you carte blanche? Because if those are the rules I'm supposed to play by, I'd like to know now and save myself a lot of time."

He felt a smile nip at the corners of his mouth. That's precisely how he would have handled the situation—find out the ground rules, then on to pitched battle.

"Brady wants a success. I don't think he's interested in the details."

She snorted out her disgust. "And you want another notch in your marketing guru belt?"

His email program chimed, letting him know a new message had come in. He quickly opened the note and attachment from Mary and hit "print." While the LaserJet spit out papers, he looked at Frankie, ice in his eyes.

"I don't need another notch in my belt for this or anything else," he said. He saw her gaze lift to the wall beyond, where a photo hung of him in uniform being awarded a medal by the president. She didn't comment, but her face reddened. "Here, look this over. I printed two copies." He handed her one set of papers while he took the other.

Immediately, she protested. "Brady will never take part in something like this!" She tapped the page with the executive producer's statement. "And trust me, you don't want him to. He'll bungle the names of characters and be unable to answer questions about stories. He's hands off when it comes to management."

"He's already agreed," Victor said drily. Would the whole meeting go like this with her questioning every single move? Better to nip that tactic in the bud. "Look, Frankie, I have one strategic interest in all this, and that's to save the show. It's personal. Clearly whatever the past bosses have been doing isn't working. And now there might not be enough time to let whatever tricks you have up your sleeve play out."

"Tricks?"

"Poor word choice. What I mean is that you might be the best head writer on the planet—and from the work of yours I've seen and what I've been learning about this process, you certainly have the goods— but it takes time to build audience share. So whatever magic you have planned for *Lust* might take too long to make a difference."

Her face paled. "Mom'll be so disappointed," she whispered.

"What?"

"So the show *is* being canceled," she said, as if she had known the news all along.

"Not yet, but closer than it's ever been. As I told you earlier, Pendergrast's board is weak on supporting its sponsorship. What I didn't tell you is how weak."

"That's happened before," she said like a little girl clinging to hope that the school picnic wouldn't be rained out when the weatherman's forecasting hailstorms.

"Yeah, well, things have changed." He didn't want to get into his aunt's deteriorating health. "I'll be honest with you. When I first thought of helping out, I wasn't sure if something could be done quickly enough. Building market share takes time and careful planning. Pendergrast's board is impatient."

She interrupted. "So they put a fuse on it?" Her eyes widened.

He evaluated. Should he reveal the full scope of the board's deliberations? Aw, hell, why not? There were no state secrets there.

"One vote. That's all it would have taken to pull sponsorship." He heard her swift intake of breath. "We meet again next quarter."

"Three months."

He nodded. "See what I mean? It's tough to turn things around in that short time, even if you are a whiz head writer."

She smiled just a little.

"So this opportunity…" He held up the pages.

He saw her face soften. Maybe now she'd see him as an ally and not as a threat.

"Okay, okay," she said. "I get it. The show's strapped to the train tracks and the steam engine's barreling down."

"Apt metaphor for a melodrama."

"But, Victor, it's not ego driving my objections. I have a *real* problem with this. Two problems, really. The thief story was lame to begin with. Even if we get viewers in with the copycat thief in real life, they won't stay once they see how bogus the story is. The writing team would have told you that, too, if they hadn't been so keen on impressing you."

"I didn't catch that from them."

"Well, Raeanne mostly. But listen, my second reason for objecting, and it's a big reason, is that I still have a really big problem with the whole public safety issue." She threw up her hands.

Victor relaxed. Her defenses were down, and she was being co-operative. No pitched battle, after all. Good. He was tired.

"Are you or have you ever been involved in security issues?" he asked with a smile.

"No, but I know you have." She shrugged to the photos on the wall.

He nodded. "I think we shouldn't second-guess the police. If they think the story should stop, then we consider it. Nobody's asked for that."

"What exactly did your police contact say when you told him we'd be keeping the story?"

"Her, not him." She was a former G.I. Jane, someone who'd served with him. And he hadn't told her they'd be keeping the story. He'd deliberately not brought it up, because he didn't want to cede their decision making to outsiders. Hadn't done so with the community relations officer she'd put him in touch with either. "Nothing," he told Frankie. "Wasn't a point of discussion." Which was true.

"If we even suspect the police want us to drop this, we drop it," she said, staring straight at him.

"But we don't push them down that path," he countered.

She nodded almost imperceptibly, then looked down at the papers. "First things first. We'll deal with the press conference. And then we talk about the story."

"I'm in."

"Brady's statement is too long. Too many multisyllabic words."

"You know him best." He grabbed a pen. "Shoot."

She made some quick suggestions for changes to Brady's statement and his own—as a member of the board and now the staff, he'd be speaking, too, but only briefly. After that they spent an hour brainstorming ideas for the thief story. Although she'd not given the thief much thought, he was very impressed with her ability to quickly concoct several stories that worked on multiple levels—as ways to pull in different demographics and as an engrossing tale. The thief was a Robin Hood type, she suggested, just trying to help out those less fortunate.

It was nearly midnight when they were finished. He wouldn't let her go home alone. Grabbing his jacket and keys, he whooshed down to the garage and drove her through rain-shining streets to her Chelsea place.

"Nice wheels," she said, making herself comfortable in his black Jaguar's leather seat.

"Gets me where I want to go."

"Nice digs, too," she added. "I should have mentioned it."

"I do all right."

"Yet you served in the military," she prodded. Her curiosity must have gotten the best of her.

"We all rebel in our own way," he answered.

"So you had that kind of parent, too," she said. He turned sharply to look at her, but her face was staring straight ahead, a soft smile catching the glow of streetlights.

"Two of them actually. Fine people in their own way. And you?"

"My father believed in freedom. Especially from raising a kid."

"But your mother?"

"My mother is a nurse. She says the sixties were a luxury the lower classes couldn't afford."

He laughed. "I'll have to remember that."

"Where are your parents now?"

He did a mental rewind to recent emails exchanged. "Mother's in Tibet. Father's in Mexico."

"See what I mean?"

"What?"

She gestured to the car. "Your parents could afford 'the revolution.'"

"Not sure I get your point." But by then they'd arrived at her building. "Let me walk you up," he offered.

"No, that's okay."

He remembered Luke Blades was there and wondered if that was the reason for her hesitation.

"Thanks for the ride, though." She opened the door and prepared to exit, stopping herself as she thought of something. "Oh, just to be clear—I won't be asked to speak at the press conference, right?"

"Not planned. Why?"

"I hate public speaking."

"No problem."

She left, smiling. He watched her enter the building, waggling her fingers at him to signal she was okay. A few seconds later, he saw the light go on two stories up in a street-view apartment.

When he drove home, he couldn't get the sound of her voice or the smell of her perfume off his mind.

Chapter 5

"YOU'RE SLEEPING WITH LUKE Blades?" Gail Warfield nearly spit out her cappuccino as she sat across from her friend at a coffee shop near the network building, a rendezvous Frankie had set up in a late-night voice mail. "About time you got your mind off Brian! Speaking of which, that character on *Lust*—the millionaire's son who wrote poetry so bad it made me choke I was laughing so hard—that was Brian, wasn't it?"

"No! That wasn't Brian! And that character's gone now anyway!" Frankie stared into her coffee, her eyes wide. Sure, Frankie had written that character's breakdowns, but that was when Jack was head writer, and he'd loved Frankie's stories. He wouldn't have accepted it if it hadn't been good in its own right. And he hadn't known Brian at all.

"And I'm not sleeping with Luke. He's just sleeping on my couch!"

Okay, so she would have slept with him if reason, in the form of a phone call from Victor, had not prevailed. Frankie shivered at the close call—for lots of different reasons. She wasn't into one-night stands, and while sleeping with Luke would have technically made it a two-night stand separated by many, many months, the principle was the same. She'd been vulnerable after her bad day and a little tipsy after one glass of wine poured on top of too much stress. She wouldn't let that happen again.

Although the purpose of this meeting was to dish over Frankie's ex, with Gail offering appropriate amounts of friendly comfort and withering scorn, Frankie had begun by asking Gail to guess who was sleeping in her apartment for a spell. Gail had first guessed "Brian," which had annoyed Frankie. At least Gail was suitably impressed that it was hard-muscled Luke.

Gail and Frankie had met at an author reading at Columbia. Although she had been studying law, Gail was a book lover. They'd discovered they had similar backgrounds—both had come from humble beginnings and were intent on "making it." Gail was from the Midwest and had the peaches-and-cream complexion and full figure of a dairy maid. Her blonde hair was naturally curly and framed her face in graceful waves.

Before Frankie could say more to Gail about her new roomie, her cell phone chimed, Nory's number lighting up the display. There was only one reason Nory would call this early, and sure enough, when Frankie answered the phone, her supposition was confirmed. Nory was calling in sick. As always when someone was out for the day, Frankie wondered if Nory had a job interview.

If she did, she was covering well. Actually, it wasn't Nory who was sick. It was her boyfriend, who'd come down with what Nory thought was the flu but might be pneumonia since he'd been traveling lately and had been on a plane with some fellow who was coughing his lungs off. Not to worry, she told Frankie. She planned on asking lots of questions of the doctors and nurses as research for upcoming stories. The entire time she talked, country music played in the background, some song Frankie didn't know but whose singer sounded familiar. She made a mental note to ask about it later—the lyrics were sure to turn up in Nory's breakdowns.

Nory had other news, too, which she breezily offered, perhaps to demonstrate her loyalty.

"You know Tom's cousin—the one who's a stage manager? A *stage* stage manager, I mean. For the theater."

Frankie was sure Nory had told her at some point about her

boyfriend Tom's cousin, but whatever she'd said about him was lost in the fog of Nory prattle that Frankie often just nodded her head to. Nory might be quiet in writers' meetings, but she could be an unstoppable font when talking one-to-one.

"Well anyway," Nory continued, "Tom's cousin is going to stage manage for that big *Hamlet* revival coming up. And guess who they're thinking of for the title role?"

Having just played "guess who" with her friend Gail, Frankie jumped to "Luke Blades."

"How'd you know?"

Frankie sat up straight. She hadn't been serious. Luke Blades playing Hamlet? Good lord, what was the world coming to? That would be like… like casting Clint Eastwood in a musical.

But Clint Eastwood *had* been in a musical—*Paint Your Wagon.* Didn't matter if it had flopped. Nowadays, investors wanted star power for box-office mojo and managed to work with the star's limitations. Luke could very well get the part. And if it were one of those modern, jazzed-up versions, Luke could be the epitome of the brooding prince. Hadn't they spent years polishing that image for him on *Lust for Life?* Frankie felt her jaw tightening.

After thanking Nory for her intel, Frankie snapped her phone closed and stared at Gail. She was an entertainment lawyer. Maybe she'd heard something.

"What do you know about a new *Hamlet* being pulled together? And Luke's part in it?"

"Lucky for you, honey, the rat bastards putting that production together aren't using our services," said Gail. "Otherwise I could only speak in hypotheticals. But since the producer is using someone else… well, yes, I did hear through the grapevine that they think a soap star would be a great publicity stunt, and they have contemplated your very own Luke Blades."

"And you didn't tell me?"

"Hey, I just heard yesterday, and I called your secretary to get to you, but you were out."

Ah yes, the ever-efficient Kayla. Frankie wondered precisely what words one would have to use to get Kayla to pass along an actual message. "But Luke as Hamlet?"

Gail laughed. "I know, I know. But I hear they're doing a Sophia Coppola job on it. Keeping it in the period but with modern music in the background and a modern sensibility. Cutting gobs of dialogue."

Of course. Frankie could see Luke now in tights and codpiece, *Lust for Life* fans staring up at it, er, him from the front rows.

"If he's under contract," Gail continued, "you could probably make life difficult for him."

"His contract's up for renewal next month. I thought it would be a slam dunk." She didn't get involved in contract negotiations, but she was keenly aware of each actor's renewal time and how it could affect the stories if things went bad.

Damn. She felt betrayed again by a man's success. First Brian was leaping to literary stardom with his novel, *To Love Faithfully and Well*. And now Luke was about to leap—healed leg and all—onto the stage, taking on one of the most revered roles in theatrical history. It felt like they were leaving her to languish in the backwaters of the creative ocean.

She sighed heavily, feeling like the outsider, the girl who'd had to learn about great poets and great authors and great playwrights at college, who'd not known how to pronounce words like *posthumous* and *mischievous* and *substantive*, who'd had to prove she was an equal. But she wasn't really, was she? She was still the girl in that knotty-pine basement, still wrapped up in *Lust for Life*.

"I'll check with my producer and see what's up," Frankie said, trying to sound like she was really in control. She changed subjects to the original purpose of their meeting. "Have you read Brian's book?"

Gail reached over and patted Frankie's hand. "We were sent an advance reader copy."

Why the sympathy? Was it as stunning as the critics said?

"Is it any good?" Frankie asked. Although Brian had shared bits and pieces of the novel with Frankie when they were married, she'd not read the whole thing. And she had no idea how much any of it had changed since his first versions.

"It's okay," Gail said, looking away.

"What? You can tell me if you like it. I won't be hurt or anything." But actually she would be, and Gail knew it. It would be so much easier if Brian's book were shallow and strained and pretentious—just like him.

"It's not that." Gail looked at her and held her hand as if poised to release bad news. "There's a character in it..."

Frankie froze. *Oh no. Brian hadn't. He couldn't have.*

"Me? He wrote about me? Oh, god. Tell me it's not awful. Tell me I'm not a dragon lady." She shook her head. Sure, they'd had some bitter arguments after she'd discovered his infidelity. But once the legal machine started in motion, it was all postmodern amicability. She'd been good to him, even generous.

"No, no, it's not awful at all. It's just that... well, it's just kind of odd reading about this character and recognizing you." Gail pulled her hand away, relieved that Frankie wasn't going to burst out sobbing, and finished her coffee. "It's kind of flattering, really. The character—Francesca—"

"He used my name?"

"Your name is Frances, not Francesca."

Frankie rolled her eyes. "Go ahead. Tell me how great I am in his book."

"Francesca is this childlike character—a redhead, like you—who comes from a poor background and makes it big but can't let go of the fact that she thinks people are always looking down on her."

Frankie's face flamed. "You think that's flattering?"

Gail smiled. "You have to read it. Francesca is very likable. She's sweet. She's bright. She's a hard worker. She's funny."

"Just like me!"

"That's what I mean. It's not unflattering."

"But you said she has a chip on her shoulder!"

"Yeah. But that doesn't mean you do, Frankie!" Gail's smiled dropped. "Don't be oversensitive about it."

"You mean don't have a chip on my shoulder about it." Frankie couldn't believe Gail was being so blasé about this. Her ex had parodied her in print—in a book likely to become a bestseller, read by tens of thousands, millions—probably by more people than those who watched *Lust*. Not fair.

"Look, I'm obviously not describing it well. I can give you my copy. I'll have a messenger bring it over." Gail picked up her purse and started rummaging for money for a tip. "Besides, how can you be upset? You do the same thing with Brian, modeling characters after him. What was that millionaire poet's name anyway? Keith something."

"I told you he wasn't Brian! His name was nothing like Brian's. Not like, like, a Francesca."

"Oh, I thought of Brian as soon as I heard the name Keith. As in Brian Keith, the old actor. Remember, you and I talked about how good he was in the original *Parent Trap* movie? We both saw it on TV, and… well, shortly after that Keith appeared on *Lust*. You know, you should be careful about that stuff, putting people from real life into the show. Somebody could sue."

"Maybe I should sue Brian."

"You have a good friend who's a lawyer," Gail said, smiling, but then looked at her watch.

Frankie should be going, too. She had a lot to do before this blasted press conference.

"That's why you wanted to meet," Frankie said, pulling her purse up as well. "To break it to me in person about Francesca."

"Kind of," Gail said, standing. "But we haven't met in a while. I wanted to catch up."

Frankie suspected that meant Gail had more news to divulge. "How's Michael?" Michael was a fellow lawyer Gail had been dating for nearly a year, an odd relationship that was hard to read. Frankie was never quite sure if they were committed to each other or just marking time.

"He's okay."

"You're hiding something." They both stood by the high tables.

"You're in a rush. We can talk later."

"Did you guys break up?" Frankie asked, reaching out to touch Gail's arm. Man, here she was so focused on her own inner turmoil that she might have kept Gail from spilling her own.

"No. Well, not yet. It's just that…" Gail brushed a lock of hair from her eyes. "I've made friends with someone."

"Ohmygod, you've met someone else! Who is he? Quick, tell it, girl. I have to run!" Frankie was glad to hear the news. Michael was taking way too long to make up his mind about Gail. Gail was a catch, and any man would be lucky to land her.

"He's in marketing, works for himself, is dark-haired, tall… and about twenty years older than me."

As Gail described her new "friend," Frankie's smile froze. It sounded like Victor. Why should that bother her? She worked with Victor, that was all. She'd worked with him for almost forty-eight hours, not a lifetime. And it didn't matter anyway if it were a lifetime.

"But it's just friends for now, really. We have a lot of the same interests and belong to the same book club. That's how I met him."

"Victor Pendergrast belongs to a book club?" Frankie asked.

"Who?" Gail tilted her head, confused.

"Sorry," Frankie said, recovering. "What's your friend's name again?"

"Stuart Kominski."

Frankie exhaled with relief. "Well, keep me posted, will ya?"

The two friends said their farewells, and Frankie double-stepped it to her office in the building next door.

―――――

Victor was already in. She went past his office on the way to her own and saw Bob hurrying in, coffee in hand. When she arrived at her own room, Kayla was nowhere to be found, but she had left a note saying she'd be late. *Well, that's a step in the right direction*, thought Frankie. Another someone—probably Bob—had slipped under her door a neat folder of the materials for the press conference, prepared for Publicity per Victor's instructions. So said the note scrawled by Bob and clipped to its cover.

Frankie slid into her chair after tossing her trench coat on a nearby coat tree. She finger-combed her unruly hair, made even more unmanageable by the damp weather. Good thing she didn't have to participate in this dog-and-pony show today. She'd been in such a rush this morning to get to her meeting with Gail that she'd dressed hastily, grabbing from her closet a see-through beige chiffon blouse over satin chemise, paired with another of her collection of shades-of-black suits. She probably looked like a nun with libido problems. She undid the tight collar button while she looked through the press packet, nodding as she saw each correction she'd suggested included.

She reached for her phone to call and compliment Victor when it rang.

Serena's hushed voice came over the phone. "Mr. Stephens said to pass this along to you. It's Ada Martin."

"Who?"

"Rachel Toland's agent," Serena said in a voice that conveyed her disgust at Frankie's ignorance. Rachel played Terri, the mysterious princess in Donovan's life, the seductress waiting for her prince's appearance in their nuptial bed.

"I don't deal with agents," Frankie said.

"Mr. Stephens said this was something you needed to know, too." With that, she clicked off, allowing Ada through the line.

"Frankie? Brady Stephens said you should be among the first to know—our Rachel is pregnant! Isn't that wonderful? She and her husband are expecting twins!"

Frankie gulped. "Twins?"

"Can you believe it? She's three months along. I was telling Brady that I know this'll play right into your plans, though," Ada gushed. "With Donovan and Terri now together, you can just write in a little baby Reilly for the happy couple."

If it were only so easy. Now that Donovan was out of baby-making commission and into kidnapped mode, it would be at least two months before they would even tape a marriage consummation scene. By that time, Rachel's baby bump would have her looking like the stress of separation from her beloved had added pounds to her lithe frame. Twins? Sheesh. She'd be big as a blimp in no time. And lucky to be able to keep filming through the entire pregnancy. And at the end of this nightmare would be maternity leave, meaning Rachel would be off the show for at least six weeks. Frankie did a quick calculation. She'd be lucky to have the Terri/Donovan duo together for a month, during which time they'd have to do high medium shots, or Wardrobe would be using lots of flowing blouses, big coats, and handbags the size of Texas. And this was assuming that Luke Blades, their walking-impaired Donovan, didn't jump ship to play the Danish prince. Good lord, what a mess.

Thanks a lot, Ada. And thank you very much, Rachel.

After this bit of good cheer, she opened her email account to see that Marketing had sent her a report on ratings for the past several months. An easy trend to spot there. A neat downward line. They were losing market share steadily. And Mary from Publicity had emailed to say *Soap Opera Digest* wanted to interview her about this—was *Lust for Life* in danger of being canceled? Their ratings were so low that the magazine was considering dropping them from the ratings roundup each week. Mary wrote, "I'll brief you after the press conference."

When she looked up, Victor was standing in the doorway. How long had he been there?

"Come in, come in." She waved her arms at him, which made a button on her gauzy top pop open. That's why she rarely wore this thing. With her right hand, she rebuttoned it while Victor sat in a chair in front of her desk.

"Bad news," she began before Victor had a chance to say why he wanted to talk. "We might be losing both our Terri and our Donovan." She filled him in.

Victor addressed the Luke problem first: "If he's under contract—"

"His contract is being renegotiated now." This stung more than she was letting on. Maybe it was because she'd opened her home to Luke and had been about to open her heart. Now she felt he was stabbing her in the back. The least he could have done was told her he was going to stab her in the back.

"You could recast."

"That's tricky business. And it's best to have the character leave and then come back."

"He's kind of leaving now, isn't he? The kidnapping. You could cover his head."

She leaned back into her desk. "Not bad. We were going to blindfold him as it is."

"Just put a sack on his head."

Frankie chuckled. "He'd love that. No trademark rugged jaw,

muscles working furiously… but we can keep him shirtless. And just look for another actor with great pecs."

Victor nodded. "Appeals to a good demographic."

A cloud entered this sun-dappled speculation. "Uh-oh. Thought of a problem." She frowned. "Your aunt Gussie is particularly fond of Luke. And he's been very shrewd about feeding her inner fan girl. Sends her flowers and candies regularly. Had her visit his dressing room a couple years back. Asks for advice."

Victor grimaced, nodding. "I think he has her private number, too."

"How well do you know your aunt?" Frankie asked.

He looked surprised. "She raised me," he said as if she should have known.

Frankie's eyebrows lifted.

"Parents divorced when I was young," he continued. "Mother went hostel-hopping in Europe while Dad hitchhiked to San Francisco."

"Must have been nice."

Victor bristled. "Hardly."

The blush of dismay warmed her cheeks. "I meant nice enough to have the cash to bum around like that. That's what I meant last night… oh, never mind." She couldn't seem to express what she really meant lately. Maybe that's why she worked in soaps and her ex was becoming a literary star.

"What do you want to know about my aunt?" Victor asked, wariness coloring his voice.

"Would her affection for Luke override her other passions?"

"You mean for dogs?" He relaxed.

"Exactly."

"It might not." Victor smiled.

They talked for a half hour more, but not about the thief story nor about the press conference. Instead it was all about Luke, his place on the show, and how to secure it or cut him free. With Hamlet dangling in front of him, Luke might want to try to renegotiate his contract with a generous leave of absence policy in it. But *Lust for Life* couldn't afford that. They'd have to replace him or create a blockbuster story where he might—or might not—be killed.

While they talked, Frankie's respect for Victor grew. Not because of his grasp of the challenges of soap writing, but by his strategic thinking. He might not know how many pages equaled a half hour, or how to leave enough wiggle room in a plot in order to change direction on a brainstorm, but he did know how to use information and power to get what he wanted. They might be able to keep Luke on the show without so much as a whisper to his agent or a change in his upcoming contract. By the end of the conversation, she felt like a conspirator. They were laughing and joking together, and he asked her out for dinner—very slyly, almost casually, really—as if it were something they did regularly and he was just confirming the time.

"I…" She didn't know what to say. Dinner? And why not? She wasn't starting something with Luke. Really, she needed to kick him out. He'd betrayed her already. At least she was speeding up the process. It had taken three years to discover Brian's perfidy. She'd uncovered Luke's version in twenty-four hours. Goal!

"I'll owe it to you," he said, a shy grin on his face.

"Why?"

"Remember when you asked last night about speaking at the press conference?"

Goose bumps formed on Frankie's arm. *No, no, no.* "Yeah?" she asked tentatively while thinking of how, if she worked fast, she could run past him, around the corner, down the hallway, and to the stairwell in less than a minute.

"Brady can't be here. Some last-minute thing in California. He's on his way to the airport."

Dammit. "What about his assistant?" Frankie asked before remembering that the assistant producer had quit shortly after Brady had taken over. He'd not yet filled the slot, relying on Serena, Bob, and even Frankie to act in that capacity as needs arose. "There has to be someone else! I'm not qualified! I can't do it. I hate public speaking!"

Victor leaned into her desk, staring intently at her as if he were a mesmerist trying to put a patient into a trance. "Don't worry. I'll coach you through it. It's nothing." He looked at his watch. "We have about an hour. C'mon. I'll help you. It's a snap."

It wasn't a snap. It took time to get really comfortable at public speaking, and this wasn't the venue in which someone should learn. It was going to be adversarial. His leak had appeared in the morning papers—it was already up on the Drudge Report—and every article referred to *Lust for Life* as "struggling" in some fashion or another. The *Post* piece even described it as "about to be canceled."

Miffed at Brady's absence after the man had agreed to this strategy, Victor decided the best way to deal with Brady was to forget about him. As far as Victor was concerned, Brady had to go. He wasn't committed to the show. It needed a producer who really cared about whether it lived or died and who wasn't always looking over his shoulder or two miles ahead for the next opportunity.

"All you have to do," Victor assured Frankie, "is read the statement we were going to have Brady use. We're having it redone in the press packets to be yours."

"Do I have to say where Brady is?"

"No. We're not even going to mention him," Victor said grimly. "If it comes up, I'll say he's traveling. Don't worry. I'll answer any questions."

"So all I have to do is read this and step aside?" Frankie's hand shook as she held the paper in her hand. She stood in front of him, prepared to rehearse.

Victor rose and placed his hand on her arm, steadying it.

"There will be a lectern," he assured her. "Familiarize yourself with the statement so you can look up from time to time. Bob will print it out in fourteen-point type so it's easy to read. It's short. Give it a try."

She did give it a try, hyperventilating so badly that she looked like she was going to pass out. Again, he came to her, this time putting his arm around her shoulder.

"Close your eyes," he said soothingly. "You've just read your statement. You've moved to the side. I'm speaking. It's all over. You're calm. Nobody hurt you. There you go. Now, try it again."

She did. With the same result, except this time her voice shook.

"Didn't you have to do any public speaking in school?" he asked, bewildered.

"I was a writer, not a speaker!" she huffed. "Why do you think I chose writing? So I wouldn't have to speak!"

She crossed her arms over her chest, which just caused another button on her blouse to pop open. That had been happening through-out the session, immediately drawing his gaze to her milk white skin under the transparent shirt. Maybe someone in Wardrobe could find a replacement? And her hair—yes, it had a charming, girlish quality to it, like something from a pre-Raphaelite painting—but it might not play well on camera.

His cell phone vibrated while Frankie tried another read-through. "Keep practicing," he said while stepping into the hall to take the call. It was his aunt, her voice sounding frantic and afraid.

"Is something the matter? Do you need help?" he asked.

"Yes, yes, I do. Something terrible is happening. That wonderful boy Donovan Reilly might be in jeopardy. He's such a sweet child. You must do something, Victor. Don't you have some friends who could break him free?"

Victor mentally cursed Luke Blades. He was probably already laying the groundwork for getting what he wanted during contract negotiations. How else would Aunt Gussie know they were contemplating a kidnap story for Donovan if Luke himself hadn't divulged it?

"Good idea, Aunt Gussie. I'd better get on that. I'll see you this weekend."

"What a delightful surprise! I'll have Dane make up your room."

He calmed her down by the time he got off the phone, but his own anger at Luke Blades was at a fever pitch. Luke was exploiting a vulnerable old woman whose mental abilities were fading. He'd talk to his aunt about changing her private phone number when he saw her this weekend.

Another thought cut him, too. How did Luke Blades hear of their story ideas? Probably through Frankie.

Chapter 6

THE PRESS CONFERENCE WOULD *have started okay,* thought Frankie as perspiration beaded on her upper lip, *if it hadn't been for Luke crashing it.* As in literally crashing.

Just as Mary had finished the introductions and Frankie had started repeating to herself, "You'll be okay. You'll be okay. Just ten minutes, that's what Victor said. Try not to pop the buttons on your blouse, don't breathe too fast, but don't forget to breathe," Luke had entered the back of the room and stumbled over a microphone wire.

Ka-boom. All control vanished as reporters scrambled to help him.

"Luke!" An anguished cry from the doorway stopped them all in their tracks, as a redheaded angel of mercy swooped into the room to tend to the fallen actor.

That's no angel of mercy, Frankie realized, squinting at the gal. It was Kayla!

Kayla?

She'd changed her hair color and was dressed in a white skirt and blouse with a white scarf around her neck.

What the…?

"We should help," Frankie mumbled to Victor, before rushing through the gaggle of news reporters to see if Luke was okay.

Not only was he okay, he was holding court.

"Can't comment for sure on the Hamlet thing," he said, dusting off his leg as Kayla helped him with his crutches. "But should have an announcement soon. The show's been great about it so far. Don't anticipate any scheduling problems." Then he looked up at Frankie and smiled. "Right?'

Frankie blushed with rage. *Dammit.* He'd deliberately sabotaged the press conference so he could get his Hamlet job on the record along with her promises to accommodate his time off. She'd look like Scrooge the distaff version if she said anything other than "How proud we are of our top actor, Luke Blades."

Someone was sticking a microphone in her face, waiting for an answer.

"Uh…"

Victor stepped in. "The character of Donovan Reilly is currently a key component on the show," he said. "We're sorry we can't have Mr. Blades stick around, but he needs to get checked out after this latest fall."

With a strength that looked both heroic and yet effortless, Victor grabbed Luke's good side and glided him from the room. Frankie scurried after, unwilling to stay by the lectern without him. As they left the room, she heard Mary telling everyone they'd get started in a few minutes.

In the hallway, Victor didn't hold back.

"I don't know what you thought you were pulling in there," he whispered harshly, "but I'll deal with it later." He let go of Luke's arm. Kayla rushed to stand by him, her face a mask of worry.

"And what are you doing here?" Frankie asked. "In that getup?" She pointed to Kayla's outfit and hair.

Kayla handed her a phone message about Brady Stephens not being able to make it that morning. As usual, Kayla was a dollar short and a day late.

"She was auditioning for a part," Luke said, not hiding his anger. "She's only a temp, after all."

"Wha—" Frankie tried to compute this. "Only a temp?"

Kayla nodded.

"For two years?" Frankie asked, thinking back to when Kayla came on board. Why didn't she know this? The boss should know this. And she was the boss. Why did she have to keep reminding people about that? And what about the—

"Auditioning?" Frankie asked. "For what?" At least this explained the woman's constant absences, her lack of dedication to her job, her "studying" at her desk.

"For the role of Florence Nightingale," Kayla said defensively, stroking Luke's arm. "In a play directed by Mishka Palonovitch. Luke told me about it."

Frankie looked at Luke, who shrugged and said, "My agent passed it on."

"We don't have time for this, Frankie." Victor looked at the door to the room where the press conference was set up.

But Frankie was undeterred. She'd get to the bottom of this. Kayla was an aspiring actress…

"Is this the guy directing *Hamlet*, this Mishka Palomino—"

"Palonovitch," Kayla repeated slowly as if Frankie herself were slow. "He won a Tony last year for *War Songs*."

When Frankie registered a blank, Luke said, "The musical set at Walter Reed Hospital. All the soldiers are in wheelchairs. Big dance number at the end of act one."

"So you both want to run off and do stage work with this comedic genius," Frankie said, disgusted.

"Comic?" Kayla matched Frankie's disgust and raised her one. "*War Songs* is a very moving tragedy about the perils of modern life as seen through the eyes of the wounded warrior. I find new levels of irony and insight every time I see it. I cry each time, too. Reviewers say—"

Frankie held up her hand. "Save it." She glared at Luke. "If you're so interested in stage work, buster, maybe Donovan Reilly isn't such an integral part of the show."

"Frankie, now's not the time." Victor grabbed her by the arm, but she shrugged away.

"And as for you," she said to Kayla, "if you're interested in acting, why didn't you tell me? I could have arranged an audition for *Lust*." Well, maybe, maybe not. But hell if Frankie would look less than magnanimous.

Kayla's reaction was anything but grateful. "Thank you, but I'm not ready to settle yet."

"She's done some small parts off Broadway," Luke explained.

But Frankie didn't hear. *Settle? Kayla wasn't ready to settle for* Lust? Red-hot rage lit up her body and her voice as she turned to face Kayla. "You're not willing to settle for acting on a daytime serial?"

"You see, this is exactly why I didn't say anything," Kayla said, her tone sweetly condescending. "I knew you'd offer to help, and, as I said, I'm not really interested in your kind of work yet."

Inside, Frankie was an erupting volcano of hurt, anger, and outrage. Kayla, the secretary—the very bad temporary secretary, at that—thought her art was too good for Frankie, that her art was better than Frankie's art. What was the world coming to?

"I... I...," Frankie sputtered, unable to give voice to the cauldron of indignation choking her throat.

"Come along," Victor said through clenched teeth. He grasped her arm and wouldn't let go. "We can deal with that later." He steered her toward the press conference door. She called out over her shoulder, "*Lust for Life* is moving and touching! Just as moving as any dancing wheelchair farce that that Mucho Parmigiano can come up with! Just as good! Just as touching! *Lust for Life* is art, too! Damn good art!"

This last bit carried into the room as they entered, triggering the first question from a reporter.

"Ms. McNally, is that the reason why you're not pulling the thief story, because you're unwilling to sacrifice your artistic vision for public safety concerns?"

Frankie bumped Victor out of the way, rushed to the lectern, grabbed the mike, and leaned forward, causing the top two buttons on her blouse to pop open.

"Let's get this straight, bub," she hissed at him. "Art doesn't rob people. People rob people!"

—ww—

"Art doesn't rob people. People rob people."

Victor winced as Frankie uttered those words. He managed to come to the lectern after that, explaining that *Lust for Life* had no intention of jeopardizing public safety.

"We're obviously very proud of the show. But we're committed to being good public citizens, too. We intend to cooperate with the police fully and in good faith."

It didn't matter what he said; Frankie pushed him aside to take more questions, her jaw set tight, her eyes narrowed. She was in the worst possible mood to be diplomatic, but there was no wresting the mic away from her.

"If you're so proud of the show, Ms. McNally, are you also proud of its ratings?"

"Ratings, schmatings. Ratings and quality often don't match," she said to the third-rate cable news reporter, "as I'm sure you can personally attest to from your own experience."

"Do you think the show has taken too many chances on controversial stories?" asked another reporter, this one from a wire service.

"What stories? Give me specifics," she snapped.

The reporter reddened, clearly not a regular watcher.

But another newswoman piped up. "Like when Monica had an abortion, or Jason had AIDS, or Pete announced he was gay." She was from the soap press. "Are you saying that Middle America just isn't ready for those gritty stories?"

Frankie straightened. Another button on her blouse popped.

"I'm saying"—she jabbed the lectern to emphasize each word—"that's just unadulterated crap." Someone in the room snickered. "I know Middle America. I *am* Middle America. *Lust for Life* does best when it stays true to each character's… 'gestalt'," she said fiercely. "Yeah, that's right. Their gestalt. Did you think I didn't know what that meant? As long as we writers set up the backstory and motivations for characters, the audience will follow them anywhere, even if it's to moral decisions that don't necessarily jibe with those the audience would make. We lose the audience when we cease to respect their natural sympathy for the characters and impose our own sermons, or, rather, plots—no matter how ennobling or hoity-toity—on the characters' lives."

She took a breath. She continued, speaking calmly now, extemporaneously, articulately, passionately, for nearly a quarter hour. It was a writing seminars course on the importance of character development, molded over the needs of a daytime serial. Victor was not just impressed. He was awed. She loved this show. She loved what she did.

But just as he thought they were out of the woods, a slim, scruffy-faced reporter who'd come in late asked Frankie once more about the thief, implying that if she was so proud of her work as a writer, she must also be proud of her work in aiding and abetting a criminal. He'd even gotten her name wrong, calling her Francesca, not Frankie or Ms. McNally as the other reporters had done.

"Art doesn't rob people," she repeated, this time with little vehemence. "People rob people." And the last two buttons on her dainty blouse popped open. Her cleavage was on full display. Cameras clicked right and left.

Victor rushed to the lectern. "Thank you all for coming. If we have any more news to share, we'll be sure to alert you. The police's community relations number is in your packets."

He grabbed Frankie's elbow and hastened her out of the conference room before reporters could corner them for more.

Mary from Publicity nodded her approval as they hurried down the hall together.

"That was pretty good," Mary said. "I think we'll get some great earned media from this. Frankie, you're quite the firecracker."

"Who was that last fellow?" Victor snarled, looking over his shoulder. "He came in late."

Mary glanced at her notes and shook her head. "I'm not sure. I'll find out." She left them to return to the room of reporters, most of whom were already gone, headed for the elevators.

"I blew it," Frankie said, looking down.

"Anything but," Victor told her, still propelling her forward away from the crowd. "You were magnificent!"

Victor guided her around a corner to the stairs so they wouldn't run the risk of bumping into reporters. One flight down and they were at Brady Stephens's level.

"Come on," Victor said, leading her to the executive's suite. "Brady won't mind." He breathed a hello to Serena and whisked Frankie into Brady's quiet and empty sanctuary.

"Have a seat," Victor told her while he headed to the liquor cabinet by the far wall. "You need a drink." *And so do I*, he thought, pouring two glasses of Scotch and water.

"It's awfully early for this," she said, accepting the drink nonetheless.

"As Nory might write, it's five o'clock somewhere. Cheers." He held up his own glass and sipped. "I never would have guessed you were afraid of public speaking."

"I guess I got carried away." She put her glass down without drinking. "It's just that I can't stand it when people look down their noses at… the show."

No, not the show, he thought. *At you. And I don't blame you for feeling that way.*

She looked down at her open blouse and, to Victor's disappointment, refastened the buttons. "Did that last guy call me Francesca?"

"Yeah. Couldn't even be bothered to get your name right."

Frankie groaned and closed her eyes, which Victor took as just more angst over her performance. He started to reassure her but was interrupted when Mary burst in.

"Here you are!" She held out a business card. "I got that reporter's name. E. J. Dewitt. Not a television or news reporter at all. He's a—"

"Book critic," Frankie gulped, not even looking at the card. Victor grabbed it.

"Writes for the *New Yorker Journal*," Frankie groaned again. "In-depth pieces. Very prestigious. Very respected." She fell back on the low couch in the room, grabbing a pillow and placing it over her head, muffling her voice. "I might not have heard of Mishka Pishka, the famous director, but I know who E. J. Dewitt is."

"Frankie?" Victor asked. "Are you sick?"

"No, no, no," she said, her voice muffled through the batting. "No, make that yes, yes, yes. I'm sick all right. Sick at heart. My life is an open book and my ex just published it."

She explained Brian's book to Victor—what she knew of it anyway—and then asked if she could go home for the rest of the day. By now it was close to noon. They'd started the press conference late, been interrupted by the Luke and Kayla show, and it had gone longer than they'd expected.

Mary had left the room when a page from a reporter called her away. Frankie suspected she wasn't at all interested in Frankie's personal problems. As far as she was concerned, Brian's book meant more publicity for the show.

Now Frankie sat up, her hands still wrapped around the pillow for comfort. "E. J. Dewitt is relentless," she said. "He's probably going to do a piece about Brian's new book and he's researching it. He's probably going to write everything I said in that damned press conference!"

"So what? You were great," Victor said.

"Doesn't matter." She punched the pillow, pretending it was her ex. "Brian painted this picture of me—of Francesca—that's apparently less than flattering." Yeah, so what if Gail had said the opposite? If it showed her with a chip on her shoulder, how could anyone say that was flattering? And so what if she did the same thing to Brian? It wasn't really the same thing. Not on a soap. Two different animals. Both in the same artistic "zoo," if you will, but two different cages, two different animals. Really.

"So Dewitt will use whatever I said—great or not—as evidence." As evidence that she was a bumbling television writer appealing to the masses while Brian breathed the rarified air of literature. *Dammit.* She wanted to breathe that air, too. Weren't they all supposed to have access to the same air? Wasn't that what America was all about—soap opera fan and literature lover as equals?

She wanted to go home and immediately start working on her own novel, something with a protagonist named Grian from a family named Blaigcand with connections to… to Nazis… Nazis, Salem witch burners, and… and… politicians. She was sure she could finish it by midnight if she wrote nonstop. She could do it. She'd always written well under pressure. She'd probably written the equivalent of five novels while at *Lust for Life.*

That depressed her. She sighed.

"Look, this isn't your problem." She stood, swaying a little from blood rushing to her feet. Victor rushed to steady her. "I can deal with it on my own."

Serena appeared at the door. "Kayla is trying to reach you, Ms. McNally. She said a Mr. Dewitt is waiting to see you."

Kayla at her post? Only E. J. Dewitt could do that. Or maybe she was there setting up new auditions. A light went on in Frankie's head. That's why the voice mail was so strange. She'd been trying on different voices! But why the dyed hair? Wasn't that a bit drastic for an audition?

"What color is Florence Nightingale's hair?" she asked Victor.

"I don't know. Why?"

Serena cleared her throat, waiting for an answer to Kayla's message.

"I can't go down there." Frankie froze, looking this way and that, as if searching for hidden doors.

"Tell Kayla to say Ms. McNally is in a meeting," Victor said. Serena disappeared.

"You have to face Dewitt eventually, even if only to say 'no comment.'" Victor still had his hand on her arm. It felt good. He was strong.

"I need to think about it. I need to read Brian's book." She remembered Gail said she'd send it over. She wondered if it was down there on her desk now, wrapped in brown paper. Maybe Dewitt was making a note about that. Was there anything else incriminating in her office? A bobblehead of Mr. Spock, a plastic fern, a scented candle in a martini glass—great. She went to Brady's desk and punched in Kayla's number.

"Kayla, if a package arrives from the law firm of Sloane, Moore, and Ryan, please have it brought up to me in Brady Stephens's office." She clicked off before the secretary could question her.

"You're just going to hang out here all afternoon?" Victor asked her. "I thought you wanted to go home."

"Maybe." It *was* comfortable in this office. Maybe she could nap here. Maybe she could live here. She'd redo it in French country with a few Tuscan touches in the window treatments. How long would Brady be gone?

Victor looked at his watch. "I have a better idea. You have any plans this weekend?"

Her plan this weekend was to curl up in a fetal position with a blanket over her head—after first changing her name and looking up who qualified for witness protection. She shook her head.

He pulled out his cell and dialed a number, telling someone named Dane that there would be two guests tonight. "Make up the Rose Room."

"C'mon," he said. "If you need anything from your office, I'll have Bob retrieve it. I can drop you at your apartment to get some things. We can spend the time plotting out what to do about Luke and Donovan and how to handle Dewitt. And I've been thinking that it's time to have a casting call for the thief."

Chapter 7

Donovan broke through rope ties on his wrist and pulled the blind-fold from his eyes, panting from the effort. His lean, muscular upper body shone with perspiration from the exertion. He glanced back and forth, sweat flinging from his curly hair. No one was about. This was his chance.

Dammit. He wouldn't be stopped.

"Sabotage," he murmured to himself as he struggled with the last of his bonds, unloosing his legs. "You don't know sabotage. I'll avenge myself, you... you shallow, pontificating, holier-than-thou scumbag. You thought you could grab what was mine? You thought you could hurt me? I'll show you what hurt is. If it's the last thing I do. I'll show you I'm as good as you, bub!"

But in the distance... a sound he'd dreaded. Barking. They'd let loose the dogs. He slipped back the safety on the gun he'd managed to hide in his waistband.

"I was never fond of dogs," he muttered under his breath. "Especially golden retrievers. Especially that rogue of the litter, Kayla."

FRANKIE WAS THE ONE who penned the breakdown about Donovan's distaste for golden retrievers. She'd insisted on those lines about sabotage, even though they'd yet to completely flesh out the reasons for Donovan's kidnapping. Victor wasn't sure how a sabotage situation would work its way into it, but she was the writer.

She'd written with an almost hysterical glee, but then again she'd had a Scotch before dinner and a glass of wine with it after not eating much at all. And then there was the brandy afterward. Victor winced when he thought of what had triggered that as he sipped his coffee the next morning in his aunt's Connecticut home, staring out broad windows toward the sun glistening on the field beyond.

It was a measure of Frankie's absolute terror of being dogged by that E. J. Dewitt fellow for an interview about her ex's book that she'd agreed, with little protest, to get away for the weekend. Then again, he'd sold her on the idea by telling her how she'd finally get a chance to meet the great Augustinia Pendergrast. She probably figured it was her opportunity to influence the power behind the curtain.

It didn't matter how he'd lured her here. She was here and he was glad of it. Not just because it meant an uninterrupted weekend pounding out *Lust* problems, which seemed to double by the minute. No, he liked Frankie, and he wanted to get to know her better. That was awfully hard to do at work—or with Luke staying in her apartment, dammit.

He would have preferred, however, that their weekend had started in a less foggy way.

After dinner the night before, they'd retired to the sunroom to catch the news. Station after station was running the story of their press conference, with one sound bite showing up in every story:

"Art doesn't rob…"

Click.

"…people…"

Click.

"People rob…"

Click.

"…people." And shortly after that, Frankie's blouse had popped another button.

With each channel switch, Frankie's eyes had widened. He'd offered her brandy then. And suggested turning off the set when they saw the ACLU lawyer on *The O'Reilly Factor* debating some law and order expert on whether *Lust for Life* had the right to continue with such an "irresponsible" story. When one expert suggested that the head writer come on the show to explain herself, Frankie had visibly paled.

To get her mind off that maelstrom, he'd clicked off the TV and suggested they go into the study, where they could bang out some ideas for Donovan and Teresa. That's when she'd dived into the golden retriever stuff with maniacal fury. That she could control, he speculated, so she went at it with gusto.

He smiled. His aunt Gussie had been thoroughly charmed by Frankie, enough to remember her name throughout the dinner and even the fact that she worked at *Lust*.

At the thought of his aunt, a worry creased his brow. After he'd made sure Frankie was settled in her room, he'd taken Dane aside into the study for a serious talk. Dane had been with his aunt for nearly two decades now, starting out as a butler and now acting as manager of the household.

Victor knew Dane had no family, but he did have a partner he was devoted to. It was becoming increasingly difficult for Dane to use his time off—he was too afraid of leaving Gussie alone. In fact, Dane spent his days trying to keep track of her, never sure she wouldn't be wandering off somewhere. Victor had authorized the man to begin interviewing home nursing staff, but it would be difficult to do because, although she was forgetful and disoriented most of the time, his aunt Gussie had a keen instinct for anything with the whiff of medical care about it. If she sensed that anyone was thinking of infringing on her freedom with well-meaning "caretakers," she demonstrated the depth and breadth of her stubbornness, a trait he usually admired. Dane, therefore, would do the interviews away from the house.

Victor heard a door close upstairs. Not his aunt. She'd had her coffee and was doing needlepoint in the sunroom while listening to the morning news. It must be Frankie.

He quickly turned back to the granite island and made sure the coffeepot was full, then set out a cup and plate for her on the table by the bay window in the breakfast nook, swiping a rose from a bouquet in the hall and placing it in a small glass vase in front of her place setting.

Pleased with his work, he was startled when his aunt crept up behind him.

"My, doesn't that look pretty," she said, holding his arm. "As pretty as the girl it's for."

If there was one thing Frankie McNally did not feel that morning, it was pretty. She woke up in a panic, wondering where she was and if she'd died and gone to heaven. It sure as hell felt like she were lying on a cloud.

But her throbbing head quickly brought her back to earth and reality. She stroked the downy duvet on top of the feather-soft Egyptian cotton sheets, and her first thought was that Teresa, on the show, would feel right at home in these digs.

She was in a bright, cool room with a rose-patterned wallpaper—the Rose Room, that's what Victor had called it when he'd phoned someone the night before to set this up. Or was that ten years ago? *Oh, my head...*

She slid her feet to the floor from the fifty-foot perch of the bed, grabbing her silky robe before heading to the bathroom that was part of this suite. She'd thrown things in a bag at her apartment with such haste she'd not even bothered wondering where traitorous Luke was. Huh—probably setting up press conferences about how valuable Donovan was to the show, or holding meetings with his agent about how to get more time off.

Holy cow, she thought, as her vision and memory returned. Even Brian's family didn't live this well. Everything was neat and clean and expensive looking. Antique furniture, brocade drapes, soft woven rugs on hardwood floors that looked like they'd been laid during the Revolution, a fireplace on the far wall.

In the bathroom she stared at herself in an oval-framed mirror and could have sworn her headache was visible as a pulsating halo around her crown. Nope, that would just be her messy hair, which she swiped out of her eyes with one hand, groping in her cosmetics bag with the other searching for her bottle of aspirin. *Not fair,* she thought, *I didn't have that much to drink.* Cold comfort—she wasn't used to drinking. She was a one-glass-of-wine-with-dinner kind of gal. She gulped down two pills and then brushed her teeth. Finally, she headed for the shower. In a quarter hour, she was feeling nearly human again. After donning jeans and a sweater and pulling her unruly hair into a ragged bun at the nape of her neck, she took several deep breaths, reminding herself that McNallys were as good as anyone, and descended the stairs to the floor below.

—◠◠—

"Oh." The manservant, or whatever he was called, stared at her as she rounded the threshold. She looked behind her to make sure bathroom tissue wasn't sticking to her rump. "You don't need to use the servants' staircase," he said. "You can use the main one."

Well, lah-di-dah, she thought, *a house so full of itself it has a servants' stairway.* Yeah, yeah, she knew about them. Brian's parents' house had one, too. She just didn't think it mattered which one you used. It certainly hadn't mattered enough to her to figure out which was which.

"Closest," she murmured. "Next time I'll use the—"

"No matter," he said, smiling. "I just didn't want you to think you had to use that one."

And why would you think that? she wondered as she gritted her teeth into what she hoped was a pleasant but somewhat patronizing smile. *Why would you assume that Frankie McNally would assume she wasn't good enough for the main stairway, huh?*

"Coffee's on. I could get you some," he said, pointing to the kitchen.

At the sound of voices, though, Victor appeared. "That's all right, Dane. I've got it covered." He looked at her and grinned. "You sleep okay? That room can get cold."

"Yes," she said. "I mean, no. I mean the room wasn't cold. I slept fine." Warmth flooded her face. Oh good. That would help her headache, which had started to recede.

"C'mon, let me get you some grub." Victor led her around the corner across miles of granite-and-stainless-steel-decorated kitchen to a small room that seemed to butt out over the back, where acres of land swept up to a dusty forest, tree branches empty of leaves. As she sat down, Victor appeared at her elbow, coffee pot in hand, pouring her a steaming cup.

She sipped. And revived. And noticed a brilliant red rose in a crystal vase in front of her, nearly causing her to spit out her java.

When Victor saw her eyes widen in surprise, he chuckled. "I'm sorry. Thought it would brighten the table. Forgot it had other meanings now." He whisked it away, placing it on the counter.

As he asked her what she'd like for breakfast and fixed her toast when she answered, she studied him. Like her, he wore jeans and a sweater, some off-white cable-knit thing that looked like it came from an exclusive shop. He was happy and self-confident, just as he was in the office, but there was something else about him here in his natural habitat. It was a mischievousness, an impishness, as if a practical joke were just around the corner. Her gaze fell on the rose as she nibbled her toast. Was Victor capable of taking a joke too far? Or, rather, coming up with what he thought was a joke and using it to promote the show? Rose Room, rose on the table, rose left by the thief…

No, he couldn't be… he wouldn't have.

"After you're finished, I thought we could go over some of the breakdowns for upcoming shows, bat some ideas around," he said, leaning against the counter sipping at his own mug of coffee. "And I have some marketing ideas I want to run by you."

"Mm-hmm," she said, swallowing. Maybe she could do some sleuthing later, looking for black ski masks and *Jewel Thieving for Dummies* books.

He plucked thoughts of the jewel thief from her mind.

"I think we should do a casting call for the thief, for example," he continued. "It's a great opportunity for publicity."

She sighed. "But Victor," she said, trying to corral her head-thumping thoughts into a coherent argument. She had to be forceful with him. That was the key. "I'm still not happy with continuing the story. I don't think I've adequately communicated that. I should have made it clear from the start. We should dump the story as soon as possible. The publicity we've snagged so far has been fine, but enough's enough. I don't think we should prolong this thing." There, she'd been forceful and decisive.

"I agree."

What? He agreed with her? She waited for the other shoe to drop.

"I trust your judgment. If you don't think the story has potential—separate and apart from its publicity possibilities now—then it definitely should be dumped. But I'm not talking about continuing the story when I say we should have a casting call for the thief."

"You've lost me there."

"Look, a casting call doesn't mean we have to keep the story. It just means we get some airtime on the news. It doesn't mean we actually have to hire an actor to play the thief."

She considered this, but then she actually heard the morning's news blasting from a TV in a nearby room, and there was that danged sound bite of her again telling America that "art doesn't rob people; people rob people."

"I don't know, Victor. Like I said, enough's enough. I'm beginning to wonder if all this publicity is a good thing," was all she said.

He crossed his arms and stared at her. "Of course it's a good thing. I'm sure our ratings will spike next week as folks tune in to see what all the chatter is about."

"Please tell me I'm not going to have to go on any talk shows."

He chuckled. "We'll manage to avoid that, I'm sure."

"Yeah, just like you avoided having me speak at the press conference." She gulped down more coffee. "How'd that work out for you?"

"Point taken," he said. "But don't worry—I think it will be to our benefit to refuse to do the talk shows. It will keep the story alive if they think we're avoiding them."

"You know, you're kind of scary." Finished with her toast, she dabbed her mouth with the napkin in what she hoped was a ladylike way, then put her dishes in the sink just as she would at home. So what if they had servants here? She would still be polite, just as her mother had taught her. She misjudged the depth of the sink, though, and dropped one of the plates, cracking it. She gasped, looking at Victor wide-eyed.

"Uh-oh. That was a family heirloom."

"I… I… can pay for it." By mortgaging her mother's house.

"Relax, Frankie." He smiled. "I was just kidding!"

Okay, maybe she was a little on edge. "Where's your aunt?" she asked, looking around.

Victor shrugged toward the sunroom, where the crackle of a television emanated.

"I should say good morning," Frankie said, thinking of the etiquette boxes she needed to check off. "And then I'd like to check my email. My laptop's upstairs."

"No problem," Victor said, leading her beyond the breakfast nook into the sunroom, which was true to its name. Drenched in bright light, it sat on the southwest corner of the home, its tall, wide windows abutting the roof and overlooking those shimmering fields beyond. Gussie Pendergrast sat in a pale blue skirted chair, her white hair straggling from its curly bun, her head bent over a needlepoint design of golden retrievers romping in a field. Several meticulously finished needlepoint pieces decorated the northern wall, which was also crammed with family photos. Frankie thought she caught a glimpse of a younger Victor in a dashing uniform, a crooked smile on his face as if to say, "Yeah, I'm a hunk, what of it?"

"Good morning, Mrs. Pendergrast," Frankie said.

Gussie looked up, her eyes clouded with confusion. She quickly glanced at Victor as if seeking help, and her nephew just as quickly provided it.

"Frankie and I will be in the study, working on *Lust*." His voice held a worried edge.

At the mention of the soap opera, however, Gussie's face relaxed, losing the tense look of befuddlement. "Oh, yes, I remember," she said, turning toward Frankie. "I hope you were comfortable last night. And I hope you find something wonderful for that darling Donovan. He's such a sweet boy, you know. He sent me flowers last week—just to let me know he was thinking of me." Her eyes twinkled. "I think he was afraid I'd be jealous of that lovely Teresa. But I only want Donovan to be happy, of course."

Gussie's lively talk about the show, and her blending of reality with fantasy, didn't surprise Frankie. She'd already known it existed and had witnessed it firsthand last night at the dinner table when Gussie had talked at length about various characters as if they were her best friends.

"We better get going if we're going to get anything done," Victor said, the same worried edge there. He touched Frankie's elbow and steered her toward the door. "You can check your email on my computer, Frankie."

"I'll tell Dane to make you some sandwiches," Gussie said as they left. "But let's have dinner before the fireplace in the parlor, shall we?"

—⁓—

"She's a sweetheart," Frankie said as they entered the dark, book-lined study in the front of the house. She flopped down in the huge burgundy leather chair behind the desk, already clicking her way through a Net browser to her email.

"She is that," Victor agreed, sinking into a wing chair in front of the desk.

"But you know, I expected to see a whole kennel full of dogs here, given her love for them."

"Her last one died last year. I've promised to help her get another, but I keep forgetting to make the time."

"She doesn't remind you?" Frankie asked, logging on.

"She keeps forgetting, too.

His voice sounded so sad that she turned away from the screen to look at him. He sat with his elbows on the armrests, his hands clasped together in front of his face, but he couldn't hide the worry there. His brow was heavily creased and his mouth was turned down as if he was distracted by dark thoughts.

"You're worried about her," Frankie said. "I don't blame you. It's hard to see those we love get older. Things start falling apart as soon as you hit fifty." *No, no, she didn't just say that, did she?* Victor was probably at least fifty, maybe somewhere just shy of fifty-five.

"Uh, what I mean is that with some people," she continued, trying to redeem herself, "with people who have, you know, health problems and the like, things start falling apart. I mean most people are pretty vigorous into their fifties and even beyond. But with some other unfortunate souls, well, things can start falling apart even earlier, maybe even in their thirties. I mean look at me, I'm terribly out of shape, and I don't eat right, and... and, well, I mean, it's the really bad stuff you need to worry about, stuff like diabetes and heart problems and... and, well, like Alzheimer's, for example."

As soon as she said it, it burst into her mind like an electric light-bulb pinned to the ceiling above her head blinking, "Rude, rude, uncouth, uncouth!"

Gussie Pendergrast wasn't just "forgetful." She had Alzheimer's. That's why Victor was so worried. Oh. Dear. God. Could she get any more insensitive?

"Oh, Victor, I'm so sorry. I just realized—your aunt. She isn't just forgetting things, is she?"

"No, I'm afraid it's a bit more serious than that."

"How far along is she?" Frankie leaned forward.

Now that the cat was out of the bag, Victor relaxed, letting his hands drop to the armrests. "She was diagnosed last year. She takes medication. Or, rather, Dane sees that she takes it."

"Well, it must be working," Frankie said, hoping to cheer him. "She's an absolute encyclopedia when it comes to the show. Why, she remembered things about some of the characters that even I'd forgotten. I should have written them down."

And here, another epiphany exploded in her brain. Gussie Pendergrast's only sense of continuity was the show. When she'd seen Frankie in the sunroom, she'd not remembered who she was until Victor mentioned they'd be working on *Lust* together. At the mention of the soap, Gussie had lost her air of confusion.

That was the real reason Victor was working on *Lust for Life*—for his aunt!

She studied his rugged face and his muscular build straining against the sweater. Here was a man, a rebel in his youth who joined the Marines rather than lead the aimless life of his radical chic parents, but whose understanding of loyalty—the Semper Fi of all those few, proud souls—meant staying true to the woman who'd been there for him over the years, helping her hang on to rational thought with the only thread she had. Here was a man willing to learn everything he could about a soap opera he probably cared little about just so his aunt could live in this world a bit longer and not in a cloud of confusion.

She felt like crying. She felt like embracing him. She felt like asking him how he had learned to be that way.

"Looks like you have a lot of email," he said, pointing to the screen, where a long list of highlighted messages was visible.

"Oh. Yeah." She turned toward the computer, trying to think of something appropriate to say, something comforting and under- standing. When she looked at the screen, however, her heart shifted gears from warm sympathy to cold, hard fear. Virtually every message concerned the jewel thief story and her performance at the press con- ference. And the vast majority of them were from strangers.

"Oh my god," she said, clicking open a few and skimming the mes- sages before retreating in horror to the next note and the next note.

Victor got up and walked behind her, resting his hands on the top of the chair. "Is that your personal email or your office account?"

"Office," she managed to gulp out. "I thought I'd check that first."

"It might overload the server," he murmured. "I should call IT." He reached past her to grab a card from his open attaché case on the desk. She could smell him as his arm brushed hers—not aftershave, just the clean scent of a fresh sweater recently warmed by the sun and some soap. Finding a number on the card, he immediately dialed it on his cell, leaving a message for someone to call him back. He did this with several other numbers and then asked Frankie if she minded if he looked at her email.

"I promise not to read anything personal," he said, sliding into the seat she had vacated as they exchanged places. He made quick work of dumping all the thief-related emails into a folder, which he emailed to his own account. When he was finished, only a few dozen messages remained, one of which she immediately recognized as coming from E. J. Dewitt. She groaned when she saw it. Victor noticed it, too.

"You know, I really think you should talk to that fellow," he said. "I could coach you."

"Just like you did—"

"Maybe this time you'll actually listen."

"I listened! At least I wasn't nervous."

"I did tell you, if you recall, only to say enough to answer their questions."

"I *was* answering questions."

"You answered as an adversary, not as a communicator. That's what got you into trouble."

"Oh, so I just need to be a communicator. When I figure out what that means, I'm sure it will satisfy Mr. Dewitt."

"You shouldn't worry about satisfying him. Only about communicating your point of view." He leaned back and looked up at her, a smile teasing at his lips. "What is your point of view anyway—on this book your ex wrote?"

"I… I don't know, I haven't read it yet!"

"Well, then. You have plausible deniability. Just tell the fellow you haven't read it, and that you wish your ex well as you do any aspiring writer."

"It has a section in it, though, about me! Or some caricature of me. A Francesca character."

"I'm surprised his editor let him get away with that," Victor said.

"Knowing Brian, he probably never told her his ex-wife's name. He probably didn't tell her he had a wife who then became an ex-wife." Why were they talking about Brian when they had so much else to do? "Look, that's my personal problem. We have other problems we need to tackle, problems with the show, with Luke."

Victor grabbed a legal pad and pen while Frankie paced. For the next half hour, they batted ideas back and forth for the main characters. They argued over direction. They laughed as they thought up diabolical twists that would satisfy viewers while scoring needed power points with the actors. They expressed mutual frustrations over the lack of time to adequately develop some plots, given the show's precarious ratings. Frankie was quick to notice that Victor took notes during this session, deferring to her as head writer, as the leader of the team. Even so, she continued to be impressed with his knowledge of the show—he'd studied hard, obviously—and his quick wit. He often finished a sentence she'd started, or came up with an idea she'd wished she'd thought of. They were on their tenth page of notes when Victor's phone rang, the return call from IT.

He made quick work of suggesting the man check the show's server to make sure it wasn't overloaded due to incoming email on the thief story, and Frankie could tell from Victor's side of the conversation that the show's website had been receiving an unusually high number of hits. What was even more promising was the number of hits on the "Watch Old Episodes" portion of the site. They were drawing in new viewers!

But this good news was followed by something that dampened Victor's mood, if his tone and demeanor were any guide.

"No, been working all morning so I hadn't looked," he said into the phone. "Really? Oh, I see. I'm looking for it now. Thanks." And after he hung up, he clicked his way to the Drudge Report and on to one of the top stories at the site. Frankie caught the headline from across the room and rushed to read it with Victor: "Soap Thief Strikes Again."

"No!" Frankie reached up and grabbed her hair as if that would make this nightmare end. "I knew it, I knew it! Victor, this has to stop!" She didn't need to read the story to know what it said, but Victor read it for her. A jewel thief—or the jewel thief—had struck again the night before, robbing a wealthy doyenne of her jewels while she was attending a fundraiser for the opera.

"I'm going to stop it myself right now. I'm the head writer, and I have the authority." She reached beyond him to the phone on the desk, intending to call Brady Stephens, telling him either the thief story ended or she would quit.

But before she could even lift the receiver from its cradle, Victor's strong hand rested on her arm.

"Not yet," he said, which she considered a victory. He wasn't saying no. Just "not yet." She pulled her hand back, but he kept his warm paw on her arm, a sensation, she realized, that she liked a great deal.

"Let me make a call first," he continued, releasing her. "I know you think I'm just continuing this story because I want the publicity. But I really do worry that pulling the plug on it abruptly could lead to some sort of psychotic break for the real thief. Raeanne had a good point about that. I have a friend on the local police force who's done some profiling. Let me call him and talk to him. We can both talk to him."

She swallowed and sighed. It was the responsible thing to do. As guilt swamped her when she thought of the poor woman whose home had been invaded, she reminded herself that she didn't start this fire, that it was a story concocted by the earlier writer. *Jack—where is he?* she wondered. Was it possible that he was pulling this stunt? She mentioned the possibility to Victor, but he shook his head.

"I thought of that, too, and checked it out myself. Jack's been giving seminars on television writing at some hotel in the Caribbean for the past six weeks."

"Nice work if you can get it," Frankie said, revising her cosmetics-selling fallback plan should the *Lust* job go bust.

Victor dialed his friend's number and soon had a cheerful man on the line, someone Victor obviously knew from many years ago, probably before Frankie was even born. After exchanging pleasantries,

Victor explained the situation and put the fellow on speakerphone so he could talk to both of them.

"Well, this is awfully limited information, Vic, so it's hard to say what a person like this might do. But I think it's safe to say this fellow—and I would assume it is a fellow if the character on the show is one—is unhinged. So treading lightly is the best advice I can give you," the man said.

Frankie stepped forward and spoke into the speakerphone. "But how big a risk is it if we just stop the story? What will this guy do?"

"He might just crawl back into his hole. Or he might step up to something more attention-grabbing."

Frankie's stomach turned.

Victor put the next question. "So what would you recommend?"

"Like I said, I'd tread lightly. I wouldn't do anything with the story that you don't want the real thief imitating. I'd emphasize his gentle side, his kindness. After all, if this thief is imitating your thief, give him some good qualities to mimic."

"We can do that," Frankie said, glad to have something positive to hang on to.

A few minutes later they were off the phone, and Frankie was thoroughly convinced that ending the story could carry as much jeopardy as continuing it. Dammit, she'd wanted clear answers. Instead she was left with this... this murk.

Frankie walked to the window, rubbing her arms in the chill. The front of the house, which this room faced, was a lovely landscape of tall trees and elegant shrubs. A graceful driveway curved around to its front door. She thought she saw stables and other outbuildings to the east, including a pool house and a now-covered in-ground pool. This was quite the estate.

"Don't worry," Victor's soft voice said into her ear. He was standing right behind her, the realization of which sent a shiver up her back, prickling the hairs at the nape of her neck. "We just need to keep our thief a polite, gentle soul. Until the police catch the real one."

She mulled this in silence. Writing this thief story would feel like providing a blueprint for the real thief. That was the kind of thing that filled his poor aunt's addled mind, reality messed up with fantasy.

Using the show as an example the thief could follow, a template, a model, wasn't such an outlandish idea. No more outlandish than turning Donovan into a golden retriever–hating rapscallion in order to break Gussie's bonds of affection for him. What if the real thief was like Gussie, looking at the show as if it were connected to his own life? They could emphasize the thief's abhorrence of violence, making him a veritable Gandhi of thievery! They could hammer his absolute insistence that he only rob empty homes when no one was home! They could make him the kindest, gentlest, noblest creature in Crestview.

As this idea took hold, excitement built. She would handle this story herself, very carefully. She would make sure that not a whiff of badness swirled around the thief. Why, she'd practically make him a saint, robbing from the rich to give to the poor. She turned with such speed that she practically fell into Victor's arms.

"I can do it."

He smiled. "I'm sure you can," he said, and with a sudden spontaneity that surprised them both, he hugged her.

And then something happened. He stared at her eyes with such intensity that she almost looked away. But there was something in those dark irises that mesmerized her with their vulnerability. His lids lowered, as did hers, and he kissed her.

She melted into his arms as his lips, dry from the cold weather, brushed her own. One kiss led to another, this one deeper and more searching, and she quivered as she responded to his sure touch, pressing into him, her hands feeling the hard muscles beneath his wool sweater. But she felt his body tense as he hugged her tighter, guessing that was the moment when discipline won out over desire. He relaxed his grip and pulled back.

"Carried away for a moment," he said, his voice husky. He looked down.

"Yeah. Yeah. So was I. Lots of tension we've been under." She still felt the memory of his lips against hers.

"Exactly.

She cleared her throat.

He looked at his watch. "Let me get Dane. We should eat something. Some lunch."

"Your aunt mentioned sandwiches."

"Yes, yes. I remember." But he didn't move, as if he knew moving would mean shifting from the fantasy of the previous moment into the reality of their work.

"We could go to the kitchen," she suggested. "He doesn't need to wait on us."

Victor smiled. "That *is* his job, you know. To wait on us."

"Well, I mean..."

"The kitchen is brighter," Victor said. He gestured toward the door, and she strode to it, knowing as she walked that his gaze was locked on her rear.

Chapter 8

GET A GRIP.

The phrase repeated itself like a tape loop through his head as he pulled out the sandwiches Dane had made; as they checked on his aunt, who was dozing in her chair in the sunroom, her lunch tray by her side; and as they made small talk over their own lunch.

Get a grip. Of course you were attracted to her. She's young and pretty and smart. And funny. And sweet. And kind. And...

Get a grip.

"So you went to Wellesley?" he asked, trying not to look into her eyes. They were too tantalizing. "My daughter went there." *That's better. Remind her how old you are. Remind yourself, for god's sake. Get a grip.*

"Long time ago," she said after swallowing. "Do you have milk? I love milk with a sandwich."

Of course, he thought as he got up to fetch it. *Milk with your lunch, just like a child.* Why, she was young enough to be his child. He had a daughter who could be friends with this woman, in her peer group.

"Courtney liked Wellesley but found the atmosphere a bit rarified," he said. That was it—*remind yourself she's young enough to be Courtney's friend.*

"Was it? I mean, for me it was. It's reassuring to hear it was for someone like her." She gulped some milk. "I mean, I don't know her. But I assume she's like you. I mean, I assume she would have fit in more than me. More than I did, I mean." She blushed, a warm pink filling her face that laced out into capillaries beyond her cheeks. She was charming, as his aunt Gussie had said, and his aunt didn't take to just anybody—if they weren't on *Lust for Life*, that is. She'd not been fond of his wife, that was sure. He'd avoided bringing Linda here.

"You're probably tired," he said. "And Aunt Gussie will want us to spend some time at dinner—she doesn't have many guests, so I should warn you that this evening's dinner is likely to be a more formal affair. We don't need to work all afternoon. You can walk around the grounds, take a ride, read, just nap. Whatever you want."

"Formal? I didn't bring anything fancy," Frankie said, panic furrowing her brows. "Not even a dress."

He waved his hand. "No, I mean she won't want to see us in jeans, that's all. But I shouldn't impose. You can wear whatever you like." He saw her relax and watched her graceful fingers brush a lock of hair from her eyes.

"Well, why don't we take a break?" Frankie suggested. "We did a lot this morning."

⁓

Gabe had been the one who captured her heart as a girl. He was the one every young woman in town wanted. And he wanted her. She remembered Carla's look when she'd shown up at the party with Gabe on her arm. She'd been wild with jealousy. Faye smiled at the memory, rolling over in her bed, arms crossed under her head.

Then she frowned. Gabe had danced with Carla at that party and let Carla think she had a chance. He had a habit of doing that, letting girls think they could have him.

She heard a car pull up and went to the window, peering past the lacy curtain to the scene below. It was him again, that stranger—dark hair, dark eyes, with muscles that shouted, "Don't mess with me." He'd wanted to buy the tavern, and she'd thought he was crass and arrogant. Then she'd found out why—he'd been trying to save it from an unscrupulous mortgage company. He had not been arrogant at all. He'd been kind.

He must have sensed her gaze and looked up at her, those dark, liquid eyes penetrating the window, finding her heart. She shivered and stepped back, pulling his card from her pocket and reading it for the hundredth time.

Victor.

———

No, not Victor. Grayson. Hunched over her laptop on the bed of the Rose Room, Frankie backspaced and typed in the right name. *Faye, I know exactly how you feel, honey, finding out Grayson is not who you thought he was, finding out he's a better man than Luke.*

No, not Luke, Donovan. *No! Not Donovan, Gabe! Good grief.*

She ran her fingers through her hair. For the fortieth time since returning to her room, she wondered if a cold shower might be a good idea.

She'd already tried to nap, but had tossed and turned instead, fantasizing about what Victor must look like under all those clothes. She remembered the feel of his muscles, the scent of his skin.

She got up and decided to opt for one of the other activities Victor had suggested—a walk. Maybe that would clear her head.

So she spent another half hour tramping around the perimeter of the estate, afraid to wander too far without Mapquesting the way home, and still unable to shake her feelings of unease. Jeez, she'd gone from wondering at breakfast if he was the jewel thief to wondering at lunch if he wore boxers or briefs. How had *that* happened?

"It happened," she muttered to herself as she trudged around an icy fountain, "because you've been stung by Brian, and even though your affection for him is long dead, the wound was deep and he managed to open it again, and then Luke made you realize how much you were missing a man, and the whole thing combined to make you vulnerable to the strong magnetism of a man like Victor Pendergrast."

Logical. Rational. Sensible. She breathed a sigh of relief to have figured it out.

But she then found herself obsessing over Victor's "strong magnetism"—specifically, the way his tongue had felt in her mouth, the way his hands had felt around her, the way his cheek had bristled against hers—and was no more calmed down upon reentering the Pendergrast mansion than she had been when she left it.

Instead of heading upstairs to have a do-over with the nap idea, she skirted into the study to take a peek at her personal email, since she hadn't been able to get her laptop to recognize the estate's wireless network. *Never checked my voice mail either,* she thought, thinking of her cell phone in her purse upstairs.

Her personal email box was empty except for some spam and a message from her mom reminding her to bundle up in the cold weather and suggesting she visit for Easter if she could get away, and a note from Gail saying she'd seen the news and thought Frankie looked great. She did a quick reply and logged out, feeling oddly lonely that her office email box had been jammed full of messages from strangers, yet her personal one had been nearly void. What did that say about her social life? To cheer herself, she did a quick stop by the show's site before heading up to her room.

Her jaw nearly fell to the floor when the site came up. A long, red rose now decorated the right side of the home page with the message: Who will be next? The "Watch Old Episodes" link was more prominently displayed, and a stat counter, which they previously eschewed because of its potential for embarrassment, now graced the lower left corner. Millions had visited the site. Millions.

Victor must have directed the website folks to make the changes. He seemed to be able to snap his fingers and get things done. Was that what he was doing with her—snapping his fingers and having her drool over him?

She couldn't think about it anymore. She went upstairs and retrieved her cell, clicking through five messages from E. J. Dewitt, three from other reporters, one from Brady congratulating her on the press conference, and one from Luke, pitiful and worried, asking when she'd be home.

—⁓—

Although she was on edge all afternoon, wondering about their next work session and whether Victor would be tense around her, Frankie discovered that her worries were groundless. Victor was nowhere to be seen until very late in the day, and then, after an apology and no explanation, he suggested they could talk about the show "later."

But later shifted into dinner, which meant they didn't discuss the show again that day. Maybe he was avoiding her?

Frankie didn't have a formal dress, but she had managed to neaten up her chiffon blouse over satin chemise, letting the blouse hang open. Black slacks and gold jewelry completed her ensemble. And she let her unruly hair hang free about her shoulders.

They talked about the show during dinner in front of a crackling fire, a conversation led by Victor. Frankie now understood why. His aunt Gussie was lively and engaged throughout the meal, as long as they were chatting about Crestview and its inhabitants.

Because the conversation settled on the show, she and Victor were actually able to get some more work done by batting around a few ideas about peripheral characters—they were both wise enough not to say too much about Gussie's beloved actors lest she dig in her heels about a story they suggested.

After dinner, they retired to a media room, where they watched an old Cary Grant comedy, Victor nestled next to her on a comfy couch while Aunt Gussie fell asleep midway through in a recliner by another crackling fire.

And then it was off to bed, where all Frankie could think about was how warm and enticing Victor's thigh had felt next to hers a few moments ago.

―――

A light snow fell in the morning, and Victor wanted to hit the road before the weather got bad. He welcomed the snow—it would mean putting distance between him and Frankie, and he needed to clear his head. But his aunt had insisted on Dane setting up a Sunday brunch, forgetting about the departure plans a mere fifteen minutes after Victor had shared them with her. He was willing to insist on leaving, but Frankie, sympathy welling her eyes, suggested they stay, pointing out that she was hungry.

After that delay, the farewell was difficult. His aunt appeared at the door, rattled that they were leaving so soon. It was clear she was muddled on when they'd arrived. Victor could have sworn she thought they had just pulled up. He had to work very hard to keep her from feeling they were snubbing her by leaving as soon as they'd arrived.

Then, once they hit the road, it took them nearly four hours to make a trip that normally could be done in a little under two. Slippery roads had led to accidents and clogged highways. Several times, he'd had to pull out of a skid himself. On one of those occasions, Frankie had reached over and grabbed his arm.

They didn't talk much on the way into the city. She was lost in her thoughts—he suspected that they were about the show and her ex's book—and he was lost in his and intent on driving. So when they finally pulled into the skyscraper-lined caverns of New York, he felt cheated. Without realizing it, he'd looked forward to a comfortable talk on the way home.

"We never did finish mapping out ideas for the thief story," he said, not looking at her, his arm draped over the steering wheel as he waited at a stoplight.

She sighed. "We should do that. It was the purpose of the weekend. And I don't want to go in to the team without a clear path. It will be bedlam otherwise." She sounded so defeated, he turned to look at her. The milky light from the snow only made her face look paler, her reddish hair a cloud around it. When she turned to him, he looked away.

"Okay. Which is it—office or my place?" he asked, putting the car in gear as the light turned green.

She let out a mock shiver. "Brrr... office will be a refrigerator on Sunday. They turn the heat down for the weekend."

"My place it is."

—∿—

So they didn't end up talking about the show. He fixed her some tea and they talked. They talked about his aunt—Frankie offered to speak with her mother, a nurse, about how to locate good home health workers. "You have to be careful," she told him. "There are a lot of good folks out there, but there are some who don't really care all that much for the people they're supposed to be watching." And they talked about her ex-husband's book, with Victor suggesting again that she not allow herself to be brought down by someone low enough to pull such a stunt.

"You're a great person, Frankie. And you shouldn't need a novel to tell you that," he said, leaning back on his sofa and staring at the snow outside.

"What makes you say I do?" She leaned forward.

"Well, you're upset by the opposite—a novel saying you're not so great. You shouldn't care either way. You define yourself. You don't let other people do it for you."

"Spoken like a true marine."

"Hey, it's in the manual." But she was considerably more cheerful, so he offered to make her some dinner as the sky turned pink and then gray. He lit a fire in the corner fireplace but wasn't so obvious as to turn on mood music. He didn't have to. She browsed his CD selection and put on some Sinatra while he cooked a simple dish. She even lit the candles on the table before they sat down.

Afterward, when they were putting the last dish away, she ended up in his arms again. He wasn't sure how it happened—if he'd enveloped her, or if she'd cozied up to him. She'd reached up to a shelf next to him and teetered when she came down off her toes. He'd caught her and then—then all bets were off.

His lips found hers, his arms circling her while her hands found his waist. She smelled sweet and fresh, and he could only think how much he ached for her in every cell of his body. He was afraid to move, afraid he'd do something he'd regret. Or maybe he was afraid he wouldn't do anything—and then regret that. He murmured her name. *Frankie.*

He stroked her hair, kissed her again, ran his hands up her back and onto her buttocks, pushing her toward him, feeling his need grow, feeling her respond with equal passion, her hands, her tongue, her lips... *Frankie.*

He'd been with women since his divorce, sure. But he wasn't a casual love-'em-and-leave-'em kind of guy. He didn't bed a woman unless he thought there might be something there, something to build on. He couldn't help it. He was wired that way. Now he was on the verge of making love to her, hoping there was the possibility of love there. And as he held her in his arms, afraid to breathe, he couldn't help feeling that he was getting too old for this. Too old to have his heart wounded. She was a different generation and possibly even a different mind-set. It might not mean the same thing to her as it did to him. He was too old for this.

He stopped, gently pulling away with an effort of will that made his head spin.

She looked up into his eyes. Was she evaluating whether he was crazy?

"I… I'm sorry. I shouldn't take liberties," he said.

She laughed. "Victor, you're so formal."

Formal? That made him feel old, too.

"I should take you home," he said, turning away. Had he just made a fool of himself? If he had, he would reclaim his dignity. "I'll just grab my keys." He headed for his room. He'd splash some cold water on his face before they got going.

Chapter 9

"SURELY HE HAS OTHER places he can stay!" Victor's hands gripped the steering wheel with such force it looked like he believed it would fly off into the stratosphere if he relaxed his hold.

Frankie was still trying to figure out what exactly was going on between the two of them after that Second Passionate Kiss, and here they were in the midst of their First Big Argument. Seemed like they'd zoomed past the whole "Declaration of Undying Love" part, not to mention the unforgettable lovemaking that went with it. Damn, she would have liked the lovemaking, even if it was a bit early in the relationship.

Victor had suggested, as he'd driven her home, that she might want to suggest Luke make other living arrangements. He'd started his case with work-related arguments—she was head writer, Luke was an actor on the show, she needed to set a tone, Luke shouldn't be privy to what might be happening with characters, etc., etc.

But when Frankie had knocked down those points easily—she didn't bring work home, Luke respected her position, and he didn't answer to her anyway, etc., etc.—Victor became sullen, driving most of the way to her place in silence. Finally, when he pulled up in front of her apartment building, he opened up again.

"What if you decide you want to invite someone up?" he asked.

"If I want to invite *someone* up," she said, smiling, "then Luke has to find something to do for the evening." *Besides,* she thought, *"someone" might have his own really nice digs.* She shivered involuntarily, wondering what kind of bedroom was in those digs. She'd not explored.

He didn't respond to this, and she got the impression he was silently arguing with himself.

She was tired, too tired to intrude in his internal disagreements. "Luke will find another place soon enough," she said, grabbing her bag from the backseat. "Stay put. No need to see me in." She thought of leaning over to kiss him, but decided against it when she saw his stony look forward. She'd half expected him to protest her command to stay put and was disappointed when he didn't. "I'll see you in the office tomorrow," she said as she exited the car.

She heard him drive off as soon as she entered her building. *So much for that,* Frankie thought, scrambling for her key as she rode the elevator up. *At least you're expediting things now—the first kiss and the breakup all in one weekend.*

Confused, dissatisfied, and annoyed, she had to admit she did want to be alone and was already resenting having to share her space with Luke. She was in a bad mood when she opened the door to her place and in a worse mood when she looked around. In contrast to the clean digs she'd left—thanks to Luke's goodwill—she now looked at a living room that could have doubled as a disobedient teenager's crib.

Clothes were strewn over the sofa and chairs, toiletries were scattered on the table, and a half-eaten carry-out pizza perched precariously on the window sill. From her bathroom, she heard the sound of the shower running.

"Luke!" she yelled, her ire punching up the volume to air-raid-warning levels. In a few seconds, the water stopped and Luke appeared in the doorway to her bedroom, towel wrapped around his waist. He leaned on the door jamb for support.

"You're home," he said, taking a step forward before remembering his leg was in a cast. He gripped the door frame. "Christ,

Frankie, I thought you were kidnapped or something. I called you, but you didn't answer."

"Don't tell me you called the police!" she said.

"I called about everybody else," he said, anger coloring his voice. "Raeanne, Hank, even Kayla. Nobody knew where you were. Kayla thought she saw you leaving with that old dude, Vincent."

"Victor."

"Victor," he said with obvious disgust. "Well, you should have told me. I hardly slept at all worrying about you, dammit."

For a moment, her heart melted. Luke had been genuinely concerned. Then she remembered what he'd just said—he'd called everyone but the police.

"But you didn't call the police," she pointed out.

"No. I didn't. I thought I'd wait until tomorrow, see if you'd show up at the office or something. Took a lot to hold off calling."

How sweet of him not to trouble the police like that until he was absolutely positive she had spent an entire weekend in harm's way.

She pointed to his cast-swaddled leg. "I didn't think you were supposed to get that wet."

"I just stick it outside of the shower stall." He grabbed at his towel, which was fast unloosening as he moved around.

Wonderful. She'd probably find a puddle of water outside the shower now. A headache was beginning to form above her eyes. Was it too early to go to bed? She needed to curl up into a fetal position like she had planned on Friday. She took her bag into her bedroom, which was now steamy from Luke's shower, and unpacked. Her stomach growled, and she realized that she hadn't eaten much at Victor's, so she went back into the living room and grabbed a piece of pizza. Luke was now dressed and flopped on the couch, looking through a script. She noticed that he'd made a quick attempt to tidy up.

"What's that?" she said, pointing to the pages he was studying.

"A play."

"What play?" she asked between gulps.

"Nothing special."

"*Hamlet*'s not good enough for you? You're doing something else?" she asked, stunned. She now regretted not getting more advice from Victor on how to handle Luke.

"No, it's nothing I'm interested in. It's something Kayla's doing. I promised I'd read lines with her this week."

Frankie pondered this.

"How often do you do that?"

"Whenever she asks me."

"Well, how often is that, Luke?"

He stopped, looked up at the ceiling, moving his fingers as if counting. "Oh, maybe once a week or so."

Once a week or so—probably more than that was Frankie's guess. A picture began to emerge. Her temp secretary wasn't just interested in acting. She was interested in Luke, disappearing throughout the day to run lines with him when he was on set. Now Frankie regretted not talking to Victor about her Kayla problem. She would have to speak with HR first thing. If Kayla was a temp, she could be moved to another office. Maybe one dealing more closely with the actors, since that's where her interest was.

"You should start looking for somewhere else to stay," she said, wiping her hands.

He looked up, his eyes registering surprise. "I won't be in this cast forever."

"But you will be for at least six weeks. That's a long time." At his hurt look, she continued. "This is a tiny apartment. Not meant for two."

"Is this because of Vincent?"

"Victor. No, it is not because of Victor. And even if it were, that's none of your business." But it was because of Victor. He was the one who'd planted the seed to get Luke to move on.

"Victor and you are seeing each other, aren't you?" His voice dropped, and he swallowed.

What was this? Luke was interested in her? No, it couldn't be.

"Victor and I are coworkers," she said. Yes, she always lusted after her coworkers. It was part of her mental prep for writing every day. Kissing them was part of that, too. Exactly what was that kiss about in Victor's kitchen anyway? It certainly had felt like more than a coworker kiss to her—not that she went around kissing coworkers. Eww—she thought of Hank. Maybe Victor was used to getting his way with women. But, no, he'd been the one to pull away. Oh, god, this was confusing. *Can't think. Can't think.*

"It has nothing to do with Victor—you finding another place to stay. I'm the one who thinks it's wise."

Despite the fact that Luke was a rugged guy, Frankie could have sworn it looked like his eyes welled with tears. Could he turn that on in an instant? With actors, you never knew. After a moment of silent staring, he pulled out his cell phone and punched in a number, leaving a message for some unnamed friend to call him, he needed a favor. He repeated this at least five times. After try number three Frankie retreated to her room, sat down with her laptop, and started pounding out breakdowns as ideas popped into her head.

─w─

"But my dear, you're only a child," Sister Marie said, coming around her big desk to sit beside Faye. "You hardly know what you want to do tomorrow, let alone for a lifetime."

"But I do know, Sister." Faye leaned forward, tears glistening in her eyes. She sucked in her lips and looked up, trying not to cry. Her eyes fixated on the statue of the Blessed Virgin in the corner of the room.

"I'm old enough to know I want to join you," she said after her emotions were under control. "I've had enough of the world. And men."

"Is this what this is about?" Sister Marie patted Faye's hand. "A man?"

"No!" Faye's vehemence surprised even herself.

"Are you sure, my dear? You can tell me. You can tell me anything."

"Oh, Sister, yes, it's about a man who's tender and strong and does good deeds."

"Why, dear, that doesn't sound so bad."

"And a man who's young and handsome and vulnerable and sometimes sweet."

"My, my, he sounds like quite a dashing hero! What on earth are you upset about? Has he hurt you—this tender and strong young man?"

"It's the other one who's tender and strong."

"What?"

"The younger one is handsome and vulnerable."

"I'm not sure I'm following you, dear."

"The older one is tender and strong and does good deeds. I mean, he's handsome, too, but not in the same way as…"

"As the younger one?" The nun recoiled. "So it's not about one man."

Faye burst into sobs, falling into the nun's reluctant arms. "Yes, yes, you understand! It's not about one man. It's about two."

Her sobs quieted, she looked up into the nun's eyes. "But you'll still take me, won't you?"

Chapter 10

HER HEAD WAS STILL throbbing the next morning, making it difficult for her to focus on what precisely she needed to do—not just with the show, but with Victor and Luke. She had started the weekend with no relationship prospects and she'd ended it with...

Well, with what? With a couple of caught-in-the-moment kisses with Victor and some friendly concern from Luke. Maybe she was reading more into each man's attitudes than was really there. Victor was a man's man, and even if Frankie wasn't a *Playboy* centerfold, she wasn't an ugly duckling. It could have been that he was... well, starved for affection?

No, no—not Victor. She couldn't imagine him going without a woman interested in him. He didn't need skinny, freckle-faced Frankie McNally to satisfy his manly desires. Maybe he really was interested in a relationship.

Okay, what about Luke? He'd made her a nice meal last week. They'd begun to engage in some hanky-panky while she was vulnerable and under the influence. And he had been genuinely worried about her and sincerely wounded when she suggested he move out. Was Luke interested in pursuing something with her? Was she interested? If so, which man was she interested in anyway? Who was she?

Not Frankie McNally, that was for sure. She decided it wasn't a good day to be Frankie as soon as she breezed into her office, past Kayla's empty desk, scrambling to catch her ringing phone.

"Is Frankie in?" a male voice asked.

Because she was in a bad mood, she answered tartly, "Who wants to know?"

After a pause, the voice continued, "E. J. Dewitt."

Oh, crap. "No, sorry, this is her secretary," she said in a sing-songy Swedish accent. "Ms. McNally isn't here yet." And then, in a moment of inspiration, she continued, "She's probably picking up doughnuts for the staff. Or some shtrudel. Ja, she brings in the shtrudel often, makes it herself."

"I thought you said she was picking it up."

Damn.

"Sometimes she picks it up, sometimes she bakes it. What a wunnerful, wunnerful woman Miss Frankie she is. Very kind. And schweet. Oh, and very self-confident. Most self-confident woman I've ever met, too. No, how you say it, chips on her shoulder."

"Say, when is she due in? I could stop by."

"Well, I, uh… she has meetings most of the day."

"But she has to be in her office part of the time."

"She's, uh, doing the good works other times, at the soup kitchen, the homeless… home. Ja, such a schweet woman she is."

"Okay, thanks." And he clicked off.

And Frankie immediately gathered up as much stuff as she could fit in a box and began searching for an empty cubicle or office where no one—especially E. J. Dewitt—would find her, muttering under her breath along the way.

"I'm chased out of my home and now out of my office. No wonder I nearly landed in Victor Pendergrast's bed," she hissed as she rounded a corner—nearly colliding with Raeanne and dropping her box in the process.

"Gosh darnit, I'm sorry about that," Raeanne said, bending to help her retrieve items that had fallen.

"No problem," Frankie said between gritted teeth.

"Were you just talkin' about Victor?" Raeanne asked, trying to sound casual. "I thought I saw the two of you leavin' together on Friday. Did you two go out? It was a lovely evenin' for it, so bright and crisp. Say, I was wonderin' if you knew when he'd be comin' in."

Frankie studied Raeanne. Today the woman was dressed in a snug, silky violet turtleneck over gray slacks. She might seem all dewy Southern innocent, but she probably would love to get the juicy gossip on Victor. Frankie had the distinct impression that Raeanne had no doubts about whether she'd like to pursue a relationship with him.

"No, I don't know," Frankie said in response. And she sashayed past Raeanne before the woman could ask any more pesky questions.

A few minutes more of aimless wandering led Frankie to an empty space, a nine-by-nine room with no window, a cleared desk, and a dusty bookcase. It would have to do. She plopped her stuff there, making a quick beeline back to her original office to retrieve more stuff before E. J. Dewitt showed up to stalk her.

She was so absorbed in her Dewitt-avoidance task that it wasn't until she heard Victor's voice near the elevator, talking to Nory, that she realized her new work digs were located a mere dozen feet away from his spacious office.

"Dammit." She scurried into her little prison cell and closed the door before he could notice she was there.

Once inside, she pulled out her cell and left two messages.

One for Kayla: "Look, if you're really into this acting thing, here's an assignment—I want you to use a Swedish accent all day today. I'll explain later."

One for Human Resources: "How do I get a temp worker reassigned?"

The cubby Frankie had found to work in might have shielded her from E. J. Dewitt and others on the staff, but it was an airless chamber that only worsened her headache throughout the morning. She managed to get very little done except obsessively checking her voice mail and email after sending around a broadcast note saying she'd be working out of the office that day but available for messages.

Kayla emailed her twice to say an "E. J. Dooit" was waiting to see her, and, yes, she'd used the Swedish accent, but it had caused a problem when a dialogue writer who spoke Swedish checked in.

Frankie didn't respond to those. When she got a note from Kayla about eleven saying "Mr. Dooit" had left and wanted her to call him, she opened her door and breathed a sigh of relief—*mostly* because she could actually breathe again. Fresh air, that is.

But it wasn't long before her open door became a magnet for trouble. As she burrowed into a long breakdown she was writing for Faye, a noisy clop-thump, clop-thump alerted her to Luke's presence on the floor. She got up to close her door, but it was too late. He saw her.

"There you are! I've been looking for you all freaking morning. Have you been demoted or something?" His face was red, but not just from the effort of hobbling around searching for her. He was furious. In his hand was a piece of paper, which he now began to wave in her face.

"What the hell are you doing to me, Frankie? Kicking me while I'm down? First, you kick me out, and now this! I thought you were a better person than that. I'd expected that type of thing from Brady or even Jack, but you?"

"What? Huh?" She grabbed the paper, and now his fury spread to her more quickly than an epidemic on a cruise ship. It was the breakdown she'd worked on at Victor's place, the one where Donovan expressed his disdain for golden retrievers. With rising anger, she also remembered Victor's arguments of the night before—reasons why Luke shouldn't stay with her. Reason A: she might bring work home. She'd protested that she didn't. Well, she'd made a liar out of herself already.

Pinching her lips together, she stared daggers at Luke while she folded the paper in quarters, took the two steps inside the room, and placed it on her desk. Luke followed her into her box.

"You went through my things!" she accused him. "How dare you! You must find another place to live!"

"I didn't go through your things. I found that"—he pointed to the paper—"on the floor by the door this morning. You must have dropped it. Frankie, how could you? This show is my lifeblood, my anchor. This show defines me."

My lifeblood, my anchor. Hadn't Donovan said those words to Teresa several episodes back when declaring his love for her? Frankie shook her head to bring her focus back to reality and away from the fantasy of *Lust.* "No, Luke, the more appropriate question is, how could *you*?"

"How could I what? I told you I wasn't snooping. I just found the paper. I thought it was something you might need."

"That's not what I'm talking about. If the show is so important to you, if it is your 'lifeblood,' if it's what makes you want to get up in the morning and makes you long for night so that you can be in her arms…" She stopped. Now she was quoting Donovan on the show. She shook her head and tried again. "You're going to be Hamlet. You crash the press conference to make sure the media knows you'll be playing the Danish prince and that we'll be letting you do it. You don't give a crap about the show. You only care about your career. You can't possibly do both Donovan and Hamlet."

Luke rolled his eyes. "So this is what it's about. I get an opportunity—an opportunity that'll make things better for the show, get it more attention, I mean—and you stab me in the back for it."

"Luke, it's not an opportunity for the show if you're not on the show! You're signing to do a Broadway production, for god's sake. That eats up a lot of time, buster. And, unlike your character on *Lust*, you don't have an evil twin who can help you get both jobs done!" She sat on the edge of her desk and stared back at him, her arms crossed over her chest, so close to him that her toe nudged his injured leg. "Sorry," she mumbled, retracting her foot.

"It's a limited gig, Frankie. If I did it, it would be a three-month thing, and then someone else would step into the role, and I'd only play it on weekends. My agent is trying to work out a deal where I can still stay on the show and keep everybody happy." His voice softened. "I love the show. I… I thought you'd respect me more for doing something like *Hamlet*."

Her jaw dropped open. Luke cared if she respected him?

He went on. "I mean, Hamlet's a terrific role and I value it, too, but I thought you'd like seeing me in this kind of thing."

She cocked her head to one side. Was he saying he was trying to impress Frankie, the boss? Or Frankie, the woman? She remembered his first night in her apartment, when he'd obviously been interested in the latter. This made a blush warm her face that triggered feelings of confusion. Had Luke just taken advantage of her to get what he wanted on the show—a flexible schedule so he could play the brooding prince?

"Don't give me those bedroom eyes, Luke Blades, thinking you'll roll me the way you tried to roll me last week," she said. "You actors are all alike. You want what you want when you want it. I'm ashamed to admit I almost fell for it, too."

Now it was Luke's turn to be stunned. His mouth fell open, then closed. He swallowed. He attempted to take a step back, but moving in reverse with crutches was a skill he had yet to master. When he started to stumble, she rose to help him, grabbing him by the elbows to steady him. He swayed, leaning back, then forward, and grabbed her shoulder as one crutch fell away. Before she knew it, he was leaning in to bestow on her a sweet kiss, his lips brushing against hers with a feather-light touch, just enough to tantalize, followed by a full-bore smack, the kind of kiss she'd seen him give Teresa on the show a dozen times. Despite her best efforts, she felt a shiver tingle her backbone.

"I've always been interested in you, Frankie," he murmured, "ever since our night together. I never understood why you didn't call me back."

"Call you back?" She gulped, trying to remember every missed call of the past two years. She retrieved his fallen crutch and handed it to him.

"Yeah, I left messages for you. With Kayla. The go-to gal for all the writers. Lost your cell number."

With Kayla? Oh, no. With Kayla! Now the picture became even clearer. Kayla was really smitten with Luke, getting him to run lines with her any chance she could grab. And when she'd sensed he was interested in Frankie, she'd conveniently neglected to give her his messages.

Oh no—another thought jangled her nerves. Kayla had dyed her hair red recently. Was that because she felt Luke's interest in Frankie growing? Was Kayla trying to look like her?

Now Frankie was the one needing something to steady her. She reached back for her desk. She looked at Luke, and her heart melted with… something. With sympathy. The darling—he'd carried the torch for her when he could have had any flaxen-haired, blue-eyed, implant-enhanced actress or fan girl he wanted. When he could have had crazy Kayla, who would have done anything for him. Frankie had misjudged him. And she'd missed an opportunity. Her head started to pound again.

The pounding was matched by a quick knock on the door. Victor filled the doorway. One more step in, and they'd be doing a remake of the stateroom scene from *A Night at the Opera*. She saw him do a quick glance between her and Luke. They were awfully close together. But it was a small room.

"I thought I heard your voice in here. Market research shows a spike for Friday," he said, his voice clipped. "And Web hits have shot up, too. If this continues for another couple days, we're in a trend. A good trend." He handed her the papers, which caused Luke to move to the side.

Frankie looked over the reports—not just the normal ratings but a private survey Victor had ordered. Victor wasn't exaggerating. Their market share had taken a tremendous leap forward. It could be a fluke, of course. They'd have to wait for today's numbers and tomorrow's, but...

"Wow, this is unbelievable," she said.

"Like I said, we need to wait for today's and tomorrow's, but I have a feeling we'll see the same trend." He didn't move, his hands clasped in front of him, the soldier-at-ease stance. Luke, meanwhile, managed to scoot behind him toward the door. Victor didn't make room for him as he passed, forcing Luke to do an awkward hopping slither.

"Talk to you later," Luke called to her as he limped away.

But Frankie hardly noticed. She was too absorbed in the numbers in front of her and their implications. The press conference had occurred right before the show aired. These numbers had to be as a result of that. It was wonderful. It was horrible. It was still a moral dilemma that hung over her like Damocles's sword. She wanted this problem to go away!

"We should have that casting call," Victor continued, repeating his earlier suggestion, one they'd never resolved. But before Frankie could protest, her cell rang and she couldn't ignore it. It was the network VP of daytime programming, Iris Carrington.

"Frankie, darling, I hope you don't mind me calling you on your cell. Your secretary gave me the number—what a delightful woman, by the way, but I always thought Oslo was in Norway, not Sweden. Anyway, I just wanted to congratulate you personally on *Lust's* numbers. They're phenomenal. I don't think we've seen anything like it for twenty years!"

Frankie listened, unable to quell her feelings of pride, as Iris went on to congratulate her on the press conference again as well. So what if the thief story was a moral and ethical minefield. So what if her performance in the press conference had been less than stellar. It didn't matter—*Lust for Life* was climbing out of the pit, and Frankie was there to hoist her up and set her on the right track. She couldn't wait to tell her mother. Looking at Victor, she knew that he, too, was happy for his own family's *Lust* fan.

As soon as the phone call ended, Victor spoke. "Did you ever work out any thief breakdowns?"

"No, I… I…"

"You could assign it to Raeanne," he said, no-nonsense. "Or even Nory. I'm not sure Hank would be up to it. And I heard him on the phone, saying something about setting up an interview."

Frankie rolled her eyes—Hank was always trying to get work for a friend. "No, no, they have other assignments. I like to sketch out new directions before handing them off anyway. Otherwise, too many chefs, you know." She really didn't want to hand off this story.

He nodded. She became acutely aware of how close he was to her. Damn, but this office was small. Every visitor who came into it was practically having intimate relations with her. She tried to casually neaten a lock of hair she felt tickling her cheek.

Victor smiled. "Let me take you out to dinner tonight to celebrate. *Lust* is turning a corner."

The way he said it, it didn't sound like he was talking about the show. Dinner with Victor. A real "date" of sorts. Was that a good idea? Hadn't he warned her of relationships with coworkers when talking to her about Luke? There was truth in that warning. But still, this was tempting. She wouldn't mind at all going out with Victor in a nonbusiness setting. She imagined something upscale. And then she imagined something upstairs—in his bedroom. She trembled inside. Which, in this small room, meant he noticed. *Dammit.*

"I wanted to apologize for last night," he said. "I don't want you to think I'm trying to take advantage of you."

She warmed with a blush. "What makes you think I wasn't trying to take advantage of you?" she asked with as much hauteur as she could muster. But, being from the suburbs of B'more, she wasn't used to mustering hauteur, so it came out sounding like a dirty joke poorly told.

Victor seemed to bristle.

"Is that what you were doing with Luke?"

He'd seen them! Her eyes widened. "Were you spying on me?" Holy crap, she had one guy going through her things and another spying on her!

"Your office is a mere ten feet from mine. I happened upon you. What are you doing in this janitor's closet anyway?"

"It's not a janitor's closet."

"Bob said the head janitor used to use it for his afternoon nap."

"Used to?"

"He got fired."

Great. Another "head" somebody getting the ax. Maybe it was the job title.

"It's only temporary," she said, gesturing to her new space. "While my office is… is being remodeled."

"As in having the E. J. Dewitt removed?"

Her blush deepened as he struck a bull's-eye. "It's only temporary," she repeated, trying to ignore how silly she must look in his eyes. To deflect his silly rays, she went on the attack. "And it still was none of your business what I was discussing with Luke, which, by the way, was just business."

"Fine," he said, his brusque tone replaced by amusement. "Then we'll just discuss business at dinner. I'll pick you up at seven." And he turned and headed back to his own luxurious, spacious, non-former-head-janitor's-closet office.

So much for a "nonbusiness" date with Victor.

Chapter 11

VICTOR STRODE BACK TO his office, nodded to Bob, and closed his door behind him before sinking into his comfortable desk chair. His blood was still pumping from his encounter with Frankie, a combination of frustration and anticipation. His intention had been to get something going on the right foot, away from the office. But when he'd seen Luke... that smug, egotistical actor...

Luke was taking advantage of Frankie, and she was too nice to see it. He had to save her from that manipulator, or at least warn her...

He threw a pencil on the desk. Who was he trying to kid? Yeah, Luke angered Victor. But it wasn't really because he was afraid Luke was manipulating Frankie. It was because Victor was afraid Frankie would find Luke more appealing, since he was actually in her peer group.

Peer group—cut the bull. Age group. Luke was younger. But Luke was just an empty-headed actor.

An empty-headed, *heartthrob* actor.

Dammit, I'm jealous. That's high school stuff.

He stood and stared out the window at slushy streets and blue sky. What exactly was his plan here—woo Frankie until what?

He was a goal-oriented man. It was one of his strengths. While others talked, Victor Pendergrast did. Charts and surveys and market reports were all well and good, all valuable tools of the trade, but they were just tools used to construct a product, reach a goal. That's what set him apart from others in his field who could fill pages and hours with endless blather about messages and branding that didn't push a product or achieve a goal. Victor focused on goals.

"So exactly what is your goal here, Victor?" he whispered to himself, hands in his pockets.

Maybe that was the wrong question. Maybe a better question was, what was Frankie's goal? She had been burned by her ex-husband, who was still managing to hurt her. Victor might just be the rebound affair. This thought both comforted and unsettled him. If he was just a fill-in until she was emotionally back on stable ground, Victor didn't need to worry about goal setting or commitments. But if, on the other hand, he ended up wanting those things…

A soft knock at his door interrupted his thoughts. When he turned to answer it, the door opened and a man stepped in, a man Victor recognized after a nanosecond as E. J. Dewitt.

"Sorry to barge in," E. J. said, "but your secretary was away from her desk."

"*His* desk."

"Oh." The reporter walked into the room before Victor had a chance to chase him away and plopped down in the chair in front of his desk. "I just wanted a few moments of your time. I'm E. J. Dewitt—"

"I know who you are," Victor said, visibly irritated. "And I don't have a few moments."

The man was undeterred. He was already flipping open his reporter's notebook. "Look, I can't seem to get through to Ms. McNally about her ex-husband's book, but you obviously have some sway here—being a Pendergrast—so maybe you can talk to her. I'm telling you, she won't regret talking to me. I'm not out to skewer her. Anything but."

Intrigued, Victor walked to the front of his desk and leaned against it. "Tell me more."

E. J. looked up at Victor with an exasperated hangdog expression.

"I've read the book. I've done my research on Brian Aigland. His family had an in with the publisher. I'm not sure a similar author would have had his book see the light of print. I'm not a fan. Okay?"

Victor smiled. He remembered the advice he'd given Frankie—to talk to the reporter, sticking to her own talking points. Dewitt was going to write the story, no matter what.

"He did snag a good review."

"Yeah, one. Others have not been so charitable."

"Off the record," Victor said. "Anything I say is off the record... or as an anonymous source."

Dewitt scowled. "Okay. If that's the best I can get."

Victor relaxed. "I haven't read Mr. Aigland's book, but I can tell you about his ex-wife."

———

Frankie couldn't stay one more second in her closet. She'd tapped out all she could into her laptop about Donovan, Terri, Faye, and the other inhabitants of Crestview. She plowed all her irritation at Victor and Luke and E. J. Dewitt and Brian into her story treatments. She picked up her cell and called Kayla, who answered on the first ring!

"Is that reporter around?"

Kayla paused as if looking for the man. "No, I don't see him," she said in a singsongy accent that sounded half German, half Italian. Criminey, no wonder Kayla asked for help with auditions. Sounded like she needed it.

"Uh... you can drop that," Frankie said.

"Jawohla—I mean, okay."

"Thanks." She clicked off and opened her door, heading for her real office, passing Victor's closed door along the way, nodding to Bob, who caught her attention as she went by.

"Did you want me, Ms. McNally?"

"What? No. Why?"

"Someone called me a few minutes ago, saying you wanted to see me in Mr. Stephens's office."

Frankie shrugged. "Nope, wasn't me. Or anyone I know."

She turned the corner and saw a shadow on the door of her office. Someone was in there! Had Kayla lied to her? Was the reporter waiting for her?

"Psst! Kayla!" Frankie whispered to her secretary from the corner, where she could beat a fast retreat.

Kayla looked up. "Yes, Ms. McNally?" she asked in a clear, resonant voice.

At the mention of Frankie's name, the shadow on the door grew until its owner stood in the doorway—Raeanne! Frankie breathed a sigh of relief and came out of the shadows.

"Nothing," she said to Kayla as she headed toward her door.

"What's up, Raeanne?" Frankie noticed the woman was carrying a folded paper. "You have some material for me? That was fast. I was going to call a team meeting for later today to go over new Faye material, so if your plate is clear, that will be fantastic." She closed the door as they entered her office, then quickly opened it again to tell Kayla they were not to be disturbed under any circumstances. Couldn't take any chances with that sly Dewitt fellow.

She turned her attention back to Raeanne in her office. "I was also wondering if you thought we should be looking for some new dialogue writers, if you know anybody who's looking for work. The thing is, you need to get experienced people and not just throw a net out, especially since *Lust* is just now hitting a stride." Frankie sat down and gestured for Raeanne to do the same. "Okay, show me what you've got there." She held out her hand, and Raeanne gave her the folded paper.

"It's not a breakdown, Frankie," Raeanne said softly. "It's a letter of—"

"—resignation!" Frankie read the short, professional note where

Raeanne thanked the *Lust* team, talked about how much she'd learned, and expressed her gratitude to Frankie. My goodness, it read like an Oscar acceptance speech.

"This is so sudden," Frankie stammered. "I didn't realize you weren't happy. I mean, you seemed like you enjoyed your job." But in truth, Frankie hardly knew the woman. The team wasn't much of a "team." It was more like a group of reluctant passengers on a lifeboat.

Building team spirit—there must be books on that. She made a mental note to call HR back about transferring Kayla. Suddenly she felt the need to keep as many people in her little lifeboat as possible.

In her defense, crises had prevented any team-building exercises, even if she'd known what they were. And now it was too late for Raeanne. Crap. She was probably the best of the bunch, too, even if Frankie was intimidated by her good looks and smarts.

"I've been thinkin' about it for some time," Raeanne said, not looking at Frankie. "When Jack was here, actually." Her voice sounded congested, as if she'd been crying.

"Well, uh, I… I'm really sorry to see you go," Frankie stammered. She looked at the letter again. "You don't say how much time you're giving us. Could you hang on until we find a replacement?"

Raeanne looked up and smiled. Her eyes looked swollen. She *had* been crying. "Well, within reason."

Suddenly, Frankie realized that a crucial piece of info was missing from Raeanne's resignation letter—where she was going. Usually, you only resigned if you had another job.

"Will your new employer mind waiting a bit?" Frankie probed.

"Maybe not, if it's not too long."

Jeez, the woman was coy. Only the direct approach would work. "Where exactly are you going, if you don't mind me asking?"

Again, Raeanne looked down, examining her perfect French-manicured nails. "I'd rather not talk about it right yet."

Frankie's face flamed as if the woman had slapped her. Was

working at *Lust for Life* so odious that Raeanne had to leave even without another job? Or did Raeanne have money stashed away? Or had she come into some cash? Raeanne did do some freelance writing under a pseudonym, Frankie knew. Book reviews, some articles, even a short story that was…

Ohmygod. Raeanne wasn't writing a book, was she?

"Uh," Frankie said, clearing her throat, "are you working on a novel or something?"

Raeanne laughed. "Why, shut my mouth, Frankie, isn't every writer?" Still laughing, she stood and shook Frankie's hand. "I've loved workin' with you and wish you the best. I'll stay on while you search, but let's not make it too long. Say, no more than six weeks? I'd prefer sooner, if possible. Don't want to make this painful." She squared her shoulders and lifted her head as if it were a matter of personal dignity not to stay on too long.

And she left, with Frankie asking her to close the door behind her.

After Raeanne was gone, Frankie sank into her chair and cursed. Losing a talented team member was bad enough. But Raeanne's secretiveness was worse. What on earth could the woman be doing that she wouldn't want to reveal it to Frankie? Maybe she should call Human Resources and find out if employees were required to say where they were headed when handing in their resignation.

She thought of Raeanne's cheerful response to her question about whether she was writing a novel. "Isn't every writer?" Frankie said to the empty room, imitating Raeanne's soft drawl.

"Well, no, Raeanne, not every writer is working on a novel in which they not-so-thinly disguise the identities of those they've worked with so they can make fun of their every fault and place on display their every peccadillo. Not every writer is that shallow, that needy, that…"

Uh, didn't she do those things on the show?

Yes, but it was a *soap opera*! Not a novel. Different animal. Same artistic jungle, yes. But different palm tree, different animal. She really needed to think of a better metaphor for this situation.

Dammit. Maybe she *should* be writing a novel.

If she wrote a novel, what would it be about? She had just as much talent as Brian, maybe more. She knew she had more discipline. My god, she churned out page after page after page for *Lust* every day. Brian could barely force himself to write three pages a day when he was working on his novel, and only when he felt "inspired." How exasperated she'd been, coming home to see him playing solitaire while his manuscript remained untouched.

Shouldn't have encouraged him, she thought. Then there'd be no Francesca haunting her.

She turned to her computer, clicking into office email. Raeanne might be leaving, but she was still a fastidious worker. There, in Frankie's inbox, was Raeanne's breakdown of the story involving Terri's mother. Frankie clicked open the attachment, scanning the story, nodding her head at how Raeanne had taken something boring and made it interesting.

Terri's mother would leave Crestview because she "didn't want to be humiliated any longer by the unrequited love of the count, whom she'd overheard talking with that young hussy he was infatuated with." Nice touch, Raeanne.

Finished with that, she went shopping online, choosing even more management books, promising herself she'd whittle the list down at some point soon.

A knock at her door jolted her upright. Oh crap. She shouldn't be in this office. Maybe if she was really quiet…

"Frankie, are you in there?" It was Nory's voice.

"Yeah, yeah, come in."

Nory entered, dressed in a layered peasant skirt, white eyelet blouse, and makeup that made her look human. Huh? She held out a paper to Frankie.

"Oh no, not you, too," Frankie said, expecting to read another resignation letter.

"What?"

But instead, Nory was handing her breakdowns for the next month's episodes involving Donovan and Terri. Except for some references to things like "winners at a losing game" (Rascal Flatts) and "he ain't seen me crazy yet" (Miranda Lambert), it was good stuff. Frankie nodded her head as she read it.

"I would have emailed it to you," Nory said, "but I wasn't sure if you'd get it. Nobody knew where you were."

"You even managed to throw in some jewel thief stuff," Frankie noted. "It's good, but we're not sure yet where we're going with that."

"Oh. I thought we were casting for it."

"What gave you that idea?" Sure, Victor had talked about it, but they hadn't okayed it. Or rather, *she* hadn't okayed it.

"When I was looking for you, I checked in with Vic, and Bob said he was busy with someone and after that he'd be meeting with the casting director to set up the thief casting."

Vic? Setting up the casting?

"Thanks, Nory. That will be all." As Nory turned to leave, Frankie had another thought.

"Nory—"

"Yeah?"

"I like the new look." Yes, that was the ticket—let staff know she noticed them. Compliment them, appreciate them. Surely this advice was in a management book somewhere.

Nory beamed. "Thanks, Frankie! I've been writing some songs on the side and decided I should get into the whole country gestalt, if you know what I mean."

Gestalt—had Nory seen the press conference news? Of course she would have. And if Nory was writing country songs on the side, did that mean she'd be handing in her resignation soon, too? Would everyone be jumping from the lifeboat?

Nory left, and Frankie just stood there, thinking and stewing. She couldn't focus on what to do to keep Nory right now. She had other problems to think about. One in particular. She ran her fingers through her hair, counted to ten, marched to the door, looked both ways and didn't see Dewitt, then stomped down the corridor to Victor's office.

She breezed past Bob, who tried to stop her, and strode into Victor's office. Steam could have been coming from the top of her head she was so mad.

But as she opened the door, she stopped in her tracks.

E. J. Dewitt! Yucking and yacking it up with Victor!

She did a quick 180 and left the room so fast she hoped they wondered if they'd really seen her. "Frankie!" she heard Victor call after her, but she was in the stairwell before anyone could find her. She hightailed it to another floor, one not even connected with *Lust*, and was roaming hallways looking for a place to hide when her cell phone jangled. She immediately recognized her friend Gail's number and answered.

"Are you alone?" Gail whispered into the phone.

"You have no idea how alone," Frankie answered, heading into a ladies room. "What's up?"

"I need to talk. Can you meet me for lunch?"

Frankie looked at her watch. The morning was flying by.

"Sure." It would be good to get out of the office and away from Dewitt. "You sound upset. Anything the matter?"

Gail sniffled. "I am upset. I think I'm pregnant."

Chapter 12

"THANK YOU SO MUCH, Victor." E. J. Dewitt stood and held out his hand to shake Victor's. "If you could convince Frankie to talk to me, that would be great. I am on deadline, though."

Victor smiled. "I'll do my best. I was glad to help." He walked with the man to the door. After Frankie's appearance and fast retreat, Victor had used all his powers of persuasion to keep Dewitt from including the incident in his story. He had assured Dewitt that he would deliver Frankie as an interviewee.

At the door, the reporter stopped. "Say, I have a pal who writes for *Variety*. He says Brady Stephens is in line for a network job."

Victor inwardly winced. Of course Brady was looking for another job—it made perfect sense. Brady Stephens was an absentee producer. That was one of the show's problems, no top leadership. It was one of several items Victor wanted to address eventually—after the current crises passed. But he certainly didn't want to discuss it with a reporter. He kept up a good face for Dewitt, smiling and clapping him on the back. "This business is filled with rumors," he said.

"When Stephens leaves, they'll probably ask you to be exec producer. Will you take it?"

"Highly unlikely. I'm not interested—if the position were even open."

They said their good-byes and Victor went back to his desk, ready to tackle the thief casting. But he couldn't help thinking of the tidbit of gossip Dewitt had just passed along. If the executive producer slot came open, Victor could think of only one person who should take it, but she'd have to see herself as executive material first, before anyone else did.

One of your skills is public persuasion, he thought. *Persuade her she's worth it.*

—⁓—

"Gail, honey, can you hold on a sec? I'm getting another call." Frankie had been hunched in a corner of a bathroom stall for the past ten minutes listening to her poor friend cry, rambling in virtually incomprehensible ways about the future, about her boyfriend, about her job. Maybe she'd be calmer at lunch.

"Hello?" Frankie said to the new caller.

"Frankie McNally? This is Sami McAllister from *Soap Opera News*. I was calling to talk about the spike in ratings at *Lust for Life*."

"Oh, yes, we're thrilled. We hope every new viewer will stick with us. We're confident we can keep them with our terrific stories." She went on like an automaton, just as Victor had told her, sticking to the talking points even when the reporter tried to steer her toward talking about the social responsibility of ending the thief story, stopping herself from repeating her "art doesn't rob people" line and saying instead that she was confident the police would catch the thief in short order.

Eager to get back to Gail, she told the reporter she had to go.

"One last question, Ms. McNally. Is it true that you are the model for the Francesca character in your ex-husband's bestselling novel?"

Frankie inwardly growled. "No! And I'm sorry, I really have to go." Nearby, a toilet flushed. *Damn.*

"Was that—"

"I have to go!" She clicked off and back to her friend.

"Gail, are you still there?" Frankie was greeted by silence. She checked her messages—a text had come in while she'd been on the phone with the reporter. It was a short note from Gail saying where and when she'd meet her.

—⁓—

Refreshed and sure the coast was clear, Frankie stood in Victor's office a few seconds later. She'd hurried past Bob after determining E. J. was gone and now faced Victor across his desk.

"You're arranging a casting call for the thief?"

He sat with his reading glasses on, looking over the same notes Nory had given her. That only added to her fury. "And why are you reviewing those breakdowns? I just looked them over!"

He took off his glasses and gestured for her to sit. She ignored him.

"I thought we agreed to cast the thief. It doesn't mean we need to use the actor. But a casting call will mean more publicity." He held up Nory's papers. "As for these, Nory couldn't find you so she emailed them to me."

"She found me. I read them. And I'll fix them and send them to dialogue writers without your help. We might be shorthanded, but I am still capable of handling these things."

"Shorthanded?"

"Raeanne turned in her resignation."

"Did she say why?"

"No. Only that she'd been thinking about it for a while, even when Jack was head writer." That sounded defensive. She changed subjects. "Get back to the casting call. I know we talked about it. Or, rather, you talked about it. I listened. I didn't okay it. We have to work out a system here. Just talking about something doesn't mean 'so it is written, so it shall be done.' I actually have to say those words—I mean, say that something should be done, before it is actually done."

"All right. What's the system? Do you want me to go through Kayla? Design a permission slip? I could have Bob do that." He was being sarcastic, which just made her angrier.

"No, how about you just wait for a simple 'yes, let's do that.' That shouldn't be too hard."

He started to say something, stopped, took a breath, then in a steady tone said, "All right. I've started the ball rolling for a casting call for the thief. I was going to meet with the casting director about it, too, but can probably handle it with a phone call. You can conference in. I can set the casting up for later this week, maybe as soon as tomorrow or the day after tomorrow. Since we discussed the benefits of this casting call, which in no way commits us to continuing the thief story in the long or short term, may I proceed? Or do you want to be included in the setup?"

She pursed her lips. She narrowed her eyes. "Yes," she said through gritted teeth. "I mean, no. I mean, yes, you can proceed, but, no, I don't need to be included in the setup. Just tell Casting we want someone with an average build, since we don't know yet who this thief is going to be. Someone who could double as any of the male stars on the show."

And she turned and walked slowly out of the room, back toward her office, her head held high.

———

The black-garbed stranger crept through the Kendall mansion, pocketing valuables along the way. He heard a noise and stopped in his tracks, looking up.

He cursed under his breath.

"The house was supposed to be empty! I never agreed to rob houses that weren't empty!"

———

The black-garbed stranger crept through the Kendall mansion. A noise came from above, then a voice.

"Is that you, Terri?" Anne Kendall cried out.

The thief looked up, muttering. "Terri? Why would the princess be here? Who made that decision?"

—-^^—

The black-garbed stranger crept through the Kendall mansion. A light went on beyond the hallway. The thief stopped in his tracks.

"I know the butler said Anne Kendall might be home, but I never agreed to that! I never said, 'Yes, let her stay home!'"

—-^^—

The black-garbed stranger crept through the Kendall mansion, pocketing valuables along the way. The creak of floorboards upstairs made him stop in his tracks. He waited and listened. He moved forward.

"Just like I planned. No one else is in on this but me. I'm the leader of this operation, the king of this jungle, the head of this zoo…"

Frankie growled as she hit "save." She wasn't getting anywhere with these thief audition scenes. She didn't know what she wanted. Yes, she did. She wanted all of this to go away. She looked at her watch. She would take her time walking to the restaurant and clear her head before meeting Gail.

—-^^—

Victor put down the phone with the casting director and made a note on his calendar. He stood and stretched. He'd grab a bite and get back to work. First, he'd tell Frankie about the casting call, maybe even work on her to talk to Dewitt. He had not had a chance to even broach that subject when she powered into his office a little while ago.

What an infuriating woman. So capable, yet so self-sabotaging. Yes, she certainly should be calling the shots on a policy decision like the casting call, and, yes, he probably had misunderstood, taking her lukewarm lack of resistance to the idea as a "full speed ahead." He was a "get it done" kind of guy. But her insecurity with her authoritative role always made her reproaches seem weak. She had to learn to change that if she was to be considered upper-level management material. *Dammit, Frankie, why are you so insecure?*

Maybe he should research that. Go to a bookstore, buy Brian's novel...

He turned, grabbed his Blackberry off the desk, and headed out the door.

"I'll be out to lunch," he said to Bob.

Chapter 13

FRANKIE HAD A CHICKEN Caesar salad that she hardly touched for lunch. Gail had salt-water-drenched nachos. That's because she cried through the whole meal, so much so that Frankie found herself wondering if passers-by would think she was inflicting mental torture on her friend.

But this worry was back-shelved as a bigger worry took its place. Gail wasn't just worried about being pregnant. She was worried about...

"I mean I made this one mistake—just one mistake—with Stuart! And now this. But it can't be Stuart's baby. I mean, if I'm pregnant. Oh, god, please don't let me be pregnant. But if it's Michael's. Well, Frankie, that's just it. This whole thing has made me realize I really love Michael. Not Stuart." She sniffed and blew her nose. "And I want a life with Michael."

Frankie swallowed and bent her head to one side. Gail had rambled like this for a half hour, and all Frankie could do was offer the figurative shoulder to cry on. She recoiled at the idea that Gail had betrayed her true love. She thought Gail was better than that. Did everybody cheat? It was depressing. But at least Gail was filled with remorse.

"Are you going to tell Michael?" Frankie finally asked.

"I don't know. I guess I'll have to if..." Gail shook her head back and forth as if wiping an imaginary window with her mop of hair. "But if not, I think I shouldn't have to. He has to commit to me. Exclusively."

"You mean you've been dating for a year and he's not been

exclusive?" Frankie took a sip of iced tea, her eyes wide with confusion. She thought Gail was stronger than that. Of course, she'd also thought Gail had some ethics.

Judge not, lest you be judged, Frankie. Didn't you jump into bed with Luke after your divorce? That certainly wasn't because you thought of him as relationship material. Then again, maybe he was, and you didn't know it because you never got the messages from Luke. But dammit, Luke could have been more persistent. Maybe he wasn't telling the truth about leaving messages with Kayla. Maybe she should check with Kayla on that—assuming she could find her secretary.

She focused back on Gail, who was looking at her through watery eyes. "I don't know how you'd define our relationship. Michael hasn't suggested anything longer term than just dating. I know I have a decision to make." Her face crumbled. "But that's all moot if…"

Frankie reached out and put her hand over Gail's trembling fingers. "Oh, honey. Maybe you should take one of those tests." Inside, she was reeling from what Gail had just let slip—Michael hadn't committed to Gail. Gail deserved better than that. No wonder she'd wandered.

Gail nodded. "I know. I'm working up my courage. I'll buy one after lunch." She wiped her eyes. "The irony is that Stuart doesn't want children. He told me before we… well, did it. He wanted to make sure I understood that any relationship with him wasn't going to lead to that. I guess he had some bad experiences with women who wanted more." She barked out a bitter laugh. "As if wanting not to have kids were enough to make it so."

"How old is he?"

"Just fifty-two, it turns out. But he just doesn't want to deal with kids at his age." Gail took a weak nibble of her lunch. "I don't blame him. I think I read somewhere that older men's sperm isn't as healthy. So your baby can have problems." At this thought, her eyes welled again.

"What brought you and Stuart together?"

"We had our book club, and he was walking me home—he's very chivalrous—and we were talking about books in general. I'd had a hard day at work, and he was so sympathetic—sometimes Michael isn't so willing to listen. And I invited him up for a glass of wine and one thing led to another…"

Frankie played the scene out in her mind, and her harsh judgments left her. Gail had been lonely. Stuart was chivalrous and sympathetic. Frankie could have fallen just as easily.

"This whole thing is teaching me a big lesson," Gail continued. "I need to know my own heart before I end up giving myself to someone. And I have to be clear on what I want. And what I want is marriage and children. Children have always been a part of that dream, you know? Maybe it's because my own mom was a mom first and foremost. I just never thought of any other possibility for me. So finding out Stuart wasn't on that same page eliminated him immediately."

Well, not immediately, Frankie thought, but she kept it to herself.

"What about Michael—does he want those things?"

"I think so. I hope so. But I intend to find out. I do love him, Frankie. This thing with Stuart taught me that. But it's also taught me not to waste time with someone who doesn't want the same things." Her resolve back, she ceased crying.

"What about you?" Gail asked. "Any progress with Luke?"

"Huh?"

"He's staying with you. I thought you might get something going there."

"No, no, nothing." She was about to say he wasn't interested in her when she remembered that actually he was. "Actually, I found out he did have a thing for me."

Gail's mouth formed a happy "oh" and she leaned forward. "Frankie! That's terrific! I thought there was something more there."

"Don't get any ideas. I'm really not interested anymore." She wasn't, was she?

"Somebody else caught your eye?"

She thought of Victor. Victor of the old, damaged sperm. No, she didn't want to say anything about him right now.

"I'm footloose and fancy-free. Married to my work." She smiled.

They finished what they were going to eat of their meals, grabbed the check, and then Frankie accompanied Gail to a drugstore to buy the pregnancy test.

—⁓—

Gail wanted to take the test in private, so Frankie said good-bye to her friend a few blocks from the network building and walked slowly back to the office, her mind a muddle. Gail might be in a heap of trouble if that test came up positive, but she had figured out something important. You need to decide what you want from a relationship and ditch anyone who is just wasting your time.

That had been the problem with Brian, she realized with aching sadness. She'd been unwilling to confront the fact that he hadn't wanted the same things she had wanted. He didn't want family life and children and the vacations at Ocean City, Maryland, the Thanksgivings playing Monopoly, the trips to the mall, the nights watching *American Idol*.

He didn't even want happiness. Not the kind of happiness she wanted, the normal kind. He wanted some other brand, something weighted down with importance. She had spent too much time pushing her ordinary desires aside, trying to emulate and embrace the gravitas of Brian's crowd. It had been her crowd at college, too—well, except for Gail, really—and once she'd arrived there, she figured all of that angst was something to aspire to.

She heaved a sigh as she tugged open the lobby door. "That's your problem. You knew what you wanted. You just didn't have the backbone to demand it."

—\/\/\—

Victor could speed-read through bland reports and digest complex material with diligent attention to detail. But he felt like he had to use toothpicks to keep his eyes open when reading through Brian Aigland's "masterpiece." More than once as he sat at his desk, feet propped up and coffee at the ready, he felt like throwing the thing across the room, or at least taking it back to the bookstore and asking for a refund.

How did this stuff make it into print, let alone onto a bestseller list? It was turgid, aimless prose, mostly navel-gazing narcissism. The protagonist was a soulful graduate student who falls in love with a coed while engaged to another woman who supports him and acts as his muse.

Way to go, Bri. By making Frankie a "fiancée" in the book, you get rid of some of the guilt associated with committing outright adultery on the woman you married.

The portrait of Frankie, though, was vivid enough to make Victor smile. Brian had captured her foibles, her insecurities, even the way she stared incredulously at those with whom she disagreed. It would have lit the fuse of jealousy if Victor weren't so unimpressed with the protagonist in the book, a shallow and morally challenged antihero. What had Frankie seen in him?

Maybe he needed to answer that question before he went any further with her. Maybe answering it would provide the key to helping her learn to roll past her insecurities and use her talent and intelligence to get ahead.

He picked up his coffee cup to sip on the energy-boosting brew, but it was empty.

"Damn."

He stood, stretching and yawning. He wouldn't bother Bob for more. He'd go get a cup on his own. It would wake him up. Then it was back to business. Brian's stupid book could wait till later.

———

"What?" Frankie stood in front of Kayla's desk, hands on her hips, staring.

"Mr. Dewitt said Mr. Pendergrast said you'd talk to him," Kayla recited. "So I penciled him in for three o'clock."

"Well, unpencil him."

"I can't. He said he'd be out all day and would just stop by in time for the interview."

Why, that devious snake. Of course he'd be incommunicado until the moment of the interview. Wouldn't want Frankie canceling it.

Too bad.

"I have something important at three. So when he comes, you'll have to tell him I'm not here and you made a mistake."

"Oh." Kayla looked confused. "I won't be either."

Well, that was more progress—Kayla planning an absence from her desk. Usually they just occurred capriciously.

"Kayla, we have to talk. You're never around when I need you, and I don't think you're giving me all my messages." There, she'd said it.

"I have a callback," the secretary said, looking jubilant.

"For Nightingale?"

"For Female Crowd Member Three." Kayla said it as if it were Lady Macbeth.

Frankie growled inwardly. "All right, all right. As to Dewitt, leave a note on my door. Oh heck—I'll do it." But she didn't leave the note on her door just yet. Instead she paraded down the hall toward Victor's office, ready to ream him out over this betrayal. It was bad enough he'd talked to the reporter. But to offer her up? If she was going to go after what she wanted, this was a good place to start. What she wanted was a man who wouldn't stab her in the back. That shouldn't be too much to ask.

"He's not in," Bob said as she stormed by. "But he should be back any second."

She didn't say a word but strode into Victor's office to wait. Damn, but it was nice in here. Lots of space and a great view. She might have to requisition this office. He could have her old one.

She walked to the windows to look out at the city. As she passed Victor's desk, her gaze fell on an open book with an artsy dust jacket sporting a tiny photo of a keyhole through which you could make out an idyllic pastoral scene. Brian's name was set in banner type across the bottom!

A shiver chilled her, starting at her toes and creeping up to her scalp. Okay, here it was. She knew she'd have to pick up a copy sooner or later. She'd never received a copy from Gail. She grabbed the book with only her thumb and index finger, as if it were capable of inflicting harm. Eventually she hoisted the thing up with both arms. It wasn't that thick a volume—Brian didn't have the patience or diligence to tap out anything too long—but it was a hardcover, awkward to hold with one hand while the other was holding her nose.

Her heart pounding, she started flipping through the pages, looking for references to Francesca. She didn't have to go far. On page twenty Francesca made her first appearance. Holding her breath, Frankie read. And slowly exhaled as she absorbed a not-unflattering description of a "smart and quirky coed." Relieved, she sank into Victor's chair and continued to browse, page after page flying by as she searched for references to her personality.

Not all of it was bad. In fact, a good portion of it she could live with. The physical descriptions were certainly appealing. And—as far as she could tell—he'd mercifully left out any sex scenes between

Francesca and the protagonist. Then again, she thought, she wasn't sure Brian would be able to write about sex very well. He wasn't a particularly macho man in bed.

She was relaxing into a state of grateful relief, twisting a hair around her finger as she read, when she came upon a passage that set her bolt upright in the chair and shot fire into her cheeks.

"Francesca," Brian had written, "was my first real love, I realized with great regret, and I knew I'd never forget her. But she wasn't my ultimate soul mate. She had so much promise. But so many stunted hopes and misdirected aspirations. I knew I couldn't save her."

"AAAAArrrrrrrgh!" She threw the book on the floor and stomped on it, penetrating the cover with the spike of her heel. "You rotten, arrogant, smug, crap-faced, no-talent—"

"Hey! I paid good money for that!" Victor entered the room, coffee cup in hand, taking bold steps over to his desk, where he set his cup down before retrieving the battered book from the floor.

"You're enriching him! You could have gotten it at the library and not paid a cent."

"I didn't want to wait that long." He dusted off the book and set it on his desk. "And it's not that bad, Frankie. That's why you should talk to Dewitt."

"Not that bad? Not that bad?" She stared wild-eyed at him before realizing that this stare was described by Brian on page fifty-seven. She consciously relaxed, searching for stares he might not have written about.

"How would you know anyway?"

"If you mean how would I know you well enough to determine that this portrait in the book is mostly caricature? Come on, Frankie, give yourself some credit. It doesn't take long to figure out you have more depth than that." He pointed derisively to the book.

She was touched but not assuaged. She said nothing.

"Francesca is not you," Victor continued.

"She's enough of me to have reporters stalk me about it!"

He waved his hand in front of his face, dismissing the idea. "Gossip column stuff. Besides, it's not completely unflattering. There are lots of great—"

"Did you miss the part about my… my…" She picked up the book and quickly found the page she was looking for—the number was engraved in her mind—then read aloud the passage about "stunted hopes and misdirected aspirations."

To her surprise, Victor barked out a laugh.

"It's not funny." She glared at him. "And I'm not either."

He shook his head. "No, you're not what I'm laughing at. I'm laughing at him!" He pointed to the book in her hands. "'Stunted hopes?' Don't you think he might be describing himself?"

"His hopes are hardly stunted. He achieved success with this… this…"

"Piece of baloney." Victor's smile faded. "Look, success comes in different flavors and different stages. "I had Bob check, and this book is only on one bestseller list, one compiled by surveying New York–centric bookstores. It's not on radar screens nationally. And it's getting mixed reviews. Some are downright pans." At her confused look, he continued. "I had Bob research that, too."

"But still," she said, "he's accomplished a goal."

"So what? Is it your goal? Did he cheat you out of your goal?"

Good question, Victor. Too bad I don't know precisely what my goal is.

Victor pointed to the novel again. "Take it. I don't want to read any further. Then let Dewitt interview you about it. Trust me—he's not falling into the fan category. You'll find him sympathetic. I can suggest talking points."

She didn't agree outright, but she did let Victor coach her, hugging the book to her chest as she listened to him advise her to say how happy she was for any writer's success, how she'd not had a chance to read the book yet but a friend had told her about it, that she was sure writers used aspects of those they knew to draw characters in their books, but she was confident that Brian wouldn't have used a novel to inflict pain on her, because who would be that cruel?

"And then turn the conversation to *Lust for Life* and what you're doing here to turn things around," Victor finished.

"Dewitt is a book reporter!"

"Doesn't matter. 'Reporter' is the key word. He'll write about *Lust* if that's all you talk about. Talk like you did in the press conference."

"You mean the 'art doesn't rob—'"

"No, no. Not that part. The parts where you were explaining the show's rationale. You were magnificent then, Frankie. You know this show, this genre, like no one else. You make soap operas sound like epic Greek poetry."

She fell silent, thinking about what he'd said. She did love to talk about *Lust*, how her love for it had started in her girlhood. She was comfortable on that territory.

"What if he asks about the thief?"

"Just don't go there. Tell him that the issue is unresolved and you can't say anything about it at the moment but will be happy to share information as it becomes available."

"I don't know…"

"He's not going to give up, Frankie. And if you put him off, then he might start buying into this silly portrait of Francesca that your ex has drawn. Until he gets to know you, the real Frankie, that's all he has to go on."

For the first time, she started to imagine herself doing a successful interview with Mr. E. J. Dewitt. Victor was right about talking about *Lust*. If she got the conversation to that field, she'd be off and running. It would be great publicity for the show, even reaching a demographic they didn't ordinarily touch.

"I'll think about it," she grudgingly said.

"Don't wait too long. His deadline's coming up."

And he had a three o'clock scheduled with her already. She didn't tell Victor that.

Her cell jingled in her pocket. One glance told her it was Gail. "Gotta run!"

—∕∿∿∼—

She picked up the call in the hallway, and Gail screamed into the line as soon as Frankie said hello. "It was negative! Negative! I'm not pregnant!"

"That's great, Gail." Frankie walked fast down the hall, around the corner, past Kayla's empty desk, and into her office, shutting the door. "You must be so relieved."

"You have no idea. I mean, I probably should have assumed it was okay—we were awfully careful, considering Stuart doesn't want kids—but you can never be sure. I think I probably was experiencing so much guilt over Stuart that I messed up my system."

"So, what now?" Frankie sank into her chair.

"Now I talk to Stuart. Tell him it's over. Or, rather, that there's no future for us."

"What about Michael? You're still not going to confess?"

Gail paused. "No. But I am going to tell him I want more from him."

"You must be worried about that one."

"You know, not really. It's strange, but I feel like a burden's been lifted off me. We've been seeing each other for, what, a year now? And part of me kept or keeps waiting and waiting. So not waiting will be a relief, no matter what. I'm in charge of that. Not him."

"Tell me how it goes."

"I really appreciate your listening to me gnash my teeth about it today. I probably made too big a deal of it."

"It was a big deal, Gail. And I don't mind. What are girlfriends for?"

"Well, they're for giving advice. So I hope you don't mind if I dole some out now. I've been thinking about what you said about Luke—how he was crushing on you."

"Gail, really, I don't think—"

"Hear me out. I remember when you and he hooked up. You felt the way I did about Stuart—glad and guilty at the same time. You thought it was a rebound thing, and you didn't want to do that to somebody else. And so you were relieved that Luke didn't pursue it."

That was only partially true. Frankie remembered telling Gail those things at the time, but that was to save face more than anything. She had secretly waited for Luke to call. Sure, she got over it quickly when he didn't—or, rather, when she thought he hadn't—but some part of her had hoped for a connection.

Gail went on. "Well, you're not on the rebound now. You've healed up quite nicely from the split with Brian. It's time to take a chance, Frankie."

"What about goal setting? I thought that's what I should be doing."

"Take a chance on going for your goal—right. And I assume the goal includes a relationship."

"I'll think about it." Why didn't she tell Gail about Victor? What was keeping her from revealing that relationship possibility?

They said their good-byes, and Frankie turned to her computer, clicking into the word-processing program. She would finally write those thief audition scenes. She couldn't be thinking about relationships or Luke or Victor or even what she wanted from men or love.

Chapter 14

THE PROBLEM, FRANKIE DECIDED, after she wrapped up the thief audition scripts, was that they didn't even know if there was any money in the budget for this character. Sure, they could probably squeeze out enough for a day player—someone who was only paid for the spots he did. But what if they went in another direction that turned the thief into a new character, one who became a part of Crestview's ongoing stories? That would require the bucks for someone on salary, and it would have to be approved by the powers that be.

Frankie had been trying to get the green light on hiring a new character for ages. Even when Jack was head writer, she'd made the case for it. It would give her and all the writers more freedom if they knew they could bring in another cast member, opening up doors to whole new stories instead of continually retreading the ones they now had. But Brady Stephens had fought her off so far. Each time she requested money for a new actor, he'd help up his hand swami-style and said, "No can do. Network's breathing down my neck as it is to cut the bottom line. Until the ratings go up, Crestview's residents stay as is." Except he'd said "Craneview's residents." Brady was not a detail person as far as the show went.

"Now I have the perfect excuse to get you to give me a new actor," she thought, printing out the pages of the thief audition script after emailing it to Victor and others. "Ratings are going up and the thief story is hot. You don't need to know that the new actor might not be the thief. Hopefully that story will be long gone by the time I'm ready to introduce a new character to Crestview."

She picked up the phone and dialed Brady Stephens's number, only to be told by honey-voiced Serena that he wasn't back from his West Coast trip yet.

"He was delayed," Serena cooed. "Do you want to leave a message?"

"When will he be back?" Frankie asked.

"I'm not sure."

Not sure? Serena knew every move Brady Stephens made. Most of the time, she told him what moves to make. Serena was hiding something.

"No message. Let me know when he returns, though."

After hanging up the phone, Frankie stood and looked out the window. Brady was an absentee producer to be sure, but this was ridiculous. Was he being fired? And did this have anything to do with Raeanne leaving? It just seemed odd that both Brady's mystery absence and Raeanne's resignation were falling at the same time.

A soft knock at her door interrupted her thoughts. "Come in!"

Hank poked his head in, as if afraid to step inside without an invitation. "I'm sorry to disturb you, Ms. McNally—"

"Frankie."

"—Frankie, but your secretary was away from her desk, and I wasn't sure if you were in or working from that other mini office."

She waved him in. "What's up?" She hoped *he* wasn't planning on resigning. He walked into her office and sat before her desk. The poor fellow's wrinkled shirt looked liked he'd pulled it from the dryer, where it had sat for a week, and his khaki pants were frayed at the hem. His dark, curly hair had a windswept look—or, rather, a wind-tunnel look—with one large lock falling onto his forehead.

But he did have a BlackBerry, which he held before him, as if consulting it for notes.

"Do you remember I mentioned to you a cousin of mine who's an actor?"

"Yes, of course." But she didn't. At least, not at first. As Hank talked, she vaguely recalled his bringing it up.

"Well, I hate to be a pest about things, but I did want to make sure to talk to you again, because I know how busy you are."

Poor Hank. He probably had to screw up a lot courage to talk to her again.

"Is he working?"

"Well, yes. He's in sales."

"No, I mean is he working in the field, acting?"

"He's had some auditions. And he was an extra for a while in that musical with the veterans in wheelchairs."

"Ah, yes, *War Songs*, directed by the great Mickey Mousekvoya."

"You know it!" Hank seemed genuinely pleased.

"So you want to know if *Lust* has anything for him."

"Well, yes, Ms. McNally—Frankie—if it's not too much trouble. Is anything coming open soon? I really need to get back to him."

At least Hank's cousin didn't think acting on *Lust* was "settling."

"Maybe there will be something." She thought of the case she wanted to make to Brady for a new hire. And she didn't mind giving Hank a heads-up on that. Lots of folks at the show had friends and relatives interested in acting and they were alerted to auditions, or had words put in for them. It still all came down to whether the auditioners had the acting chops.

"What's his name?" Frankie asked, smiling.

"Thane Galahad," Hank said.

Frankie choked back a laugh.

"It's not his real name," Hank explained. "He said he wanted something heroic for the stage."

Galahad was certainly heroic. "I'm going to be asking Mr. Stephens to include money in the budget for a new character," Frankie said. "I don't know who it will be yet—even if it's going to be a guy—but as soon as I decide, I'll let you know, and Thane can have a go at it."

Hank's face beamed with gratitude. "Thank you so much, Ms. McNally. My mother will be so pleased to hear this. And so will Thane. Thank you, thank you." And he backed out of the room as if she were a royal presence.

She looked at her watch. Damn, time was zooming by. She liked to catch the show, and it was almost over. She could view it later. Right now, she would talk to Victor. Maybe he knew where Brady was. And even if he didn't, he'd be a formidable ally when she did approach the executive producer.

—⁓—

Bob was away from his desk when Frankie came up to Victor's office, eliciting a curious sense of satisfaction in her. So she wasn't the only one with a disappearing secretary. She knocked briskly on his door and stepped in, ready to urge—nay, order—Victor to contact the executive producer to make the case for a new character on payroll.

But as soon as her mouth opened, she shut it again. Victor wasn't alone. Raeanne sat on the edge of a chair in front of his desk, her shapely legs crossed and a tissue in her hand. A tissue?

"Come on in, Frankie," Victor said.

"I don't want to intrude," Frankie said. "Looks like you were in the middle of something."

"No, we're finishing up." He looked at Raeanne as if to confirm this. Raeanne stood, smoothing her slacks.

"Were you telling him about your resignation?" Frankie said, sounding more snappish than she'd intended. She couldn't help it. She wanted to know what was going on.

"As a matter of fact, we did talk about that," Victor said, standing as well. He was doing his gentlemanly thing again, standing when a woman stood. "And Raeanne has some good news."

Thus prompted, Raeanne looked at Frankie and said, "I've decided to stay. Victor convinced me. He's been so kind." Raeanne looked over at Victor, her large eyes blinking fast.

Frankie was relieved. Or at least, she knew she should be. If Raeanne wasn't leaving, that was one less task for Frankie to handle. But how did Victor convince her to stay? Frankie looked at Victor, but he merely smiled like the Cheshire cat.

"That's great news! Just great news," Frankie said, trying to think of something else to add. "Glad to have you back on the team. Not that you'd officially left, of course."

"Thank you again, Victor," Raeanne said, walking around to Victor. She stood on tiptoes and planted a kiss on his cheek. "You did me a great kindness with this little talk." She smiled at Frankie as she left the room, a smile that seemed to say she'd scored some victory.

When she was gone, Frankie looked at Victor. "How on earth did you do that?"

"It wasn't so hard." He sat down as Frankie sat, putting his hands behind his head and stretching back in his chair. "I merely asked her to reconsider."

Victor wasn't telling her the full story.

"You must have turned on some heavy-duty charm."

"I've been known to be charming." Again, the grin.

"What did you promise her?"

"A good working environment, success…"

"C'mon. More money? Did you get Brady to up her salary? Because if you did without telling me, I'm going to be ripped. I want to go after Brady for another budget item. It's what I came to talk to you about." And she outlined her idea of using the focus on the thief as a way of getting the producer to okay the new hire.

"I think that's an excellent idea," Victor said, leaning forward. "Tell me what you want from me."

"I want you to grease the wheels by (a) finding out where the hell

Brady is, and (b) letting him know we have to cast the thief soon, because the story is making the ratings go like gangbusters."

"So you're now on board with using the story to achieve your goals?" He smirked.

"What? It's not the same thing as using it to spike ratings! It's—"

"The same thing."

She didn't want to argue. And it didn't matter who was right anyway, as long as she achieved her purpose.

"I have to run," she said, rising. Victor stood, too.

"You have that appointment with Dewitt," he reminded her.

"Right."

She turned to go, but his soft voice stopped her at the door. "And don't forget—we have a dinner date."

"A business dinner," she said, not looking at him.

She raced back to her office, clicking on the TV to catch at least the last part of the show. On the screen, a Terri and Donovan flashback played—scenes from their tumultuous courtship. Terri was crying her eyes out to her mother after finding Donovan in what she thought was a compromising position with the conniving Colleen, a step-niece of Anne Kendall. Colleen had been working in cahoots with another character, Beaumont, who wanted to bed Terri.

"I… I thought Donovan might not be right for me, but, but… I never thought it would be because he would cheat." She sobbed, leaning into her mother's embrace.

Frankie remembered writing that scene. It was right after finding out about Brian's affair.

"There, there, darling. Are you sure there wasn't a mistake?" Terri's mother asked.

The very same question Peggy McNally had put to her heartbroken daughter.

"No, Mother, I saw with my own eyes… oh, it was awful…"

Frankie mouthed the words with her and felt her eyes welling with tears as Terri collapsed again into sobs. She'd said those words, too, about Brian. She'd come home early one day and seen with her own eyes the evidence of his betrayal.

The door burst open and Donovan appeared, dragging Colleen with him. "Tell her," he shouted at Colleen. "Tell her how you set me up! Tell her how you worked with that conniving Beaumont."

Oh, how wonderful it would have been had Brian been set up by a scheming woman and not really been unfaithful. No broken heart then.

But would she have been happy? Frankie clicked off the remote, pushing memories aside. She was pulled out of her melancholy by a text message from Nory.

Chapter 15

Nory needed to talk to her about vacation. Oh no, was Nory planning on being out in the near future? Was no one as committed to *Lust* as Frankie was? Nory could have come and talked in person, but she always preceded her requests with electronic communication. Frankie was sure she'd find a similar email from Nory when she checked her inbox.

"She probably wants to run off to some island with that no-good boyfriend of hers. He's probably telling her that working for *Lust* is a betrayal of their communal principles," Frankie growled to herself as she sat at her desk.

"I'm sorry, are you on the phone?" A gentle male voice came from the doorway. Frankie looked up. Dewitt! He was here. Early. She hadn't even decided—truly, surely, firmly—that she was going to meet with him after all. Her palms began to sweat. Should she make an excuse? *Aw shucks, E. J. I really did want to talk, but I had this emergency call about a special meeting of this mentoring group I belong to where we talk to young girls about* unlimited *hopes and* directed *aspirations."*

Dewitt didn't wait for an invitation. He stepped into her office, careful not to look too intimidating by clasping an old brown raincoat and his reporter's notebook and tape recorder to his chest. He dropped his pen as he got to the chair, apologizing for being such a bumbler.

"Hey, no problem. I'd rather be a bumbler than a loser," she said.

He looked up and smiled. "You're talking about Francesca."

"No, no. What makes you think that?" She smoothed her hair, trying to tame its frizz, pulling her hand away as if touched by electricity when she remembered how Brian had described Francesca doing the same thing when she was nervous.

"Look, Ms. McNally—"

"Francesca… I mean Frankie."

"Frankie, I'm not here to do a hit job on you. I just want some backstory for my piece on Brian Aigland's book. That's all." He flipped open his notebook and put his recorder on the desk, punching the on button.

Frankie cleared her throat. "Uh, you better move that closer. I'm a low talker." She grabbed it herself and placed it smack in front of her, flipping the switch off while she was at it.

"I want to hear about you before I ask about Francesca. Tell me about your life here at *Lust*, how you got here, was it always a goal, what you hope to accomplish."

And she was off. She didn't need Victor's talking points. She didn't need coaching. All she needed was someone asking her about what she did.

She talked about the art of storytelling, about how that's what originally drew her to *Lust*. She talked about her mother and what a bond the show created between them. Yeah, some of the stories were outlandish, but that was the challenge of it—to make the outrageous believable, to take characters who committed adultery and baby swapping, or engaged in nefarious backstabbing plots and betrayals, and make an audience like them. Not like them in the sense of wanting to be friends with them. But like them enough to want to hear their stories.

Every day, Frankie told Dewitt, she woke up asking herself one question: How do I get them to listen to my stories?

He asked her about her favorite story—she had to think about that but ultimately chose a crazy one involving an ingénue who gave up her true love to do nursing work in the Congo. She wept for days, she said, as she wrote those breakdowns, and fan mail was heavy, all in favor of the plot, which originally had been driven by a popular actress' exit from her contract.

She talked and talked, unaware of the time passing or the sun fading, or Dewitt running out of paper (no danger of running out of audio tape).

Finally, he brought the conversation back to the book.

"Have you read it?"

"No." That was partially true. Oh hell, honesty was the best policy. "Okay, I'm human. I did skim it looking for Francesca."

"What did you think?"

She laughed. "I liked how pretty she was." Then she paused, growing more serious. "But didn't think in the end it was a portrait of me at all."

"Because of the less than complimentary sections?"

"Because it was a cartoon character, not a real person. The characters on *Lust* are more real." Even the outlandish ones she drew were more real than this Francesca. Even the Keith character. Well, at least he was funny.

After a few more perfunctory questions, he closed his notebook and said they were finished. He grabbed the recorder, looking at the "off" button and shaking it, and stood.

"You should write a novel," he said. "Sounds like you'd do a bang-up job."

She stood and shook her head, waving the air dismissively. "Pshaw," she kidded. "I'm not a novelist. Not a literary writer, I mean."

"What exactly is that anyway?" Dewitt asked, his tone more serious. "I've been trying to figure it out, and I've been writing about authors for seven years now. Don't sell yourself short. You've got stories to tell. Isn't that what a book is all about?"

He wished her farewell and was off. She sank into her chair, relieved.

It was a business dinner, right? So she wasn't going home to change. She'd go straight to the restaurant in her black silk pantsuit and lime green satin blouse, after first daubing off the spot of jelly from the afternoon doughnut she had consumed after E. J. Dewitt left. Damn, but it was hard drying that thing using the hand dryer in the bathroom. She'd have a backache for weeks.

She brushed her hair, trying it in a twist, in a clip at her neck, and finally putting a thin hair band on it even though she thought it made her look a little too prep school. She refreshed her lipstick and reapplied some blush and powder, topping off her ladies room toilette with a quick spritz of a knock-off perfume.

"That will have to do, Frankie, m'girl," she said into the mirror.

She hurried back to her office, stuffing her bag with dialogue sheets that she still hadn't read, as well as the thief audition scenes. Satisfied that she wouldn't be early and might even be a few minutes late, she left, grabbing a taxi almost as soon as she stepped to the curb.

Right after she'd given the driver the address and sank back in the seat, her cell buzzed. Luke. What was he calling for? Oh no—not to announce his departure, she hoped. She hadn't been too harsh on him, had she?

"Luke, what's up?" she answered, perky and hopeful.

"Nothing much," he said in such a quiet voice she had to put her finger in her other ear to hear him. "Just wondering what your plans are for dinner. I could make something."

So he hadn't found another place yet.

Or not quite.

"I have a friend who can let me have a sublet, but not until next weekend at the earliest," Luke explained.

"Oh, that's great. Thanks for telling me." The restaurant was a mere three blocks away, but the traffic was slow.

"So I was wondering if you'd like…"

Honking and horn blaring blocked out his last words as a battered Chevy plowed into the back of a Ford station wagon two cars up. The taxi driver cursed.

"That's okay," she said to the driver, her hand over the phone mouthpiece. "You can drop me here."

Back to the phone, she said, "Luke, I have to run. We'll talk later, okay? Thanks for letting me know about the apartment."

———

She stepped into the restaurant, one of those upscale bistro things in Midtown fronted by flower boxes, now bare of blooms, diners' shadows flickering across candles through smoky glass windows. Tugging at her collar to make sure it was straight, she walked into the foyer, scanning the crowd as she gave her name to the maitre d'.

But there was no need. She caught Victor's gaze across the room at the same time that he saw her. He stood, smiling, and she headed for his table in a cozy corner by an exposed brick wall.

"I see you're ready to work," he said as she hoisted her heavy bag onto an empty chair. She sat down before he had a chance to come around and hold her chair for her.

"Well, it *is* business," she said, looking at the pale coral, perfectly ironed tablecloth, the lone calla lily in a smart crystal vase, and smelling something that set her taste buds drooling. "I brought the thief audition with me. It's moving fast, so we need to finalize it tonight." No, she didn't need him to finalize it. She'd already finalized it. "Rather, I thought you'd want a copy. I've revised it and have a few versions to use."

While he looked over the pages she handed him, they both

ordered wine and some appetizers. As soon as the wine came, she started to relax.

"These are great," Victor said, putting the papers down and taking off his reading glasses. "Much better than some of the dialogue on the show itself. Your background shows."

Frankie blushed. She did pride herself on being a topnotch dialogue writer, knowing not only how things sounded when they were said but also how particular actors would say them and what their memorization styles were. She knew some of the actors learned only their own lines, giving scant attention to any of the lines of the others in a scene. This caused problems for scriptwriters intent on crafting clever parallel constructions or repetitions to be hammered by one actor and then another.

If an actor wasn't paying attention to the previous line that was said, he didn't always emphasize the right word. Frankie knew that and planned accordingly. That's why she often included actual dialogue in her breakdowns. Her scriptwriters knew if they saw such passages, they were to incorporate them into the actual script.

For this new character, the thief, she'd struck out in several directions, writing a scene that could be read as a deranged madman or as a Robin Hood or as a suave miscreant in need of redemption. Victor obviously appreciated the nuances.

"I spoke with Dewitt, by the way. It went well."

"Excellent!" He raised his glass to her. "I really think he'll treat you fairly. I didn't sense he had an ax to grind."

She smiled. And then lapsed into an awkward silence. Now what? What were they doing? They'd kissed twice. But she was trying to pretend this was just a working relationship. How did you do that? Maybe the thing to do was to cut it off entirely, until they were finished pulling *Lust* out of the trash bin, and then start clean. What had she been thinking when she fell into his arms?

But they were terrific arms. She admired the broad cut of his shoulders, the strong wrist and hand poking beyond a perfectly laundered cuff. She wouldn't mind pursuing something with Victor. She shivered.

"You cold?" he asked.

"No, no, I'm fine. I just need to—"

"Victor!" A woman's voice cut through the diners' hum, a voice that was dark and insistent. Victor turned around, and Frankie looked up.

A handsome woman approached. Six feet tall, with the confident look of someone who owned horses or other expensive things, she had sandy blonde hair knotted in a twist that looked as perfect as it looked casual. She wore a heavy sweater and hip-length jacket over dark pants and tall boots. Maybe she had been riding earlier. Frankie wouldn't have been surprised to see a crop in her hand.

Victor stood and kissed the woman on both cheeks.

"Linda!" His greeting was so warm and welcoming that Frankie wondered for a second if she were a guest Victor had forgotten to mention. "I just saw Courtney the other night."

"We have lots to talk about," Linda said, holding on to Victor's sleeve.

"Courtney says she doesn't want a fuss."

Linda laughed. "She wants a fuss, trust me. She just doesn't want to say she wants one."

So this was his ex. Frankie felt left in the shadows, wondering if the stain really was out of her blouse, and feeling oddly overdressed next to this casual yet oh-so-perfect woman who was old enough to be her… well, older aunt at least. She looked like she'd thrown on her clothes that morning, tossed her hair in a clip in the afternoon after her ride, and was now sun-kissed and rosy-cheeked, bright-eyed, fresh, and just right. She was "doesn't try at all," and Frankie was "tries all the time" in the good looks department.

"Oh, excuse me, I didn't introduce you. Frankie," Victor said, "this is Linda Darlington." And to Linda, "Frankie McNally, head writer at *Lust for Life*."

Linda held out her hand, smiling, and said a quick hello before turning back to Victor. "That's your aunt's show, isn't it? I thought it had gone off the air!"

"No, no, still hanging on," Victor said cheerfully, but Frankie could tell he was inwardly gritting his teeth. "Are you waiting for someone? Care to join us for a drink?"

Now Linda looked down at Frankie. "Wendell's here some-where. I'm just in the city to pick him up. We're having a bite first. Thanks, but you clearly have business to discuss." Just then a man as distinguished looking as Linda was attractive appeared, the maitre d' leading him through the crowded room. With wavy gray hair and model-rugged face, he looked perfectly groomed in his tweedy jacket and silk turtleneck. "Looks like he's here!"

Quick hellos and intros followed, and then they were gone—the "Most Perfect Couple in Connecticut Come to Visit New York City."

"My ex," Victor explained, sitting down with Frankie.

"I gathered."

"And Courtney, our daughter, she's getting married. Just found out." It was a subject that clearly didn't make him all that happy.

Come to think of it, it didn't make Frankie all that happy, either. She was thinking of seeing a man old enough to have a daughter in her "friends" category. She wasn't from a place where people dated men who had daughters her own age (or thereabouts). In Frankie's neck of the woods, age groups stuck together like classes on a field trip.

After they ordered, more awkward silence ensued. Frankie wasn't sure she wanted to hear more about Courtney. But Victor opened up anyway, telling her how he and Linda had had Courtney when they were "too young" but that she was still the best thing that had ever happened to him.

"I think I married too young," Frankie said. "I didn't know what

I wanted." That made her sound ancient. She wasn't that far from that "too young" person. Victor was. "I mean…"

"Same here," Victor concurred. "And I thought I was so sure, too." He laughed at himself.

She turned serious. "Is that why you and Linda split—you grew up and apart?"

He took a sip of wine. "You could say that. She certainly grew apart."

"You mean like Brian—my ex?" She looked into his eyes, which held no pain.

"Yes."

So Linda had betrayed Victor, just as Brian had betrayed Frankie. She wondered if he still carried the torch for her, though. They did have a daughter together. And she was so much more his type than Frankie was. She was sophisticated and sure of herself, the kind of born-with-it sure of herself that no person or situation would ever knock down. Could it be that Victor had never really gotten over Linda but was too proud to forgive her?

"She married the guy?" Frankie probed. "Was that him?" She shrugged her shoulder back toward the room where Linda and Wendell had disappeared.

"She did marry the guy, as a matter of fact, and Wendell is not him. For all I know, Wendell's a friend. She divorced her second husband five or six years ago."

"For Wendell?" Frankie said as the waiter arrived with appetizers. After he left, she continued. "Looked like a relationship."

Victor shrugged, tearing off a piece of bread, staring at Frankie as if trying to figure out how to say something. "When Linda and I divorced—even before we divorced—it was over between us. After a couple bumpy post-divorce years, we settled into a cordial relationship because of Courtney, and now we're amiable, but not close, friends."

"So you had no bitterness over her…"

"Adultery." He swallowed some bread and shook his head. "Anger, yes. Bitterness, no. I might have fallen out of love with Linda, but I don't accept betrayal. You make a commitment, you stick to it—until you openly sever that commitment."

"Wow, that seems harsh."

"You would have taken Brian back?"

"No." She was surprised at the speed and vehemence in her answer. But, no, she had felt the same way about Brian's transgression. It was something that couldn't be fixed. Even though she, unlike Victor, still had had feelings for her spouse when the betrayal had occurred. She knew, though, that she'd never be able to trust him again. Not that he'd asked her to.

"I never thought I would be a divorcée," she said. "I always imagined the forever thing."

"It's not a bad idea, you know. The forever thing."

She smiled. "I guess you thought so if you had a kid together."

"Best thing of all."

"I imagined that as part of the forever thing."

"With Brian?"

She paused, the question hitting her like a punch to the gut, because she had come to realize what a catastrophe that could have been. Had she ever thought of him as potential parent material? Maybe at the beginning. Like all women, she thought she could mold him into what she wanted.

"At some point."

Dinners arrived and they dove in, both of them hungry. Their talk was now exclusively about their hopes and dreams and pasts, with no business or show discussion entering the umber glow of their intimacy. Frankie was feeling mellow and comfortable, patting herself on the back for ultimately giving herself permission to come to dinner with Victor. She wasn't crazy for liking him. He was a damned likable guy.

As desserts of panna cotta with raspberry sauce and chocolate were set before them, Victor brought up the business end of their dinner.

"I hate to spoil this with shop talk," he said. "But I think we can get the extra actor budgeted, and you should proceed as if it's okayed."

"Brady said yes?"

"Brady will say yes."

"I also want to hire some more scriptwriters," Frankie said, leaning forward. "We have a fair team now, but there are some weak spots. Plus, after Raeanne's resignation, I'm thinking backups are good."

"Raeanne's not resigning, remember."

"Yeah. I'd love to know what you promised her on that."

He smiled. "I think if we talk a few more minutes about the show, it will qualify as a tax write-off or an expense account dinner." He pulled out his credit card as he spoke.

"Okay, I have more ideas."

He stared into her eyes. "We could discuss them over brandy. At my place."

—⁓—

But in the end, they didn't do much discussing, and Frankie knew they wouldn't as soon as she agreed to go to his apartment. She'd affirmed that decision in the cab, when a fast turn around a corner had her tumbling against his strong arm, and he'd looked at her and leaned in and kissed her with such intensity and need that she thought they'd both explode. *You just don't make that kind of connection often*, she thought to herself as his breath trembled against her neck. *Not the kind where you can't stand the thought of letting the opportunity pass, of never feeling him against you, around you.*

So after they'd made some token small talk about the Faye character at his place, she was in his arms again, making it clear she was ready to make the next step into his bed.

And what a step it turned out to be. He was a magnificent lover, not hesitating a moment once the path was clear, stripping off his clothes with his gaze locked on her, helping her with her blouse buttons, removing her bra and straddling her with the lean, hungry look of an animal. He was strong and sure, sensitive but not simpering, thrusting with vigor until they both reached an ecstasy she didn't remember feeling with Brian... or with Luke for that matter. Was it Victor or her particular needs? She didn't know. All she knew was she felt so damn comfortable in his arms, so damn happy to be in his bed.

As she stared at Victor's strong shoulders and muscular pecs, she was overwhelmed with tenderness. So what if he was twenty years older? He was a good man. So what if they came from different social strata? They shared the same values. So what if he had a daughter her age? The union that produced that happy event was long over.

He sensed her gaze and opened his eyes, smiling. "I'm not a one-night-stand kind of guy."

She smiled. "That's good to hear."

"What I mean is, I like you a lot, Frankie. I..." He stopped himself and chuckled. "That sounds sophomoric." He turned more serious. "What I mean is, I think I'm falling in love with you."

She thrilled to hear those words coming from this man. He wasn't a youngster, miserly holding back his feelings, or, worse, doing the opposite—prematurely gushing about undying affection while in the throes of lust. He was a thoughtful man who said what he meant. It was refreshing. He would expect the same level of honesty from her.

"I... I think..."

He put his finger on her lips to stop her. "Don't. If you're not sure, don't make it up."

Her heart melted. In that instant, she would have declared undying love for him. But she heeded his advice and held back.

He was right. She should be sure before uttering those words. They should mean something.

"All right," she said at last. "I think it's safe to say that I'm very, very attracted to you. And I want to continue this and see where it goes."

He reached over, grabbed her, and pulled her face to his for a kiss. It was the type of kiss that signified something, sending a trembling of fear and anticipation through Frankie's torso. *Do you want this?* a voice kept asking her. Before the night was over, they'd made love again, a slower, less tempestuous union, but no less satisfying. If anything, it produced more heat than their first explosive coupling as they tantalized each other with the climax that was to come.

He wanted her to stay, but she insisted he take her home. As she waited for him to finish dressing, she looked around his apartment, noticing the photos of Courtney for the first time. After meeting Linda, Frankie could see the resemblance. There was one picture of the two of them on horses. Frankie hadn't been wrong about that assumption.

"Pretty, isn't she?" Victor asked, pulling on a sweater as he came into the living room.

"Mm-hmm. You must be proud." Frankie put the photo back on a shelf.

"She's pretty special, too. You'll have to meet her."

He said it very casually, but Frankie took note of its significance.

"She's an only child?"

"If you're asking if I have any bastard children anywhere, the answer is a rock-solid no."

"Wow, you're certainly sure of that one! Cue the long-lost son's appearance." She laughed, but noticed Victor wasn't joining in. "Uh, I mean, on *Lust* that's how it would play."

Victor grabbed his keys. "Well, if any more progeny of mine started turning up, there'd be a malpractice suit to pay."

—∿∿—

Linda had suggested it, Victor told Frankie on the way home. Courtney had been a difficult birth—nearly killed Linda—and they both decided not to have any more children. Victor had no problem being the one to go under the knife. Oh, he'd had a regret or two after the divorce, but none since then. He'd brought one beautiful child into the world and counted his blessings.

Frankie listened politely, asking a few questions she thought were acceptable, but all the while thinking, *He can't have children, he can't have children, he can't have children.* Forget about damaged sperm. His were permanently dammed up.

Despite the fact that they were nowhere near the "forever" part of a relationship, Frankie couldn't help but remember Gail's earlier words about deciding what you want. Frankie wanted children, dammit. And any man who even came close to stepping onstage in her "forever" fantasy had to have that possibility. She felt cheated, gypped, a victim of false advertising. *I mean, c'mon, he's a virile, macho hunka hunka burning love… but with the seed pods disconnected. Shouldn't there be some sort of disclosure form about that?*

A confused good-night kiss and she was back in her apartment. Luke was asleep on the sofa, and the table was still set with the remains of what had obviously been intended to be a romantic meal.

She went to bed and dreamt of babies, her own babies, a whole passel of them. But when the father came in to see his brood, his face was obscured by shadow.

When she woke up, she made a resolution: Think; don't feel, think.

Over the next few days, she would avoid Victor and Luke (as much as she could in her small apartment) and try to figure out what the hell she wanted.

Chapter 16

"Get these effing thieves out of my way!" Maurice yelled as he brushed past a hallway of black-garbed actors, many of whom were mumbling or orating the words on the audition sheets in front of them. "I have a show to direct!"

Frankie rolled her eyes at Maurice's display of ego. He was miffed because he wouldn't be in on the auditions and had had very little impact on the direction they were headed with the character anyway. She wasn't even sure he knew they were making the character a full-time possibility.

Anyway, she had bigger fish to fry. In one hand she held a coffee cup. Under her arm was a morning paper. Victor was right—they had generated more publicity with this casting call. And the thief had struck again! She would have called Victor with her big news, but she'd left her damned phone at home that morning and had been on the go since getting in.

Besides, she'd been working her avoid-men-who-might-be-relationship-material strategy the last few days and had hardly spoken with him, even when he'd asked her out the night after their tryst—*Sorry, no can do, have to see an old friend.* Mostly she avoided asking herself how that was working for her and what she really wanted.

She headed through double doors at the end of the hallway, into a quieter room where a lone actor, in black jeans, tee, and vest, recited her words: *"It isn't about the money. It's about something more."*

At a table facing the actor were four people—the casting director, a young assistant, Nory (per Frankie's request—she'd decided Nory should be the backup breakdown writer on this), and Victor. Not too far from him was an unnamed cameraman taking digital video of the scene.

She and Victor exchanged knowing glances, laden with meaning. Just seeing him after their night together sent smoldering heat through her veins. She had avoided running into him the last few days and was glad of it. She was too confused. Now she was glad he'd stopped her that night from blurting out confessions of love prematurely.

Even if she *was* in love with him, did she really want to pursue a relationship now that she knew about his… snip-snip thing? Part of her was heartbroken over that, and she needed time to process it all.

It was a good thing he'd been working on this casting call setup the past two days, pulling it together in record time. He'd tried to talk to her alone a few times, but she was a master of avoidance—the E. J. Dewitt episode proved that—and she had managed to be out or on her way somewhere each time he'd stopped by. It had been hard, damned hard, but she couldn't think straight when he was too close. All she could do was feel.

"*…Money isn't the solution to every problem, you know…*"

Frankie slammed the papers on the table, making the thief and everyone else jump.

"Okay, I'm sure now. I might have backslid with all that mumbo jumbo about the real thief having a nervous breakdown. But I won't be a part of this. I might not have high standards, but even this doesn't meet them. This has to stop." She pointed to the story of the thief robbing a condo the night before.

Victor looked down and raised an eyebrow.

"Uh… I can read the other version," the actor said, holding up the alternative scripts Frankie had penned.

"I don't mean you," she said. "Just wait a sec."

She grabbed Victor's arm. "Come here." And led him back into the hallway. As they walked out together, she couldn't help feeling a frisson being so close to him again. *Get a grip, Frankie! One night in his bed and you're besotted!*

She did a mental head shake to clear her thoughts, pushing her libido aside. "Give me your police contact's name and number. I simply cannot let this go on. I can't live with myself!" Frankie hissed at him in the hallway as a murmur of thief lines hummed in the background.

Give me your jewels and you won't be hurt...
...Money isn't everything. Love is more important...
Diamonds aren't your best friend now...
Don't patronize me. I won't be talked down to...
...your jewels and you won't be...
...isn't everything...
I won't be talked down to...

"Shut! Up!" Frankie yelled into the corridor. Noise stopped. Dozens of eyes looked at her, some from behind ski masks.

"You were saying?" Victor said through gritted teeth.

The blush rose hot and fast on Frankie's face. She pursed her lips and mumbled, "Not here," indicating he follow her. Through the double doors they wandered, around the corner until they were in the foyer before the stage set. The red light wasn't on. In the morning they'd be rehearsing, not taping.

"Look, I understand your jitters," Victor said, preempting her rant. "But you committed to this strategy. Reluctantly or not, you committed. And the casting call barely made it into mainstream media since the setup was so fast. It was just on some websites and a cable news show Tuesday night. The real thief probably didn't even see it."

"First of all, I think we have to assume the thief keeps up with all things *Lust* related, no matter how obscure. And secondly, I can change strategy any damn time I want. Not changing strategy is a bad strategy. How'd that work out for the folks on the Titanic, huh?"

"For god's sake, Frankie, the thief probably would have struck even if you hadn't okayed the auditions."

"For all we know, the thief could be sitting in those auditions!" She flung her arm out toward the hallway around the corner just in time for it to hit Luke Blades smack in the face, who hobbled into view at that moment, the blow sending him careening toward the wall as his crutches fell with a clatter.

"Oh my god, Luke! I'm so sorry!" She rushed to stabilize him, grabbing him by the arm on one side while Victor reached for him on the other. When he was upright, Victor handed him his crutches.

"Wow, Frankie, you've got a punch." Luke rubbed his jaw.

"What are you doing here today?" she asked.

"I'm shooting the kidnap scenes. They're fitting them in right after rehearsing."

That was right—Frankie had okayed it what seemed like a lifetime ago.

Before he ventured onto the set, he pulled something from his pocket—Frankie's phone!

"You forgot this. Found it on the counter." Handing it to her, he left.

"Thanks!" she yelped before he disappeared through the door.

Victor scowled. "I thought he was moving out."

"He is!" Frankie roiled at Victor's change of subject. "And it simply isn't your business anyway. It's not like we're—"

"Sleeping together?" Victor said.

"Ms. McNally!" Another voice joined their private conversation. Frankie looked up and Hank stood just five feet away. How long had he been there? What had he heard?

"Frankie. For god's sake, will you please just call me Frankie?" she snapped.

But for once, Hank was not intimidated. Color flaming his face, he stepped forward, hands grasped in front of him, and took a deep breath. "Frankie, I really have to express my deepest disappointment and sadness. You promised me just the other day that you would let me know of any cast openings, and now I see we are in the midst of a major casting call, and yet you cruelly and flagrantly ignored my request—unless I received a message I don't yet know about—to be notified of such a casting call." He breathed fast, as if he'd memorized this speech and was glad it was over.

"What?" she asked, genuinely confused.

"My cousin Thane," Hank continued. "I told you he was looking for work, and you promised me you'd let me know of any auditions. And I promised him, too."

She hit her head with her hand. Crap. She'd completely forgotten.

"I'm so sorry, Hank. But don't worry. This role isn't really being cast. It's just a huge publicity stunt." She glared at Victor.

"It might end up being cast," Victor countered. "And stunt or no, you agreed to do it."

"Frankie, Frankie," Hank said. Now Frankie wasn't so sure she liked him using her name. "My cousin Thane is a fine actor whose day of fame is surely just around the corner. I offered him to you, professional to professional, and you coldly ignored my generosity. I can't say how disappointed I am in you. I thought we had an agreement." He was getting better at this. A sense of injustice rolled off his tongue.

"Hold on, hold on," Frankie said. "I'm not disrespecting you, okay, Hank? You're great. You do great work. Don't get any ideas of taking off or"—she looked at Victor—"I'll have to sic this fellow on you. Tell your cousin's agent to give me a personal call this afternoon. I'll get him in to try out. But don't get his hopes up. This role might not be cast after all." And she stomped through the double doors to the set just as the red light for taping went on, eliciting a curse from the director that could be heard throughout the entire building.

―⁓―

Two hours later Victor was still fuming over Frankie. But by that time he had figured out the root cause of his anger. It wasn't the back and forth over the thief. He'd always understood that her attachment to that story and his publicity attempts was tenuous at best and would require constant upkeep.

No, it was that damned Luke Blades showing up with her cell phone, a reminder that the fellow was still sharing her apartment. And bringing her the phone was, in a way, an act of intimacy, a gesture saying, "I'm looking out for you, kid." Meanwhile, he'd been unable to spend any more time with her, not even one-on-one meetings to go over show-related material. He knew she was avoiding him.

"Dammit, you're too old for this." Too old to be hurt.

But that was just the thing—Frankie made him feel youthful. Not just because she was so much younger than he was, but because she was lively and fresh and vulnerable and, well, dammit, he was in love with her. He was experienced enough to know his own heart. This wasn't just a schoolboy infatuation. There was something about her that answered something in him. Dammit to hell, but he was too old for this!

He slipped in a DVD of the day's thief auditions and started clicking through black-garbed actors mouthing their lines. But his mind wasn't on it. He was thinking of Frankie and him, of how they were both similar but from far different social strata. Her father had been a free-love hippie type. His parents had been beatnik-generation wanderers. Both Frankie and Victor had rebelled against that lack of structure by seeking it. She'd embraced academic achievement. He'd found solace in military order and duty. That duty had even seen him through the years after the divorce from

Linda when he avoided any kind of commitment to a woman so as not to upset his relationship with his daughter, made fragile at the time by the rupture of the marriage.

Now no duty called, at least not in that part of his life. And he felt... at sea. He liked rules. He liked order. He liked predictability.

His phone buzzed. Bob's voice cut through as soon as he picked it up.

"Burton Gilroy is returning your call," Bob's voice announced softly.

"Good. Put him through." Victor leaned back. Burton was a brother of a fellow Victor had served with. Now Burton worked in Hollywood, a mid-level executive with a competing network. That was one thing about the military—you met a lot of people and forged strong bonds.

"Burton, thanks for getting back to me. Must be early out there!" Victor said, segueing into small talk about Burton's brother and then his own interim work for *Lust for Life*, the Pendergrast family's pet project. "Look, the reason I'm calling is to get a handle on when Brady Stephens will be starting on his new project for you. Just trying to work out some scheduling, and I can't seem to raise him yet on his cell." Always best to pretend you have information you don't have in order to shake more free.

―᷍᷍᷍―

"The what?" Frankie stared at Nory while clicking the thief auditions playing on her computer to "pause." Nory, dressed in fringed skirt and boots, stood in the doorway, fresh script pages in hand. She'd been going to email them, she told Frankie, but she'd marked them up. But as usual with the mysterious girl, she'd come to Frankie's room with gossip as well as work.

"*The Hate Game*," Nory said. "That's the name of it. Brady is going to produce and own a piece of it."

Frankie scratched her head, unbelieving. "Is he ever coming back?"

Nory shrugged. "It's some reality thing, like *Survivor* and *Amazing Race* and *Top Chef* all rolled into one."

"*Top Chef?*"

"And the hook is that the contestants are put into groups from the get-go, competing against each other."

"Groups?"

"Yeah, like all the Catholics together, all the Jewish people, all the blacks, the Koreans…"

"Ah… I see." *The Hate Game.*

"Brady's really excited about it. Should be a big splash on TMZ by tonight. I heard he's taking a page from you all with that."

"What?" Frankie seemed incapable of anything but one-syllable questions.

"He's using controversy to spark interest. He thinks the thief stuff you're doing is brilliant." Nory shifted her weight. "I mean, that's what I heard. Tom has a friend in marketing at…"

Frankie stopped listening as Nory prattled on about Tom's friend of a friend of a friend and how Tom was now working on a new project with a docudrama-meets-*Borat* kind of feel and Nory really thought this would be his big break.

"When does he start this *Hate Game* thing?" Frankie asked.

Again Nory shrugged. "Dunno. Might have started it already."

"And you say TMZ will have it tonight?"

"Think so." Nory nodded. But did not move.

"Something else?"

"About my vacation…"

"Oh! Sorry—I thought I'd approved it." In the hubbub of the last few days, it had slipped Frankie's mind. She vaguely remembered the dates Nory had suggested—one week a month hence.

"A whole week—you usually only take a day here or there."

Nory looked down, smiling. "We're going to Nashville."

"Really? That's great, Nory!" Frankie quickly okayed the vacation, happy to know Nory was going to get to see her country heroes.

But as soon as Nory had left, Frankie's goodwill turned sour. Hadn't Nory told her recently she'd been toying with writing some country tunes herself? Good grief—Frankie had probably just okayed a job hunting expedition for the girl. Another one over the edge. Damn.

As soon as Nory was out the door, Frankie didn't look over the scripts or continue viewing the thief auditions. Instead, she picked up the phone and called Mary in PR to let her know that a truckload of crap was headed her way with Brady's resignation hitting the press before it came through internal circles.

"Oh, thanks, Frankie, for the heads up, but I already knew."

"He told you?"

"No, Victor just called. He told me. You guys are really on top of things."

Victor already knew? *And for how long?* Frankie wondered. Victor might have professed his love for her, but he was awfully sly around the office. Could she really trust him? She rang off with Mary and clicked the thief auditions back on. Drone after drone after drone appeared on the screen, all mouthing the words she'd written, but none of them lighting a spark.

"Assuming you'll use the character anyway," she growled to herself.

Oh, who was she trying to kid? She wasn't forcing the thief stuff to stop, because she was invested in the character now! All her protests were just bluster. As soon as she'd started writing the auditions, the fellow had begun to take shape in her mind, become flesh and blood, a part of the Crestview community, its story. She would cast him, all right. She just wanted to get past this ghastly business with the real thief.

A soft knock at her door had her clicking the computer to "pause" again. "Come in," she yelled. Kayla was gone an awful lot the past few days. Frankie hadn't seen her once.

Hank stopped in, looking sheepish. "I'm sorry to disturb you, Ms. McNally."

Oh, so they were back to "Ms. McNally."

"No problem, Hank. Come in. I still haven't heard from your cousin's agent, by the way."

"Well, that's just it. I called Thane—that's my cousin—and, well, I've been meaning to let you know, or, rather, I thought you assumed, but, well, I'm acting as his agent."

"Oh, I see." She smiled to herself. So Thane didn't have an agent and was using his cousin for the job. Some people thought getting into TV and theater work was as easy as showing up and saying they were ready for their close-ups. They thought good looks was all it took. It would make sense that Hank, a fresh-off-the-farm type himself, would have a cousin with those same sensibilities. She wondered if he even had the looks. Hank was not a bad-looking fellow, in that Jethro Clampett naïf way of his.

"Don't let that fool you, Ms. McNally—me being his agent, that is. Thane's been serious about acting ever since he was the infant Jesus in the living nativity. It's just that, well, he knows this is something I'm interested in, so he let me have a try at it." Hank strode across the room and put an envelope on her desk. "There are his photos and resume."

Frankie stared at the envelope and then at Hank. His cousin had let him agent him because he knew Hank was interested in that sort of thing. First, Nory running off to Nashville, and now Hank running off to William Morris. Was there anyone at *Lust* who enjoyed their job and wanted to stay here?

Speechless, she opened the envelope to appear polite and interested, pulling out the eight-by-ten glossy and neatly printed resume. She had to suppress a chuckle. Thane had listed all of his work experience—not just the acting. Every job the guy had held since high school was on there, with references.

"Not bad," she said, scanning the photo of a good-looking guy with the same wild eyes as Hank's and an oddly familiar look to him. "But he still needs to call to set something up. I mean, you need to set something up. Look, call the casting director. I'll let him know to expect to hear from you. I promise."

Hank beamed. "Oh, thank you, Ms. McNally. I'll just step out and tell Thane. I mean, I'll step out and call him."

"Wait a sec," she said as he turned to go. "Have you seen Kayla around lately?"

"Why, yes, I saw her just a few minutes ago."

"When you came in to see me?" Kayla had not been at her desk then. Was Hank covering for her?

"No, before that. Over in Production. That's where she's working now."

Crap. HR had actually listened to Frankie and transferred Kayla.

When Hank left the room, Frankie picked up the phone and talked to a very sweet, but very flustered Sylvia in Human Resources, who explained that Frankie had only requested Kayla be transferred and not that Frankie get a new secretary.

"Well, I want her back," Frankie said. A disappearing secretary was far better than a disappeared one. "And I want her back now."

After hanging up the phone, she looked at Thane's photo again. She was surprised it was an actual publicity photo and not some digital pic taken at the beach last summer. Very nicely done, actually, with Thane leaning into the camera, his rugged chin resting on his fist. What was it that was so familiar about him? She stared, searching the photo for clues. Thane was wearing a plain turtleneck with a designer logo on the neck, one earring, tousled hair…

Hey, wait a minute! She fumbled through a file drawer and pulled out Luke Blades's publicity photo. Same pose, same turtleneck, earring, and hair! Even the facial structure was similar. If it weren't for those wild eyes… the two could be twins.

Ohmygod, ohmygod! Possibilities tumbled through her mind like skiers in an avalanche. Sure, they'd killed off Donovan's "evil twin," but it had been one of those open exits where the audience might not be sure he was really gone. The schedule had been a bitch for Luke—playing double parts. And now he wasn't even capable of playing one part with his broken limb.

Ohmygod, ohmygod! This is perfect!

Frankie shot up from her chair and ran to the door. "Hank!" she called out, but he wasn't there. Kayla, however, was coming around the corner with a box of belongings. For once, someone had done something ASAP when Frankie had asked for it ASAP. This truly was progress.

"He just left," Kayla said.

"Was he with someone?"

Kayla nodded, shuddering. "Yeah, some creepy guy that was like a cross between Hank and… Luke." She made a face as if she'd sucked on a lemon.

"Help me find him!" she called to Kayla as she ran off down the hallway, pulling her cell phone from her pocket. A Luke doppelganger could solve so many problems—get them out of this stupid kidnap story, give them a great premise for the thief.

"Please, oh, please, let him be able to act," she murmured to herself as she flew around a corner. And why didn't she have Hank's number on speed dial? Whatever number she had, he wasn't answering. She called the casting director instead, alerting him to Hank's imminent call, telling him she wanted to be there for the audition. Why hadn't Hank mentioned the resemblance? Did he not see it himself? Mmmm… with Hank, maybe not.

Chapter 17

THE NEXT MORNING VICTOR picked up a dozen roses on the way into work, planning to leave them on Frankie's desk. They weren't just because he was trying to woo her—which, he'd decided, was what he needed to do. Yes, some good, old-fashioned wooing, with all the trappings. She'd been treated shabbily by her ex and by who knows how many other feckless lovers. He would show her how a man should treat a woman.

But the roses were also a celebration gift. He'd had a call from his inside source at the police station. They'd brought in a suspect in the thief case—it could all be over and done with soon, allowing Frankie's conscience to rest easy. His source said this was a solid lead, so Victor was sure they'd be fielding calls from the media soon. He was already forming the words of a statement as he made his way up to his office—he would talk about how this "nightmare" was over, pointing out how *Lust* would continue to go on to entertain millions in the years ahead, and hinting at an exciting story line involving the soon-to-be-cast role of the thief on the show.

His heart lightened. Maybe when this damned thief thing was resolved, Frankie and he could get past the tension it generated and into smooth riding with their relationship. According to the market research surveys he'd ordered, *Lust*'s ratings were holding and growing. He was confident that Frankie could lead the show to more successful times. He had a plan for that, too, now that he knew Brady Stephens was soon to be out of the picture.

"Bob, could you have Raeanne come see me sometime this morning?" Victor asked, walking past his secretary toward Frankie's office. "And call Mary in Publicity. Set up a meeting with her and Frankie and me ASAP."

He glided around the corner and into Frankie's office. She wasn't in. Good. He'd leave the flowers and explain them later.

As he set the vase down, his gaze landed on a publicity photo on Frankie's desk. It was Luke Blades. A wild, slightly off version of Luke, that is—probably taken years ago. What was Frankie doing staring at a photo of Luke? Despite himself, Victor felt himself heat up with irritation. It was the type of thing a fan would do—moon over a photo of a star.

Please tell me you're not doing that, Frankie.

A hastily scrawled note beneath the photo read *thief audition*, with an afternoon time and the day's date.

What the hell did that mean? They'd seen all the thieves they needed to see. Was she considering having Luke try out for the thief? It was one thing to turn his character, Donovan Reilly, into the thief, but he'd never agree to actually audition for the part. It would be a slap in the face.

Victor smiled. Good. Maybe Frankie was smacking Luke Blades in the face.

He left.

———

Frankie wasn't smacking Luke Blades in the face. In fact, she was doing anything but. She was back at her apartment, trying to convince him to stay in town for a few days, because he wanted to go off to a friend's cabin in Vermont for an extra-long weekend, since he wasn't shooting anything more until next week.

"But that might change," Frankie said, her hands on her hips. She stared while Luke threw clothes into a duffel bag in her living room. He'd told her first thing he'd be going—he'd gotten permission from Maurice.

But Frankie wanted to audition Thane and see if he was good enough to use in a thief/evil-twin story. If he was, she might need Luke to hang around to retape some of the kidnap scenes to reflect a new direction, and that would have to be done pronto. Then she wanted to do an audition scene between Thane and Luke, to see what the chemistry would be like and if it would ignite whole new possibilities for stories.

She just didn't want to alert Luke to this possibility. Yet. In addition to all her other plans for this audition, she had one sneaky motivation as well. She wanted Luke to see his lookalike and wonder what the future would hold for Donovan if a Donovan-like actor were also on the show.

She thought she'd had it all set up, too. Thane was scheduled to come in at one, and Luke had originally been scheduled to come into her office for a meeting about "direction for Donovan" around the same time. Her plan had been to catch the audition—it shouldn't take long—taking Luke along with her. And it had taken some maneuvering to get this stupid Thane audition on the books, too. After all of Hank's pleading, it turned out that Thane's "real job" meant he had a tight schedule and couldn't get away easily. She'd only managed to shake his hand and get a measure of him when she'd run after him and Hank on a wild goose chase. Good voice, nice manner—if a little "off," like Hank.

"And just what are you going to do at a ski resort anyway?" she asked when Luke didn't respond to her. "Sit around as the 'after' picture?"

"Huh?" He looked up.

"You know—before and after." She pointed to his cast. "Forget it. I really wanted to talk to you this afternoon about, you know, Donovan and where he's going and—"

"You're here. Can we talk now?"

"Well, no." She glanced at her watch. "Because I really don't have time now. I have to be at a… another meeting. To discuss Terri."

"Boy, she's already looking blimpy, isn't she?" He shook his head, then smiled at Frankie. "I'll be back in a few days and we can talk till the cows get home."

She sighed. And decided to try a different tack. "Do you have to go? I was kind of getting used to having a man around. Made me feel protected."

"I thought you wanted me to find another place to stay!"

"Well, yes. Long term, of course." This was going nowhere. She could just insist he come in, but that would ruin the effect. She was ruining it enough already. "What time's your friend picking you up?"

He shrugged. "Noonish."

"Have him pick you up at work. I promise we'll be done by two!" Okay, maybe three, but he didn't need to know that. He grudgingly nodded, and she went back to the office.

———

At the office later in the day, Frankie sneezed for the fifth time in one hour. The roses on her desk were not only incredibly fragrant but also pollen laden. Or maybe she was no longer used to the smell of fresh things after living in the city for so long. The roses had brightened her mood when she'd come in that morning, but now they were annoying her. She'd spent hours distracted by trying to figure out who sent them, but none of the suspects on her list would have acted anonymously. She picked up her phone and buzzed Kayla.

"Kayla, do you know who dropped off this vase of flowers this morning?"

Silence, then, "What flowers?"

Frankie heaved a sigh. "Never mind."

As soon as she hung up the phone, though, she rebuzzed her secretary, wanting her to remind Victor of the one o'clock audition.

"This is *Lust for Life*'s administrative assistant, Kayla Johnson. Please leave a message after the beep." Damn. She was on the phone. Frankie stood and stretched. She had just enough time to grab a quick sandwich from the vending machines around the corner. It wasn't gourmet, but it would keep her stomach from grumbling during the audition. She'd stop by Victor's office first, reminding him of the one o'clock.

Victor welcomed Raeanne into his office and asked if she'd like a cup of coffee. When she shook her head no, he nodded to Bob, who hovered at the door, indicating he could leave. Victor didn't go back to the chair behind his desk but sat instead in one of the comfortable chairs in front of it, directly across from Raeanne.

"When we talked before," he began, smiling, "I told you that if you stayed at *Lust*, there might be some exciting opportunities."

Raeanne blushed and looked down at her nails. "Yes, I was very happy to hear that."

"From what I understand, you've done great work here," he continued.

He knew Raeanne had been cagey about where she was headed, but he'd done some digging. Brady Stephens had offered her a job as assistant producer on the start-up show he was grabbing. Victor had been shocked when he'd first captured this tidbit. Although he didn't know Raeanne well, he'd sized her up as a pragmatic, sensible, but ambitious woman. Hitching your wagon to Brady Stephens might be ambitious, but it was hardly sensible.

He could understand her reluctance to go public with that information. She wanted the jump up; she just didn't like that she had to hold her nose to do it. He had been gratified that she'd so quickly given up the Brady Stephens opportunity when he'd suggested there might be more promise staying at *Lust*.

"I try my best," she answered, again not looking at him. She seemed uncharacteristically shy. Maybe she was nervous about what he had to offer.

"Every breakdown I've seen of yours is exceptional," he said. "Clean, well thought out. Ready to go to dialogue." He'd learned quickly to recognize those skills.

Now she did look at him and batted her eyes. "Why thank you, Victor. I do try. I started as a contract scriptwriter, you know." She leaned forward and patted his hand, a friendly gesture, except she did let it linger a moment too long. She was Southern, though, and perhaps friendlier than most.

He nodded, pulling his hand back. "It shows. You understand what needs to be on the page to set the scene."

"Well, when I was a lowly scriptwriter, it used to take me eons sometimes to figure out what they wanted from some of the breakdowns. I'd end up watchin' old shows over and over to catch the context, which ate up a lot of time. So I try to fill my own breakdowns with lots of motivational information. I've rarely had to reject dialogue pages as a result." She was looking at him now, obviously proud of her work. She leaned forward again, but this time it merely revealed more of her shapely figure.

"Have you ever thought of advancing… beyond just a team writer?"

"Well, I do hope to land bigger and better things." She tilted her head in a coy gesture and smiled.

Now he leaned forward. "I'm sure you've heard about Brady leaving," he said. "Which isn't a bad thing." He watched her. She continued to smile at him. "Brady has his strengths, but storytelling like this isn't one of them. He's more suited to… oh, I don't know, maybe some silly reality show destined to last half a season before being yanked, embarrassing itself out of existence."

He wanted her to know she'd made the right decision giving up the Brady Stephens opportunity. She nodded.

"No, it's not a bad thing that Brady will be leaving *Lust for Life*," he continued. "It needs new direction, someone who really cares about it, someone who can step up to the plate and direct and shape its future. Someone who cares about stories, who takes the time, like you do, to get things right."

She was fixated on every word, nodding and swallowing hard.

He beamed a grin at her. "Sure you don't want a cup of coffee or something?"

"Uh, some water would be good."

He stood and went to the door, opening it and asking Bob to fetch water for Raeanne and coffee for him.

"Anyway, I pity the poor souls who get involved in Brady's start-up. Lots of people think those things can be stepping stones to bigger jobs. But they can be career killers, too. You end up hiding them on your resume and trying to account for the hole in your work life." He shook his head. Okay, enough of that. He had sufficiently let her know she was making the right call. "But say, I'm not here to talk about Brady. I'm here to talk about you."

She nodded, now smiling at him. "Yes?"

"With Brady leaving, there'll be a shake-up here, like I said. Nobody can make any promises, of course, until official word comes down, but the head writer slot might be open."

The head writer? Frankie stopped outside Victor's office. Was he offering her job to Raeanne? Was this some sort of joke?

Her breath came fast, and she clenched and unclenched her hands, trying to get sensation back in her fingers. She put two and two together and kept getting three—Raeanne in her job, Victor pulling the strings, and Frankie out on the street selling cosmetics.

But now things were starting to make sense. Raeanne had been evasive about where she was going. Then Victor had sweet-talked her into staying. He must have promised her that something would open up. Then Frankie had slept with Victor. Then she'd given him the cold shoulder. My god, was this repayment for that? Giving her job away?

Despite her best efforts to remain calm, she felt unshed tears sting against her eyelashes. Injustice stabbed. And this was more than unjust. It was traitorous. At the very least, Victor could have told Frankie first. He could have broken it to her gently: My dear, you are so talented, so skillful, but Raeanne has more of what *Lust* needs...

Crap. A horrible thought flitted through her mind. Maybe he'd bedded Raeanne, too. Maybe all his talk about falling in love was just talk. *Sweet-talking men are everywhere, Frankie, m'dear.* And with his advanced age, he probably had years of experience with it. Why, he probably had the equivalent of a PhD in sweet talk.

But still, this was a low blow, to have him giving her job away. She was good at it, dammit! She was a fine writer and knew *Lust* like the back of her hand. Surely she'd proven that a thousand times over since Victor had come on board a short while ago.

So what if she didn't have terrific leadership skills? She was learning, and working to learn more. She had all those books on her to-buy list! And she was constantly leading the team in her own way. Okay, maybe more like nudging and prodding. Like a tugboat, really. But that was a form of leadership. Didn't tugboats eventually lead big fat ships into safe harbors? Why didn't people celebrate the lowly tugboat, huh? Why was it always about the big shiny ship with its huge bulging... towers? Tugboats were important! Tugboats were necessary! Tugboats were leaders, too!

The Tugboat Theory of Executive Management—maybe that was the book she needed to write...

"Can I get you something, Ms. McNally?" Bob stood before her, holding a cup in each hand and looking at her oddly. Like Natasha on a spy mission, she was leaning up against the wall right next to the door.

"Uh… huh… no, thanks." She relaxed her stance and looked at her watch. "Just, uh… catching my breath. Have to go… busy… like a tugboat, pushing big boats to harbor. Important work…"

He still looked at her oddly. "Do you need to see Mr. Pendergrast?"

She squared her shoulders. "No. Just remind him of the audition at one. That's all."

—⁓—

"Give him a prop to hold! Or put someone in the scene with him. Don't just feed him the lines from the table!" Frankie barked at the casting director. She was in a foul mood, still stinging from the overheard conversation in Victor's office. She was glad to be so busy, though. It kept her from dwelling on his betrayal.

They'd been at it for a half hour. Thane Galahad was so close to being just what they needed, but it was that tiny piece that was missing that seemed crucial. He said the lines okay. He looked okay. He moved okay. All of that would have been enough, would have been something they could work with, but there was this indefinable "offness" to him that had her suggesting different takes.

She couldn't put her finger on it. Maybe it was that wild look in his eyes, the same one that seemed to come over Hank occasionally. Maybe it was the creepy resemblance to Luke. She had to keep blinking to remind herself that this wasn't Luke. Maybe it was the voice. Thane had a velvety baritone, so soft that they had to keep telling him to speak louder. It had an odd Southern accent to it, too, that he obviously tried to hide. So sometimes he would say, "I want your valuables," and sometimes he would say, "Ah want your valuables." If they hired him, which Thane would they get?

Making the audition even more difficult was Hank. He lurked in the corner, a clipboard in hand, smiling as his cousin performed, taking his role as agent extremely seriously.

"You know, you don't have to stay," Frankie whispered to him. "I think your cousin is doing fine."

"Oh, I do need to stay. I am acting as his agent right now." Hank wrote something on his clipboard.

She just stared at him. She'd created a monster. Then she leaned over and whispered in the ear of Nick, the casting director. "I need to talk to you. Let's step outside."

The burly man stood, taking off his earphones and following her into the corridor. She smiled at Hank as they retreated. "We'll be right back. Need to talk to him about something else."

She looked over at Thane. "Just keep running the scene. Try it different ways. Sad. Angry. Happy. Anything you can think of!" She flew out of the room with Nick behind her.

"What's the matter with him?" she asked as soon as the door closed. Through a two-way mirror, she could see Thane begin the scene again. But the sound was off, so it played in pantomime. He must have been doing "happy," because a smile as bright as Times Square lit his face. They both stared at him, appalled yet unable to look away.

"That is what's the matter with him," Nick said, pointing to the enthusiastic Thane. "He's like a big puppy dog that doesn't know when to stop jumping on you."

Frankie put her hands on her hips. "But we can ratchet that back, right? He's so damned close to being perfect! If we can just figure out what it is that makes him a bit off, maybe we can fix it. Maybe with good direction…"

"Good direction—say, is Maurice leaving?" Nick asked, refer-ring to *Lust*'s current director. At first Frankie thought he was being sarcastic, but then realized he was being perfectly sincere. Everyone assumed people were leaving *Lust* and looking for opportunities to move up. Just like that quisling Raeanne, or Kayla, or Nory… or even Hank!

"No," she said, quickly qualifying it with, "not that I've heard of, anyway." She turned her attention back to Thane. "If Thane had some coaching, maybe he would be right." She sighed, watching Thane now switch to "sad." He was holding his hands to his head as if tearing his hair out.

He looked just like Luke, sure. But he would require so much coaching that paying another actor to get plastic surgery might be cheaper. She voiced this last opinion to Nick, who chuckled.

"Oh, he beat you to that. Turns out our wacky boy here already had plastic surgery."

Thane seemed to have moved on to some unrecognizable emotion now, rolling his eyes to the ceiling and clasping his hands to his chest.

"What? He had surgery to—"

"Yup. To look like Luke. He loves the show. Has watched it forever."

"Ohmygod." She felt like she *had* to offer him a part now. He'd gone under the knife just to look like his hero! She'd heard of this sort of thing before, but had never come face to altered face with it.

Her thoughts were interrupted by a click-thump, click-thump as Luke Blades himself rounded the corner.

"I thought we had a meeting. Kayla said you were down here!" he said as he came into view.

Luke's gaze went to the window, and then he did a double take as Thane launched into yet another rendition of the scene, this one some exaggerated method acting style with brooding stares and furrowed brows.

"What the…?" Luke hobbled over to the window. He looked at Thane. He looked at Frankie. He looked at Thane again. He looked back at Frankie. "What are you doing here? Are you recasting Donovan? I'm getting my agent on the line."

He shuffled a little as he tried to retrieve his cell phone from his pocket. "This is a low blow, Frankie, something I'd never have expected from you. Cheap shot, that's what it is. Cheap shot. I want to improve myself doing *Hamlet* and you pull this stunt!" He gestured to the window and almost fell.

Frankie stepped forward. "Not recasting. Just a possible double while you're out of it, that's all." But of course it wasn't all, and she was glad he was seeing it that way. *Take that, Luke Blades. You're not irreplaceable.* But she hadn't expected him to reach for his agent immediately. She had just hoped for a quick reality check.

"I was thinking maybe we could bring back the twin," she said in a more conciliatory tone. "Remember what fun that story was? Remember all the fan mail?"

Luke nodded, remembering, loving the memory.

"But remember what a bitch it was to learn all those lines? The long shooting schedule? You could never do that if you were working on Broadway, too. So I thought we could use good ol' Thane here…"

Thane was throwing himself against the walls, playing the scene as if he were a lunatic.

Frankie cleared her throat. "Uh, in fact, while you're here, I was hoping you could run some lines with him. You know, like you do with Kayla from time to time."

Thane bounced off the mirrored wall, startling them all.

Luke was shaking his cell phone as if that would make the reception come into play. This deep in the building it was hard to get a signal.

"Say lines with him? You want me to help my replacement get the job? That takes balls, Frankie." He laughed, a bitter Donovan-was-just-betrayed laugh. "And here you were telling me you wanted me to stay at your place because you liked having a man around."

Another male voice cut through the scene, but this one was

Victor's. He, too, showed up, just in time to hear Luke repeating Frankie's lie about wanting Luke to stay at her apartment. "Are you talking about staying on the show?" he asked pointedly, but it was quite clear he'd heard Luke correctly.

"No, I was talking about…"

"Of course he was talking about staying on the show," Frankie said, stepping in front of Luke. "That's what this audition is about. Keeping Luke—or, rather, Donovan—on the show while Luke is incapacitated. I wanted them to run lines together, in fact." She gestured weakly to the window.

Thane was now writhing on the floor. Was this some sci-fi take?

Victor stared. They all stared. "Who is that?" He turned to Luke. "Your brother?"

"Hell, no. That freak is no relative of mine."

The door opened, and Hank stepped out on the tail end of Luke's line.

"What did you just say?" Hank asked Luke.

"He said…" Frankie searched for something diplomatic. "He said that that meek man was not related to him. Because, you know, Luke is not the shy, retiring type. And your cousin is obviously a very modest man for having such… such enormous talent."

Thane was now skipping around the room performing the scene as if he were a child.

Hank seemed mollified. "I was wondering if you were going to ask him to do any more, Ms. McNally, or if you've seen enough."

Oh, she had seen more than enough. They all had. Thane was sitting on the floor sucking his thumb in between lines, playing the scene as an infant. Someone had to stop him.

"I just wanted him to read with Luke, since Luke is here," she said, inwardly cringing.

"Why should I read with him?" Luke asked. "If you hire him, you hire him."

"I want to see the chemistry," Frankie said.

"Chemistry? Is there some story coming up you want to tell me about?" Luke asked, staring at Thane, who now appeared to have dropped into a coma-like trance, mouthing his words at the ceiling.

"Well, if he does become the thief, and then the two of you play..."

"The thief has been caught," Victor announced.

"What?"

"Huh?"

"No!"

This last came from Hank, who didn't wait for any further explanation but rushed back into the audition room, presumably to tell his cousin.

Frankie turned to Victor. "You knew this and didn't tell me?"

"It's not official. And I haven't had a chance to talk to you. You're very hard to get hold of these days."

"Is that why you were talking to Raeanne earlier?" Frankie asked, unable to keep an accusatory tone from her voice.

"What?" Victor asked.

"Does this have an impact on our thief?" Nick asked, but no one seemed to be listening. "Are we casting this character or what?"

"Damn. I was hoping I'd get to play him in a scene," Luke said. "I had it all worked out in my head."

Frankie ignored him and went back to Victor. "I can certainly understand how meeting with other writers would take precedence over talking to the head writer—or should I say *current* head writer—about something as trivial as whether or not a hazard to public safety that originated with a story on our show has been taken care of!"

Victor crossed his arms over his chest and glared. "I told you, it's not official yet. I was going to check in with my contact after the audition. But I did leave you some flowers to celebrate early."

"Oh, so those were from you!" she said. "Thanks. I enjoyed looking at them when I wasn't sneezing."

Hank burst through the door with Thane right behind him.

"As my cousin's agent," Hank announced, "I have to demand that he be given a shot at another character, since the thief has now been caught. You have wasted his precious time, and I think it only fair that he be allowed to try for another slot, now that the thief is leaving the show."

"The thief was caught in real life!" Frankie shouted. "Not on the show! Can't you get that through your heads! They are two different animals."

"Funny how you wouldn't listen to me when I told you that," Victor grumbled.

"How did they catch the thief?" Thane asked, so softly that no one heard him at first.

"I don't know," Victor answered. "Like I said, it's not official. But as Frankie has pointed out, it has nothing to do with whether we continue the thief on the show. That decision is in her hands."

Silence dropped over the scene. They all stared at her, Victor daring, Luke annoyed, Nick waiting for orders, Hank confident in his new role, and Thane... Thane was glancing from one to another with his body perfectly still, making him look like a doll with googly eyes.

She breathed fast, wondering what to say. Where was that "Little-Tugboat-that-Could" attitude when she needed it? She had enjoyed working up the various thief scenarios. She had become invested in the character, just as Victor claimed. It would be good to continue it so that *Lust* didn't have to quickly wrap up a loose end in some non-credible way. And if the real thief were no longer a problem...

Victor's cell phone buzzed. How did he get reception down here? Did he have some special satellite hook-up? He took the call.

"Uh-huh... Yeah... Oh, I see... Yes, yes... No, that's okay. Thanks for letting me know." He flipped the phone closed. "That was my police contact. The thief hasn't been caught. The suspect they had in custody had a rock-solid alibi for two of the three burglaries. The real thief is still out there."

"Yes!" Thane's muted voice whispered.

Chapter 18

"Well?" Victor stared at Frankie. "What's your decision about the thief? Does he stay or not?"

"And does Thane get to play him?" Hank added with unusual confidence.

Just a second ago, Frankie was ready to give an unqualified yes to continuation of the thief. Once she'd gotten into writing his character, she started to see a story emerging from the mist of imagination. He was quirky but good-hearted. He had a past—she hadn't decided exactly what it was yet, but it involved some sort of heartbreak or hard times—and he wanted to do good but somehow had snapped. He never harmed anyone. He just wanted to make a point, to let the poorer people of Crestview know that someone was looking out for them.

Now those stories evaporated as she once again thought of the real thief and the public safety hazard he posed. And they'd been so close, so close to having the thief problem go away—the real thief, that is—resolving her moral dilemma once and for all.

Victor didn't wait. "Let me know when you finally make up your mind." He turned and walked away, pulling out his cell phone in the process. She could hear him talking with Mary, the PR gal, telling her to work up a stand-by statement in case news broke about the suspect being caught and released, saying the show was disappointed, along with all New Yorkers, that the thief hadn't yet been caught, but had every confidence that the NYPD would bring this scofflaw to justice.

"We will keep the thief," she called after him. "And Thane will play him!"

Hank and Thane started jumping up and down. Luke mumbled something and limped away. Nick looked at her as if she were crazy. She left the scene, hurrying after Victor.

—w—

He had grabbed the elevator before her, so he was sitting behind his desk when she stormed into his office a few minutes later. There was no avoiding Victor now. This was war. She didn't wait to be welcomed or to be seated. She stood in front of his desk, ready for battle.

"The thief stays, in case you didn't hear me," she said. "And I'm hiring Thane to play him."

"So you've made that decision on your own." His tone was businesslike. She couldn't read him.

"Yes."

He said nothing.

"You're still angry," she said.

"It shouldn't matter what I am. You've made the decision." He looked down at his desk as if he were calming himself. Then, in a more pleasant voice, he said, "I'm glad you made the decision."

"With Brady not here, I'm going to do what I want. And I want that Thane character."

"He *was* a character from what I could see." Now he sounded more natural, the old Victor. He'd moved past his irritation. Good, so would she. Another notch in her leadership belt—dealing with the annoyed coworker. She relaxed.

"But he has precisely the right kind of quirkiness I want. Viewers will love that. We haven't had an oddball type on the show since 1999 when we had a palm-reading scientist. Anyway, I can think of a long, drawn-out intro that will have viewers guessing if it's Luke who's the thief or this new character. And we can use him to double for Luke while he's recuperating. Long, shadowy shots. I can get him into the sack with Terri and set up her on-show pregnancy to parallel her real one. Many problems solved at once and no sacrificing the integrity of the story."

"You really think you can get this Thane fellow up to the level you need?" Victor leaned back. The anger had vanished completely, and he was back to helping fix the show's problems. No pitched battle necessary.

"He won't have many lines at the outset. If he doesn't get up to speed by the time he does, we'll replot."

"That's gutsy."

"We have to take chances if we're going to turn this ship around." With her reference to a ship, Frankie recalled her earlier vision of her leadership style and her anger over Victor's talk with Raeanne. "That's how I roll, Victor. I take chances, yes. But I don't bark out commands. I push and nudge. Like a tugboat. Tugboats are the... the... the leaders of the harbor team. And I'm the leader of this team. I'm the tugboat of *Lust for Life*." Why did that not sound leaderlike?

Victor smiled. "Yes, you are, Frankie. And a very good tugboat indeed."

Was he making fun of her?

"I'm glad you agree. Because I don't think tugboats should be passed over for big, shiny... yachts with lots of big, bulging... bilges... who might be on the harbor team but are hardly capable of pushing the big ships to safety."

Now he looked confused. "Am I missing something here?"

"I mean that I may not be as glitzy and charismatic as say, a Raeanne, but I am certainly capable, in my own dogged and skillful way, of leading this show to success. And I don't think that just because I'm not out there tooting my own horn constantly—"

"Actually, tugboats do toot their own horns."

"Well, this tugboat does not. And just because I'm not out there honking up a storm with look-at-me spandex tops and blonde-above-the-scalp hair, I shouldn't be glossed over if a shake-up in the harbor team occurs." There, she'd spit it out. Whatever "it" was.

Victor smiled again and leaned into the desk. "Sit down, Frankie."

She thought about it. And then sat down. She leaned forward on the edge of the seat, just like Victor was doing. She looked serious.

"It's funny you should mention a shake-up, because *Lust* is about to have one," he began. "Brady Stephens is leaving."

"I know."

"And that means the show will be in need of a new executive producer."

"The network will probably field candidates," she said.

"But Pendergrast Soap, as the main sponsor, could have a large say in that decision if the right word were placed to the right people." He threaded his hands together.

"Of course."

"And my plan was to talk to you about whether you'd be interested in the job. Because if you are, I would say that right word to the right people."

She blushed. She sat up straight. She swallowed.

"And I'd suggest to you that keeping Raeanne on as a head writer in that case would be a wise decision."

She nodded. "Good continuity. I know I can work with her. And she's a good writer with leadership qualities."

"Exactly. But she was getting ready to bolt. So in order to keep her around long enough to allow you to choose her for head writer, I talked to her. I didn't make any promises. But I did let her know that promotion was possible."

"That was risky. You didn't know if I'd approve!" She bristled as it all sank in, Victor making all these plans for her. On the one hand, Victor was flattering her by offering her the possibility of Brady's job.

But on the other hand, he was acting like the grand puppet master by also offering Raeanne the possibility of the head writer position should Frankie move up. The executive producer, whoever he or she was, should be making that decision, or certainly having substantial input.

"What happens if I don't want to choose her?" she asked, her tone sharp, her leg starting to bounce and her fingers tapping.

Victor raised his hands in the air. "You just said she'd be perfect!"

"I said she'd be good," Frankie corrected him. "And as executive producer, I'd certainly want to be in control of that decision, whether Raeanne or someone else were to fill the slot." She glared at him. "What sort of promise did you make her anyway?"

"None! I was careful not to do that. I merely told her there might be an opportunity."

"Just like you're doing with me now."

"What I'm doing is trying to save *Lust*—the job I came here to do."

"I thought you said we were to work as equals."

He opened his mouth, closed it, looked away, shaking his head just the tiniest bit in frustration. "I don't think I ever used those precise words, Frankie. That was always your assumption."

"So we're not equals. I've been laboring under a misperception." She stared at him through narrowed eyes. "You're really my boss."

He sighed heavily. "In a way, yes. It's been a somewhat flexible arrangement, which is why I didn't use a heavy hand."

She stood. "So I guess I just slept my way to the top."

It was as if she'd slapped him. He straightened.

"No!" He stood, too, his fingers tensed in anger at his side. "How could you think such a thing—about me, about yourself?"

She could think it because she was Frankie, ex of Brian Aigland, daughter of Peggy McNally, who'd been abandoned by her man. She could think it because she was mad as hell to realize she'd been operating under the wrong premise, thinking they were working side by side when, in reality, Victor considered himself her superior no matter what he mumbled about "flexible arrangements."

So he'd been patronizing her, pretending not to be the guy in charge, letting Frankie, the plebian, think she was a member of the Roman Guard. What fun that must have been for him—to watch her acting as if she were his equal. Nothing made her angrier than condescension. She'd had enough of it in her life already, from snooty professors to snooty classmates to a snooty husband and his family. She wouldn't take any more.

"It's over," she said. "Whatever you and I were starting—it's over as of this second." As the words came out of her mouth, her heart sank a little. *You don't know what you've got till it's gone*, the song said. It was true. "If I get the promotion, I'll know I got it because I deserved it."

Victor's face was a mask, but she noticed he swallowed hard. He came around to her, as if to see her out.

"You do deserve it, Frankie," he said, almost in a whisper. His eyes shone. "I didn't ever intend to make you think otherwise. I…" He took both her hands in his. She felt the warmth of his fingers, his body heat, his breath. She closed her eyes in anticipation. But at the last second, he stopped himself, that solid discipline kicking into gear, and pulled back. "I'm sorry I gave you the wrong impression."

He shook her hand, as if she were nothing more than a business associate.

―⁓―

"Mom, I think I'm in love." An hour later, Frankie was on the phone in her office with her mother. She'd called her as soon as her blood had stopped pumping at gusher speed and she could breathe again. She hadn't realized how much she was beginning to care for Victor until she broke it off with him.

Yeah, she was still mad at him, but mad the way lovers are—aching to make up, with all the perks that went with that. She'd spent an hour fuming and fussing in her office, rattling off the many reasons to be angry with him—she was justified in her wrath, of that she was sure. But why had it hurt so damned much? Because she'd begun to care for him, that's why.

"Really?" Her mother's tone was cautious. Frankie had been in love before—with Brian Aigland.

"This is different, Ma. This guy is… well, he's…" And she went on to discuss Victor's background in the Marines, his chivalry, his smarts, his good looks, his accomplishments. On this last point her mother was unusually perceptive.

"My goodness, Frankie, either this fellow is some kind of child genius or he's—"

"Older. Yeah, he's older. My guess is he's fifty-something." And she sighed. Because she knew what the next question was going to be. It didn't take long.

"Does he want more children?"

"Well, it's not so much a matter of 'want,' Mom." And she told her mother about the vasectomy.

"Oh," was all her mother said. Damn. Frankie knew she probably wanted grandchildren. So did Frankie! Well, children first, that is.

"I don't really know if he wants children," Frankie went on. "We didn't pursue the subject once I learned about the—"

"Snip-snip," her mother finished for her. "Are you sure he's the one?"

"I don't know. I mean, I guess I want to find out." Of course, there was that little part about the breakup five minutes ago. Why had she felt compelled to share with her mother the story of her affection for Victor just after she'd given the fellow the heave-ho? So she went on to explain that situation as well.

Her mother laughed. "So you're calling to tell me you think he's the one—right after you've given him the boot."

"It's not really the boot. It's more like… the slipper." She smiled at her mother's laughter. "It's just that I don't want people thinking I slept my way to the top. And he's pretty powerful around here, being the sponsor of the show and all." Whoa, she'd just admitted to her mother that she'd slept with Victor, not something she usually discussed with her despite their close relationship.

Peggy McNally was nonplussed, however. "Very noble of you, my dear. But I'd say the only person who needs to feel sure you didn't sleep your way to the top is you. Screw everybody else." She paused. "Not literally, of course."

"Yeah, yeah, I guess that's true, but…" But what?

"Are you sure you didn't cool your jets because you have other issues? Like maybe this kid thing?"

Frankie didn't say anything, but that didn't stop her mother from continuing. "I mean, honey, we both know that even if you're pure as snow, some folks are still going to think you got where you are because you're an attractive woman."

"Thanks, Mom."

"No, listen. No matter what a good girl you are, there might be some gossip who thinks you went to bed with someone to get ahead. You have to learn to get past that. So if you really wanted to be with Mr. Methuselah—"

"Victor."

"With Victor, I don't think office water cooler talk should matter. The question you need to ask yourself is, is there something else bothering you? Is it the kid thing?"

Why'd her mom have to be a buzz kill? Here she was all hot and bothered with the realization that she was falling in love—albeit with the guy she just broke up with, but, hey, that was just a minor detail—and her mom had thrown a big dumpster of water on those embers.

"Does it matter to you? That you wouldn't be able to have kids with him?" Peggy McNally pressed her daughter.

"I don't know." She turned and stared out the window. Yeah, it bothered her. But in her "bother" priority list, the Victor-as-boss thing had taken precedence. She would have to focus on the kid thing eventually, though, if she got to the make-up-after-breakup point. Maybe that's why she was talking to her mother. Maybe she was trying to figure out if there should be a make up.

"All I know is he's everything I thought Brian was. He's protective. He's strong. He's sure of himself. He's"—good in bed, no need to share that—"honest and brave and… and he takes care of his elderly aunt, Mom. It's really very touching."

"Think about it, Frankie. If you're taking a break with him, it's a good time to evaluate how much it would bother you not to be able to have kids with him."

"They can reverse vasectomies, you know." At least, Frankie was pretty sure they could. Hadn't she seen a medical show about that? Or maybe it was a story they'd done on *Lust*…

"But you don't know if he'd want to do that, right? Because you never talked about it."

"It's not exactly dinner conversation, Mom." And it wasn't as if they'd had much of a relationship anyway. They'd slept together once. They'd shared some intimate kisses.

They'd connected, dammit! Wasn't that enough?

"If you're serious about this guy and you want kids, you have to have that conversation at some point. Otherwise, you shouldn't waste your time. Take a deep breath and ask yourself if you want to have that conversation, and how you'd feel if he said 'no dice' to reversing the slice." She snickered at her little joke. "Maybe it'll help you decide what to do."

Her mother sounded like Gail. Gail had decided the same thing—not to waste her time if her man wasn't going to step up to the plate. There was something liberating in knowing one way or another if it was going to work instead of building up these fantasies and being disappointed when they didn't come to pass. She'd built up fantasies with Brian, that was for sure.

"What should I do—have him fill out a questionnaire?"

"No, but there are ways to find these things out."

"Yeah, like in the middle of a writers' meeting. Right after we discuss Donovan and Terri's pregnancy, I can turn to Victor and say, 'What about you, Vic? You want more kids? And if so, what are you prepared to do to get them?'"

"Donovan and Terri are going to have a baby? That's great! I knew that was gonna happen sooner rather than later. But how you gonna pull that off if Luke can't, you know, perform?"

Frankie smiled. This was comfortable territory—the show. She relaxed. "Shhh… don't tell anyone. The actress who plays Terri is preggers and we're writing it into the show. As for Luke…" And she was off, telling her mother what was up with *Lust for Life*, who was slated to be with whom, how they were going to use a double for Luke, and where the stories were headed. Frankie's very real problems faded into the background.

By the time she got off the phone, the day was ending. She didn't want to go home just yet, though. She was still aching in her soul. Instead, she turned to her computer and began pounding out ideas for the show.

—⁓—

A very pregnant Terri rubbed her swollen belly as she sat in the Kendall mansion living room. When Anne Kendall entered the room, Terri stood, but the matriarch waved her back to a seat.

"I see it didn't take long for you to get in the family way," Anne said acidly. She went to a nearby sideboard and poured herself some water. "It's that Reilly boy's, I presume."

Terri noticed that Anne Kendall didn't offer her anything to drink. "Why, of course it's Donovan's!"

Anne eyed her over her crystal glass. After she sipped, she walked to a chair opposite Terri and sat down. "At one time it could have been my late son's child."

"No, it couldn't have been," Terri said. "Since Roger had a vasectomy."

Anne stared at her. "What?"

"He never told you?"

"Is that why you left him?" Anne Kendall visibly whitened, her hand fluttering to her throat, obviously surprised by this bit of news.

Terri paused, then shook her head no. But Anne Kendall could tell in the girl's hesitation that it had played a role. Her son had lost a princess because of that surgery. He would have died a happy man if Terri had stayed with him.

"I just came here to tell you how happy I am," Terri continued. "No stunted hopes or misdirected aspirations for me. I'm happy at last. Gloriously happy."

Anne softened. She sighed and eventually patted Terri's hands. "Of course. And I'm happy for you. You're aglow with joy, just like any woman would be in your condition—loved and in love, and carrying your beloved's child. I understand why you chose Donovan, my dear. I hold no grudges."

Chapter 19

VICTOR WENT HOME THAT evening with an empty heart. What had he been thinking—starting a relationship with someone who could be perceived as a subordinate? He knew better than that. If you're in a position of power, you don't become sexually involved with those who need that power to further their own careers. You don't start something with someone who might fear saying no.

And then there was the whole business of whether he really was her boss. Sure, he'd thought of himself that way when Brady had let him in, but he'd quickly surmised that the best way to work with Frankie was to do it on as equal a footing as possible. He was good at sizing people up, and he'd sized her up as needing to know she was still somewhat in charge.

"Somewhat," he snorted to the empty room. "You know better than that." He'd fooled her, knowing at any moment he could have pulled the plug on whatever she'd wanted to do. He should have been clearer from the outset. And he shouldn't have gotten involved with her. He was too old for this.

He threw his keys on the counter and pulled a bottle of Scotch from his liquor cabinet, tossing in a few drops of mineral water and downing the whole thing in one swift gulp like a cowboy standing at a saloon bar. With the liquor warming his chest, if not his soul, he walked to the windows and stared at the dark evening.

He could try again once this gig with *Lust* was over. Start fresh, with no work relationship interfering. But he had this nagging feeling that something might get in the way. Not something. Someone. Luke had known her longer. Luke was attractive. Luke was talented.

Luke was… young.

The age difference with Victor must have crossed her mind. It certainly had crossed his. He'd never seen himself falling for a younger woman. He'd always thought if he settled down again it would be with someone from Linda's set, or maybe a fellow soldier's widow, someone who understood who he was.

But Frankie understood. That's because she was, at heart, the same kind of person. She was a realistic dreamer. Except for the mistake of marrying that jackass Brian. But they'd both made mistakes in that regard. They'd both married people who ultimately betrayed them. Another bond.

"Dammit," he said out loud. "Maybe you just aren't that into me."

Suddenly he couldn't stand the thought of time on his hands. It wasn't that he had been a social animal before Frankie. He had just been content. He would read in the evening or go over marketing reports for whatever company he was consulting for. He would go to the theater or opera as part of charity fundraisers. He would meet Courtney for dinner. Increasingly, he would head out to visit his aunt.

His aunt—another kind of guilt washed over him. He had not called her today. And hadn't checked in with Dane about how the search for a caretaker was going. He flipped open his phone and dialed his aunt's number. It rang and rang. No answer.

He tried her cell number, even though he knew she never used it. He'd bought it for her months ago, and she kept it in a drawer in her bedroom. No answer there either.

She didn't go out anymore. And she was a light enough sleeper that the phone roused her. He tried her main number again. And again. He tried it four times. Still no answer. His blood began to pump fast, and his palms started to sweat. He quickly looked through his phone's directory for Dane's personal phone and dialed it. Voice mail. He left a message.

"This is Victor Pendergrast. I've tried to reach my aunt and no one answers. Could you please call me back as soon as possible?"

As worries started to build, he wondered if he should hit the road for Connecticut. If so, it shouldn't be with a glass of one-hundred proof in his system. He made himself a cup of coffee and found enough in the fridge to cobble together a sandwich. He flipped on the news, only half paying attention while he waited for a call back. He would try his aunt and Dane again in a half hour if he hadn't heard anything.

Twenty-five minutes later, his phone rang at last.

"Mr. Pendergrast, sorry for the delay. I was actually meeting with a potential caretaker. I think she'll work out well, in fact, and I'd like you to meet her," Dane said. "She's the fifth one I've interviewed. I'd about given up on finding someone suitable."

Victor breathed a sigh of relief. "So Gussie liked her?"

"I don't know yet. I thought I'd do these preliminary interviews first, and then after getting your okay we'll find a way to have Gussie meet the person or persons we like best."

Worry returned, creasing Victor's brow. "Gussie isn't with you?"

"Why, no. I'm home. Just got in."

"She's not answering her phone," Victor said.

Dane didn't say anything at first, but then replied, his voice filled with uncertainty. "It's possible she went to bed and didn't hear the phone."

"Has she ever not answered when you called?" She always answered when Victor called, even if she'd been heavily asleep. The phones in the house were numerous and very loud.

"I don't call often, of course, because I'm usually right there, but, no, she might take a while to answer, but she will answer. Did you let it ring a long time?"

"At least twenty times."

"Did you try recently?"

"I was just about to." Victor paced to the window, gritting his teeth. This didn't feel right. "I'll try now and get back to you." He hung up the phone and dialed his aunt again, letting it ring a long time. Still no answer. He called Dane back and gave him the news.

Dane didn't hesitate. "I'm twenty minutes away. I'll go check on her."

"I'll head out, too."

"There's no point in that," Dane said, his voice muffled. He must have been donning a coat. "I'll call you as soon as I get there."

"Look, I wouldn't mind visiting her anyway. I'll head over. You've got my cell number. Call me as soon as you find out anything."

With growing anxiety, Victor threw some clothes in a duffel bag, drank some water and threw a couple bottles in his bag, heading for the door.

He had no doubt he was sober. His blood was racing through his veins like a NASCAR auto in the lead. His heart pounded fast and furiously, and he warmed from the adrenaline rush of worry.

He made it on the road in record time, heading for the interstate out of the city in less than an hour. He was just pulling onto the highway when his cell buzzed. He hit "speaker," knowing Dane would be on the other end.

"I've called the police. She's not home, Mr. Pendergrast. The front door was unlocked, and she left a note for me saying she'd gone to look for 'Donovan.'" He paused. "I'm sorry, Mr. Pendergrast. I really thought she was okay. She seemed better the last time I was here."

Victor gripped the wheel. "I'm going to give you a name of someone I know on the force. Give him a call. And call my lawyer. He might know an investigator." He rattled off the names. "Call me as soon as someone arrives. Turn on all the outside lights. Call the neighbors." Dane had already done some of those things, but the more Victor could think of, the better he felt. "I'll be there in an hour." If he avoided speed traps, he'd be there in far less time.

—◊◊◊—

Frankie entered her dark apartment and flipped on the switch. The living room and kitchen were neat and clean. Luke had had the decency to do that before taking off for the weekend. She wondered if he really did have a ski weekend planned or if he was trying to make her feel his absence. Wasn't that supposed to make the "heart grow stronger" or something like that?

Did she miss him? She missed somebody, that was for sure. She'd gone from having two guys after her to having none. One she'd kicked out and the other she'd broken up with. And which one should she try to reconcile with anyway? She'd not even given Luke a chance. Maybe she should have let him into her heart more. He was her age. He could have kids.

She threw her attaché bag by the couch, then poured herself a glass of wine and looked in the fridge. Some cheese and grapes. How romantic. She popped some grapes in her mouth and pulled out the cheese, searching for crackers in the cabinet. With the box under her arm and the cheese and grape plate in one hand and her wine in the other, she plopped down on her sofa, clicking on the TV after settling her makeshift dinner on the cushion next to her.

The news flickered past her while she halfheartedly ate. Maybe her mother was right. Was it really necessary to give Victor the kiss-off? There would always be talk at the office. She shouldn't let it bother her. If Victor's inability to have children bothered her, well, that was a whole other kettle of embryos. She needed to resolve that. She couldn't just assume he wasn't willing.

First step, Frankie: find out if he'd even want to have more children.

Second step: find out if he would be willing to go under the knife again.

Oh, preliminary step before these steps: make up with him.

She finished off her wine and went to get another glass. She brought the bottle back to the living room.

By the third glass, she had rehearsed an entire conversation with Victor.

Frankie: So, Vic, remember when you introduced me to your daughter?

Victor: Yes?

Frankie: I was thinking how great it would be to have more like her.

Victor: Well, there is that little vasectomy thing in the way.

Frankie: You do know they can be reversed, don't you?

Victor: I had heard, but had never investigated.

Frankie (pushing several brochures about the subject across the table to him): You might want to look these over. It's a painless procedure.

Victor: Why thank you, Frankie. This is wonderful! I'll look into this right away!

Frankie: So you'd like to have more children... if you met the right woman?

Victor (eyes sparkling): Yes, most definitely.

By the end of the third glass of wine, she was dialing his work phone. When she got his voice mail, she left a rambling message:

"Hey, Vicco, good to talk to you. Really sorry about that goofy convo we had in your office. Don't know if we really need to go that far. I mean go all the way. With a breakup, I mean. And I was wondering, well, if we could talk about some more things. Like your vasectomy. I just thought, you know, it's something we shouldn't be afraid to talk about."

After the phone call, she set her glass aside and leaned into the pillows, glad to have accomplished something important.

She fell asleep a few minutes later as the news anchor announced that the jewel thief had struck again.

Chapter 20

AT FOUR O'CLOCK IN the morning, a team of searchers that included Victor and Dane found Gussie Pendergrast sleeping under a pile of horse blankets in the stable of a neighbor's estate. She was bright and happy when they woke her, only slightly dehydrated and minimally affected by hypothermia. She refused—with a display of indignant stubbornness that brought a smile to Victor's face—to go to a hospital, pointing out that her nephew and Dane could take care of her.

When questioned about her midnight stroll, she had a vague memory of going to "look for someone," but either was cogent enough to hide the fact that this "someone" was a fictional character or had forgotten the nature of her quest.

Within an hour of finding her, Victor and Dane had her settled into bed, a warm toddy by her side and her favorite dog-embroidered wrap around her shoulders. He told Dane to join him in the living room for some coffee.

Victor could breathe again. The hours he'd spent looking for his aunt had been among the worst in his life. He would never have forgiven himself if something had happened to her. During those long, cold, dark moments as he walked over frozen fields and along empty country roads, he had questioned himself on his latest strategies. He was so sure that keeping *Lust for Life* going was a good idea, so happy when he'd lit on this idea to prolong a sense of continuity in his aunt's life. But had he just been putting off the inevitable?

He should have been out here 24/7 helping Dane find a caretaker Aunt Gussie would tolerate. That should have been his number one job. He suddenly realized why Frankie had wrestled so much with the public safety issue of the thief. If someone you know has been hurt, you don't fool around. Frankie had seen that potential with the thief story. He would trust her judgment more in the future—if there was a future for him and *Lust*.

"You said you think you found someone to watch her," Victor said, handing Dane a mug. Dane sat in front of the fire that Victor had lit. The fellow was worth his weight in gold.

"She's a retired nurse," Dane explained after taking a sip. "Very motherly but not… smarmy, if you know what I mean. I don't think Gussie would tolerate that."

Victor knew exactly what he meant. His aunt didn't suffer fools gladly. He nodded and Dane went on.

"She—Viola Conway—is a widow with grown children. She loves to read mysteries. She had some responsibility when she was in nursing. Was a head nurse and then taught for a while. She's a no-nonsense type but no Nurse Ratched. She loves dogs. But here's the icing on the cake—she adores *Lust for Life*. Has watched it for ages. Never minded taking the late shifts, because it meant she could catch the show."

Victor smiled, but only a little. His preoccupation with saving the show might have led to his ignoring this caretaker issue for too long.

"How do you propose we get around the fact that my aunt loathes the idea of having a companion?"

Dane shrugged. "I think we might need to bring on some tough love, Mr. Pendergrast."

"Call me Victor." He should have given Dane that liberty long ago. The man took more of an interest in his aunt's well-being than his own father did. He'd left a message for his father hours ago and had yet to receive a call back.

"Well, Victor, I think that we can't beat around the bush anymore. She either accepts a companion or…" He shrugged again, and Victor knew what it meant. Or they looked at institutionalizing her.

"You're right. There's no soft-pedaling it. I'll handle talking to her. I'll bring in Dr. Baker. She trusts him, looks up to him."

Dane looked into the fire. "You know what would make it easier?" He smiled. "If you could get someone on that show to convince her."

"You mean one of the actors, coming here?" It made Victor shudder to think of involving someone like Luke, or any of the stars, in his personal business. If he let them into Gussie's life, there was no telling what damage they might do in the future. No, he didn't like that idea at all.

"I mean through one of the stories," Dane said. "Have someone convince someone like Gussie to take a companion."

Victor looked into the fire, thinking about it. There was the Anne Kendall character—she was around his aunt Gussie's age, or at least was a matriarchal type. She was widowed and childless since her only son had been written off the show in a mysterious car wreck years ago. There were certainly enough parallels. But the character of Anne Kendall was of a sturdy, healthy woman. The actress who played her was nimble and spry.

"I don't know," he murmured. But he continued to think about it.

"It's the one thing we have going for us—Gussie's interest in the show. It really brightens her day when it comes on. I watch it with her, you know. I have to say it's been pretty darn good lately."

Victor nodded. Yes, ever since Frankie had taken over as head writer, it was pretty darn good. He looked at Dane. "So you think if someone on the show has to be convinced to take on a companion, that would be enough to convince Aunt Gussie to do the same?"

"Maybe not alone. I'm just thinking that our urging, combined with the show and maybe an introduction to Viola Conway—all of that together could be the tipping point," Dane explained.

"Let me think about it," he said to Dane. They finished their coffee, and Victor insisted that Dane sack out in a guest room. Dawn was breaking, but Victor might be able to grab a couple hours' sleep.

—⁓—

"I know it's a weekend, but I want to know if you check Mr. Pendergrast's voice mail!" Frankie leaned into Bob's vacant desk, his phone pressed into her ear. She'd risen at seven with a numbing ache but enough memory of the night before to recall her embarrassing message on Victor's office phone. This is why she was a one-glass-of-wine-with-dinner gal.

It had occurred to her during her third cup of coffee that morning that maybe good ol' efficient Vic allowed his secretary/administrative assistant to retrieve his voice mail for him. The thought of Bob listening to her ask questions about Victor's vasectomy made her want to upchuck.

She'd raced through a shower and changed, then took a taxi into the deserted office in search of Victor's voice mail password. Surely if he allowed Bob to get his messages for him, good ol' efficient Bob would have it written down somewhere! *Please oh please oh please oh please!*

But, no, Bob was so efficient that he locked up his damned desk.

"How cynical you are, Bob!" she'd said to the empty office as she tried a paper clip in the lock. "What were you thinking—people are going to try to steal things from you?" The paper clip broke. She used another one to try to jiggle the broken part free. *No can do.*

That's when she'd noticed the directory on Bob's pristine desk. The directory of top management for *Lust* plus team writers, etc. Decision makers. Office, home, and cell phones. She flipped it open and her heart soared. Yes, it included secretarial numbers, too, and

Bob had added his to the list. She dialed his number without thinking about what she'd say. While she dialed, a piece of paper slipped out—contact information for *Days of our Lives*. That was odd...

"Ms. McNally, I don't think I can give out that password. I'd have to check with Mr. Pendergrast first. Is this an emergency?" He sounded drowsy, and she thought she heard another voice in the background.

So Bob did check Victor's voice mail! *Oh no oh no oh no!* "Well, it sort of is an emergency—but I don't want you to disturb Mr. Pendergrast. I just need the password, that's all."

A long pause.

"Are you still there?" she asked.

"What message is it you need to get?"

"Uh, one that I left about something that... that's not true... and it might, it might upset him to hear it, and it's kind of sensitive material that I really don't want getting out at all."

"Mr. Pendergrast is not a gossip, Ms. McNally. And neither am I."

"Oh, no, I would never think that he was a tattler of any sort. Nor you! But this material, well, it really shouldn't be shared at all, seeing it's not true. Why, it could even have ramifications with Homeland Security, you see, because it deals with the police and the thief story, and so I really think it's the most responsible thing to get rid of this message immediately."

"You mean it has to do with the thief striking again?"

"What?"

"It was on the news this morning. He apparently struck unusually early last evening—around seven, the police think."

Frankie's stomach sank. Things just got worse and worse.

"I'll look into that. I mean, I will certainly make sure that *Lust for Life* is acting responsibly. But that brings us back to this message."

"Look, Ms. McNally, unless you want me to contact Victor about giving you his password, I think the best thing would be for me to retrieve the messages, and when I get to the one from you, I'll just hit 'delete' without listening."

She didn't like that very much, but Bob was a play-by-the-rules guy, right? So he would stay true to his word, right? He wouldn't listen to the message. He'd just delete it. He had to do that. It would be cruel not to. He had just assured her he was not a gossip!

"Ms. McNally, I give you my word. I'll just delete the message without listening to it."

She sighed. "Okay, Bob. As soon as you hear my voice, you just smack that 'delete' button, okay? It's critical that you do this. Absolutely critical, I tell you. If you listen to it, well, I'll have to kill you."

Twenty minutes later, Frankie was sitting at her own desk, a mocha from the nearby Starbucks in hand and several newspapers in front of her. She quickly found the story of the latest jewel thief burglary, and her heart raced as she read the report: "…Mrs. Eunice Pepperdine, a widow and heir to the Pepperdine oil companies, discovered the theft when she returned to her apartment to retrieve a shawl she'd wanted to take to the opera. Police believe she may have missed encountering the burglar by mere minutes…"

Oh my god. What if that poor old woman had run into the thief? What would he have done? What harm would have come to her?

Frankie put her coffee down and stood, pacing to the window. Sweat beaded on the brow of her pounding head. She wouldn't be able to live with herself if someone were hurt by this thief. It wouldn't matter how many times Victor tried to convince her that it wasn't *Lust*'s fault. In her heart she would always wonder if pulling the thief story from the show would have somehow made a difference.

She ran her fingers through her unruly hair. She crossed her arms. She blinked fast.

And she let out a growl and a curse.

She wasn't afraid of going up against Victor. No, her scruples could take that fight, and she knew she'd best him this time.

She had a real fire in the belly to do what she believed was right in this case. And that was pulling the story. She'd waffled before because she'd begun to associate *Lust*'s thief with the real thief—a harmless eccentric who posed no real risk. But this near-miss story of the widow had brought that fantasy crashing down into hard-rock reality. The real thief could be dangerous. And no one should encourage him.

It wasn't these thoughts that had her muttering curses, though. It was the thought of giving up a character she now really liked, one she'd fully embraced. When Victor had convinced her to let things ride, to even cast the darned character, she hadn't been able to stop the creative juices from flowing. That was the real reason for her back-and-forth on the story. Deep down, she'd wanted to keep him all along.

She turned back to her desk and pulled up the various notes and breakdowns she'd worked on ever since the thief had begun to grow in her mind. She'd written some more since the Thane audition. And what she'd written had mirrored his personality—slightly off but not dangerous, a quirky spirit who could turn into a sprite, an imp, or just a sweet love interest for one of Crestview's inhabitants.

She read through each page, saying farewell to her lovely thief. She had even coined a name for him—Heathcliffe Chamberlain. Heath for short. It was both manly and different.

With a trembling finger, she hit the "delete" button. It had to be done. She couldn't worry about what Victor would say. With Brady out of the picture, she was the captain of this ship. Not just of the tugboat, but of the ship itself, dammit.

She then looked up Mary's number—the gal who did PR—and left a message saying she needed to talk to her immediately about the thief story. "It's urgent."

She thought of leaving a message for Victor but didn't want to bollix up the arrangement she'd made with Bob to erase her previous message. She could call Victor on his cell, of course, but she didn't want to risk that call triggering a check of his office voice mail before Bob had a chance to work his erasing magic. Victor would fall in line. This thief business had to stop.

Maybe it was a good thing they'd had their little "breakup," she mused. Maybe it was clearing her head.

There was another person she needed to call, though, and that was Thane. They wouldn't be needing his services now, at least not for the thief. Maybe to double for Luke? No, she didn't think so. They could get any stand-in for that, as long as they didn't show his face.

She sighed, rummaging among her papers for poor Thane's photo and resume. She would talk to him personally, assure him they'd notify him of the first opening.

As she stared at his photo, she remembered what an odd duck he'd been. Just like his cousin Hank. Still with that whiff of the farm on him, and an overeagerness to please and grab attention that put goose bumps on your arm. He'd calm down if he stayed in the business.

Where is your phone number, Mr. Thane Galahad? She looked at the resume and found the number at the top of the page. As she dialed, she looked closely at his work experiences for the first time. He'd listed all of them, after all, not just acting gigs. She smiled, seeing his stints at fast-food places and retail outlets, all with the reason for leaving as "to pursue better career opportunities." As she punched the last digits of his number, she read his description for his current job: *Salesman, RightMight Security Systems: Sell home alarm systems to upper-income single residents...*

Aww, poor Thane schlepped around the condos and apartments of the rich and elderly crowd trying to sell them on protective electronic equipment. He probably got along with those old blue-haired ladies with his backwoods politeness and eager-to-please attitude. Frankie guessed he did well. A lot of widows and spinsters would be charmed by him…

With a snap, she hung up the phone before it rang through.

Widows… Thane probably saw a lot of them in those neighborhoods. Widows like the one who was just robbed.

No, it couldn't be. She was still under the influence of the hangover. She needed to drink less. No, maybe more. If she drank more, three glasses of wine wouldn't make her crazy like this, imagining all sorts of wild things.

Speaking of wild, wasn't the thief kind of a kook? Wasn't he a fan of the show, leaving roses for his victims just like Lust*'s thief?*

An obsessed fan. A fan who was going to great lengths to show his devotion to…

She looked at the photo again. Thane had gone to great lengths to look like Luke, too.

Thane was crazed. He wasn't just eccentric. Thane was a nut. *Ohmygod ohmygod ohmygod.* It was right under their noses. Thane was not just some off-the-farm naïf trying too hard to impress the *Lust for Life* team. Thane was… the thief! *Ayayayayay! Holy Mother of…*

Her heart pounding now and her hands shaking, she looked for another number instead. The police. She had to tell them. She had to let them know that…

But what would she say? What exactly was her evidence? That he'd had plastic surgery to look like Luke? That his acting style was over the top? That he had wild eyes and was quirky?

Yes, officer, I'd like to report a bad actor.

A bad actor who was eccentric. The city was filled with quirky people. They weren't criminals. If it was against the law to be slightly off-kilter, half the city's residents would be in jail. Not enough. Not enough.

She couldn't just turn Thane in. She would be setting the show up for a lawsuit. Hell, she'd be setting herself up for a lawsuit. There was a chance he was innocent, after all. *Think, Frankie, think.*

Hank. She had to talk to Hank. But why? What could she find out? Thane's alibis for the nights in question? What he was really like? Whether Hank himself had his suspicions? She just didn't know.

She looked for Hank's number and dialed anyway, not quite sure what she'd say. She'd play it by ear once she got the fellow on the phone. He was acting as Thane's agent, after all.

Her heart in her throat, she adopted a cheery tone as soon as she heard Hank's friendly voice on the line.

"I'm sorry to bother you on a Saturday, Hank."

"Ms. McNally? Is anything wrong?"

"Well, sort of. I'm just in the office catching up on some work, and I'm afraid I have some bad news about the thief."

"Oh, dear. I saw the papers. It's awful, don't you think?"

She breathed a sigh of relief. Hank saw the danger, too.

"Exactly. And I'm afraid, upon reflection, that *Lust for Life* just can't continue that story after all. It's not responsible. I have a call into PR about it, and we'll be issuing a statement."

"Oh."

And after a pause, he repeated, "Oh, I see. That means that my cousin—"

"Precisely. I'm afraid we won't be able to bring him on full-time. I'm not even sure there will be any day work for him, either. I'm having to rethink how we pull the plug on the story. It might not be necessary to cast it to do that."

"I understand," Hank said in a voice so mournful that Frankie was afraid he was going to cry. But she used his mood as an opening to talk about Thane.

"I was going to call your cousin myself," she continued. "I thought he should hear it from me personally."

"Thank you, Ms. McNally." Hank sounded like he was sniffling.

"Do you think he'll be really upset?" she asked, tiptoeing up to the subject. "I mean, are you worried about your cousin?"

"Oh, yes, I am worried about Theodore." Hank's words came fast, as if he were relieved to have someone to talk to about this. "Theodore's his real name, you see. He changed it when he decided to come east as an actor. Anyway, he hasn't been doing so well with the acting, and I know his job doesn't pay that well, but he seems to be spending too much money, as far as I can see. I visited him the other day to help him prepare before his audition—I hope you don't mind, but I took the time off; I'll make it up to you, don't worry—and anyway, he lives in this tiny little one-room over in Brooklyn, but he had what seemed to me to be some expensive… things. And we Glenn people are very frugal. I think he was counting on this job to, you know, pay off his debts, because I can't see how he can afford all that… stuff."

Her face warmed. "Back up, Hank. What stuff? What kinds of luxuries are we talking about here? Expensive clothes, furniture… bling?"

"You mean like big gold necklaces and such? Oh, no, nothing like that. But his shelves were full to bursting with those expensive soups, and his freezer had all those frozen dinners that cost so much. I mean, he could be cooking for himself for far less…"

Her heart sank as Hank droned on about Thane's profligate food spending. Where Hank came from, Stouffer's was a luxury. She actually could relate to that. She remembered the days when she and her mother would feast on TV dinners as if the meals were gourmet treats. Thane, or Theodore, might have opted to pay a few dollars more rather than cook from scratch, but that was hardly evidence he was living off the proceeds of pawned jewelry.

Of course, if he'd pawned the stuff, there'd be a trail of some sort. He was probably hording it. If Frankie's theory was correct, he wasn't stealing the stuff for money, but for glory.

Into these thoughts, Hank's recitation of Thane's fiscal improprieties intruded.

"…and my goodness, he had so many fresh flowers in there it smelled like a funeral parlor…"

She sat up straight, the blood once again coursing through her veins. She pressed the phone tight to her ear.

"Flowers? What kinds did he have?"

"I don't know flowers, Ms. McNally. I know vegetables, but not flowers. My mother grows those. I can't tell a daisy from a dahlia."

She didn't want to ask outright if they were roses. She didn't want to tip him off. Hank might be a little dense on some things, but he could be incredibly astute on others.

"Me, too. I'm not so good with the flower thing. I guess that's why I'm not a florist." She looked up, her gaze resting on the bouquet that Victor had given her when he'd thought the thief was caught. "Did you see the bunch I got last week? They're pretty dried up now."

"Oh, yes, those were beautiful. Thane had some like that here. Some were all dried up, too, and I threw them out."

Roses. Thane had roses in his apartment! So many that Hank had had to get rid of the dead ones. Frankie's eyes widened.

"How well do you really know your cousin, Hank?" she asked softly.

"Well, we were never really close growing up," Hank answered. "We'd see each other at holidays and the like. When he came to New York, I tried to take him under my wing, of course, because my mother asked me to."

"When your mother asked you to look out for him, did she mention any, oh, problems he might be having?"

"If you mean spending problems, like the ones I just mentioned, no. She did say that he was very sensitive, and my aunt Miranda—that's his mother, of course—was worried that he was, oh, at the end of his rope, so to speak."

"What did she mean by that?"

"Well, I didn't push her on that, Ms. McNally. But I think she meant that Thane had been working a bunch of jobs and not settling down. You see, he took a lot of jobs just so he could get a good schedule to watch the show. He's a big fan, as you know. But then I started sending him DVDs of the show so he wouldn't have to do that. I hope you don't mind."

"Not at all."

"It's really nice of you to be trying to help, you know, soften the blow for Thane," Hank said. "Are you sure there isn't something coming up on the show he would be right for? I'd already told my mother he got this job, and I'm sure he shared the good news with my aunt."

Her mind racing, she thought of the phone call she would next be making to Thane. Now she was back to wondering if retracting the job possibility from him would tip him over the edge, just as Victor had worried that pulling the thief story would have the same effect. The fellow seemed reasonably mild-mannered, but one never knew…

"Let me look through my notes, Hank. Maybe there's something… I just need to think about things. I'll call you back, I promise, before or after I talk to Thane. But don't say anything to him until I have a chance to work some things out."

"Oh, thank you so much. I'll wait for your call."

She had no doubt he would do just that, probably sitting by his phone all day.

For hours she paced and wrote, wrote and paced, picked up the phone, put it down again, screamed at the phone, screamed at the computer, screamed at Thane. When Mary from PR called her back, she put her off, telling her she'd have more information in a day or two.

She felt completely alone. She couldn't share this with the police—not unless she was sure. She couldn't share it with Victor—he'd want her to go to the police. Not to mention the fact that she still wanted to avoid talking to him until she was sure Bob had deleted that awful message of hers. She couldn't share it with her friend Gail—she was a lawyer and might have ethical responsibilities to report Frankie's suspicions. She couldn't tell her mother—she'd call the police herself if she thought Frankie were involved in something risky. She couldn't tell a living soul. It was all on her to figure out what to do.

She paced some more. She wrote some more. She browsed websites looking for legal and ethical advice. She reread Thane's bio. She went out for a sticky bun. She calmed down.

She had a plan.

After hours of this torture, she finally placed the call she'd been dreading, her hand shaking as she punched the buttons.

"Thane? This is Frankie McNally, the head writer at *Lust for Life*." Her voiced trembled, so she spoke more forcefully. "I need you to stay put so I can messenger over some new dialogue sheets, okay? We'll be doing some fast work on the thief, and I need you to spend all your time studying."

Oh, Thane was all too willing to devote every second of his weekend to working on his new part. Frankie was relieved. He wouldn't possibly rob another soul for the next forty-eight hours as long as she could spin out thief scenes for him to study. She'd bought some time. Now she just needed to figure out what to do with it.

Sister Marie looked up from her prayers. Was that someone at the door or just the wind rattling the hinges? The convent and orphanage were so old and the nuns so poor, everything was in disrepair. She quickly crossed herself, putting her rosary away in her pocket, and walked to the foyer. Sister Helen joined her from another room.

"I thought I heard someone," Sister Helen said.

"So did I." Sister Marie pulled open the heavy oak door with its decorative stained glass windows, letting in a blast of snow.

There, on the front steps, was a huge box. The two women struggled to bring it inside. Sister Helen immediately knelt and began ripping it open.

"Oh, Sister, look!" She held up a stuffed animal, and then pulled out another and another toy. "For the children! They will have a merry Christmas after all!" Tears filled her eyes.

Sister Marie, however, was less sanguine. She stepped over to the door where something had fallen when they'd dragged in the box. It was a perfect ruby-red rose. She picked it up, letting herself smell it before taking it over to Sister Helen.

"Do you see this?" she asked Sister Helen. "This gift is from the thief!"

Sister Helen stopped rummaging. "Oh, no." She stood, clasping her hands together. "But surely we don't need to deprive the children of these presents."

"We can't accept ill-begotten goods!" Sister Marie cried.

Sister Helen went to her, touching her arm. "Maybe they aren't ill begotten."

"They're the fruit of a sin, Sister. They're the result of thievery!" Sister Marie declared.

"But what if the sinner were to confess his sin… and do penance?"

"You mean to one of our priests?" Sister Marie asked.

"No, to the police. What if he turned himself in to the police?" Sister Helen pressed.

"Why, then he'd no longer be a sinner. He'd be a hero!"

Outside, the dark figure of the thief lurked in the shadows, listening to the conversation through the drafty door.

"Turn myself in?" he whispered into the dark. "Be a hero…"

Chapter 21

IT WASN'T EASY. EVEN with Dr. Baker's help. Even with Dane's and Victor's persuasive power. Even with Viola Conway's considerable charm as well. Gussie Pendergrast might be suffering from beginning-stage Alzheimer's, but she had enough of her wits about her to know when her nephew was trying to strong-arm her into doing something she didn't want to do. And she didn't want to admit that she needed live-in help, certainly not nursing help.

For several hours Victor had been talking to his aunt about Viola moving in. It was a bright Sunday morning, and light streamed through the tall windows of the sunroom. His aunt Gussie sat primly in a favorite chair in the corner, the Sunday crossword puzzle on her lap and an erasable pen in hand ready to attack it. Yes, her mind could still be incredibly sharp. And so could her tongue.

"For the tenth time, Victor, dear, I simply don't feel comfortable having someone chase after me like a nanny. It makes me feel like a child." She picked up her reading glasses and perched them on her nose. "Dane is perfectly capable of attending to the household needs. I don't want to add staff."

"Dane has a personal life, Aunt Gussie. He can't be here constantly." Victor paced to the window, hands in pockets, and looked out.

"Nor would I want him to be here constantly. That's just the point!"

"But you need… someone." He sighed. Although he'd explained to her several times how she'd wandered off in the night, he got the impression she didn't quite believe him. She had little memory of the incident, and what she did remember she waved off as "sleepwalking" that wouldn't happen again.

"You're overreacting," she said to him, studying the puzzle in front of her and jotting in a word. "I know I'm getting older. But I'm not losing my senses." She said this with almost bitter finality, as if she refused to admit to herself that she could be in serious medical trouble. This is the way it had been since Dr. Baker had diagnosed her. She'd stubbornly refused to accept the verdict, assuring them all that she was merely getting old, not demented.

Victor watched her, her head bent over the puzzle, her small hands quickly filling in blanks. She'd always been an independent soul who cherished her privacy. He couldn't blame her for not wanting to give that up.

"If you don't allow Ms. Conway or some other suitable companion to stay with you, you know what will have to happen, don't you?"

She looked up, her face pale.

He smiled, putting her at ease. "I'll have to move back in with you."

"Be my guest, Victor. I'd love to have you!" She grinned, calling his bluff. She knew he'd never institutionalize her. Hell, he knew he'd never be able to. She'd fight him legal tooth and nail on that one, and he'd admire her every step of the way. No, his aunt was going to stay just where she was. He merely had to get her to agree to a live-in nurse.

He sat on the ottoman near her knee. "Tell me what you didn't like about Ms. Conway."

"Oh, I have nothing against her. She was very pleasant, in fact."

"You had things in common."

"Yes."

"And she assured you she would give you your space."

"I'm sure they all say that at the outset."

"What about a trial run at least? Say, a couple weeks?"

Gussie took her glasses off and stared into her nephew's well-meaning eyes, her own gaze sparking fire. "I know you mean well, Victor, but this is getting tiresome, and I'm going to have to ask you to stop pursuing it. Or leave."

—◆◆◆—

But he didn't leave. He could be just as stubborn as his aunt. He made an ostentatious show of staying, in fact, calling his realtor and loudly talking about selling his condo so that he could "stay with his aunt." He ordered Dane to draw up a menu of healthy low-carb meals instead of the heavy sauces and old-fashioned dishes his aunt preferred. And he made another performance of arranging for exercise equipment to be moved into a front parlor. All of these activities his aunt watched with silent, pursed lips. She wouldn't give in.

It was a battle of wills, and ultimately he knew he wouldn't win. With her fading memory, she would not recall how long he'd been underfoot, diminishing the impact of his strategy. He had to do something else.

That evening, he wandered into the kitchen for a snack as Dane prepared a cold supper.

"You don't usually work Sunday nights," Victor commented, opening the fridge and grabbing a carrot stick.

"I arranged to take off an extra day this week, so I thought I'd put in some time now."

Victor nodded but inwardly grimaced. His aunt probably didn't even remember the arrangement. Yet one more reason a Viola Conway was needed.

Dane put a platter of chicken and salad on the counter and went to the pantry for a tray.

"Victor, I hope you don't mind my bringing it up again, but I really do think you should consider that other idea I suggested."

"What other idea?" Victor munched on the carrot, trying to remember.

"Using the show," Dane said. He brought the tray to the counter and started arranging dinner on it.

The show. Damn. He still needed to contact Frankie about his thoughts on letting the thief story go. "I'll think about it."

After Dane left, Victor had a quiet dinner with his aunt in the sunroom. He didn't press her on the companion idea, but did probe her on the show, asking her which characters she most admired, which stories she found most interesting. To his surprise, she didn't identify with the older Anne Kendall at all but was fascinated by the new Faye story.

"That Faye has some big decisions ahead," she said seriously, sipping at some tea Victor had made for them. "A younger man or an older one."

Victor smiled at his aunt. "Which would you choose?"

She didn't answer right away, but stared into the distance as if remembering something. Victor thought she'd lost the train of their conversation, but she voiced an opinion a few moments later.

"I think you are a remarkably accomplished man whose spirit is always young."

Victor stiffened. What was she talking about?

"How is that lovely young lady you brought here—her name was Faye, too, wasn't it?"

"No. Frankie was her name." He stood, removing the dishes from the table in front of them. She was confusing the show with real life again. But wasn't that what he wanted her to do?

"Do you admire Faye?" Victor asked her. "I mean, do you trust her? Would you listen to her advice?"

His aunt laughed. "Faye is one of the most down-to-earth

characters I know," she said, a dreamy quality coming into her voice. "She's a salt-of-the-earth type. Yes, she'd be quite the catch for you."

———

He tried reaching Frankie that night, but she didn't pick up her phone. He left a message for her, promising to say more in an email.

"I know it's a lot to ask," he said to her voice mail, "but I'm at the end of my rope with my aunt. I've got to get her to agree to a live-in companion for her safety's sake. And I think the only way to do it is to have Faye argue for the case. I'll drop you some notes."

In his follow-up email his notes were rambling and sketchy. He apologized again for the favor he was asking, telling her wouldn't ask for it if he could think of another way to handle the situation. He needed the Faye scene inserted in an upcoming show right away, which would mean throwing off the whole schedule, a huge favor to ask of an already-overburdened writing team, especially Frankie. And since they'd had no setup to the argument that Faye would need to make to reach his aunt, the task was doubly challenging. He didn't tell her about his aunt's brush with misfortune. That would have made his note an epistle.

At the end of his email, he remembered the thief—"Do what you want with the thief. I won't stand in your way or issue any objection if you want to pull that story. I'm taking a few days off, but you can reach me on my cell. Thanks. Victor."

Chapter 22

THE REASON FRANKIE'S CELL phone was off Sunday evening was because Luke insisted she turn it off so she could relax. When he came home from his "ski trip" late that day, he found her curled up on the sofa with a wet cloth on her head, nursing a migraine.

"Let me make you dinner," Luke said, hobbling into the kitchen and pulling out the only protein she had available—a half dozen eggs.

She didn't protest. She was glad he wasn't irritated with her any longer. "I can't believe you can cook so well," she murmured under her damp cloth.

"I'm sure there are lots of things you don't know about me, Frankie McNally."

She heard him pulling out a pan and knew she should offer to help, but her head was throbbing too wildly to do anything but lie very still. The headache was her own stupid fault. She'd worked herself into a state of nervous exhaustion on Saturday, trying to figure out (a) how to determine if Thane really were the thief, and (b) trying to figure out a way to get him into the hands of the police if he were.

She had managed to buy herself time with Thane by constantly feeding him new material to learn. He'd be so occupied with that, he wouldn't be able to swipe some poor woman's jewels. She must have done up a dozen scenes over the course of Saturday and early Sunday. She knew she was okay when Thane plaintively asked her in a Sunday afternoon call if she thought there would be any more revisions. The fellow was up to his eyeballs learning material, some of it only a few word changes, but she'd insisted he be letter perfect when he showed up on Monday for a shoot.

And just what would that shoot be? What on earth could she write that would have an impact on this deranged man's psyche? She should just go to the police.

No, if she went to the police and Thane wasn't the thief, then she would have ruined him and invited a lawsuit.

On and on and on it had gone until she was pretty deranged herself. Scampering through these big worries like a puppy constantly tripping her feet were thoughts of Victor. Why hadn't he called her? Surely he'd seen the news about the latest robbery. Was his ego so damaged by her desire to cool things that he was backing off of all contact? Way to go, Victor. Way to go, Frankie. You know how to pick them.

"Frankie, sorry to bother you, but could you reach this for me?"

Frankie lifted the corner of the cloth and saw Luke pointing to a shelf above the stove that held spices and canned goods. She dragged herself up and shuffled to the kitchen, pulling down the dried red peppers Luke couldn't grab because of his balance problem.

"No offense, but you look awful," Luke said, beginning to crack eggs into a bowl.

Frankie yawned and pulled a cola from the fridge, downing two aspirin with the bubbly liquid. "No offense taken." She ran her fingers through her hair. "Rough weekend."

"Victor here?" Luke asked, trying too hard to sound casual.

Frankie smiled. He was jealous. "No. In fact, Victor and I are not an item. I didn't think it was a good idea to have an office romance."

She saw Luke relax, just a subtle loosening of his shoulders. The guy was still interested in her. He probably had gone away that weekend to get her out of his hair or teach her a lesson or both. She leaned against the fridge, grabbing a piece of cheese from some he'd grated. Standing made her head feel better.

"I spent the weekend working," she said. "I've got some big problems to iron out." She didn't think it wise to confide in him about Thane.

"Nothing with Donovan, I hope," Luke said, swirling eggs into a pan.

"Don't worry—Donovan's story arc remains the same."

"What about that crazy guy—the double?"

"Nothing for you to worry about."

Luke turned toward her, grinning. "So that was just a stunt to get my goat?"

"Not really." Well, maybe a little. But the "crazy guy" was presenting a whole set of problems now that she didn't want to talk about with an actor on the show, even if said actor was sexy Luke Blades, who seemed to be itching to lend her the proverbial shoulder to cry on.

"That doesn't sound like you're sure," Luke probed.

"I'm sure, I'm sure." She sighed. "There are issues with that character but nothing that concerns you."

"Is that what caused your meltdown?" He shrugged toward the couch where she'd lain all afternoon.

"Partly." And partly wondering why she'd not heard from Victor.

Luke flashed her a sympathetic smile. "If you put some plates on the table, we're ready to eat."

———

Maybe it was the food. Maybe it was the rest of the cola she downed with the food. Maybe it was the great conversation. Whatever the reason, not only did Frankie's headache lift during dinner but she actually felt relaxed and good about herself by the time the last crumb was consumed.

She'd scrupulously avoided talking about her problem—Thane and the thief—which had forced her to really talk to Luke, to get to know him. She discovered he'd never envisioned himself as an actor. He'd started out wanting to be an athlete. He was good at golf, skiing, baseball, and figured he'd go off to college and get some degree in sports management, landing as the head of a chain of fitness centers throughout the country.

He had never had a chance to put those entrepreneurial skills to work, though, because once he was cast in a local television commercial in his hometown of St. Louis, Missouri, his career as an actor took off. More commercials followed, including one that went national, and he was asked to go to New York to audition to be the voice and face for a men's cologne. He landed the gig, but the ads never ran when a corporate decision refocused the company on clothing. Luke was ready to head back to Missouri and sports when the commercial's director called him to cast him in a pilot for a TV series. It, too, failed to launch, but by then Luke had been bitten by the acting bug.

"So I bumped around New York for a while, then went out to L.A.," he said. "And the rest, as they say, is history."

That part Frankie knew. He'd done more commercials, some day parts on California-based soaps, a walk-on here and there on prime time, and finally landed the short-lived but dramatic part of a young but terminally ill murderer on an obscure cable show that lasted a half season. It was enough to bring him to the attention of *Lust*, which was looking for a new heartthrob and thinking of rapidly aging the character of a then pre-teen Donovan Reilly.

"Do you miss it? Home, I mean," Frankie said.

"Not so much anymore. I did at first. You really do feel like an outsider here. And in L.A., too. You know, when you're not from here."

She knew. She still did feel that way. You can take the girl out of the suburbs, but...

She looked at Luke with fresh eyes. She'd always lumped him into the category of narcissistic actor, too risky for a relationship. She knew he'd had several girlfriends over the years at *Lust*, including a relationship with a leading lady that caused complications when the two split offscreen but were still linked on-screen.

Maybe Victor was a stepping-stone relationship, and she should take a chance on Luke?

Whoa—rewind. Where had that thought come from? She took another sip of cola—*probably from your fatigue*, she thought as she gazed at Luke's strong chin and shoulders, his tan face, his crinkling eyes.

"So what are your goals?" Luke asked her, after sharing how he wanted to "gain respect" in the acting world by doing stage work, like the souped-up *Hamlet*. At least he didn't think working on *Lust* was "settling," the way Kayla viewed it.

"If you'd have asked me that a couple days ago, I would have said 'write a great literary novel,' but now I don't know." Or maybe she did know but didn't want to spill.

"Your ex's book," Luke said, making the link between Frankie's comment and Brian's accomplishment. "I heard it has some great stuff in it about you."

"Depends on what you mean by 'great,'" she snorted. She stood to clear the table.

"You really do want to write a book?"

She put plates in the sink and came back for more. "Actually, no. I think what I want to do is make *Lust* work—for the show itself and for me."

"You want to move up then? To Brady's job since he's leaving."

She chuckled. "Word travels fast. Yeah, I wouldn't mind being considered for that job." She took the last of the glasses and cutlery to the kitchen and filled the sink with sudsy water. Luke hobbled over after her, grabbing a dish towel and leaning against the counter to balance himself.

"Better hurry up and let the powers that be know you're interested," Luke said.

She tilted her head to one side, wondering what he knew. "What does that mean?" She handed him a rinsed plate.

"I heard Raeanne was lobbying for the job," he said.

No, not that job. *Her* job.

Or maybe... was it possible that Victor had also hinted to Raeanne that Brady's job could be hers? She mentally shook her head. Those thoughts were dangerous.

"She doesn't have the experience." She handed him another plate.

"She has other things, if you know what I mean."

Good looks, charm—sure, Raeanne had those. But they wouldn't work on Victor, and the network execs were too far away. Right?

Luke dried a glass and set it on the plates. "She's been hanging around Victor a lot."

Frankie's ears burned, but she focused on the dishwashing. "They had a meeting to discuss her future at the show," she said, trying to sound casual. "I knew about that."

Luke laughed. "Just one meeting?"

She ached to ask him more but was afraid of giving away the depth of her feelings. She washed the last glass and drained the sink while he dried. Finally, she turned to him, "Raeanne and Victor? I don't see it."

He smirked. "I guess you don't."

⁓

That evening she sat up in bed with her laptop and read Victor's note. She'd just retrieved his voice mail. His voice had sounded ragged, immediately triggering a pang of sympathy. Poor fellow sounded awfully low. She shouldn't have let Luke fill her head with jealous thoughts about Victor and Raeanne. There was no Victor and Raeanne. Really. *How silly to let your paranoid fantasies go there.*

Still, she approached his request with mixed feelings. It *was* an awful lot to ask to insert a new scene in the schedule that was slated to air in the coming week. She wasn't even sure she could do it. She didn't have her notes at home, but she went to the show's website to refresh her memory about what had just played and what was to come. Some Donovan and Terri scenes—shot before Luke had broken his leg and leading up to the honeymoon that was not to be. More of the Faye/Gabe/Gabe's father triangle. Those were the big stories on tap with some secondary tales brewing in the background ready to pop to the front when they heated up.

Faye was the one they needed to use for this, Victor had said. Faye was sweet, vulnerable, on the cusp of falling into deep love. Gussie probably saw that and was anticipating it, even if she wasn't sure which man Faye would choose.

"Hmmm…" Frankie tapped her chin with her index finger. "Maybe the way to reach you, Gussie, is to threaten to pull Faye's story." She began typing a breakdown for a very short scene, lasting no more than a minute. They might even be able to squeeze it in just by shortening reaction shots in other scenes.

Pleased with her work, she hit "send" and went into the bathroom to brush her teeth and wash her face.

When she returned, she was happy to see an email from Victor, already responding to her note. Her cheery mood vanished as she read his grateful note:

"Frankie, thank you so much for putting this together. It looks great and should do the trick. I hope you don't mind, but I'm copying Raeanne on this. I thought we should bring her into the loop to flesh things out…"

Chapter 23

"DID YOU KNOW THAT Victor Pendergrast had a vasectomy?" Kayla whispered to Frankie as Frankie breezed by her secretary's desk the next morning. It sounded as if Kayla had come in early just to share this news. But if Kayla knew this news, it could only be because…

"Who told you?" Frankie stopped at Kayla's desk.

"It was—"

"Bob?"

"No!" Kayla seemed genuinely shocked by that possibility. "It was Luke. Talked with him this morning." She looked down. "I asked him to run lines with me today. Hope you don't mind. I'll let you know when I take my break."

Progress on the secretary front, but Frankie didn't have time to enjoy it. My god, if Luke knew about Victor's medical history—the news must have traveled like a wildfire. Who else knew? Who had Bob told? Bob. Why, that two-faced, traitorous snake! He had listened to her message to Victor before deleting it!

She remembered how Bob's desk had been locked up like Fort Knox when she'd come in on Saturday. But of course he was a jerk! A man who thought people were going to steal his number-two pencils obviously had a devious mind himself. Why on earth had she trusted him? What else had he shared?

She didn't have to wait long to find out. As she left Kayla's desk, the secretary said, "They can be reversed, you know. You were right about that. My father is a doctor."

Frankie's face flamed as she closed the door to her office. She had to stop these rumors before they got back to Victor!

She didn't have time for that worry, though, because her phone rang as soon as a sigh escaped her lips. Raeanne's soft tones purred over the line, causing Frankie's muscles to tense.

"I'm sure you saw Vic's memo," Raeanne drawled. *Vic? Since when had he become Vic to Raeanne?* "And I hope you don't mind, but I took the liberty of writin' up the scene myself. I could also call the network and get the okay if you'd like."

No, she would not like. She was still the leader of this team, thank you very much.

"I'll handle that. And just email me your pages. I have some of my own."

"I think it's so sweet the way Vic is doing this for his aunt," Raeanne continued.

"Yeah, real sweet."

"Why, he must be desperate, the poor man. I can't imagine how frightened he must have been."

Frightened? "Uh, yeah, it must have been awful," Frankie said, improvising.

"It's a good thing they found her when they did. She could have died of exposure!"

Frankie's skin chilled. So Victor wasn't asking for this favor out of the blue. It had been precipitated by a crisis, a crisis Raeanne knew about but Frankie didn't.

"Where did they find her again?" Frankie pressed.

"In a stable—can you imagine?"

Ohmygod. Poor Victor. No wonder he wasn't in. No wonder his message had sounded so choppy and disorderly, so unlike him. But why had he shared this bad news with Raeanne and not with Frankie?

She remembered Luke's words about Raeanne. One shouldn't

assume Raeanne was innocent. And by "one" she meant herself, and by "innocent" she meant "not getting it on with Victor."

"Just awful, just awful," Frankie tsk-tsked to Raeanne. "I'm so glad she's doing well now," she added, making it sound like she'd just talked to Victor a few seconds ago. "Especially this morning. It being such a nice morning and all." She looked outside. It was raining.

"Did you hear the other news about Vic?"

Oh, no. Here it came.

"You mean about the vasectomy." Frankie said, cringing.

"What?"

Oh, crap.

"Uh… about his past in… in Schenectady," Frankie improvised, trying to cover.

"No, not that. I heard he might be in line for the executive producer slot."

And where did that leave Frankie? It left her toting women's cosmetics door to door, that's where it left her!

"I didn't think he was interested in the show long-term," Frankie said.

"Network might be interested in him."

Of course. He was a Pendergrast, after all. Nice insurance policy there. Built-in advertising mojo when you have the advertiser's nephew in charge. Was Frankie the biggest fool on the face of the earth or what?

"Well, let me know if you need me to do anything, okay, y'all?"

"Sure thing, sweetie-pie," Frankie answered. Then, before Raeanne could hang up, she did think of something. "You know, there is one thing. I need you to call this actor, Thane, and remind him we will definitely need him today. Have him come to your office first." That would keep him out of Frankie's hair while she finished plotting her moves.

When she hung up the phone, she dialed Victor's cell wanting to talk to him about his aunt, about the show, about what the hell was going on. She mostly wanted to hear his voice and see if she could tell, just from tone and timbre, if he was sincere, if he'd meant what he said about falling in love with her, or if he'd just been playing her. As she punched in the numbers, though, Bob walked by her open door. She quickly hung up. She wanted to grab Bob and wring his scrawny neck.

"Bob!" she cried out, chasing after him.

It was better not to talk to Victor right now anyway, she reasoned as she ran after fast-moving and suddenly deaf Bob. Victor might have gotten wind of the whole vasectomy-out-of-the-bag thing. And she was sure that whatever his intentions, Victor's voice would give nothing away but would have the effect of melting or stinging her heart.

"Bob!"

He disappeared into the men's room before she could grab him.

—⁓—

Network wasn't happy. Maurice wasn't happy. Sassy Maslin, the actress who played Faye, wasn't happy. But by the end of the morning, Frankie had her okay for the extra scene. The only way she'd gotten network to give in was by telling them the scene was integral to the whole gestalt of the thief, which was sending ratings through the roof. She used a lot of phrases about story arcs and character development that didn't seem to move them and then lit on the magic word: demographics. This scene would launch a story appealing to a key demographic, blah blah blah.

As she made all these arrangements, she kept telling herself it was for Gussie's sake, not Victor's. Who knew what Victor's motives were or what his feelings for her were? In the end, she had to look out for herself. And making the main sponsor's family happy was not a bad thing to do. Her goal, she decided that morning, was ultimately to make *Lust for Life* so popular that it didn't depend on the whims of one family.

She had pages down to Production by eleven, and Maurice was rehearsing it before noon. Thank god this was a day Sassy was on the set for other scenes. Frankie would go down to watch taping in the afternoon, but she had other business to deal with first.

Namely, the thief.

After writing and rewriting and plotting and revising and pushing forward and backtracking, Frankie finally thought she had her Thane/thief strategy nailed. Yes, she would write the thief into the hands of the police. But very subtly, very subtly...

She picked up the phone and dialed. She needed Luke's help, though, if this was going to work. She would have to let him in on the plan.

"Luke, could you come in today? I have a scene I'd like you to look over, and Kayla said you were going to run lines with her anyway."

—⁓—

Luke was there within the hour, his crutches leaning against her desk. He read the pages she'd provided while munching on a sandwich. He'd picked up two on the way in, figuring Frankie wouldn't have time to grab lunch. She was touched by his thoughtfulness.

"So we tape this today?" Luke looked up at her.

She swallowed, taking a sip of coffee. "Sort of. I'm using the old soundstage on the fourth floor and having Bob pretend to be a cameraman.

"Bob?"

"He owes me." Oh, yes, he owed her. She'd made that abundantly clear when she ambushed him coming out of the men's room earlier. Bob either did her bidding, or she would tell everyone, including network, that he was applying for a job at *Days of our Lives*.

The look on his face when she'd made this educated guess confirmed it was true. He really was a traitorous snake. They all were.

"I still don't get it," Luke said. "We're pretending to tape this scene so this new guy can watch... to get the feel for the character?"

Frankie hadn't told Luke everything. She was still skittish about revealing her suspicions, afraid if she weren't correct she'd look like a paranoid fool, or worse. And part of her also wanted to preserve Thane's reputation, such as it was, in case he really was innocent. She was doing a crazy thing here. Better not to drag too many people into it with her.

"I know it's odd," she said, finishing her sandwich and glancing at her watch. Thane should be showing up in Raeanne's cubicle in a few minutes. "But you'll have to trust me on this. Thane needs to see how we work. And I need to see how he works under pressure. He doesn't have a lot of TV experience."

"I don't like this. Maybe I should check with my union rep," Luke said, finishing his sandwich and balling up the deli paper, making a perfect shot with it into the wastebasket.

"Don't be silly," Frankie said, quelling her anxiety at the dreaded words, "union rep." "This isn't a real taping. It's just... just like another audition. That you're helping with. That's all. C'mon, do me a favor." She, too, finished eating and stood.

"Okay. But how am I supposed to play this thing with my cast and all?"

"Don't worry. We'll work it out."

―᚜᚜―

Or, rather, Bob worked it out with Kayla assisting. Luke corralled her as they went by her desk, and she'd been all too willing to help. Bob and Kayla worked it out in painstaking detail, in fact. Bob was absolutely smitten with the idea of directing a scene, even if it was a fake scene. And Kayla seemed to share his enthusiasm, amplifying his thoughts, demonstrating moves and tone, and becoming so wrapped up in the process that she even turned to Frankie at one point and said, "You know, I can now see the potential of this material." Scratch a secretary and you get a director. Who knew?

"Now, lean into the chair—that's right, that's right—and say that next line looking upward, like you're appealing to the heavens, just like Kayla showed you." Bob nodded to his "assistant," and Kayla walked over to the makeshift set Frankie had set up—just a few chairs and tables arranged like a living room—and demonstrated for Luke, dramatically raising one hand to her brow, as if gnashing her teeth and rending her garments were but a few seconds away.

Frankie stood to the side with Thane, who was studying the scene with fetishlike intensity. It scared Frankie. She stepped forward.

"Uh, Bob, can we get things rolling here?" Bob was scaring her, too.

"Oh, all right. But it won't be nearly as good as it could be." He motioned Kayla back, stepped back and behind the useless camera Frankie had pulled from a corner, and cried, "Action!"

Luke began the scene, just as Bob had instructed him, pouring heart and soul into the monologue as if he had to play to the very last seat in a twelve-hundred-seat arena. He had to rely on the drama in his voice, though, because he couldn't move much without his crutches. Bob had positioned him next to a wing chair. Luke leaned against it precariously, occasionally reaching out to grip its side when his balance shifted.

"I know I can't continue striking fear into the heart of the city. It's not fair. Those poor women. My gosh, those poor, poor frightened women…"

Oops, he nearly fell over there, grabbing for the chair at the last minute to right himself.

"…so there's only one thing for me to do. Yes, I must turn myself in. I shall do it immediately, before another woman has to fear for her safety. Those poor, poor women." He rolled his eyes skyward and actually beat his breast. Frankie heard Kayla whisper "marvelous."

"I shall call the police this instant," Luke declared.

Yes, the police would have to come to him in this scene, since he couldn't go to them in his hobbled state. In fact, even getting to the phone on the nearby desk was a challenge. He inched along the back of the chair, then leaned over, groping for the phone. His first attempt was a miss, his second a near catch. Finally, he grabbed the cord and dragged the phone to the edge but nearly lost his balance when he started dialing. He gave up after punching in five digits and said the next line into the receiver as if the call had gone through.

"Hello, police? This is Donovan Reilly. If you come to the Hertzberg estate, you'll find your jewel thief. Yes, that's right. I'm the thief." Luke said it all in a Dudley Do-Right kind of voice, staring straight at the camera. "I'm the hero of Crestview, stealing from the poor to give to the rich..."

Damn, he'd reversed that. No matter, he was plowing ahead.

"...and now sacrificing my freedom to ensure the citizens of this teeming city sleep easy at night. I shall no longer be responsible for the heinous crime of disrupting the community sense of safety and peace."

Luke delivered the speech as if it were the Gettysburg Address, his voice rising and falling, his handsome profile flashing in the light he was always sure to find. All in all, it was a bravura performance, and Frankie joined Kayla in clapping enthusiastically when it was over.

"I've told you you should be on the stage," Kayla said, tears in her eyes.

"Magnificent, Luke! Really stunning!" She turned to Thane. "Don't you agree?"

Thane wasn't so sure. In fact, Thane was visibly disturbed by the scene. He looked at Luke with an envy so palpable that Frankie could have sworn Thane was turning green around the gills. Or maybe that was just the hair dye he used to get his curly locks looking like Luke's.

"I thought you said *I* was the thief," Thane said, his voice taut and barely above a whisper.

"Well, you are and you aren't. I just wanted to see first if Luke, I mean, Donovan works as the thief, because the thief is something of a hero, don't you think?" She stared at him, watching warily for reactions.

"Why, of course he is." Thane straightened.

"And Donovan is *Lust's* hero right now."

"But that's just it—the thief was going to be the hero. That's what these pages say!" Thane tapped the papers in his hand. They contained the same lines Luke had just spoken. "And... and the other pages you sent me this weekend. They all said the thief was the hero!"

Luke, meanwhile, grabbed his crutches, hidden behind the chair, and limped over to Frankie. "Do you need me anymore? I have to get ready for the taping today."

No, she didn't need him, but she didn't like having him leave either. She suspected Bob and Kayla, the "wonder directors," wouldn't be much help if Thane snapped. But she couldn't think of a reason to keep Luke around. "Thanks. You're finished," she said instead, smiling.

He hobbled to the door, and when he opened it Frankie could have sworn she saw Raeanne meeting him, talking in some intimate, secret way. Hmmm... she'd have to ask about that.

Kayla saw it, too, and rushed after him. "Don't forget about running lines with me!" They went off together.

Frankie grabbed the pages from Thane. "I had originally thought of you as the thief, but I just wanted to try Donovan first. And you know what? Luke did such a good job with that, I'm just now re-thinking the scene and the whole thief story."

Bob stepped out of the shadows. "Well, I do think Luke's direction had something to do with it."

Frankie ignored him, focusing on Thane, who appeared crestfallen. "But what about me, about my thief?" he whined.

"I don't know, Thane. Luke was just so good. Maybe we'll find something else for you. Maybe Donovan's long-lost hunchback brother."

"Ooh, a hunchback story," Bob interjected, clasping his hands in front of his face. "Who plays Esmerelda?"

"A hunchback?" Thane swallowed and frowned. "Is that a hero role, too?"

Frankie laughed. "Oh, no. He'll be something of a buffoon, I think. Comic relief."

"But the thief... *I* am the thief." His voice was pitiful and pleading.

Yes, you are the thief, Frankie thought. *But I have to get you to admit it—to the police.*

She stared at him, as if pretending to be considering a new idea. "You know, you *could* be..." Frankie said.

"Oh, no! The hunchback has so many possibilities," Bob exclaimed. "Trapped in the bell tower. Saving Esmerelda from the crowd."

Frankie pushed Bob aside and went back to working on Thane. "We could make it that Donovan is just pretending, see?"

Thane nodded his head.

"And trying to steal the real thief's—that would be your—thunder."

Thane nodded once more.

"Donovan goes to the police to give himself up—he doesn't wait for the police to come to him, see? And he gives this passionate speech, all about helping the poor and saving humanity and stopping the plague of crime that is striking fear into the hearts of innocent women."

Thane was glowing.

"And… and we even set up a big publicity push with it, too. We have you actually go to the police station—there's one near here, you know, just three blocks over if you walk to the end of the block and make a right, then look for the big gray stone building in the middle of the block, not the one with the dingy windows but the big one next door; there's a storefront church on the other side—and have your photo taken. Why, I can see the headline now: 'Local Hero Gives Himself Up.'"

Thane was practically drooling.

"Of course, Luke could be the thief and get all that fuss…"

"But that should be only me—I'm the thief! Not Donovan!"

Bob stepped forward again. "You mean Luke."

"Shh!" Frankie hissed at him. Then, back to Thane, "That's right. You're the thief. And you deserve that big pat on the back at the police station. You deserve all the glory, not Donovan Reilly. Donovan Reilly has had enough glory. And he was never that good a guy anyway."

"That's right," Thane said. "He nearly drowned his sister in that boating accident."

"Yes," Frankie agreed. "And he accidentally set fire to the Kendall estate when he was so mad at the family for snubbing his mother."

"Oh, I think he set that fire on purpose," Thane said.

True enough—at first, the writers had thought that way, too, but they changed direction when Donovan Reilly started developing a fan following. But Frankie didn't think it was the time for a discussion of *Lust for Life*'s story development.

She went on, feeding Thane's sense of injustice at having his moment of glory stolen from him. "And Donovan was in debt to that loan shark, remember? That put his whole family in jeopardy."

As she went through the list of Donovan's shady past doings, she began to wonder what women saw in him. Why did women always fall for the "bad boys," thinking they could redeem them? She really needed to change that on the show. It wasn't right.

"Donovan does not deserve this honor!" Thane said, as if ready to march off to battle.

"Are you going to kill him off?" This from Bob. Stupid, stupid Bob. Murder was not a good idea to plant in Thane's deranged mind.

"No! Absolutely not!" Frankie countered. "Why, anyone who ever thought of killing off Donovan Reilly would be persona non grata in the entire universe! Shunned, I tell you. A pariah. A leper! Unclean, unclean!"

If his demeanor was any guide, it didn't look as if Thane had taken to the "kill Donovan/Luke" idea, thank goodness. Frankie veered back to her original scheme.

"So the thing to do, I think, to really make this character pop, to make the whole world fall in love with the thief, is for him to give himself up, to march right down to the police station as fast as his legs can carry him. You know, the one around the corner, near the storefront church. After that, why, the sky's the limit as far as what we can do with this character… Here, why don't you play the scene yourself. Bob—set things up."

Thane left the phony soundstage only after Bob had directed him through a half dozen "takes" of the scene where the thief gives himself up to the police. Frankie just watched in stunned silence as both Bob and Thane got into their respective roles. She'd had no idea Bob was such a drama queen. *Still waters run deep, I guess.*

Thane even began improvising during the scene, throwing in his own rhetorical flourishes on the heroism of the thief surrendering to the authorities.

But would he really do it? *Was* he the thief? Was she just imagining things? Time would tell, and she hoped the time would be short.

She herself didn't have time to think about it. She still had to go to the shoot of the Faye scene, where she knew she'd be treated like an unwelcome guest. But she had made a promise to Victor, and she would keep it.

Chapter 24

VICTOR HAD PLANNED ON staying with his aunt all week. He knew from Frankie's emails that she was planning on writing and inserting a scene designed to convince his aunt to accept a live-in companion. He had already expressed his gratitude in a message on her cell's voice mail. And he'd told Raeanne to pass along his thanks as well.

So he thought he'd covered all his bases and merely had to wait to see if the plan worked. But then he'd received a curious message from Raeanne. She'd emailed him to say he was needed back at *Lust*, that Frankie was in over her head with something to do with the thief.

He called Dane and asked him to stay, then packed and headed back into the city, calling Frankie on the way in. She didn't pick up her cell, but he did manage to reach Kayla, who told him that Frankie was involved in something with Thane.

Thane—the actor they'd thought of hiring as the thief. Was she going ahead with that story after all? Whatever she decided, he would support it. But what on earth had Raeanne meant when she said Frankie was in over her head?

As soon as he got in, he headed straight for Frankie's office, but she wasn't in. Neither was Kayla at her desk. Raeanne, however, appeared from around the corner.

"Oh, thank goodness," she said, "you're here."

"What's the problem? And where is Frankie?"

"She's tied up with somethin' right now, but she'll be here soon.

Oh, Victor, you have no idea what's been going on. Luke told me all
about it. Let's go to your office and I'll explain."

———※———

But Raeanne didn't really explain. She rambled in that lazy Southern
accent of hers, which seemed to get thicker by the second. She had
a way of going on that made you think she was saying something
when in reality she was beating around a very big bush. In fact, her
monologue was planting doubts in his mind as to whether she really
could fill Frankie's shoes.

"…and then she gave this Thane the script, the very script she'd
had Luke just read, with Bob behind the camera—my goodness,
Victor, Bob isn't a cameraman; it was the strangest thing. Then
again, Bob does have dreams, but so do we all. Why, I had an uncle
who dreamed of bein' a carnival owner, but the closest he ever came
was to runnin' the concessions stand at the local Lions Club fair
every summer. That didn't make him a carnival owner any more
than handin' Bob a ridin' crop makes him a director. Did I mention
she had him act as director, too?"

"Raeanne, wait a sec, could you tell me…?" But he couldn't
get a word in edgewise. All he could make of this speech was that
Frankie was up to something with Thane. What on earth was she
concocting with him? Why the pretense? Was she just trying to make
him feel better after pulling the thief role from him—assuming she
had done that, that is?

Raeanne was pacing as she talked, which was making him dizzy.
He sat in one of the wing chairs in front of his desk and was itching
to get up and find out for himself what was going on. If he couldn't
find Frankie, maybe Bob would know. He'd been surprised to find
Bob away from his desk when he came in, but now Raeanne was
telling him Bob was directing a scene. Or was it he was acting as
cameraman? The world was turned upside down.

Ever since he'd stepped over the office threshold, it was as if he'd entered a *Twilight Zone* episode. The receptionist by the elevator had greeted him oddly, saying, "You know, you can have that sort of thing reversed, Mr. Pendergrast."

"Raeanne, Raeanne, stop!" He waved his hands in the air. "I don't understand a thing you're telling me. Frankie worked out a scene to tape with Luke, but she didn't actually tape it. She used Bob as a phony director and cameraman. And this Thane actor was there to witness the whole thing?"

Raeanne nodded seriously. "Why, yes, that's it in a nutshell."

"But what on earth does it have to do with anything? Why is this a crisis?"

"Well, it's like this…" She stepped forward, turning her ankle on her too-high heels, and before he knew it, he had a lapful of Raeanne Sanders, her hair tickling his nose.

It was at this moment that the elusive Bob showed up, standing in the doorway as if he were a schoolmaster who'd just caught the top student cheating on finals.

"Oh, I see you're busy," he said and walked out of the room.

Victor helped Raeanne to her feet and went after Bob.

"Wait a minute! I need you to explain something!"

Bob was at his desk, ashen-faced. "It wasn't me. I didn't start those rumors."

"What rumors?" Victor was now completely dumbfounded.

"Uh… nothing. Nothing. Nothing at all." Bob flicked on his computer screen and popped his Bluetooth in his ear. "What can I help you with?"

"What were you and Frankie up to this morning—with Thane and Luke?"

Bob looked up at Victor with a grin as wide as the Sahara on his face. "Oh, Mr. Pendergrast, if I told you, I'd have to kill you."

"Get in my office right now, Bob. If you don't tell me, I swear *I* will kill *you!*" Victor stormed into his office, with Bob following. As they entered, Raeanne exited, whispering to Bob, "Where's Frankie? I thought she was comin' up."

Bob replied, "I think she's with Luke. Taping another special scene of some kind."

Raeanne hurried away.

———

Bob had more information, all right, but it was either garbled or so crazy that Victor could hardly believe it. Although Frankie had not let Bob in on all the information she had, he got the impression that Frankie thought she knew who the thief was and was trying to "send a message to him."

"Send a message? But how? I thought you said the camera you used wasn't running."

"That's true, Mr. Pendergrast. But I think she was using Thane to send the message. She wanted him to see the scene so that he would carry the message… to whomever."

Victor felt his skin crawl. No, she wouldn't be using Thane to send a message, unless she thought he was involved in some way. *Oh, Frankie, what are you doing? You could be putting yourself in danger!*

He sped from the room, oblivious to leaving Bob hanging.

"Mr. Pendergrast, did you know that Frankie is thinking of doing a *Hunchback of Notre Dame* story? It's so exciting!"

———

It took him all of ten minutes to find Frankie, and when he did he couldn't talk to her. She was on the *Lust for Life* set, standing behind the cameras as the scene with Faye was being shot, the scene he'd requested her to insert in this week's lineup.

He watched from the editing booth above the soundstage, marveling at how elegantly she'd crafted the scene, making it fit into the flow of *Lust*'s current story, not a line sounding unnatural or out of place.

The actress who played Faye sat on a stool in the Reilly Tavern talking to Luke as Donovan, who served her a cup of coffee from behind the bar, his broken leg and crutches nowhere in sight. Only the cast and crew knew he was leaning on the bar for balance, not for effect. They were lucky that Luke could even play the scene, and lucky, too, that they still had one day before the big Terri and Donovan wedding and honeymoon scenes. The scenes had been taped, but they had yet to air.

"So what's got you all bothered, sis? Is it Gabe?"

Faye scrunched up her face. "No. It's not Gabe. It's Aunt Louisa."

"Aunt Louisa? I thought she was in the hospital."

Victor knew from his study of the show that an Aunt Louisa Reilly had been involved in a plot a year ago, a story where she'd kidnapped Donovan's stepbrother's baby, causing enormous grief in Crestview, until she was found and carted off to a mental institution. The actress who played her had carted herself off to rehab. It was her drinking and pill problem that led the show to write her character out.

"She's been released, Donny. She's doing much better. She just needs someone to take care of her."

"Then she should hire someone. She can certainly afford it."

Victor nodded. Louisa Reilly was a rich heiress, one of the few in the Reilly clan with any money.

Faye looked up at Donovan. Victor could see on the monitors that one camera was catching her doelike eyes as they glistened with tears.

"She won't hire anyone, Donny. And I can't let her be on her own. She needs a companion."

"You're thinking of—"

Faye nodded. "I can't bear to think of her on her own. She wandered away from her house recently, you know. She could have hurt herself."

"But, Faye, if you became her companion, you'd be sacrificing your life, your future…"

Again, Faye's innocent face filled the screen, her head tilted to one side, her wide eyes unblinking.

"I know, I know. It would mean… no life with—"

"Gabe."

Faye looked down and murmured, *"Or Grayson."*

Donovan, not hearing, went on, *"Don't do it, Faye. It'll be like entering a convent. You can't wall yourself up like that."*

"What choice do I have, Donny? If she won't let a companion live with her, I'll have to make the sacrifice, I'll have to give up my life and any chance at love…"

The scene went on for a few more seconds, ending with the Donovan character muttering some words of worry about strangers who might sabotage his wedding to Terri. That was a nice touch. Frankie had managed to set up the new Luke-as-hostage plot in addition to the message to his aunt.

And what a masterful message it was. When he'd asked Frankie to craft something like this, he had imagined a more direct plea—perhaps Faye or even Donovan, characters he knew his aunt loved, speaking to an older character about the need for a live-in companion. He'd expected a frontal assault, in other words, with the beloved character appealing directly to his aunt, through the other character on the show.

After watching this scene play out, he realized how awkward and ineffectual his idea would have been. It would have required a great deal of backstory explanation on the need for a companion. And later, of course, they'd have to jettison the idea of a companion as the regular stories moved forward. Even if his aunt Gussie had identified with the older character in such a scene, she would probably be rooting for resistance to a companion idea.

No, by setting up the scene between two of his aunt's favorite characters, Frankie had avoided that. And she'd surely tugged at his aunt's heartstrings with the beautiful Faye ready to sacrifice her love life for her own aunt because of the aunt's stubbornness in refusing a perfectly reasonable solution to her problem.

The scene ended, and the red light went out. Victor hurried down to the set.

"Bravo!" he said, coming up to Frankie as she left the soundstage.

"You're back!" she said. Victor wasn't sure, but he detected a note of worry in her voice, as if she weren't sure she was happy to see him. In fact, she didn't linger outside the soundstage but immediately started making her way up the hallway toward the elevator and their offices. He had to race to keep up.

"That scene was wonderful," he said, trying to break through the wall she'd erected. "I'm sure it will have an impact on my aunt. When will it air?"

"I think they can squeeze it in tomorrow. Maurice said they'd almost run a little short for that day—some actors rushing a scene. So he'll fit it in. I'll let you know for sure, though, so you can make sure your aunt is watching." They arrived at the elevators and she pressed the button. Within seconds, a car arrived.

"I'm sorry to hear about your aunt, by the way," she said as they stepped on. She didn't look at him. "Raeanne told me about how she'd wandered off."

Was that what was bothering her—that Raeanne had pulled the story out of him? He'd not meant to divulge it to her, but she'd insisted on knowing.

"I'd wanted to tell you, but didn't want to leave a message about it. Raeanne can be quite persistent." She'd dragged the details out of him when he'd reached her on the phone. He'd been reluctant to call her but when he hadn't heard back from Frankie right away, he'd gone to Frankie's deputy.

They reached their floor and the doors glided open.

She stepped off without looking at him once.

"Frankie," he said before she could walk away entirely. "Do you have a few minutes? I'd like to talk."

"Not now, Victor, I have to run. I'll catch you later! And look, it wasn't me who spread those rumors." She rushed away, as if afraid to talk.

—⁓—

He tried to connect with Frankie throughout the rest of the day, but each time he went to her office, she was either on the phone or out. He couldn't help feeling she was avoiding him. He gathered what information he could from other sources about the thief. The PR department knew nothing about the story being pulled, so she'd obviously not made a decision on that yet. He tried connecting with Raeanne again—even though he dreaded another long monologue about nothing—but all he got from her was a cryptic return message to his voice mail. "I can't explain now. Be at Frankie's tonight around seven and I'm sure she'll tell all."

Frankie's at seven? Since when was Raeanne Frankie's calendar keeper? He shrugged it off as one more crazy incident in this crazy day, and spent some time on marketing tasks, periodically checking in with Dane to make sure his aunt was doing okay and not wandering the moors.

Chapter 25

ALL HELL BROKE LOOSE about six o'clock. Hank stormed into Frankie's office, his face and eyes red. Poor fellow—looked like he had been crying.

"Ms. McNally, may I have a few minutes?" he asked and entered without waiting for her answer. He sat in the chair in front of her desk. She scooted a box of tissues toward him, and he took one and blew his nose.

"The most awful thing has happened," he continued. "And I might need to take a few days off."

"Sure, Hank. Whatever you need." She held her breath, hoping against hope that the story he was about to tell was the one she wanted to hear.

"It's my cousin, Thane, you see," Hank said. "He did something awfully stupid this afternoon. I just can't believe it. Even now, I can't believe it." He shook his head and blew his nose again.

"What can't you believe, Hank?" She leaned into the desk, trying not to look too eager or too happy.

Hank looked her in the eyes. "He went to the police and told them he's the jewel thief! Good gravy, Ms. McNally. His mother will be so upset. I have to get him a lawyer and get him out of jail and straighten this whole mess out. I can't believe he did this. What in the world made him think he was the thief? I mean, I know he loves the show and all and follows it so closely that sometimes he tells me things about characters and stories that I'd forgotten or never learned, but this is taking that kind of appreciation to a whole new dangerous level. I mean, turning yourself in to the police for a crime you didn't commit just because you love the show is ridiculous, and as his agent, I've advised him of the foolishness of this stunt."

She cleared her throat. "Uh, you don't think it's possible he really did commit the, er, crimes?"

Hank straightened as if hit by lightning. "What an awful thing to suppose! Thane is a good, upstanding, law-abiding citizen. He's never done an unlawful thing in his life—unless, of course, you count that time he stole an apple from Mrs. McGarrity's tree, but that was when he was seven and his daddy was carrying him on his shoulders. Thane Galahad is no criminal. He'd never besmirch the family name in that way!"

"But he's not besmirching the family name. He changed his name, remember? You told me." Hank's impassioned defense of Thane was making Frankie uncomfortable. What if Thane really was innocent and all she had done was prompt a crazed fan to give himself up for a crime he didn't commit? She hadn't considered that possibility. She'd only counted on Thane turning himself in if he really was the criminal.

She leaned in a little more, her voice low and sympathetic. "Do you know where he was the nights of the robberies? An alibi—does he have one for the burglaries?"

Hank again pulled himself up, as if the suggestion of Thane as the thief was a duel-inducing offense. "Well, no, I don't know that. I know I tried to reach him on one night that a burglary occurred, and he didn't call me back until way late. But that's hardly cause for a guilty verdict."

Frankie breathed a sigh of relief. Not being able to reach Thane on the night of a robbery might not be enough for a guilty verdict, but it didn't prove him innocent either. She turned her attention back to what Hank was saying.

"…I just don't understand why he would do such a thing. Here he was just on the verge of getting a good acting job with *Lust*, and he throws it all away in this bizarre act. You saw him today, didn't you? He said he was coming here for a reading or taping or something. Did he say or do anything that tipped you off? I thought he'd stop by and say hello after he was finished, but he must have gone straight to the police instead. What happened, Ms. McNally, when he was here?"

"Uh…" What should she tell him? He'd find out soon enough if saw his cousin. Thane was sure to tell him about the "taping" and show him the dialogue pages. "Well, as it turns out" —she let a fake chuckle interrupt her narrative— "as it turns out, I now recall that the scene I asked him to come in for did involve the thief turning himself into police. But, of course, Luke was playing the scene first, before Thane read the lines."

"Luke? He's Thane's hero. I mean, Donovan is his hero." Hank hit his forehead with the palm of his hand. "That's what must have set him off. He's such a fan of the show, he gets confused easily between reality and what's happening on the show, and… he probably left here still in character. He's a method actor, you see, and sometimes I know he stays in character for weeks when he's working on something. This was a real problem when he played Zorro in a children's theater production." He looked at Frankie eagerly. "Do you have a copy of the tape? Maybe if I see the scene, it will help me understand what triggered this incident and I can use it when I go to the police to explain."

She sucked in her lips. "Uh, no. Don't have a copy of the tape. Sorry." Why wouldn't her phone ring, or someone knock on her door? She had to get out of here. Sure, Hank would find out soon enough what triggered Thane's surrender to the authorities. She just didn't want to be there when he did.

"Then I'll get one from Production." He stood. "Thank you, Ms. McNally. I think you've helped me a lot. And more importantly, you've helped Thane." He held out his hand and she shook it, feeling queasy.

"No, don't thank me. Really. Don't," she murmured.

"Oh, one other thing before I leave," he said. "Kayla mentioned to me that she might be interested in auditioning for the role of"—he pulled a slip of paper from his pocket—"Esmerelda when you're ready to cast it, and I've agreed to represent her."

"Oh." So a character based on a classic heroine was good enough for Kayla. Or maybe it was her sudden epiphany about *Lust* when she was playing director with Bob. "I'll let you know about that."

As soon as Hank left, she started pulling her things together to hit the road herself. She'd check in with PR later to see if they'd heard anything on the thief. She just didn't want to be around when Hank discovered that there was no copy of the afternoon's "taping" and that the whole thing had been a ruse to get Thane thinking about turning himself in. No, she'd face that tomorrow, thank you very much. And probably have to put the word out for a new story editor.

As she grabbed her purse, a soft knock came from her door.

Now feeling that every encounter would only bring bad news, she hesitated before saying, "Come in." Maybe it would be Victor. Maybe he hadn't heard the vasectomy rumor, after all. "Come in!"

To her surprise, Kayla stood in the open door. "I was just leaving," the secretary said.

"Oh." Since when did Kayla announce she was leaving for the day? Maybe she wanted news on the casting of Esmerelda. "I spoke with Hank and told him I'd let him know when we're ready to bring ol' Ezzy on," Frankie said.

Kayla smiled broadly. "Thanks."

Still Kayla stayed put.

"Is there something you wanted to tell me?" Frankie prompted.

"Well, no. I mean, I guess I was wondering if you were doing okay. I know you and Victor were... well, close."

Frankie stood stock-still while blood coursed through every vein, warming her from head to toe. What did this mean? Was Victor so angry with her over the vasectomy story that he'd publicly humiliated her?

"Um, yes, I'm fine. Thanks." She shifted from one foot to the other. "Uh, just to be clear here, did Victor say anything in particular to—"

Kayla shook her head. "Oh, no, Victor is a gentleman. I just heard it through the grapevine. About him and Raeanne." She seemed genuinely sad for Frankie.

Victor and Raeanne? Frankie's eyes felt like they would pop out of her skull.

"You know, she was in his office and they were... well, close." Kayla's voice held deep disappointment. But of course—if Frankie were the one getting "close" with Victor, she wouldn't be with Luke. And Kayla wanted Luke.

"Well, I'm fine. Just fine," Frankie said, her voice on speed talk. "And I really have to get going, so if there's nothing else..." She found some papers on her desk and stuffed them into her attaché. She kept stuffing things in as Kayla walked out, even ramming a company phone directory in the bag before noticing what she was doing.

Damn. Victor and Raeanne? He'd already moved on. Or maybe he'd been playing her, flirting with Raeanne on the side as a backup and now trading Frankie in for the new model. Raeanne had always made eyes at him. And it was funny how she had been the one he'd told about his aunt roaming off in the night. He hadn't bothered to confide that in Frankie.

She felt a pinch. It was her heart. Not breaking, but maybe twisting on its way to breaking. There it was again. And there was a little spot of damp on the papers crammed into her attaché. Where had that come from? Her eyes. She wiped them and sniffled.

What a little girl you are, Frankie. It's not like you and Victor had anything but a... a... fun fling. It lasted all of, what? Oh, yes, one night. And you were the one to break it off, remember. You didn't want folks to think you were getting the executive producer slot because of sexual politics. No chance of that now if he's moved his "politics" to a different party.

"Maybe he'll give that job to Raeanne now, too," she said to the room, pulling the excess materials from her case and turning out her light.

But it really wasn't his to give. Yeah, the Pendergrast company had a lot to say in it. But it was ultimately network's decision, and she could make her case to them without relying on Victor to give her the extra push, dammit. She didn't need Victor. No sirree. She could do it on her own. *I am woman, hear me roar.*

Her cell jangled as she locked the office door behind her.

"Mom? I'm glad you called."

—⁓—

Her mother's voice was like chicken soup on a rainy day. Frankie sank into the backseat of a cab, splurging so she could continue the conversation she'd started in the office and continued on the elevator and into the lobby and out to the street. Ironically, on this of all days, her mother had called to reverse her position on Victor.

"Maybe that's just office gossip, Frankie. You shouldn't listen to all that stuff."

"Trust me, Ma. The gossip's accuracy reading has been off the charts today."

"Well, I wouldn't believe it until you check it out yourself."

"What—you mean catch them in the act?"

"Maybe talk to him about it, hon."

"Why are you defending Victor? Just the other day you were telling me his sperm didn't deserve me." Frankie caught the cab driver glancing in the rearview mirror and lowered her voice. "I mean, you were urging me to go for younger guys, remember?"

"Well, I've had a chance to think it over, and I decided you should go where your heart leads you. You never know what can happen in life, and you don't want to regret not following your heart. If Victor is the one you love…"

"But what about the baby thing?" Again her voice rose, and the taxi driver looked her way.

"Baby schmaby. There's in vitro. There's adoption. There's vasectomy reversal. There's cloning…"

"Cloning?"

"Oh yeah, that was on *Lust* when Brianna went to that doctor in Italy."

"That plot was a stinker," Frankie said.

"Before your time. The stories are much better now," her mother concurred. "What I'm trying to say here, Frankie, is you never know what life will throw your way. You married Brian thinking he was the one and you'd be having children with him, and look what happened— he turned out to be Mr. Beef Jerky. So if you just base your decision on who to be with on how high their sperm count is, who knows what will happen? Maybe that fellow's sperm will decide to go on strike. Maybe he'll have an accident that means he can't use his sperm. Or maybe they'll end up swimming up a different canal, if you know what I mean."

"Ooh, Mom…" Frankie whined.

"What I'm getting at is you can't plan too much. It sounds like a cliché, but you should follow your heart."

"That's what you did with Dad. Look what it got you," Frankie said.

"Yeah, it got me you, baby girl! And it was worth every single second. That's exactly what I'm talking about. Maybe if I had applied logic to the process, I'd have ended up with Mr. Responsibility and no Frankie and still a divorce."

Or maybe another Frankie. Frankie couldn't keep this existential debate straight in her head.

"There's still the little matter of Victor two-timing me."

"Well, that's a nonstarter for sure. But don't assume it's true. He sounded like a pretty stand-up guy when you described him to me before."

"I think my 'stand-up guy' barometer is busted." She'd thought Brian was one, after all.

Nope. Scratch that. She hadn't really seen him that way. She'd thought she could make him into one with the power of her love. Or, rather, the power of his love for her. But it had been too weak a beam.

The taxi pulled up to her apartment.

"Look, I gotta go, Ma. I'll keep you posted."

She paid the driver, exited, and stood on the curb collecting her thoughts just long enough for a car pulling up at race-track speed to splash a late-day puddle onto her coat.

Chapter 26

SHE FELT LIKE A wet cat by the time she unlocked her apartment door and was warmed by the sight of Luke in the kitchen cooking, the table set for two with candles and a bottle of wine. She might be in love with Victor, but it sure was nice to be taken care of by somebody.

In love with Victor—it had taken this rumor about him and Raeanne to crystallize Frankie's feelings for him. She'd been going back and forth wondering if he was the man for her, or at least worth pursuing as "the one," before good, old-fashioned jealousy had solved that mystery for her. She'd let the whole baby issue cloud her feelings, too, pushing her to view men as mere baby-making machines. As her mother pointed out, she now lived in an age where there were alternatives. What to do now? Find out if Victor was the good guy she'd believed him to be or the two-timer that Kayla and office gossip were saying he was.

"You look fried," Luke said, leaning on his crutches. "But I have something to perk you up." He looked at his watch. "Why don't you go take a nice warm bath, and dinner will be ready when you're done." He smiled.

"You know, that sounds great," she said, putting down her case and hanging up her raincoat. She sniffed the air. "And something smells great, too." She would certainly miss Luke's cooking when he moved out. And she had to ask him to leave if she was going to make a go of it with Victor. Okay, she'd deal with that after the dinner. And the bath.

"I set things up for you," he called after her. "Take your time."

She stepped into the bathroom with its 1920s black and white tile and claw-foot tub. Wow, he really had set things up. Candles glowed on the table by the sink. Bubble bath sat at the ready by the tub next to a neatly folded stack of fluffy white towels. She ran the water and quickly changed. In a few minutes, she was sinking into a warm, foam-filled, lilac-scented tub of water, worries and stress melting out from every muscle. She thought she heard a phone ring but let it slide as she closed her eyes.

Victor glanced at his watch and flipped his phone closed. He barely had time if he was going to make it to Frankie's by seven, as Raeanne had told him to do. What a crazy afternoon—the rush back to the office, the strange interaction with Frankie, the talk with Raeanne, and now, great news to share at this mysterious meeting. The thief was caught!

He pulled on his trench coat and turned out his office light. He'd just gotten off the phone with Mary in PR after hearing from his police contact. Thane was the culprit. They had enough circumstantial evidence to go with his confession for a rock-solid case.

Victor didn't have all the details yet, but of this he was sure: Thane was mentally unbalanced, and Frankie had steered him to the police. The thought of her alone with him made his skin crawl. He hoped Thane would get help rather than jail time, but he also was mad as hell that Frankie hadn't shared her plan with him. She could have been hurt.

He raced to the elevator through the now-empty office, eager to see her so he could tell her how worried *and* angry he was that she'd taken on this burden alone. And then he'd share with her his own plans for a quick press conference, announcing her role in bringing the thief into the arms of the police. Maybe that was the purpose of this meeting. Maybe Raeanne had known about Frankie's involvement, but Frankie had sworn her to secrecy. He shook his head as he made his way to the garage. He couldn't keep his theories straight. They were beginning to blur in his mind with all the *Lust* plots he'd read over the past weeks.

———

Frankie was slipping into a dream, her head leaning against the feather-soft bath pillow and her thoughts curled around the velvety sounds of a Michael Bublé CD, when she heard the doorbell buzz.

She blinked her eyes awake and sat up straight, reaching for a towel. "I'll be right there," she said, then remembered that Luke was available to answer the door. Who could it be? The lobby door was locked. Visitors had to be buzzed up first. Oh, well, it was time for her to get out of the tub anyway. She was beginning to resemble a reddened prune. She reached for her silky robe, pinning her hair up on top of her head as she walked through her bedroom into the living room.

"Who is it, Luke?" she asked, before her eyes popped out of her head, and her jaw dropped to the floor.

———

What she saw when she rounded the corner was Luke standing in the hallway, a towel around his naked body. His naked wet body. His hair was dripping and his skin glistened. *What the...?*

He was holding the door open for Victor, whose stare went from Luke to her in slow motion. She could read the thoughts that went with that gaze. Luke in a towel. Frankie in a robe. Both of them wet...

"Victor! How nice to see you!" she said in as hospitable a voice as she could muster. "Come in, come in. We were just about to—" She looked at Luke. "What are you doing in that towel, Luke? I thought you were fixing dinner!" But this only sounded fake, as if she were making up an excuse for what they really had been doing. Oh no.

"I can see I was interrupting," Victor said in a strained voice. "I thought we were supposed to meet. We can reschedule."

Meet? Had Kayla failed to tell her about a meeting? But Kayla had been doing so well lately, and seemed to want Frankie and Victor together. Frankie stepped forward, but that only made her feel more awkward, because it put her closer to nearly naked Luke, and she didn't want Victor drawing any more conclusions than he already had about… closeness… between her and Luke.

"No, no, come in. Really. Nothing is happening here. I mean, nothing is going on. I mean…"

She took another step down the narrow hall, which meant Luke moved to the side a millimeter, just enough to upset his balance—he was only using one crutch and holding on to the wall—and the loose towel around his waist slipped. If nothing was going on, someone had failed to send that message to an organ of his body that was demonstrating a desire for *something* to be going on, even if nothing yet had.

Ohmygod. She glanced at it. She looked up at Victor. Victor opened his mouth to speak, but turned and left instead.

"Victor!" she said after him as he stormed off down the steps. But she couldn't follow him to the street in her robe, so she turned around back to the apartment, confronting Luke as she reentered the hallway.

"For god's sake, put something on. What's the matter with you? What are you doing out here? Rehearsing for a porno audition?" Her anger blew away the serenity she'd felt in the tub. Now she felt only rage and disappointment… and a strange sense of déjà vu, as if she'd been in this scene before. She shook her head, cupping her hand over her ear to suction water out of it.

Luke retrieved the towel, struggling to get it around his waist while standing on his good foot. "I'm sorry, Frankie. I spilled some grease on my pants and almost burned myself. I ripped off my clothes, doused myself in cold water, and grabbed the towel when I heard the doorbell." He looked at her with puppy dog eyes. "Can you help me with this?"

Oh what the hell. She stepped over to him, grabbing the towel and cinching it tight. As she finished, she was surprised when he pulled her into a strong embrace, his back against the wall for support. His fingers kneaded her shoulders through the thin robe while his tongue licked the desire from her mouth. Try as she might, she couldn't get the image of him nude out of her mind. Luke had a spectacular body, well toned and leopardlike, ready to strike. Strike he did, pulling her closer, moaning softly as she didn't resist. She picked up the scent of his aftershave…

No, it wasn't his aftershave. It was the scent of a dryer sheet, the ones she used on her laundry, like the big fluffy bath towel he was wearing. He'd grabbed the towel, he'd said, when he heard the doorbell ring.

But the towels were stored in a linen closet in the bathroom. The only way he'd have had access to a towel to grab was if he had planted one in the living room before she got in the tub.

She pulled away. The déjà vu was still fuzzy but getting clearer.

"Why did you have a towel in the kitchen? A bath towel?" She knotted her robe more tightly and crossed her arms over her chest.

"What?" Luke looked perplexed… and afraid. His eyes were doing that little crinkly thing they did when he was unsure of his next lines.

It came back to her! Two years ago. Donovan and Terri had almost split up when the conniving Colleen set up a scene just like this one to make it look like Donovan had just made love to her! The flashback had recently played on the show in the ramp-up to the big Terri-Donovan union.

"Oh. My. God." Frankie paced into the kitchen, hitting her head with the palm of her hand. "The Donovan/Colleen/Terri triangle! No, wait! That was a quadrangle, because that fiend Beaumont wanted Terri, so he helped Colleen set it up by getting Terri to Colleen's apartment!" She turned back to Luke. "Who was your Beaumont? Who got Victor here?"

Before he had a chance to respond, she thought of the answer herself. "Raeanne!" Her mother was right. The office gossip was probably part of this whole scheme. After all, on the show Colleen had set up her "scene of betrayal" with weeks of not-so-subtle hints aimed at Terri.

"Why did you do it? Don't tell me it's because you love me."

Luke's jaw worked furiously, just like Donovan's in a scene of tempestuous lovemaking or white-hot fury.

"Is that so hard to believe, Frankie? That I might have fallen for you? But you were stuck on Mr. Empty Gonads there." He shrugged toward the door. "So caught up with him that you couldn't see straight. He can't offer you much of a future, you know. I can."

"So this is how you try to win me—by stealing a scene from *Lust*? You couldn't even think up something original?"

"It was Raeanne's idea," he said.

"Raeanne, I take it, has the same feelings for Victor."

Luke nodded. "But she couldn't get him to take notice of her when he's making goo-goo eyes at you."

Goo-goo eyes? It was a good thing she wrote his dialogue.

"Look, Luke, I'm really flattered. And I won't lie to you. I did think of a relationship between the two of us at one time. But that time has passed." She paused, trying to figure out if she'd used that line in the Colleen scene. Nope. She'd just thought of it.

"When I broke up with Brian, I was vulnerable. And I let that vulnerability lead me into a... a fling. I shouldn't have done that. I'm sorry. I had no idea it would mean so much to you. I just figured you were used to getting any woman you wanted, and I wouldn't register on your radar." She saw him nod at the reference to getting any woman he wanted. "And you know, there is a good woman interested in you. Kayla."

But she couldn't waste much more time here, stroking Luke's ego. She was sure he'd get over her. She had to talk to Victor. "I wish I could talk this out more, but you've kind of screwed things up for me, and I need to straighten them out first."

She headed for the bedroom, where she threw on jeans and a sweater and ran a quick brush threw her hair. She grabbed her cell phone and her purse and came back into the living room within ten minutes, prepared to tell Luke he needed to move out within the next twenty-four hours.

There was no need. Despite his crutches, the man worked fast. He'd changed, too, and left her a sloppy note. "Will get my things tomorrow. Staying with friends."

She blew out the candles, picked up his damp towel and hung it on a chair, then made for the street, hailing the first cab she saw.

—◆◆◆—

She reached Victor on the first ring, sinking back into the taxi after giving the driver Victor's address.

"Give me thirty seconds to explain," she began, but he stopped her.

"Don't bother. I already know." There was a laugh in his voice.

"That Luke and Raeanne were working together?"

"Yes."

"How'd you figure—"

"Oh, let's say the fact that Raeanne waiting for me outside your apartment building was the first clue. The second was when she asked for a ride. And the third was when she revealed in the car that she'd neglected to put on anything under her coat."

"Wow. Not subtle. But then again—"

"Colleen wasn't subtle either," he finished.

She smiled. "You really did study the show."

"It was probably fresher in my mind than theirs. Like a student cramming for a test, you remember everything."

"Where are you?" she asked. "I'm headed to your apartment."

"I'm in my car. Don't go to my apartment. Meet me at the office. We need to plot strategy."

"About Luke and Raeanne? I don't think we need to go that far. Revenge isn't my thing."

"No. PR strategy. I'd like to call a quick press conference about the thief—Thane—giving himself up."

"I hate those things."

"I don't see how you can avoid it, Frankie. Sooner or later you'll have to grant an interview, go on the record about it. Remember how well the Dewitt thing went when you finally gave in?"

She relaxed. "Yeah. Okay. I'll be there in twenty." She closed the phone, feeling more relaxed than when she'd first slipped into that frothy tub, then gave the driver the change of destination.

Chapter 27

THEY WEREN'T FINISHED UNTIL nearly midnight. Mary from PR came in, too, for most of the session. They banged out statements after getting the scoop from Frankie. She was surprised at how Victor's admiration for her maneuver was mixed with equal parts of anger, rooted in his fear for her safety. "What if Thane had had a psychotic break?" he'd burst out in the midst of her narrative, his face flaming. "My god, Frankie, you could have been..." And he'd looked away, his knuckles closed tight. "You should have told me. I could have helped."

No, she thought, *you couldn't have. You'd have insisted we tell the police, and I wasn't willing to take that chance with Hank's cousin.* If Thane had been innocent, he'd have been dragged through the ringer for nothing. It was better the way she'd handled it, strewing her figurative bread crumbs from the show to the police station for Thane to follow.

Three cable channels and two local ones came by for quick interviews. This time, she was completely calm and needed no talking points. She had had her suspicions about the suspect, she said to the reporters, but didn't believe they were enough to finger a potentially innocent man. So she'd decided to put her theory to the test by writing him into the hands of the police. If that had failed, she would have shared her concerns with the appropriate authorities, but she was glad it didn't come to that.

After Mary left, she and Victor watched the story air in her office, both of them leaning against her desk, his hand warmly covering hers. Each story carried a variation on the headline "Scribe Writes Culprit into Police Hands." *Lust for Life* was mentioned many times, but with no promises to continue the thief story. Oh, they would pull it—Frankie would have to let go of her wonderfully crafted stories for that character, because she didn't want to risk a copycat picking up where Thane left off. But let viewers tune in to find that out. They'd wrap up the thief story as soon as she had the Terri/Donovan tale nailed down and a couple new story arcs on their way. Each news clip sang her praises, one even calling her "the writer of the century."

"I guess your ex will find that interesting," Victor commented.

"You know, I hadn't even thought of his reaction," she murmured. And with this realization came another—she was sorry for the silly Keith stories she'd put into the show. They were beneath her.

He squeezed her hand. "That's as it should be."

As the last news story finished, she clicked off the TV. Victor stood and stroked her arm.

"Are we officially over the breakup now?" he asked.

She smiled, leaned in and kissed him, then looked at her watch. "We're officially over the breakup in twelve hours."

His eyebrows shot up, and she answered before he asked the question. "That's when network in L.A. opens," she said. "I'm going to contact them myself about taking over Brady's position."

"And what if they don't respond in the affirmative?"

She twisted her mouth to one side. "I guess I start looking for another position—where my talents will be appreciated."

"I think Pendergrast Soaps would have something to say about that." He reached out for both her hands.

"I'd rather do this on my own, without your help."

"This is business. *Lust*'s sponsor wouldn't want to see the show lose 'the writer of the century.' That's not good strategic thinking at all." He pulled Frankie into an embrace that melted her insides and her heart, his strong arms enveloping her, his strong body pressed against her. Her knees went weak, and she thought how wonderful it would be to return to his apartment for the night to… plot more strategy. But she pulled away.

"I might ask for *some* help," she said, looking up into his eyes. "About management styles." She would forget about all those books she was going to order.

"Happy to be of service." He kissed her again, setting her heart on fire.

"Hold that thought," she said, placing her index finger on his lips.

"I'll put some champagne on ice." He grinned. "I think we'll be doing some celebrating."

"Oh, I'm sure, one way or another, we'll be celebrating." *Now that I know what I want*, she thought.

—*w*—

He drove her home and walked her to the door, but she didn't invite him in. Sure, no one was around to see them and draw conclusions about using the relationship to get ahead. But it was important to her to embark on the promotion to executive producer by not sleeping with the sponsor's nephew the night before her quest began. He understood and respected her for it.

After a long and hot good-bye kiss, she was far from sleepy. She had a goal at last. A few of them, in fact.

She cleaned up the kitchen and the bathroom—the tub was still full of soapy water. She rearranged her linen closet. She wrote emails to friends she'd lost touch with. She read blogs and caught up on cleaning out junk mail.

Oh hell. I might as well get some work done, she thought, sitting cross-legged in bed in her pajamas, her laptop before her. She brought up the files where she kept *Lust* material and clicked her way into a document labeled *Faye—future stories.*

She typed and typed until two in the morning, excited by her ideas, on fire to share them with the world.

Grayson scooped up Faye in his arms, her frothy white wedding gown trailing nearly to the floor, her face lit up with desire.

"I never thought I'd love again like this," he murmured into her hair.

"I never thought I'd find someone like you," she whispered.

He strode across the threshold and carried her all the way up the curving staircase of his mansion, his strong muscles unwavering, his breath steady. When they reached the bedroom, he set her down and peeled off her feathery veil.

Looking into her eyes, now his breath trembled. He slowly, slowly, slid the straps of her gown off her shoulders, then pulled her to him so he could reach behind and unzip the dress. It fell at her feet. He reached up and removed the clasp from her hair. She shook it free. Now clad in only a satin slip, she stood before him, waiting, longing.

He ripped off his tie. She unbuttoned his shirt. He cradled her face in his hands and kissed her, his desire melting into hers. She moaned softly, placing her hands on his waist.

"Grayson, I can't wait a second longer."

In one swift movement, he picked her up again and carried her to the bed. Candles flickered on the nearby tables. Music played in the background. Her heart beat to the rhythm of his lovemaking.

"God, I love you, Frankie."

Acknowledgments

Many people assisted me with this novel. First, my husband, who helped me brainstorm this idea years ago. But more recently, I owe a debt of gratitude to Jean Passanante (of *As the World Turns*), Sarah Mayberry, and Harley Jane Kozak, a wonderful novelist and former soap actress. The information they provided was invaluable and served as the platform upon which I staged my fantasy. I hope those closely involved with soap operas forgive my stretching of the facts—I know my story merely skims the surface of reality, and I took many liberties with settings and activities of those who work in daytime drama.

I also want to thank the tireless Deb Werksman, editor of this book and shepherd of so many writers. Without her faith, my stories would remain untold. Finally, in addition to family and friends who act as cheerleaders, I thank my agent, Holly Root, whose suggestions, encouragement, and common sense have provided an anchor in a sometimes stormy sea.

About the Author

Libby Malin's May 2009 release, *Fire Me*, was chosen as one of the "Best Novels of 2009" by the website A Novel Menagerie. *Fire Me* has been called "hilarious," "inspired," "the perfect beach bag chick lit," and "laugh-out-loud funny."

Her debut women's fiction book, *Loves Me, Loves Me Not* (2005), was hailed as a "whimsical look at the vagaries of dating" by *Publishers Weekly*, called "charming" by the *Washington Post*, and dubbed a "clever debut [offering] quite a few surprises" by *Booklist*.

Writing as Libby Sternberg, she is the author of four YA mysteries, the first of which was an Edgar finalist and a Young Adult Top 40 Fiction Pick by the Pennsylvania School Librarians Association. Her YAs have been called "taut, vivid, and stirring" (*Library Journal*), "simply a delight to read" (*Romantic Times Book Club*), "lively and captivating" (*VOYA*), and "an entertaining original" (*Romance Reviews Today*).

Although writing was always her first love, Libby earned both bachelor's and master's degrees from the Peabody Conservatory of Music and also attended the summer American School of Music in Fontainebleau, France.

After graduating from Peabody, she worked as a Spanish gypsy, a Russian courtier, a Middle-Eastern slave, a Japanese geisha, a Chinese peasant, and a French courtesan—that is, she sang as a union chorister in both Baltimore and Washington Operas, where she regularly had the thrill of walking through the stage doors of the

Kennedy Center Opera House before being costumed and wigged for performance. She also sang with small opera and choral companies in the region.

She eventually turned to writing full-time, finding work in a public relations office and then as a freelancer for various trade organizations and small newspapers.

For many years, she and her family lived in Vermont, where she worked as an education reform advocate, contributed occasional commentaries to Vermont Public Radio, and was a member of the Vermont Commission on Women.

A native of Baltimore, Maryland, she now lives in Pennsylvania. She is married and has three children. Her website can be found at www.LibbysBooks.com.

Fire Me
LIBBY MALIN

"Humorous and full of heart, *Fire Me* is a sharply
written novel about life, love, and the good ole 9-5."
—*Melissa Senate,* author of *See Jane Date*

How to lose your job and find true love…

Fed up with impossible deadlines and meaningless busywork, Anne
Wyatt goes to work one day determined to resign. But that's the day her
boss announces someone is going to get laid off—and with a generous
severance package. Now Anne has one day to ruin her career...

Anne's hysterical tactics are unwittingly undermined by Ken, the
handsome graphic designer in the next
cubicle, who has his own ideas for liberation
from the corporate grind...

"*Fire Me*…had this reader chuckling out
loud." —*Lancaster Sunday News*

"For hijinxs and crazy shenanigans that'll
leave you chuckling to the bewilderment
of those around you, I highly suggest
this book." —*Love Romance Passion*

"A light-hearted romp of a book..."
—*A Bookworm's World*

978-1-4022-1757-9
$12.99 US/ $13.99 CAN/ £6.99 UK

Holly's Inbox

HOLLY DENHAM

"Unbelievably, compulsively readable."

—Nancy Homer, Bookfoolery and Babble

Dear Holly, Are you sure you know what you're getting into…?

It's Holly Denham's first day as a receptionist at a busy corporate bank, and frankly, it's obvious she can't quite keep up.

Take a peek at her email and you'll see why: what with her crazy friends, dysfunctional family, and gossipy co-workers, Holly's inbox is a daily source of drama.

Written entirely in emails, this compulsively readable UK smash hit will keep you laughing and turning the pages all the way to its surprising and deeply satisfying ending.

"A new format with compelling results… The story becomes more engrossing as fresh details come to light." *—Booklist*

"[Ms. Denham] creates a warm, comedic heroine who slowly grows a backbone." *—The Romantic Times*

"A charming, amusing, entertaining read. One of the best chick lit books of the year." *—A Bookworm's World*

978-1-4022-1903-0 • $14.99 US

Dating da Vinci

MALENA LOTT

"Delightfully affirming romance!" —*Booklist*

She knows she shouldn't take him home…

His name just happens to be Leonardo da Vinci. When the gorgeous young Italian walks into Ramona Elise's English class, he's a twenty-five-year-old immigrant, struggling to forge a new life in America—but he's lonely, has nowhere to live, and barely speaks English…

Picking up the pieces of her life after the death of her beloved husband, linguist and teacher Ramona Elise can't help but be charmed by her gorgeous new student. And when he calls her "Mona Lisa" she just about loses her heart…

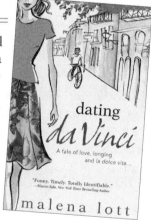

"Malena Lott's charming, heartfelt novel about how grieving widow Ramona Elise gets her groove back will have you cheering 'bravissimo.'"
—*Jenny Gardiner,* Award-winning author of *Sleeping With Ward Cleaver*

"A remarkable tour de force. This story will make you laugh, cry, and fall in love all over again."—*Single Titles*

978-1-4022-1393-9
$12.95 US/ $13.99 CAN/ £6.99 UK

An Offer You Can't Refuse

JILL MANSELL

"The perfect read for hopeless romantics who
like happily-ever-after endings." —*Booklist*

Nothing could tear Lola and Dougie apart... except his mother...

When Dougie's mother offers young
Lola a £10,000 bribe to break up with
him, she takes it to save her family. Now,
ten years later, a twist of fate has brought
Dougie and Lola together again, and her
feelings for him are as strong as ever.

But how can she win him back without
telling him why she broke his heart in
the first place?

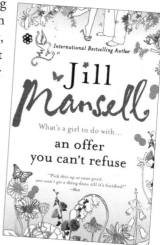

"Mansell knows her craft and delivers
a finely tuned romantic comedy."
—*Kirkus Reviews*

"A fast pace and fun writing make
the story fly by." —*Publisher's Weekly*

978-1-4022-1833-0 • $14.00 US

"Endearingly optimistic and full of attitude." —*Saturday Telegraph*

Millie's Fling
JILL MANSELL

"A super cute and wicked funny book—I thoroughly
enjoyed myself." —*Booklist*

Millie's life is about to be turned upside down…

Bestselling romance author Orla Hart decides to make her new friend
Millie Brady the heroine of her next novel, even though Millie doubts
that her boring life will inspire a steamy page-turner. But whatever
excitement doesn't happen to Millie naturally, Orla is secretly
determined to stir up.

While Millie faithfully recounts the
hilarious mishaps of her friends and
family, Orla schemes to match Millie
with the perfect romantic hero to
really spice things up. But Orla doesn't
know that Millie has deliberately left
out the juiciest recent development…

What readers are saying:

"Another sure-fire Mansell winner."

"Page-turning, truly funny, and
 heart-warming."

"The dialogue sparkles."

"I could not stop laughing!!"

978-1-4022-1834-7 • $14.00 US

Miranda's Big Mistake

JILL MANSELL

"Mansell's novel proves the maxims that love is blind and there's someone for everyone, topped with a satisfying revenge plot that every jilted woman will relish." —*Booklist*

Even the worst mistake of your life can lead to true love in the end...

Miranda's track record with men is horrible. Her most recent catastrophe is Greg.

With the help of her friends, Miranda plans the sweetest and most public revenge a heartbroken girl can get. But will Miranda learn from her mistake, or move on to the next "perfect" man and ignore the love of her life waiting in the wings...?

"An exciting read about love, friendship, and sweet revenge—fabulously fun."
—*Home and Life*

"A fantastic, fun read!"
—*Wendy's Minding Spot*

"An absolute romp of a read!"
—*A Bookworm's World*

978-1-4022-1832-3 • $14.00 US